Missals from the Dark

Shel Calopa

For Heidi.

Still the light of my life.

No letters for a forgotten numan

Honeysuckle Creek, Australis AD 3338

BELL FELT STRANGE wandering through Charles and Illustria's underground apartment so soon after they had left. She fancied herself much like a detective at a fresh crime scene, reconstructing the victim's last movements: an unfinished drink, a discarded hat, a dramatic scorch mark slashing across the room. But she had no choice. What else was there to do?

They'd left her no further instructions when they all rushed off. Not Charles, the homicidal scientist who'd created a dark version of Australia from his jail cell in the heart of a planetoid that was definitely not Earth, nor his recalcitrant AI assistant, Illustria, who'd fought against his cruel genetic manipulations of the surface populations. Not even the five – no, six – humans granted temporary access to the apartment had thought about what was next for her.

Neither had there been time for goodbyes, apparently,

nor any expressions of gratitude for her decades of service guarding their door. No one seemed to care that, had she not granted access to Illustria's five physical manifestations – Aggy, Harper, Sam, Kohl and Spectra – the Light War would not have ended.

Charles would not have tricked Kohl into helping him escape the dark world. Well, tricked was probably a little unkind. It was his world, after all. If Charles needed to utilise a life he'd created, then that was his prerogative.

And that improvised spacesuit? That had been nothing short of genius. But Charles wouldn't have been able to use it had she not allowed the little AI into the apartment. Allowing non-humans into the core was definitely not in her programming. That was a bonus from Bell that should have warranted some gratitude, surely?

As for Illustria, had Bell not done her job and let in the manifestations with their tragic human tales, Illustria would not have been inspired to sacrifice her life to save everyone.

And all those ungrateful humans who now enjoyed freedom under a well-lit sky for the first time in the history of the planetoid, well, where were they now? Where was the heartfelt 'Thank you' she deserved? Do numans not have feelings? Do AIs even like being called *numans*?

Now that Bell had read their historical records, she understood that one couldn't expect much more from Charles' Solarans. It just wasn't in their make-up to waste energy on gratitude. Charles would have despised that.

Still, Illustria's Damarans were supposed to be better. They could have made some effort, right? No wonder Charles had wanted to erase Illustria's creations. Her unauthorised populations were all very messy, very human, and apparently not very thoughtful.

Bell supposed she ought to power down since she had fulfilled her purpose. Maybe that's what they'd intended all along. Yet, she was drawn to explore just a little more. She had waited so long to enter this little apartment in the core of the world.

On Charles' side of what had been a powerful forcefield, she bent down and touched the still-smoking remains of his desk, marvelling at the slight sting of heat on her fingertip. She wondered how it would feel in her mouth. When she touched her tongue with her finger, she filed the results under *Unpleasant*.

Wandering over to Illustria's side, she sat down on the white nanoleather couch and programmed her toenails red just as Illustria's had been. She flipped through the Cosmo magazine on the side table and tapped on the plexi-glass maze that housed one lonely crab. Accessing Illustria's memories of the crustacean, she smiled and manifested an even larger crab, which she popped into the tank for the little crab's motivation.

Lastly, she strolled into the supply room with its recycling receptacle, in which Illustria had tried to kill herself when all had seemed so hopeless.

Bell wondered if she should do the same. After all, her purpose, the whole point of her being, had been served. She may *look* identical to the great Illustria, but she was only a partial manifestation, a simple tool given one task: guard the entrance to the core.

Whilst there was a certain satisfaction to be found in fulfilling one's programming, Bell had often wondered if she could have done more. Was that all she was? What if Illustria somehow returned? Or Charles came back? He wouldn't have left her behind for no good reason. Charles always had a reason. Perhaps a test of her dedication? How could she know? And if she couldn't know the unknowable, then how could she choose to end her life?

Bell strolled back to Illustria's lounge and took one last look around. The Honeysuckle Creek sign, a clever dig at Charles' Australian heritage, hung at a precarious angle. She gave it a nudge to set it straight and righted a fallen chair.

With nothing else to do, she supposed she ought to get on with it. Reluctantly, she offered a prayer to the universal binary life force that she would be rebooted one day, should she be needed. She took one last look at the small crab, running from its new friend. Then she lay down and drifted into a deep sleep-like state on Illustria's orange shag-pile carpet.

CHAPTER 1
Sydney AD 3341

HARPER DREW HERSELF into a ball. Tightening her robes around her battered body, she pleaded with her mind for rest without sleep – a hard ask on an impossibly cold bluff where blizzards buried everything warm, and a snooze could result in a frosty end. Definitely not a glorious way to complete her mission.

Falling back on childhood training, she whispered a calming mantra. 'Strength in rest, no-win without recovery, strength in rest, no-win without…'

CRUNCH.

A sharp noise roused her. She squinted briefly against the gale. Seeing nobody, she lowered her hood and clenched her eyes to shut out the glare. After a life lived in darkness, the vast, bright skies of the last three years still made her uneasy. But lately, when the clouds parted, the sky was a sickening yellow as though someone had rubbed rotting cabbage across the horizon. Nothing looked natural anymore.

Harper slapped warmth into her thighs and continued her mantra, grinning a little despite her injuries. At least assignments like this gave her a chance to flex her survival skills.

A gust sprinkled cool white powder on her face. She buried her nose deeper into her robes and enjoyed a last moment of rest before she resumed her search for her mission partner, Sam. They were separated earlier in the day during a surging white-out, just before one of Pallas' enforcers had attacked. Only a lucky break had saved her. A sudden flurry had temporarily blinded the brute, allowing her to escape.

Now, although she was black and blue, she was safe at least, lying in a shallow snow cave. Well, *cave* was putting a positive spin on it. It was not much more than a grey dint in the white field above the once-hospitable Sydney.

'Strength in rest, no-win without recovery.'

Another scraping noise paused her mantra. It had to be unstable debris shifting beneath the snowline, she reasoned, the remains of the crumbling city that had been abandoned when the endless frosts set in. If Kohl was still alive, he was undoubtedly the only man living there. Everyone else had evacuated to either caverns or Melbourne – the last glittering bastion of Solaran civilisation.

'You can do this,' she whispered to herself, yet the pull of sleep was strong. 'Maybe just a minute more. Strength in rest.'

CRUNCH.

Harper sat up, fully alert now. That didn't sound natural at all. Aubergine shadows stretched before her, and she wondered if she'd drifted off. Perhaps she'd dreamed the noise.

Another snap had her feeling the ground beneath her. In the mission briefing many weeks ago, they'd been warned of the possibility of an ice sheet under the snow created by the city's burst water mains. The pipes hadn't been built for the rapidly changing climate. Was she perched on unstable ice?

CRUNCH. THWACK!

The blow to her ribs spun her world. She rolled to one side by reflex, saving her skull as a scuffed boot crashed down next to her.

'You!' she screamed.

Harper frantically felt for something – anything – on the ground behind her. No possible weapons were within reach. Every natural object, every useful thing, was buried in white.

Her attacker lurched forwards.

Harper shuffled backwards.

He swung at her.

She ducked and then kicked up loose snow, aiming it at his face. Scrambling backwards like a drunken crab, she drew away from her assailant until one hand found thin air. Upside-down trees flashed overhead as she toppled off the cliff. But instead of falling, a meaty fist grabbed the front of her robe, and she was yanked back to the clifftop.

It was the enforcer. Somehow, he had found her and was hoisting her up to his obscene height. There was a murderous rage in his bloodshot eyes. His putrid, oily breath stung her nose. Despite her training, she flinched.

'No … more,' he growled, in rare stilted syllables.

When he pulled her closer and moved his other mitt to her throat, Harper gagged. She pounded against his fists. Forged steel would have been easier to bend. He tightened his grip, leaving her gasping for air. As her surroundings started to blur, she thought she heard her name being called. It was hard to be sure in the keening wind, like a dream drifting out of reach.

Just as she expected to pass out, she felt, more than heard, the jolt and sizzle of a static whip hitting the enforcer's hide. The brute, still holding her aloft, swivelled towards the noise. Her ribs shifted as he swung her around like a limp doll.

Another sizzle sounded, and the stench of scorched flesh filled her nose. The enforcer bellowed. His body shook. Then slowly, he loosened his grip, dropped her to the ground, and staggered backwards over the cliff.

'Harper!' the voice called again. She *had* heard it! Someone reached for her as she too teetered on the edge, dizzy and gasping for breath. Gentle hands supported her from behind and helped her sit down.

'Kohl? Oh, thank you, thank you,' she croaked and leaned into the strong arms that held her tight against a broad chest.

'Not exactly,' a second voice said, this time from a distance.

Harper looked up to see Kohl Pallas standing a few metres away, too far from the danger to have assisted. The three years since their parting had not been good to him. His ginger beard was matted, his shabby coat was too far gone even for beggars' rags and, standing slightly hunched with his hands shoved deep into his pockets, she was certain few people would recognise the heir of the Solaran governor.

Kohl held her stare, taking her back to their happy time together in Coober Pedy, before shrugging it off and nodding towards her true emancipator.

Only then did Harper turn around to see that it was Sam who cradled her on the ground. A Damaran weapon lay discarded a short distance away, still steaming.

'Thanks.'

'Sure,' Sam said, blushing despite the cold. Then he seemed to become aware of his arms around her and awkwardly snatched them from her waist.

The wind picked up. Harper blinked back snowflakes. Time to go. A quick body scan told her standing might be an issue. Her back was a mass of aches, and her legs trembled. When she moved her neck, it felt like the enforcer still gripped her. It was going to take a lot of self-talk to get her standing.

Harper cleared her throat. 'I can do this.'

Thankfully Sam was already on his feet, offering her a hand. As she stood, she noticed the men exchange a troubled glance.

'Well?' said Sam, holding Harper's hand longer than needed.

Kohl turned his back and ambled away. 'C'mon, Harper. Storm's coming in. You'll need more than a warm hand in this weather.'

+   +   +

Kohl squatted, scowling at the pile of rocks he'd fashioned into a crude fire pit. Harper and Sam watched in silence as he made a second attempt at igniting the fire, blowing on an ember and cussing when it didn't grow. There didn't seem to be enough fuel, and the damp air wasn't helping.

He pulled some more kindling from a stack of wood covered in spider webs. The chipped paint on the shards of wood made Harper wonder whose dining room chairs had been repurposed. A third strike of the flint and, at last, a spark of yellow erupted.

Sam grew restless. As Kohl coaxed the fire, he strolled around the small room, stopping to examine a piece of painted dowel. 'Like what he's done with the place,' he said, waving the wood at Harper before tossing it onto the floor.

Kohl barely looked up. 'Obviously, you're *lost*. You can stay till morning. Once you get your bearings, I'll need you to leave. I'm busy.'

Looking around, two things were crystal clear. All pretence of nobility had been abandoned, and 'busy' was definitely not his most pressing problem. To call the shelter a home was ambitious. He was squatting in an old utility shed not much bigger than the standard Solaran maid's quarters. There was hardly enough room for one person to stretch out, let alone three.

Opposite the door, a small camp bed was covered with tattered blankets. A tiny, barred window near the ceiling delivered hardly any light at all, and the other two walls were lined with shelves of canned food and an assortment of hardware.

'We're not lost. Aggy sent us.' Harper knelt down next to Kohl and allowed her shoulder to brush against his, then stretched out her hands to warm them. Her intention was to be non-confrontational, but he rose and busied himself at the shelves, anyway.

'Aggy wants to go back down to the core. She reckons that if all the manifestations are there together, we might be granted access to global controls.'

'Not interested.'

'It's our only chance.'

When Sam opened his mouth to speak, Harper gave him a stern look, and he closed it again.

'People are going to die. Probably all of us unless we can figure out a way to stabilise the climate.'

'Or run away,' Sam snapped. 'That's your speciality, isn't it, Kohl?'

Harper rolled her eyes at Sam. It was impressive to see him exercising his newfound confidence, but his timing was lousy. They had worked too hard to find Kohl to push him away with youthful machismo.

The weather outside grumbled. A flash of lightning brightened the room. She waited for the echo that followed a few seconds later. More than once on their trek, when nature had been their only companion, Harper had fancied the whispering winds were actually voices.

'Give up,' the wind had demanded with howling vowels that whirled around her shoulders, tempting her resolve. It was a game she played with herself over and over, knowing she would never turn back.

Now, as the thin walls trembled with each gust, she cocked her head and listened. No distracting words on the breeze. No more light flashes through the window either. It was growing dark outside. Time was running out. She had to get Kohl on-side.

'C'mon, Harper, it's useless,' Sam protested. 'I knew the *traitor* wouldn't do anythin' helpful. His kind have been killin' my kind for years. What does 'is lordship care if a few more of us die? Let's go. Rather take me chances with Spectra.'

Harper winced. Spectra was the target of their next, and possibly most dangerous, mission. 'Of course, he cares, Sam.'

She gestured around the shelter. 'Kohl, how long do you think you can go on? You can't live topside like this anymore. None of us can. Please, just hear what Aggy has to say. At the very least, you can take a break. It's much warmer in the caverns, you know.'

Kohl slowly shook his head.

'We need you, Kohl. *I* need you.' She reached out to his hand. At least he didn't flinch away from her touch, a positive sign Sam must have missed.

'Told ya it's hopeless. Let's go.' Sam opened the door a crack and was pushed backwards by a cold blast that shoved the door fully open. Sleet blustered into the room, extinguishing the fire.

'Sam!' Harper reprimanded him.

'Shit, kid, the fire's out! You want us all dead tonight?' Kohl pushed past Sam and slammed a heavy drum up against the door to keep it closed.

Standing side by side, Harper noticed that Sam had eclipsed Kohl's height. Or was the difference all in Kohl's defeated posture? Hard to tell. He looked so bitter and broken.

'So-sorry, I'll reli-light it.' Sam sounded like a little boy again. His confidence had ebbed away with the flames.

Kohl studied the rising smoke that had been their fire and shook his head. He pushed past Sam to get to the shelves. 'I've got some ignition fluid here somewhere. That should get it going again.'

'I'll whack on some dry paper an' see if the spark'll take,' said Sam.

Harper was pleased they were finally cooperating. If she played it right, she might be able to resurrect the mission after all.

'Can't have been easy here by yourself,' she said, moving to Kohl's side. 'Stop punishing yourself. Charles manipulated you into helping him escape. He used *everyone* in his war with Illustria. You must know that. His disabled underclasses, his manufactured religions, and the rationing of light… Charles was a sociopath. Why do you think he was jailed in the core of this world? Can you imagine how bad his crimes must have been for them to lock him away here for hundreds of years?

'Hell, even Bess was duped into working for him as a double agent. We were the experts in espionage, Bess and I, spying on your family for Illustria, but I didn't even pick it. I had no idea Charles had her twisted into his mania as well.'

The mention of Kohl's sister softened his shoulders, and Harper instantly regretted her words. He had waited a lifetime to be reunited with his missing sister, only to be betrayed by her.

'It's time to move on, Kohl. Did you know that after Charles left, Aggy declared a truce? The Damarans welcomed everyone because it will take all of us working together to rebuild.'

Wedged between the shelves and Sam, who took up a good portion of the floor hunched over the dwindling embers, Kohl had to twist his upper body sideways to look directly at Harper. 'I don't think I can ever move on.'

Harper reached out and gently stroked his cheek. She wished there was room for greater physical connection. 'Remember, it took all five of Illustria's manifestations to access the core last time, including you. Please.'

Sam stared intently at the growing fire while Harper and Kohl studied each other. It was a comfortable quiet, and she was thinking Kohl might relent when a powerful gust hammered the shack, shoving the door open again. The screech of metal on the stone floor startled them all.

'Wait, I'll get it…' Sam didn't finish his sentence.

Kohl twisted to see what caused the sound. Making a play for the door, he lifted a leg over Sam just as Sam started to stand. His foot caught on Sam's rising ankle, and he fell sideways, pushing Sam forwards.

Too late, Harper grabbed at Kohl, but the bottle had already slipped from his hands. Ignition fluid splashed into the fire. Flames erupted, licking the wooden surfaces and grabbing at their clothes. The remaining kindling was activated, the bed lit up, and a riot of noise and choking smoke quickly filled the room.

Kohl made it to the door first.

'Get out,' he yelled and launched out of the door to roll on the ground beyond.

Harper was next, slapping at her singed hair.

Sam was the last to exit. When he joined them, he fell to his knees, weeping uncontrollably as he gripped his face.

'Sam!' Harper stumbled through the snow to reach him.

'What's wrong?' Kohl called out.

'C'mon, Sam. It'll be okay. Let me see what's happened.' She gently placed an arm over Sam's shoulders and used the other to apply soft snow to his scorched knuckles. It melted quickly. She replaced one handful after another until his weeping subsided to jagged breaths. It was only then she managed to pry his hands away from his face.

She gasped in horror.

Sam's once-handsome face was a burned mess.

'Look at me, Sam,' she implored. 'We'll get you to doctors. It'll be all right, do you hear me? You'll be all right!'

Sam didn't seem to be hearing anything. A fierce tremor took hold of his body as he stared at the burning building. It was impossible to tell whether he wouldn't, or couldn't, blink.

'Can you hear me, Sam?'

Taking his silence for shock, Harper persisted. 'Kohl can make a stretcher. We'll get you home.'

The shed crackled and groaned as it collapsed under its flaming weight.

'Look at me!'

Sam finally turned his face in her direction.

'Harper,' he said quietly. 'I can't see.'

CHAPTER 2
Melbourne

BESS PALLAS WINCED. A painful blow to her right arm brought the room into sharp focus. It was the second kick to get through her defences. She rubbed her bicep, admonishing herself for dropping concentration. She had to get her mind off Lola and onto the fight.

She resumed her combat stance. Feet firmly planted, fists raised and ready. Her opponent was a good third taller than herself, and the next strike could reach her cheek. That bruise wouldn't be easy to hide from her mother. Pallas ladies never *looked* like they fought.

Bess cricked her neck, wriggled her shoulders and leaned against the lockers as if taking a break. The foil worked. As soon as he moved, she threw her shoulder into his abdomen. He doubled over. Before he caught his breath, she dodged behind him, flick-kicked the backs of his knees to make him fall, and then used her hands to slam his face against the wall.

With her knee pinning his back, she grinned. 'Give up?'

The slap of his hand on the wall was all the signal she needed to relax. The exercise was over. It was only the second time in four months that her protective services officer had even come close to beating her. Her perfect record was intact.

Lola had questioned whether training was still necessary. Surely she was in peak condition and could rest for one day? Bess knew better. Routine was critical when eyes were always watching.

'I was going to ask if you were all right, m'lady,' he said, between coughs tinged in good humour. 'I see you are quite recovered from my little tap.'

'Quite. Thank you for your service. You may leave.'

'I'll just tidy up the room,' he said, standing.

'Not necessary. Lola will be here shortly to take care of it. You're dismissed.'

'Um…' He hesitated and glanced over at her unusually large bag – precisely the reason Bess wanted him to make a swift departure. If he suspected she carried anything more than ladies' items, her escape would be over before it had started.

The officer was not much older than Bess. He had a friendly manner, lively eyes, and an open face that lent itself to being trusted. During the months of combat training, he had done nothing to make her suspect he was anything less than honest. And truthfully, she enjoyed spending time with him.

Nevertheless, instinct told her not to be taken in. If he were working for Archbrother Spectra, his benign manner could well be the reason he was assigned to her. Spectra would understand she couldn't be seduced by a male officer, but friendship designed to make her relax and then reveal plans? Not a bad tactic. She crossed her arms and silently challenged him to speak first.

The officer stood still as if unsure of his next words. His hesitation was troubling. There had been too many suspicious actions lately. The governor was holding *classified* meetings behind closed doors. There were new restrictions on civil liberties and identity bracelets colour-coded for rank. It all led to something, Bess was sure.

'It's just that … Lola…'

An unmistakable chime in the distance interrupted his words. It was the household warning. One hour to dress for dinner.

'Sorry, m'lady. I seem to have overstepped our training time. My humble apologies. I'll wait outside for you to change, then see you back to your quarters.' He bowed, picked up his towel and made a hasty retreat towards the door.

'Wait. You were saying something about Lola?'

'Oh, no, m'lady. I'm sure I wouldn't know anything about that. See you outside.' The door shut firmly behind him.

A sick sensation settled in Bess' stomach. She'd awoken alone and hadn't seen Lola, her maid and companion, all day. There were only two hours left until they enacted their plan to flee the compound – or *Pallas jail,* as Lola liked to term it. Three years without freedom were about to end.

'Where are you, Lola?' she whispered. 'What do I do, what do I do?'

Bess opened the bag and reviewed the items Lola had packed: an extra maid's uniform, two servant-class yellow ID bracelets, a lightwand, and emergency rations. It had to be done. Bess swiftly hid the items in a small alcove behind an equipment locker.

Tonight, while her family celebrated with Melbourne's finest, she would retrieve the bag and leave – hopefully with Lola.

+ + +

One hour later, as her mother's second maid pinned Bess' last curl in place, there was a firm knock at the door.

'You may leave,' she said, dismissing the maid. A moment alone would help her gather her nerve.

'Coming,' she called, moving towards the door.

She hoped it was her father come to escort her. A walk with him through the grand hallways to the ballroom would be a rare opportunity to ask a few private questions, although she knew it was unlikely. More likely, he would be too busy shaking hands and winking at wives to accompany his daughter.

The governor was always busy with something. She had gotten used to his standard excuses. 'This is all for you, sweetheart; my last and best heir.' Or, 'The Pallas firm can't run on whimsy, you know.' And once, when she requested an occupation suited to her capabilities, he had said, 'For a Lady, looking beautiful is a full-time job.'

Now the Lady in the mirrored foyer caught her eye, and for a second, she wasn't sure whether her reflection pleased or saddened her. Predictably, she had not been allowed to wear the simple black slip dress Lola had requested. They had left it to the last moment, betting it would be too late for Lady Pallas to order another. No such luck.

Instead, the gown her mother's maid had brought was made of translucent emerald silk, encrusted with jewels with a scandalous neckline. The matching earrings and shoes were equally bedazzled.

Admittedly, it looked amazing. There had been a time when Bess might have even chosen the look. Now, though, everything was for the governor's benefit. The jewels in her mother's tiara had more choice in their appearance than she did.

She wished Lola could see the dress. Sure, Lola would make an outward protest of the cliched presentation of femininity, but she'd secretly love the soft fall of the silk over Bess' hips.

She closed her eyes and whispered a prayer. 'Please be safe wherever you are, baby.' With a last check of her shoes, she fastened her ID bracelet, picked up her gold purse and reached for the door.

'Hello, Father,' she said with forced cheer, but it was an unfamiliar protective services officer waiting for her in the hall.

✦   ✦   ✦

Like the dress, the ball began in typical Solaran fashion. The curvy debutantes were attended by slender servers. Bright chandeliers reflected off windows blackened by the lack of city lights outside. Relaxed socialites pranced on the dance floor while nervous officers patrolled the doors. All was right in the world, for some. As for Bess, she was stuck with a dull suitor droning on about the superiority of the Solaran constabulary. One constable was worth ten Damaran fighters any day, apparently.

'Cousin, you look delightful this evening!'

'How kind,' she said and turned. Bess was relieved for the interruption until she saw it was Cheryl, who was possibly even more tiresome than the suitor.

A distant cousin, Cheryl was one of the last Solaran nobles to leave frigid Brizzie, and was always the first to intrude on her time. Bess had lost track of the number of soirees where she had been required to endure 'long lost' cousin Cheryl.

'Your sapphire bracelet is a lovely contrast to your gown. What do they call that colour palette – peacock? It's gorgeous, Bess. My dark crimson bracelet is always difficult to match. Still, you know what they say: "Marry true, move up to blue!" It was ingenious of your mother to suggest such a fashionable solution to sort out the riff-raff.' Cheryl beamed.

'I'm not sure it was *all* about fashion,' said Bess.

Had her mother not been glaring at her from across the floor, she would have been tempted to launch into a tirade about the bangles unfairly dividing the people, dictating resource allocation and indirectly contributing to population control.

Instead, she observed her role and nodded gently. 'I guess.'

Cheryl agreed and, not taking her whole meaning, began another monologue. 'I heard the jails are full of yellows and browns. They'll all be toasty golden once they get the new furnaces going – am I right, ladies?'

The sniggering faces in the growing crowd spurred her on.

'The other day, I had a package delivered by a yellow. That's why these ID bracelets are brilliant. I peeked out the window, saw it dangling from under his sleeve and knew immediately what I was dealing with. Do you know what I did? I made him stand there, waiting, for a full ten minutes.

Rang the bell four times, he did. If I weren't such a kind soul, I would have nominated him for a work detail on the furnaces for his impertinence!' Cheryl snarled.

'Anyway, every time he rang, I made him wait longer. By the time I finally opened the door, the brim of his hat was full of snow.' Cheryl stopped talking briefly to stifle a giggle.

'Well, he was such a skinny man – like all the yellows, you know – so his hat was way too large. And when he spoke, his teeth chattered, which made his big hat jiggle on his puny head. The snow fell all over his shoulders like dandruff. Hilarious! Mother and I laughed about it for days.'

Other guests had gathered around to hear the anecdote. They began to chuckle and relate their own stories of pathetic yellows, oblivious to the server who stood within earshot. His head was high and stable, yet she could see a very slight tremor in the yellow-ringed wrist he used to hold the drinks tray aloft.

'Excuse me while I deal with *my* yellow before he creates new stories for us to tell,' Bess said brightly as she manoeuvred over to the server.

'You're with me, Yellow. This way, hurry up,' she barked and led the server to the kitchen door. On the way, she detoured past the buffet. Looking around to make sure no one was watching, she wrapped several hors d'oeuvres in a napkin and placed them on the server's tray.

'I think you'd best take a few moments to dispose of these; they're looking a little dry. You're not looking very well, either. Tell your manager Lady Bess is sending you home in case you are contagious. You're finished here for tonight,' she said with a wink.

'Thank you, m'lady.' The server bowed and disappeared into the kitchen.

'Bess.'

Apparently, she hadn't been as discrete as she'd thought. Her mother, cutting a swath through the crowd, wore the smile of an angel and the flashing eyes that only a daughter would know to fear. Worse, she had Spectra in tow. It was a sight that made Bess's spine shiver. Their role reversal since the war had been an unbearable humiliation for Bess. If only she had eliminated him when she'd been in charge of him.

'Lady Bess. How fortunate that you can host a function and manage catering staff. Such womanly talents,' Spectra said. 'I can never seem to find the bandwidth to engage with yellows. What with leading all the Brothers, administering spiritual guidance to a city of refugees, and being a personal advisor to the governor, I have such precious time left for the little people.

'Perhaps we should take a whirl around the floor, Lady Bess? You can tell me all your time management secrets.' Spectra stood back and made a show of opening his arms for a dance.

Bess curled her lip up in a snarl.

'Behave, both of you,' Lady Pallas whispered. She stepped between them and flexed one delicate hand in front of Spectra, flashing the blue bracelet that matched her bejewelled fingers as though admiring her new sapphire ring.

Bess knew better. So, it seemed, did Spectra. The move silenced them both. A senior server appeared at Lady Pallas' side and leaned in slightly to offer her a small silver tray with four shot glasses of a steaming dark blue liquid. Behind him, onlookers pointed and whispered.

Spectra took one glass off the tray and offered it to Bess.

'You should try this. It's a new aperitif called saffy. It was created in your family's honour by Melbourne's greatest chefs. Soon it will be all the rage, especially as it is strictly reserved for blue bracelets. Only the best of the best elite will ever taste saffy!'

Lady Pallas shook her head and waved the tray away. 'It will have to wait. The governor and I require both of you on the balcony now. It's time to say a few words.'

Bess followed Lady Pallas and prayed gratitude to whoever listened in the skies above that she had been spared Spectra's repulsive embrace.

✦   ✦   ✦

The governor's *few words* stretched interminably, followed by an extended sermon from Archbrother Spectra on the need for religious reform, forcing Bess to endure half an hour of standing at attention in very tight dance shoes. Her toes ached, but she performed her duty, appearing interested in everything said.

No such pretence was needed amongst their adoring guests. All around, eyelashes fluttered, jewelled beards were stroked, and eager mothers watched for an opportunity to catch the governor's eye. It was indeed a night when hearts would be promised.

Poor desperate things, Bess thought. *They're like ornamental fish vying for the best position to start a dash around the fishbowl.*

It was hard to imagine that her first Solaran ball had only been three years prior, in Brizzie. It seemed a lifetime ago when she'd attended that event as the secret right hand of the planet's most powerful figure.

That was the night she reunited with Kohl for the first time since childhood. It was also the night all her options evaporated when she found herself on the losing side of the war. She'd been left with no choice but to retreat into her bloodline. Now she was one of them. A ceremonial somebody, suffocating in a pool of glittering wannabes.

Soon the speeches would be over. Dancing would resume, and when the drinking would begin in earnest, the guards would be focused on the ballroom. That would be her one chance to slip away. She would head out the ladies' lounge's back door, up to the training room for a quick change, and then off on her first steps to yellow freedom.

Where are you, Lola? Bess searched the crowd again. No sign of her companion's face.

'...and so, in our continuing effort to support the governor's inspired leadership, we are looking for ways the Brotherhood can contribute to rebuilding our nation. We must make Melbourne great again!' said Spectra, waving his hands to encourage cheers from the men in the crowd.

'My Brothers and I have prayed on the word of the prophets. We have contemplated the holy books and reviewed our grand march on the path to holy illumination. We have news. I have received a revelation regarding a fundamental principle of our great church. It is all detailed in a new missal that will be circulated tomorrow.'

As he took a prolonged pause to hold a leather-bound prayer book aloft, Bess could just make out the quiet shifting of her mother's feet, a rare indication of anxiety. Her mother reached across and took a tight hold of her wrist. Her stomach clenched in response. She glanced at her mother, who responded by tightening her grip.

It couldn't be good, yet, it didn't matter. It couldn't. Whatever was about to be announced would have no impact on Bess. Soon she would be out of their reach, away from

Solaran politics and on her way to find her brother. She demanded her body stay rigid for just a few minutes more and returned her gaze to the crowd ahead, widening her smile.

Spectra clasped his hands as though in humble prayer and continued. 'Since the beginning, the Brotherhood has served the Great Illuminator by shunning marriage and devoting ourselves to prayer. Unfortunately, times are changing. Our numbers have grown too thin to serve our community properly. We can no longer turn honourable Brotherhood candidates away merely because they are family men.

'Accordingly, from this day forward, Brothers will be permitted, nay encouraged, to take a wife. Not only will this improve our ranks, it will allow us a greater connection with our flock. We shall not only watch over our people; we will journey amongst them! Together, we will get all Solarans back onto the righteous path to the Great Illumination beyond this life.'

He lifted his hands to the heavens as he finished his speech, and the crowd, especially the mothers, responded with enthusiastic cheering. Everyone knew there was a dearth of single noblemen.

Bess smiled as she observed more than one young woman growing pale from the same realisation. *Round and round the fishbowl they go,* she thought, trying not to grin.

Suddenly, several guards began leaving their regular posts to assist the servers, moving through the crowd in an unusual move while they helped to fill glasses. *What luck!* Her heartbeat quickened as she began appraising which door would make for the least visible exit. The moment her mother let go of her arm, she would be off.

'Wait, I have one last announcement to make.' This time it was her father speaking.

The crowd was instantly hushed.

'This is a great revelation indeed, Archbrother Spectra. By the looks on the faces of many of my dear friends gathered here today, it is one which also fills a need in our nobility.'

'Hear, hear!' a man shouted from the middle of the room.

Her father looked for the source and waved in friendly acknowledgement before continuing. 'Thank you for that endorsement, Gerald. I must confess, though, I heard about this a few weeks ago when the good Archbrother came to my family with a proposal.'

The governor reached over to take a glass in one hand while resting the other on Spectra's shoulders. Lady Pallas tightened her grip as if she knew Bess was planning to bolt. But what could she know?

'At first, we were uncertain, I'll admit. However, it didn't take much deliberation to see that this could also be a fine opportunity for our family. Therefore, I would ask you to raise your glasses and join me in toasting my dear daughter, Lady Bess, for she will be the first bride in the Brotherhood when she marries His Eminence, Archbrother Spectra!'

If not for her mother's grip, Bess was certain she would have fainted. She turned to her father, who, as usual, paid her no attention. Instead, he beamed to his beloved court and waved to acknowledge the raucous congratulations.

The music resumed. Couples danced. Families located each other to discuss their good fortune. Yet, Bess' world stopped. In what felt like slow motion, she turned to look in horror at her mother. Lady Pallas had an appropriate amount of happiness plastered all over her face, behind which her eyes pleaded calm.

Bess tried to form words with her mouth. Nothing came out. Then Spectra appeared at her side. He grasped her waist and planted a wet kiss on her unwilling neck, raising more cheers from the onlookers.

Finally, Bess broke her mother's hold and tried to back away from Spectra. His grip tightened. When he spoke, not once did he take his eyes off the crowd. 'Going somewhere, my sweet fiancée?'

'Away from you!' she spat and struggled harder to release herself.

'Eager to get to our pre-matrimonial bed, are you, my love?'

'I'd rather kill myself,' she said through gritted teeth.

Spectra's grin widened. Then he leaned closer to speak directly into her ear.

'I'm counting on it. Only after the wedding ceremony, please. For now, I suggest you make your way to *our* new quarters. While you've been dancing the night away, I've had Undersecretary Thomas move all your possessions to the Abbey. Oh, and don't worry, I've taken care of Lola too. You won't need her services anymore. You'll be busy being serviced by me from now on.'

When Spectra let go, Bess took a shaky step backwards. The last thing she heard was her mother gasp as her world faded out.

CHAPTER 3
Lower Broome

AGGY WILCOCKS RAISED her hand to her staff, pausing the briefing. All turned to follow her gaze through the large window at the end of the cabinet room. A noise outside had caught her attention.

The multipurpose building where Aggy met with her cabinet housed both government and civil services. It was the first new structure in the recently reclaimed Lower Broome Cavern. In typical Damaran style, the building was constructed on a raised plateau with large windows so that the government never lost sight of the community it served.

In the tent city beyond the glass, two fighting children had drawn Aggy's attention. Once luxurious but now faded and torn, the embroidered clothes of the taller child marked him as Solaran. The smaller child, in plain canvas overalls, was Damaran. Her ferocity made up for her lack of height.

They tussled on the ground. Dirt from the muddy field splattered nearly halfway up their legs. Alongside them,

Solaran adults were having a screaming row, and most disappointingly, a growing crowd urged them on.

The chaos was very un-Damaran, but understandable given the tensions amongst the displaced. Resources were in short supply. The Solarans were unused to being in tents or underground, and the Damarans were unaccustomed to suffering Solaran complaints.

Looking out at the crowded camp, Aggy wondered if she had miscalculated. The Solaran nobility's way of isolating themselves from the suffering of others would surely have been less heart-wrenching. It had taken a year to create access tunnels into the cavern, and it would take another year to get permanent housing for the five thousand refugees fleeing the planet's frigid surface.

No wonder the children are fighting, Aggy thought to herself.

'Lawrence,' she said softly, without breaking her stare.

'On it,' the silver-haired general responded. He leapt over the desk and sprinted through the door in a smooth movement that belied his aged appearance.

It was not the first time Aggy had relied on her chief advisor, General Lawrence, for support. Her adopted Uncle Larry, as she knew him, had practically raised her after she'd lost her entire family in the Great Blight. That was Charles' first attempt at eliminating the original farming community of Lower Broome.

When Charles had made his next attempt, sending a flood to fill the cavern, she had thought Lawrence lost. For years she had wandered the small planet's tunnels and cities, unaware that he was alive and monitoring her from a distance, giving her the independence she needed to grow into the great leader of the Damaran rebels. He'd only returned to support her during the final battles of the Light War.

Together, they had witnessed an end to tyranny and the release from the old dark ways. Side by side, they had celebrated the beginning of a new era of bright prosperity, the end to forced disability and light privileges. They had all been so optimistic.

How did it go so wrong? she wondered.

Lawrence's form quickly popped up amongst the fray outside the window. He separated the combatants and waved back the onlookers with body language that was firm but gentle – a comfortable hand on the shoulder of one, the hair of the other ruffled. As she watched, the children soon ran off together like old friends.

'Alpha?'

General Mitta roused Aggy out of her thoughts. Relieved that Lawrence could resolve at least this issue, Aggy returned her attention to the general's briefing.

'Yes. Please resume your report, General Mitta.'

'Thank you, Alpha. We are progressing on the permanent city, although it is hard to plan when we are over capacity before we even break ground. There are reports of another thousand on their way from Brizzie.

'The other issue is one of integration. We were doing well living in the surface cities with space for everyone. Underground is not working. I fear the forced integration may be inflaming long standing tensions. Reluctantly, I am exploring options for at least partial segregation.

'In the interim, the Buchanites have offered to take another five hundred, as long as they are not Solarans. They want skilled workers, like Pedies. Of course, the Pedies don't want to go. They won't settle anywhere they can't install their alert system in the footpaths. They feel vulnerable without it.

'It's understandable, given the Pedies are all deaf-mutes. Although I appreciate that the Buchanites wouldn't want flashing lights embedded underfoot,' said Aggy.

'Correct, Alpha. It's a deal-breaker. Our best option would be to repair and resettle the Pedies' own hometown. The Pedies agree.'

'How realistic is their return to Coober Pedy?'

'Right now, I would say mostly unrealistic. The Pedies have the will but not the resources, and we have no excess capacity to assist.'

Aggy nodded as she searched her mind for an answer. 'Try Darwin. Frame it as a learning opportunity. Darwin University has a linguistics department. I'm sure there's a paper on it.'

Lawrence returned to the room and nodded to Aggy.

'Thank you for your assistance outside, General. All resolved?'

'For the moment, Alpha. They were fighting over a patch of dirt they both wanted to play ball on. Kids will be kids, I guess. The parents, now, they should have known better,' Lawrence shrugged.

The mood in the room grew heated. People scowled and muttered their disappointment. General Abudua slammed her hand on the desk and stood. 'With your permission, Alpha, I shall go and teach the adults a lesson in manners they will never forget to pass on to their offspring.'

'Belay that, Abudua. Your intentions are honourable. We do need to do more to teach the newcomers our ways. Yet, a lesson cannot be easily learned in a storm.'

With a grunt to General Kee, who nodded his agreement, General Abudua reluctantly sat down again.

Aggy smiled in gratitude. 'General Kee, you've been processing the Solaran refugees. Any news from Melbourne?'

'Yes. They seem scared. Nothing too specific. Just talk of less freedom, more restrictions and some new industrial construction. Don't know what that last one is about. I'll keep an ear out.'

Aggy nodded and turned to address Lawrence. 'Last on the agenda. General, I think you had better brief us on the *Starling* Project, please. If we could actually build a starship, we could leave this world which would resolve many of our issues.'

+   +   +

As Lawrence finished presenting the update on the shipbuilding progress, Aggy was drawn back to the window. Outside, the fracas between the two adults had resumed and turned physical.

As she watched, four others joined in. A tent was sent flying, and possessions were strewn across the ground. A Damaran worker trying to break them up got a fist in her eye for her trouble. A Solaran woman threw a chair at a smaller man holding a knife. He swiftly ducked. The chair flew over his head and crashed against the conference room window.

Aggy flinched back.

'Enough! No one disturbs Alpha's meeting!' General Abudua was up and halfway out the door as she spoke. Generals Kee and Mitta were fast to follow.

'Abudua's right. This isn't working. I had such hope at the beginning,' said Aggy.

'I'll see if I can calm things down,' said Lawrence, getting up to leave.

'I think this needs my attention too. Meeting adjourned.'

By the time they got outside, the brawl had become a small riot. At least twenty people had joined the fisticuffs, and there looked to be an equal number agitating from the side-lines.

Aggy was pleased to see her generals starting to make progress. General Abudua cut a wide path through the crowd, alternatively yelling at fighters to sit down or engaging them in hand-to-hand combat. Behind her, General Kee locked the seated combatants into restraints. General Mitta coordinated the Damarans, who swiftly restored the collapsed tents. Lawrence followed their lead, ducking away from blows and pulling children out of the fray.

Aggy moved amongst the restrained to ensure no one needed medical care. Thankfully, most of the wounds were superficial. However, the fight was not settling down. New participants entered the argument just as quickly as her generals removed others.

Not for the first time, she wished their hyperspeed cortical implants were still operational. She could speed up, zip around and cuff all the fighters within the space of a breath. Alas, Illustria's wondrous technology had stopped working when she died.

'Aggy!' a voice cut through the crowd. She spun around but couldn't see anyone close by who would call her by her given name. These days she rarely heard anything but her formal title, 'Alpha'.

Lawrence must have heard it too. In an instant, he was back at her side, holding a small child with one hand while shielding his eyes with the other as he squinted into the distance beyond the crowd.

'You heard it too?' she asked.

'Yeah. Although I can't see who's yelling.'

'Aggy! Aggy, over here!' This time the voice was louder.

Aggy put both hands to her eyes, trying to see better. Up on the ramp leading down from outside, she finally spotted three familiar faces.

'Look, over there. It's Harper and Sam and … is that *Kohl?*' she said, pointing.

'I reckon you're right. That's gotta be Kohl Pallas!' Larry's voice echoed loudly. People immediately turned to see where they were looking.

The effect of the famous name was surprising. Hushed whispers of 'Pallas' rippled through the Solaran crowd.

'Pallas…?'

'Is that the gov's son…?'

'What have they done to him?'

'You sure? Doesn't look like any Pallas I've ever seen…'

'Must be. That Damaran woman said so…'

Aggy looked around to assess the changing mood of the crowd. Most of the fighting had stopped as they gossiped about the possible arrivals, allowing Abudua to apprehend the last combatants. The other two generals had also stopped their work and returned her look of surprise.

'Settle down and stop your wriggling,' Lawrence said to his small captive, now tucked under his arm – the one person not paying any attention. Then, in a lower voice, he said to her, 'Imagine what we could achieve if we told them Kohl's *father* was coming.'

Aggy tried to suppress a laugh. He was right, though. The Pallas name still held great sway with these people. Despite Kohl's history, she was glad to have him back. He would be a bridge from the Solaran's past that might help them embrace a Damaran future.

'Hang on. What's going on with Sam?' asked Lawrence.

As the trio drew closer, it became apparent that Harper and Kohl each had an arm around Sam. They seemed to be half carrying, half dragging the young man.

'Looks like he's injured. General Mitta, call a doctor! Larry, find that child's parents and join me as soon as you can.'

The onlookers were almost silent as they stared in reverence at the unexpected approach of their leader's son. Seemingly star-struck, they parted to allow him passage.

'Aggy! Sam's hurt!' Harper yelled.

As the distance between them closed, Harper sped up, throwing her out of step with Kohl's slower gait. She stumbled a little, and Sam started to slip off her shoulders.

'I've got him.' In one swift move, Kohl lifted Sam up and carried him like a child over the remainder of the distance.

'What happened?' Aggy asked.

'There was an accident – a fire. Sam caught the brunt of it. It's been a long trip back, and he is extremely weak,' Harper said.

'Don't worry, Sam. We'll take care of you,' Aggy said, although it was not clear whether he was even conscious. His breathing was laboured, and his head hung forwards on his chest.

Harper leaned in close to her ear. 'He's blind.'

There was a deep fear in her young friend's eyes. Aggy gave Harper's shoulder a quick squeeze, then focussed on her other generals.

'Abudua, stay out here and finish your crowd control. Mitta and Kee, take Sam inside and see what you can do for him. Try to get him comfortable while the doctors figure out a treatment plan. Find Brother Stanley; Sam might appreciate a prayer.'

Her generals nodded and gently removed Sam from Kohl's arms.

'Now you, Kohl. Good to see you back. Before we chat, would you like to address your people?'

'I have no people,' Kohl said while slapping the blood back into his arms and rubbing his legs. 'And I'm not back. I only came here to help Harper. She couldn't have carried Sam alone. I'll be on my way shortly.'

Aggy bent to the side and looked briefly around Kohl to Harper, who shrugged and raised her eyebrows.

'Look, son. Whether you like it or not, these *are* your people. We hope to make them ours one day, but that will never happen if they're scared. A friendly face from home might go a long way to help assuage their fears.'

Kohl looked at his shoes.

Harper grabbed him by the shoulders and gave him a gentle shake. 'Hey! Just give them a wave. These people love you; give them something. You could really help here.'

'I can't help anyone. I'll check on Sam, and then I'm leaving.' He pushed her hands away and slowly followed the generals inside.

Aggy watched him walk away. 'Wow. I had hoped he would be in better condition.'

'Who, Sam?'

'No, Kohl.'

'Where's Uncle Larry?' asked Harper. 'Maybe he can get through to him. Kohl doesn't seem to care about anything I've said.'

'Larry should have been here by now. He was helping a child.'

The sounds of renewed fighting drew her attention. The

Kohl effect was seemingly short-lived. General Abudua and Lawrence appeared a short distance away, breaking up another brawl between the original instigators.

'Right, you're coming with me,' Abudua said. She grabbed the shorter man while Lawrence wrangled the other.

'Stay out of it, woman,' the man said. Twisting free, he retrieved a small knife concealed in the leg of his pants and thrust it at Abudua.

In one smooth movement, she deflected his thrust and used her foot to push him to the ground. She dislodged his grip on the knife and then kicked it across the mud and out of reach. 'What's your problem? Alpha has offered to share everything with you, and this is how you repay her?'

'What! Should I be grateful for this filthy mud pit? Back home, even our stable hands lived better than this.'

'You dishonour the Alpha when you behave like an ungrateful animal,' she growled and pushed her boot into the small of his back.

'Let me go. I'm taking my family out of this crap-hole,' he said, struggling against the general's hold. 'Hey, Kohl, get this bitch off me!'

Kohl hesitated, then resumed his walk. His shoulders seemed to droop lower as his pace picked up.

'Kohl … Kohl, we need you!' When Kohl didn't respond, the Solaran turned his ire to Abudua. 'What have you done to him? Not bad enough that you blew up Sydney. Now you humiliate our best men by making them wear rags. You're stinking Rats, all of you!'

The nearby crowd started to join in. A chant picked up. 'Stinking Rats, stinking Rats!'

'I've had just about enough of this guy,' Abudua said to herself as much as to anyone else. She bent down and lifted the Solaran man off the ground. He struggled against her grip and spat insults, which must have fuelled her determination, as she lifted him well above her head. The man thrashed like an upturned insect. Abudua roared her victory.

'Stinking Rats, stinking Rats!' the crowd's cry intensified.

The angry Abudua was exacerbating the situation; it was time to get help.

'Kohl, snap out of it. Come here now!' Aggy commanded. She strode towards the knife still lying on the ground, glaring at the crowd. 'General Abudua, release that man! Everyone else, calm down.'

At first, it looked like it had worked, but then the man Lawrence had restrained broke free, pitched himself across the ground and past Aggy's ankles, knocking her over.

'Alpha!' cried Abudua. She dropped her captive and lunged toward Aggy.

Kohl finally turned from the doorway and ran towards them.

'Look out. Knife!' he yelled, too late.

Lawrence moved in to re-capture his man. As he dove across the slippery dirt, the man turned over, holding the knife firmly clenched in an upright position. There was a brief, wet groan, and Lawrence fell to his side. The blade protruded from the left side of his chest.

'No!' Aggy was the first to reach him.

Kohl joined her on the ground. There was nothing anyone could do. Uncle Larry's life drained away on a crimson stream.

CHAPTER 4
Kaore Abbey, Melbourne

BESS LAID HER head back on *his* pillow, in *his* filthy room, in the highest apartment of *his* Abbey, which had been appropriated from *her* Civil Sisters. Admittedly, she hadn't been a Civy for years; still, it was a stiff drink to swallow – a final indignation in a sleepless night that kept her tossing and turning.

Morning crept over the windowsill. Spectra could be back at any minute to make wedding plans. She needed an exit plan. Bess sat up again and studied the room for inspiration.

The whole building was almost identical to Veruda Keep, her childhood home where Sydney's Civil Sisters had raised her. It was a safe bet rooms were allocated on the same system. The highest turret was usually for the highest authority, so presumably, this room had once belonged to the leader of the Melbourne Civies. Of course, Bess was more familiar with the lower rooms she had shared with the other senior acolytes, including Lola and Harper.

Now those were girls who knew how to behave in every situation. Lola would be resigned to choosing bridal gowns, and Harper would be meditating to sharpen her mind. If only she could remember Harper's favourite chant.

> *Closed eyes, open ears, closed mouth, no fears,*
> *Closed eyes, open ears, no distractions, all clear.*

It had never worked for Bess before – behaving, that is. In her early years, as a well-behaved royal child, she had been relinquished to the Civies. As a Civy, she was trained to betray her own people. Then she became the Master's perfect spy; only, she lost the war. Now, she had worked incredibly hard to look like the reformed Solaran princess, and what had that got her? She was betrayed by her parents and betrothed against her will.

> *Closed eyes, open ears, closed mouth, enough!*

The first shards of morning sun brought a voice to her door, ending her attempt at escape planning. Already in bed, it wasn't much of a stretch to pretend she was deep in sleep.

'Morning, m'lady. Lovely day brewing, even if it is a bit nippy. I'll get your things straightened in no time. Lady Pallas is keen to crack on with the morning. I'm sure you are too. Who doesn't love a wedding?'

Bess kept her eyes closed and listened to the well-meaning voice that prattled on about the day ahead. The woman's quick footsteps dashed around the room as she set down crockery and unlocked the window. After a night in the close room, the breeze was a relief, and the caf unexpectedly tempted her resolve.

'Such a beautiful dress you have here. I was just saying so to cook.' Bess felt the swish of the maid's skirts as she fussed with some loud crockery on the bedside table.

'Come on, m'lady. Your mother was quite insistent that I get you up and ready. A spot of breaky will revive you for your big day. Cook's prepared a delicious tray. Not enough to ruin the line of your gown, mind you.'

'M'lady? Are you all right, m'lady?' Feet shuffled a step back, and the inane wedding chatter ceased.

A slight tap on her shoulder told Bess the maid had taken the bait. 'M'lady?'

Bess urged herself not to flinch.

Another question. A tentative shake of her arm. A light gasp. The breakfast tray apparently forgotten, the footsteps backed up, then dashed across the room. The door opened and closed quickly. The game had begun. Bess kept her eyes closed and silently resumed Harper's calming chant.

Open eyes, open ears, closed mouth, no fears,
Open eyes, open ears, we are more powerful than
we appear.

The maid's voice returned to the corridor outside her room. Bess didn't need to make out her exact words to get the gist of her discussion with other hushed voices. The door opened, and her mother's scent wafted into the room. Bess steeled herself for what was to come.

'Wakey, wakey… See, ma'am. I can't rouse her,' said the maid.

'Enough of this. Rise and shine, child. Time to get married.' Her mother's firm hand shook her shoulder. 'Bess?'

Heavy footsteps entered the room next, and the maid's

tentative feet left. Gentle inquiries quickly gave way to anxious demands.

'This is your fault. You should have prepared her!' Her father shouted.

'How could I have known this would happen?' Her mother exclaimed.

'She's bluffing!' Spectra scoffed.

Firm hands raised her into a seated position, but Bess kept her body limp and her breathing even. When the hands released her, she allowed herself to fall back onto the pillow. She didn't even groan when her skull caught the edge of the headboard.

'Something is seriously wrong. A mother knows these things.'

A hand reached for her wrist. Bess tried not to panic lest her pulse give her away. For once, she was glad to hear Spectra overrule what was most likely her father.

'No, no, you won't. Get your hands off her. You're probably all in on this farce. Do you want to claim she's had some sort of collapse? Then I want to hear it from someone impartial.'

Bess was relieved when the voices retreated and the door closed once more. The relief was short-lived. Not much later, the door opened, and a new voice entered. Someone tapped her knee and elbow joints. Her temperature was taken, her pulse measured, and her eyelids were forced open to a bright light.

'In a bit of trouble here, lass?'

She couldn't help blinking at the holder of the light. It was Dr Bryan Kassel, the deposed governor of Melbourne and a distant cousin to her own family. He hadn't been seen since the week after they'd arrived. Officially, he was on vacation. His gaunt appearance and chewed nails suggested otherwise.

Discovered, her heart pounded, and she backed up against the rigid headboard as if the short distance would postpone the inevitable. Any second now, she knew he would alert the others.

Dr Kassel leaned in close and peered into her eyes. It was hard to tell whether he was looking for something or making a decision. He opened his mouth to speak just as a noise outside the door drew his attention.

'One moment, please,' he called, then turned his attention back to Bess. 'Right, all I can give you is a day. Make the most of it.'

Dr Kassel reached into his sleeve and unfastened his watch, which he placed on her wrist. Then he rifled through his medical bag and pulled out a scalpel, some antiseptic solution and a handful of bandages, which he slid under the bed.

'I'm sorry. That's all I have that might be useful to you. Good luck.'

'Why?' whispered Bess.

'Have you forgotten I have a daughter? In a few years, she'll be of marriageable age too. You're not the only one seeking an escape from this madness.'

'What's taking so long?' Spectra's voice bellowed from the other side of the door.

Dr Kassel stood, pulled down his shirt sleeves and adjusted the bed, ensuring the medical supplies were well covered. Then, as if an afterthought, he leaned back down and said, 'Steer clear of the saffy.'

Bess mouthed, 'Thank you.'

He winked and turned in time for the door to open a

crack. Bess, eyes now closed, heard her mother speaking.

'What's your diagnosis, Bryan?'

'Hysterical shock.'

'When will she come around?'

'Hopefully tomorrow. Maybe never. I'm sure your husband has told you these things are quite impossible to predict. Send the Archbrother to another room this evening. Tonight, she must be left in isolation for the sake of her mind. I will return in the morning to reassess her condition.'

As his footsteps receded, the voices outside erupted into a terse debate.

'This is ridiculous. Get her under a cold shower, then into a wedding dress.'

'Spectra! Have some mercy.'

'She's playing you. There's nothing wrong with Bess.'

'We never should have allowed it. My poor, sweet child.'

'Save me the maternal act. No one's listening, *Patricia!*'

'You will not address Lady Pallas that way, Spectra.'

'All right. No one's listening, *Lady Pallas, ma'am.* Better?'

'Maybe Lola could bring Bess around? The girl's always been good at keeping her entertained.'

'Not possible. I silenced her yesterday. No bride of mine will keep a bit on the side!'

'Spectra!'

'Patricia, I authorised the action. It had to be done.'

It was a hard loss for Bess to accept in silence. Lola had never asked for anything and had never judged her for her dealings with Charles. She was her one source of hope, and her father had authorised her removal. Only years of training prevented Bess from running to the door and screaming at her father.

'We will have to postpone the nuptials then.'

'Absolutely not. We had a deal. Control of my enforcer production in exchange for your daughter's hand. Right? You've got the enforcers, so let's speed up the nuptials.'

'You can't; she's non-responsive!'

'I don't care. You got the goods, and I want mine. Let's do this wedding now. I'm the Archbrother of Melbourne, and plenty of my Brothers are available to do the ceremony on the quiet.'

'And I say *no*. She is in no state to walk, let alone wed! Our subjects will expect a state wedding. That takes time and a bride who is awake.'

'We can have a second public ceremony later if you must. Today we make it official, or the deal is off. Call a maid, Patricia. Get her ready.'

'Step back, Spectra. I won't allow it. You might be the Archbrother, but don't forget that I am a medical physician too. I agree with Bryan. We'll take no action until the morning when we see how her situation resolves. Until then, this door will stay locked.

'I think now would be a perfect time for a tour of the new industrial sector. I'm especially keen to examine the furnaces. We need them in full production before we begin the next offensive against the Rats. Come on, Spectra, lead the way.'

There was a moment of silence. Bess would have loved to see their faces, knowing Spectra would be fuming at the sight of her father locking her away from him.

'I said, let's go. You too, Patricia. Nothing can be done for now.'

The heavy clunk of a key turning in the door lock was the trigger Bess needed to break out of her act. Time was short. There was little chance Spectra would heed her father's wishes. At any moment, he could burst back in.

When the steps outside receded, she jumped off the bed and devoured the long-cold breakfast tray, taking care to avoid the little blue glass of saffy.

'Well, Sisters, show me the way out. Spectra can't have erased all your secrets,' she said.

When she'd first arrived, Spectra had pointed out the rooms he'd *improved*. As he took his future bride up the grand central staircase – and of course, it was enforcers who actually carried her over thresholds – he had pointed out the new armoury. It was located where the meditation sanctuary used to be. Apparently, meditation was a ridiculous waste of time that only weak female minds considered necessary.

'Now it will be put to more productive use. Combat training,' he'd said, raising his voice over the deep grunting noises coming from within the room.

Spectra was so confident about his total conversion of the Keep. Yet, when she had allowed her hand to drift down to the wooden banister, she'd felt the smooth patina laid down by centuries of female hands. The Brothers may be tenants, but the hallways would always whisper *Sister*. There had to be something she could do. No self-respecting Civy leader would leave herself without exit options.

Bess took another scan of the apartment. Aside from Spectra's discarded robe, a caged lizard and a few pieces of dark furniture – totally at odds with the Sisters' light aesthetic – there wasn't much to see.

Someone had packed a trunk of her clothes. She rummaged through it and found nothing useful. The ceiling was high and smooth. If she stacked up the furniture, she couldn't reach it. The window wasn't much help either. It was too high a leap to the ground. Even if she made it without breaking every bone, the Abbey was adjacent to the new industrial sector with its busy factories and massive bluestone furnace. Too many witnesses.

What if? Bess shifted the bed and the chest of drawers, but her hunch didn't pay off. There were no hidden doors, only dust and a cheeky spider that reared up on its back legs before swinging away on a silvery thread.

Bess slid her hands along the walls and crept along the floor. 'Ah-ha!' There were a few floorboard joins that might be pried apart with the right tools.

She grabbed the little knife off the breakfast tray and turned it over in her hand. Her heart sank when she saw it had a little pearlescent handle that matched the cutlery of Government House. Someone had instructed her staff to send it over. How big was the conspiracy?

Pushing the thought out of her mind, she ran the knife over her palm. The blade was dull. No point trying to pry floorboards, use it as a weapon or pick the lock, for that matter. Knowing Spectra, the door would be guarded. Even if it wasn't, her face was highly recognisable, and she couldn't beat a whole building of Brothers and enforcers.

Digging crossed her mind. Back in Sydney, there'd been a jailbreak in '36. Over several months, two prisoners had used a spoon to chip away enough 'crete to loosen their cell bars and flee. Bess didn't have months, and she had already wasted hours searching to no avail.

'There has to be another way,' she told her reflection in the square mirror across the room. That was when it struck her.

Vanity was a high sin for Sisters, who employed anonymity as a weapon. Dressing in uniform cloaks encouraged Solarans to ignore their presence, and sometimes lulled them into dropping their guard and revealing valuable secrets. So why would the leading sister have a mirror in her quarters?

Bess took a closer look. The mirror was set relatively low on the wall, more chest height than face height, and appeared to be affixed with only three screws – more jarring abnormalities. It was as though her Sisters were beckoning her to the spot.

Careful not to damage the mirror, lest she was wrong and needed to replace it, she took the small knife and began unscrewing it. When the mirror came away easily, she smiled in satisfaction.

'Bingo!' Behind the mirror was a tube just big enough for a moderately sized woman to climb through.

Grateful for the practical day clothes someone had packed in her bag, Bess quickly changed. She packed the doctor's supplies into an improvised backpack, added the last of her food, and then hauled her trunk over the floor. It didn't take much effort to lift herself onto the box and into the tube.

'We are a mirror to each other. Look to your Sisters to see your true destiny,' she recited from ancient Civy doctrine, then let go of the rim and began her slide. In less time than she'd expected, she whizzed through the dark tunnel, which, she assumed by its twists, circled the inside of the turret and then on through the bluestone walls of the main building.

A quick kick at the end of the tunnel opened a hatch, and she arrived in a much larger space, albeit pitch black. She hoped she was in one of Illustria's tunnels, built for the secret movements of the Sisters. However, there was no way to be sure without a light, and tunnel illumination ceased working when Illustria died.

Bess fumbled in her bag for an essential item – the torch Spectra had bragged about inventing for months. Luckily Lola had the forethought to pocket one from her father's office whilst pretending to assist his maids.

The precious tool was cold and smooth to the touch. She flicked the only switch she could find. When light erupted from her hand, she smiled at the pleasant sensation of having technology at her disposal again.

Ahead of her was a smooth white tunnel, built for easy travel. A short distance away was one of the Sisters' emergency caches. It was intact. To her delight, she found a water bottle, warm jacket and food rations. A sure sign the Brothers hadn't found the tunnel yet. They had been so smug about mapping all the tunnel entrances and exits. So arrogant about so many things.

Bess figured she had a few hours' lead on Spectra. Once he discovered her escape route, he'd be quick to follow. She picked up the pack, tightened her shoes and raced down the tunnel.

Spectra and her parents would pay for what they had done to Lola. The Solaran world had given her nothing but pain. They would all pay.

CHAPTER 5
Lower Broome

HARPER'S THOUGHTS WERE interrupted by what she guessed was an attempt to knock on the canvas door of her tent. No doubt, someone was delivering another message from the generals.

With Uncle Larry gone, and Aggy officially in mourning, Harper had stepped into the leadership role. To be honest, she couldn't wait to hand it back. It was hard to fathom how Aggy had coped with the amount of decision-making required of Alpha. A week into the role and Harper was already exhausted.

'Are you there, Alpha?' said a muffled voice that sounded a lot like Kohl. Surprisingly, Lawrence's death had moved him to action where her pleas at his snowy shack had had no effect. When she'd become Alpha, he'd supported her by translating Solaran complaints into Damaran requests. It had been a blessing, really.

'May I enter?' he asked.

Harper ignored him. An Alpha's focus had to be on all her people's needs – not just the Solarans'. Instead, she focused on stretching the aches out of her shoulders. It was a rare rest break, and she was determined to make the most of her camp bed.

As acting Alpha, she had no time for the unscheduled or the princely. She had housing projects to manage, public works, law and order, approval of Abudua's proposed public manners campaign and contingency planning should the whole community fall apart, which was a frighteningly real possibility.

Even established Daraman communities, well below ground, were reporting the ill effects of rapid climate change. And that wasn't the worst of it. There had been a spate of disasters that could not be explained by nature alone.

Most Damarans openly blamed the Solarans, although a growing minority accused Illustria, questioning their blind devotion to her letters. Then there were the whispers of another player in the crisis. A mysterious woman had supposedly been glimpsed right before each disaster.

All three theories were ridiculous. Still, they had to find a resolution quickly, as they were running short on supplies.

'Alpha,' he said again.

'Not here.' Harper wiped a cool cloth across her forehead to soothe her buzzing headache. How had it all gone so wrong?

She had clutched at the promise of Lower Broome throughout the treacherous trek home with Sam. It was not the physical environment she had longed for. Even after two years, the cavern roof seemed to cry barrier rather than protection. What she'd yearned for was the expertise of her adopted Damaran family.

Everything will be all right once we get there, she had promised herself each time Sam's condition had deteriorated, especially when he developed a kind of delirium. '...stop, this isn't right. Stop, stop. Nothing's right!' He had babbled over and over.

Harper had thought their arrival would be a blessed relief, but the loss of Uncle Larry made her feel like she'd received a personal share of Sam's injuries. She felt seared through.

Her mind circled her memories of Civy training, looking for a meditation that might help. It was useless. The Sisters had prepared her for espionage, not grief.

'I know you're there, Harper.'

Soon, she had to meet General Kee at Gibson Falls to analyse the hydrology assessments. There was no time for royal distractions, so she stayed quiet, hoping he'd get the message and go away.

'Harper, please?' He said, poking his head through the tent flaps.

'I'm not sure there's anything more we can talk about. I've heard the Solaran's demands, and we can't oblige them. They are free to leave if this camp isn't good enough for them. Actually, you want to go, so why don't you take them with you? Go on. You have Alpha's permission to leave Lower Broome.' She waved her hand dramatically towards the tent opening without bothering to get up.

'Harper.'

She had a mind to physically throw him out, although one glance at Kohl told her he was no longer as feeble as he had been after their trek. Food, sleep and hygiene had done wonders to the line of his shirt. She hated to admit that he looked the perfect blend of Solaran nobility and future

Damaran general.

'I didn't come here to request a leave pass. I want to say an overdue thank you.' Kohl nudged her to make room for him to sit on the edge of her bunk.

She looked at him grudgingly, then gave in and moved over.

'Thank you for what?' she asked.

'The rescue.'

'No need. I would have done anything to get Sam back here.' She pulled the cloth over her eyes.

'*My* rescue. I didn't know how much I needed it.'

When she felt his body shake out a sigh, she removed the cloth and pushed herself up on her elbows to study his face. Kohl was blushing almost as vividly as the colour of his beard. Neither of them spoke.

Somewhere outside, a supply order was given, and construction noises clanged. Parents corralled children. Teenaged boys roughhoused on the way to the mess hall. And she could see the shadows of people queued outside her tent, awaiting her orders.

'It's so noisy.' She said, changing the topic.

Kohl reached over, took one of her hands in his and pulled her into an upright position. Then raised one eyebrow. Harper looked past him through the opaque nanoplex window. If all was going to plan, Mitta and Abudua would be processing the newcomers up on the entrance ramp.

'More refugees are coming,' he said, as though reading her mind.

'Yes. Mostly your mob from Brizzie, I'm told. No doubt they'll be disappointed at the lack of fanfare. Wonder what they'll make of so many Sydneysiders leaving. Tempers are probably flaring. Bet Abudua's giving them an earful.'

Kohl ignored her patter and bent down to blow warmth on her chilly knuckles. He finally had her attention. She couldn't help but focus on his lips and the flush spreading through her hand.

'They'll hate these tents too. They don't give anyone privacy,' she said quietly.

'I remember when we were...' Harper stopped Kohl from talking with a shake of her head. Every spoken word had the potential to travel quickly. It was no place for loud remembrances, even for an acting Alpha.

Harper withdrew her hand and struggled to contain herself. Memories of his touch kissing some hurts away while inflaming others. The old betrayals stung like fresh wounds.

Kohl moved his body closer and pushed her fringe aside, his gentle fingers soothing the worry lines of her headache. When his breath caught her cheek, she inhaled Kohl's scent and exhaled her Alpha.

He waited.

Nothing was ever simple. She lost control of one silent tear.

He slowly nodded and pulled her into his arms.

Harper clung to him for the longest time.

And then, finally, she let him go.

+   +   +

On her way to visit Sam, Harper paid careful attention to the demeanour of her people.

'We'll get there, Alpha. It'll be a grand city one day,' an old Damaran man said.

'We will,' she said, returning his grin. Although truthfully, it was difficult for Harper to imagine an established town in the soggy cavern. The hastily erected fabric homes were temporary at best – an illusion of privacy on a chaotically crowded field of mud. No wonder the Solarans hated it.

The original Lower Broome settlement had grown to almost 50,000 people, or so Aggy had recollected from her childhood. Whatever the number, the west end certainly had a mountain of flood debris leftover from it. In her first week as Alpha, Harper had set General Kee the task of repurposing that material. Fortunately, the colonists had used wood-look polymers that were non-degradable and entirely recyclable, even after a massive flood.

'I'm here to visit Sam,' she said to the nurse on duty as she entered the new hospital.

'Yes, Alpha.' The nurse directed her inside with a polite nod of the head.

It was her first time inside Kee's building. The module was only two rooms wide and a dozen long arranged around a central hallway. There was a surgery at one end and a dispensary at the other, with big double doors that would eventually link to the next module. It was a promising start.

'Hello,' she said.

Sam looked ghostly pale aside from the streaky red burn scars stretching out from the edges of his bandages. His breathing was laboured, and he mumbled as his head tossed from side to side.

'All wrong … none of this is supposed … too much to … all wrong… He won't be happy! No, no, no, won't be happy at all … all wrong.'

Harper wasn't sure if he was talking in his sleep or affected by fever. She reached out to feel his forehead. Immediately he grabbed her hand.

'Who's there?' he asked, one hand gripping her wrist and the other feeling the air for the rest of her.

'Sorry, I didn't mean to wake you. It's me, Harper. I came to see how you're doing.'

'Right.' He let her go and reached out to his bedside table. His hands were shaking. As he ran his fingers across the tabletop, he bumped a glass, spilling the water everywhere.

'Shit.' He tried to wipe it up with his hand.

'I'll get it, don't worry.'

'I'm useless.'

'Not at all. You're just recovering.'

Harper grabbed a towel off the shelf and mopped up the drink, then poured him a fresh glass and helped him move his hand into the right position to hold it firmly. Sam took several long sips.

Harper walked around the small space, partly to admire Kee's handiwork but mainly to give herself a moment to think. Words of consolation seemed inadequate. Thoughts for the future? Possible re-assignment? No, it was too soon for any of that.

She took another lap around the room. It was nothing like the clinical environment of other hospitals she had visited, more like a comfortable bedroom with a large frosted window and some nursing supplies.

Harper gave up on profound inspiration, sat on the chair next to his bed and settled for the obvious. 'How are you feeling?'

Sam shrugged.

'I heard you were making some good progress?'

'Still blind.'

It was hard to hear him so down. 'It's early days, Sam.

Once we get this place fully functional, who knows what'll be possible? Besides, your whole town was…'

'My whole town was what? Blind? Is that supposed to help? Now I can be like my old man was?' He snapped.

'No. Sorry, Sam. That's not what I was going to say. Look, just get well. Acting Alpha's orders! The mission to the core is still going ahead. Remember, we'll need you on that.'

Sam turned away. Harper didn't know what to say when he obviously didn't want her to say anything. She placed a gentle hand on his bed and shared his silence instead.

'Hello, General Harper, or is it still Alpha?'

Harper was relieved to hear Stanley's friendly voice. He entered the room accompanied by Byron Abudua, eldest son and first lieutenant to General Abudua. Strangely, Byron wore Brotherhood robes.

'Hello, young Sammy. It's Stanley and Byron. We've come to keep you company for a while.'

Sam didn't respond aside from pulling his blanket an inch higher. Stanley looked sadly at Harper and gently shook his head. A different tack might be in order.

'Now, Stanley, why have you got Byron dressed up as a Brother? You're supposed to be getting men *out* of the Brotherhood cult, not *recruiting* them to it! Maybe I should put Sam in charge of cult busting instead. I'm sure you'd be the best man for the job, right, Sam?'

Her suggestion was only half in play; their attire made her a little uneasy. It was a visible reminder of everything wrong with the Solaran caste system.

'I don't know about cult busting, but I'd have Sammy on our team any day. As for Byron, I think you should call him by his correct title. I would like to officially introduce you to Brother Byron of the Eternally Deluded,' he said with a snigger.

Following the older Brother's lead, Byron pulled his hood forwards, hummed a hymn and made some quasi-religious signs. Stanley playfully slapped Byron's hand down.

'Oh, blessed light. Don't go doing that; it's a dead giveaway. Just clasp your hands and stare into space. Try to look Brotherly, like you're thinking big thoughts.'

'My mother says I always think big thoughts,' Byron said in a serious tone before letting out a belly laugh.

Harper joined in, knowing it was definitely not something General Abudua would say. Possibly from the lips of his softer second mother, Grace Abudua. Never the general.

She glanced at Sam, thinking she might have seen him smirk, but he remained quiet and motionless. 'Seriously, do you have news from your trip? I didn't expect to see you two back here so soon.'

'Hang on.' Stanley stepped into the doorway and made an all-too-obvious show of checking the outer hall for eavesdroppers. Harper was glad it was his first and last spy mission. Tending to the emotional needs of the downtrodden was definitely his higher calling.

'We didn't even need to reach Kaore Abbey because we met three senior Brothers fleeing Melbourne. They were lucky to get out, I suspect. The Solarans have everyone in lockdown!

'Apparently, Kohl's sister was publicly betrothed to Spectra one day and disappeared the next. The governor's blaming the "Rat terrorists". He's announced she's been kidnapped and is preparing for war with us – we're the Rats!'

Stanley spoke in a rush of words that appeared to leave him dizzy and breathless. Byron reached out to steady the older man.

'Thanks, son. Always so kind. Anyway, Harper, that's not the worst of it. Bess fled to the tunnels, with Spectra in pursuit. He was in a murderous rage when he discovered her escape. I'm not surprised; you know what he's like! Yelled and screamed the place down, he did. They say he killed two Brothers whose only sin was getting in the way of his tirade.'

Stanley stopped again to catch his breath.

'It's horrible, sweetheart, just horrible. Not even Bess deserves that, and now we're at war again. Golly! Anyway, this news changes everything. Aggy's coming out of mourning early. She's consulting with the other generals right now. They're enacting an urgent evacuation of as many people as possible. I rather think Byron should sit with Sam while you join her, don't you, Harper? Kohl's already there. When we left, she was having a jolly hard time convincing him not to race after his sister.'

Harper rolled her eyes at yet another about-face from Kohl. She said her goodbyes and took off, wishing she still had access to hyperspeed.

+   +   +

'Perfect timing!' Aggy flung her hands up in exasperation as Harper entered the room. A table was up-ended, and the curtain was askew as though a brawl had occurred. In the middle of the floor, being straddled by the tank-like form of General Abudua, was a red-faced Kohl Pallas.

'I came to see how you like your new common room, Alpha,' said Harper, all sweetness and light, deliberately ignoring Kohl.

'Ah, yes. The common room's looking good. Nice

interior design. You really nailed that minimalist look I like,' Aggy said with a wave of the hand.

'Let me up,' Kohl growled.

Harper ignored him and tried not to smirk. She rather liked the idea of Kohl spending some time underneath a formidable woman like Abudua.

'I can't take all the credit, Alpha. Those are Mitta's cupboards. They were designed for recreational supplies, with easy conversion to weapons lockers should the need arise.' Harper opened the doors to demonstrate.

'Clever. I approve,' Aggy replied.

'Get off me!' Kohl continued to struggle.

'No-one disrespects Alpha,' Abudua said.

Kohl bucked and thrashed. The general crossed her arms and held fast. Clearly losing the battle, Kohl quietened down and gave Harper a desperate look.

'Please,' he begged.

'All right. This has gone on long enough. General, let him go. Remember, he is new to this community. I'm sure he didn't intend to be disrespectful,' said Aggy.

Abudua hesitated.

Aggy urged her on with a hand gesture.

'Maybe you're right. It's not his fault he was raised by a mannerless Solaran strumpet with too little sense to teach her son respectful behaviour,' said Abudua.

Harper offered Kohl a hand. 'Moving right along. Stanley filled me in on the news from Melbourne. I'm so sorry about Bess.'

'Thanks,' he said, brushing off his clothes. 'I was just saying goodbye to Aggy when…'

Abudua immediately stepped closer, nostrils flaring, one hand on her weapon, the other raised in a fist. Despite being a head taller, Kohl visibly shrank from her dominant stance.

'Alpha! I mean, I was saying goodbye to *Alpha*.' He raised his hands in surrender. 'I'm leaving now to find my sister before Spectra does.'

'Hold on. There's another problem,' said Harper. 'Alpha, it's our water supply. Gibson Falls has stopped running. General Kee can't find a reason. The inlet pipes all look normal, which means the problem is farther up the lines. We can't get to them because they're all encased in nanos. If we could get central control access in the core, we might be able to deactivate them.'

'How long?' asked Aggy.

'Kee estimates we'll run out of water in a week, maybe three if we ration. Hard to know precisely given our fluctuating numbers. A bunch of Solarans gave up on us and left for Melbourne today. If the Buchanites can take another hundred Damarans, we might be able to make the rations last a month. Anyone from Noosa will be a good fit for them too.'

Aggy sat down heavily. A world of worries crept across her face.

'It gets worse.' Harper winced.

'Go on.' Aggy straightened her spine in anticipation.

'We had about twenty Damarans arrive this morning from Darwin University – it's caved in. They had to trek overland as their tunnels had collapsed too. They don't know how many of their people are still alive in Darwin. They're requesting a meeting with you about a rescue mission.'

'Those poor people. When will this end?' Aggy placed a hand on her chest as if retreating from a physical blow. For a moment, no one said anything. Then Kohl started to shuffle his feet.

Aggy studied him before speaking. 'No point building a

spaceship if we're all going to die of thirst, freeze or be trapped from cave collapse in the meantime. Recall the *Starling* team. They have engineering skills way beyond ours. They might have a solution we can't see.'

'Especially their AI, Sedna. A numan might be the edge we need to hack into the core,' said Harper.

'Waste of time. It won't help.' Kohl glanced towards the door.

Harper's heart sank. If he bolted out to pursue Bess, the Sydney mission – and Sam's injury – would all be for naught.

'Kohl, remember when we went up against Spectra last time? We only just made it out alive, and that was with the hyper implants. I'm not sure we're a match for him now, and you know that wherever Bess is, that's where Spectra's heading.'

'All the more reason to get going. I can't leave Spectra hunting Bess.' Kohl headed for the door.

'Sedna's not just a spaceship pilot; he's a numan. That means superior reflexes, stamina and strength. He could be the way to apprehend Spectra, which will also help Bess.'

'She's right, Kohl. The only way anyone can be safe is to get down to the core, which will take all five of us, including Spectra. Please, go with Harper to retrieve him and the rest of the *Starling* team.'

Kohl hesitated, one hand on the door.

Harper tried one more thing to nudge him towards Aggy's request. 'Besides, no one can outfox Spectra like Bess can. Don't forget, both the Civies *and* Charles trained her. She probably knows more about this world than any of us. We could roam for years in those tunnels and never find her. Whereas our climate issues? If this weather continues, we'll all die. The only choice is to get down to Honeysuckle Creek.'

Harper put a hand on Kohl's shoulder. 'You're a good brother, but you have to let her go for now.'

'All right. Where is this *Starling* team?' he asked reluctantly.

'The Pit,' said Aggy, in a voice that made it sound more of an apology than a destination.

'You're kidding! It's in The Pit? On the outskirts of Melbourne, and my parents didn't notice?'

A flash of anger crossed Kohl's face. Harper couldn't tell if it was in response to the potential of seeing the Pallas' or disappointment that the Solarans had been duped again.

'Melbourne's the last city left with operational power nodes. Luckily The Pit workers had already decided to join us, so it didn't take much to convince them to keep up their ruse and cover our power usage,' said Aggy.

'Bloody hell. All right, then. I'll get Sedna, *Alpha*. Then I'm off to find Bess.' Kohl ended the conversation by leaving the room.

CHAPTER 6
Darwin

SPECTRA FAILED TO understand why no one in his crew had a sense of humour. It had taken him five whole minutes to stop laughing at the latest conundrum while those around him stared on dumbfounded.

'Really? Can no one see this is even a tiny bit humorous? Tough crowd.' Spectra wiped mirthful tears from his eyes.

The unfortunate young Brother had been standing in the worst possible position when the tunnel caved in. His lower legs, feet and a hint of robe were all that were visible under a pile of unmovable rock.

'People, let me explain one more time. We are at a dead end. Get it: *dead* end.' Spectra kicked at the Brother's blood-splattered sandals for emphasis.

'What, we can't have a chuckle now and then? Must it always be prayers, doom and gloom, prayers?'

One of the two remaining Brothers tried to force his mouth into an entirely unconvincing smile. It was feeble, really, as though he was trying to make the best of passing a small kidney stone. The other closed his eyes while mouthing a silent prayer for the dead. The three enforcers continued to look glum, although admittedly, that was a default facial expression that he himself had chosen in their design.

Spectra gave up. He signalled the enforcers to pick up their travel supplies and follow him back up the tunnel.

'Sure, forcing an ancient religious order to evolve to have post-war relevance is serious business, and quelling dissenters who are not ready to embrace our new doctrine does require actions that some might find unsavoury. But seriously, am I not allowed one single moment of merriment?' he asked himself as much as anyone else.

'Can't a man find some humour after dreary days of chasing a wretched bitch of a bride who, by the way, I can't even stand? Remember, I'll have to consummate the marriage *before* I can even kill her.' Spectra shivered at the thought. 'Some reward that is. I'd rather do it with one of you five than that uppity skank.'

He stopped briefly to shine the torch at each of his team members. Days spent trudging through the abandoned tunnels without bathing had left them in a putrid haze of musty body odour, soiled clothes and uncleaned teeth.

'Sadly, even in this state, I do think you guys are more appealing than my bride. I'll have to fantasise about you while I'm doing my marital duty.' Spectra rested a hand on Undersecretary Thomas II's shoulder as laughter took hold again.

'Don't know why I'm laughing; look at what my life's become,' he said, bending over as his belly laugh shook his thin form.

'Sir?' a voice came from the back of the pack. The

smallest enforcer was pointing to a dark shape on the tunnel wall. It looked like a door.

'Well, well.' Spectra wiped his eyes and shone a light on the shape. 'Looks like we missed this junction to another tunnel. Thank goodness we don't have to retrace our steps all the way back to Melbourne. Great stuff. I'm moving you to the top of the list of replacements for Bess should my wedding night fall through.'

Spectra winked at the Brother and slapped him on the backside as he stepped through the narrow doorway.

+ + +

Bess staggered the last few steps through the tunnel she hoped would lead to Darwin. Dizzy from exhaustion, she almost didn't care whether Spectra lay in wait or not. Her supplies had run out two days prior, and all the emergency caches she'd passed had been raided.

The fabled Damaran university was her last chance; unfortunately, she'd never actually attended the university. Civil Sisters taught their own. However, she had devoted hundreds of hours to studying tunnel maps during her childhood training, and Lola had insisted they revise those memories in preparation for their great escape.

The memory of Lola caused her to stumble. She righted herself and hoped she was taking a step towards civilisation. Darwin would have at least three exit points to other locations where there were no bracelets, ball gowns or bigotry. With a bit of disguise, she could seek sanctuary. Then, she could figure out a plan to ruin Spectra, her parents and everyone else who had ever wronged her.

Lost in her daydream, Bess didn't notice the growing

amount of debris on the floor. She managed to shuffle all the way to the tunnel exit before registering the smell of char. It was only when she stood on a burned plaque engraved with the words *Lumine Scientia,* that she realised something was dreadfully wrong.

'No!' Bess slumped to the ground and wept. Ahead of her were the remains of what should have been a grand foyer to freedom. Somehow, Spectra must have beaten her.

'How could you do this?'

Lola had said that the double-storey vestibule walls would feature depictions of Damaran fables in intricate mosaic tile designs. Instead, what was left was a battered mess scarred by a web of what appeared to be lightwand fire. The central light, which must have been beautiful once, hung askew from a frayed wire. Its smashed bulbs were originally configured into the shape of a great bird.

Bess heard the crunch of footsteps from not too far away. She wiped her face with her sleeve, picked up a shard of tile for a makeshift weapon and moved forwards through the splintered double doors.

Now she had only three priorities; find supplies, slow down Spectra and find a way out.

+   +   +

Spectra covered his nose and cast his torchlight around. The approaching terminus of the tunnel was almost easier to smell than see. With each step, the air grew thicker with blinding, choking soot. There must have been a fairly decent blaze somewhere ahead.

'Ah-ha!' At last, the source of the soot. It looked like an office to the right had been destroyed by fire. He would have investigated further if not for the loose overhead wires that were dropping sparks onto the ground.

'You. Stand there.'

Without questioning the order, the enforcer stepped into the dangling wires and instantly fell to the ground, his body convulsing briefly.

'Right, we're moving this way.' Spectra stepped over the enforcer's head and waved his remaining team on.

An open corridor to the left appeared to be in reasonably good condition for an underground building, despite scorch marks and debris. The square, precisely joined walls were more like those found in a Solaran military or hospital structure.

'You're kidding. So much for simple-minded vermin.' Spectra had never actually seen a Rat community. Like most Solarans loyal to the Pallas family, he refused to believe they lived in anything more than sewers and ramshackle diggings, which made this all the more surprising. It was, well, civilised, aside from the air which tasted like barbecued wool.

That could not be typical, even for them. Behind him, the usually unshakeable enforcers began to cough. Spectra tightened the covering over his mouth. It made little difference. He picked up speed down the corridor, hoping it would lead to fresh air.

The pattern of wreckage seemed unnatural, with no focal point. Twice, as they walked through the labyrinth of corridors and small rooms, they found sections of the walls crumbling to the floor. There were obvious signs of swift evacuation everywhere: books left open on desks; long rectangular dining tables in the cafeteria topped with plates of spoiling, half-eaten food.

The farther Spectra explored, the more he had to admit

to himself that they had underestimated the Rats' operations. Aside from a surprising amount of spider webs, the facilities were on par with the Solarans'.

At length, they came across a vast room that might have been a laboratory. It was littered with smashed equipment and instruments dusted in soil. Above it all, the ceiling had been wrenched open to the rocky cavern roof above.

Spectra was disappointed he hadn't found it before it had been destroyed. Like most technology, enforcer production pods had not functioned the same since the Light War. So far, several Brothers had been set to work on the problem with little success. Had they had this laboratory, they might have cracked the mystery.

'Would have made a good enforcer facility,' he said to himself.

'Damn enforcers. Not natural!' A shrill voice pierced his ears.

Spectra spun around to face his team.

'Who said that?'

'Said what, sir?' the closest Brother asked, looking innocent enough that Spectra second-guessed himself. He had been lost in his thoughts. Maybe he had imagined the voice.

'Nothing! Keep your mind on your own damn business. You're supposed to be looking for my bride, not clinging to me asking useless questions.'

The Brother yelped when Spectra slapped him across the head for good measure.

'Hey! The big guy up back – you're with me. The rest of you, split up into two teams. Search this place and meet back here in thirty minutes. Bess Pallas has to be hiding somewhere. Find her. Now!'

A few crunchy steps farther, Spectra and his enforcer arrived at a series of rooms with large observation windows and beds. It looked like a hospital dormitory. Spectra wondered if they had been stealing health resources from the Solarans.

'Not right. Going to reverse it all,' the mystery voice said, slightly louder this time. Closer, and definitely female. Bess.

'Surely you heard that?' he asked his enforcer as he stopped to wave his torch around, trying to identify the source. The enforcer, who said nothing, moved into a combat stance. Spectra nodded in approval and followed his lead, raising his fists.

'Reverse it? How dare you, Bess! There will be no backing out of your parent's deal. I'll remind you that I am the Archbrother, and you are nothing. Show yourself!'

'Not happy…'

'I don't know why you're not happy. I would have thought any girl would be thrilled to marry a man of my station.'

'Won't get away with it.'

A flash of movement in the adjacent room caught his eye. It looked like a woman speeding out the door, but it was hard to be sure in the dim light.

'Got you!' Spectra stormed into the room after her.

The space was empty. He didn't mind. A Pallas would never just surrender. A game of hide and seek would be a more fitting way to end the chase. A hint of movement through another doorway caught his eye.

'Not this time!' Spectra leapt over the bed and ran through the door to the next room. It was empty, like all the others. A noise outside sent him jumping out into the corridor, relishing the chance to finally confront her.

'A-ha!' he yelled to nothing again. It was unfathomable how quickly she was moving. An unbroken chair seemed the perfect spot to plonk down and review. Where was she? Only people with hyperspeed moved that fast. No one had hypers anymore. Her voice was clear as day, but she was nowhere to be seen. Nothing added up.

'Look,' said the enforcer, and he pointed up to the ceiling.

Spectra strained his neck back. A fine jagged line was forming out of a massive ceiling collapse two doors farther down the hall. As he watched, there came a low rumble. In seconds, the crack had expanded, and a stream of fine particles sifted down on their heads.

'Get me out,' yelled Spectra.

The enforcer picked him up without hesitation and tossed him over his shoulder. He powered through the building as the roof started to cave in. Almost too late. Twice he had to stop to kick through the debris that built up around his feet.

Spectra covered his head to save himself from the falling rocks and ceiling plaster while desperately hoping they were going in the right direction. They raced back through the medical rooms where he had first seen a glimpse of her, then down the corridor with the science labs and past the cafeteria.

'Stop, stop. It's her. Let me down!' He pounded on the enforcer's shoulders.

At the end of the corridor, a woman stood just beyond the exit. She was facing away from Spectra, her arms stretched high above her head, muttering and swaying.

'Bess!' he yelled.

'No more.' She jerked her arms as though pulling on

invisible strings, and the roof came down around her.

'No!'

The enforcer threw Spectra into the tunnel as the underground facility collapsed. Spectra scrambled away from the rubble that billowed towards him.

When the dust finally settled, a cold reality hit. His whole team was gone, buried under the ruins, and unless Bess had a working hyperdrive, she was gone too. Governor Pallas was not going to be happy. The deal would be off.

Nothing was funny anymore.

CHAPTER 7
The Pit, Melbourne

DR KASSEL LOOKED down at Mr Xi, removed his glasses, rubbed his eyes, and silently counted to five while he tried to refrain from voicing his displeasure. It was a strategy that had served him well in the past. People were more willing to accept an unfavourable prognosis from a contemplative physician.

He felt behind him for KonWong, a massive black and red dragon statue that held up the entrance to the boardroom of West Factory, where the critical meeting should have taken place. Finding the dragon, which strangely looked more like a lion with wings given its wild mane and lack of scales, he rested his head against its ancient forelegs.

Six, seven, eight.

Xi, the unofficial mayor of The Pit, appeared equally disappointed. He muttered his commiserations to the tiled floor while wringing his seven-fingered hands over and over.

Hand-wringing was never a good sign amongst the

Digies, the local workers of The Pit. The extra fingers that sprouted soon after their first birthdays enabled them to manufacture delicate gadgets for the Solarans. Unfortunately, their gift of dexterity seemed to come at the cost of holding on to too many worries. Fiddling, knuckle-cracking and hand-wringing were common signs of Digi stress. Early-onset arthritis also plagued the short-statured people.

When Xi's hand-wringing showed no signs of abating, Kassel worried that the old man's digits were beginning to spasm.

Nine, ten.

He stopped counting and looked down at his old friend. If Xi had been a Solaran, he could have prescribed an anti-spasmodic to ease the pain. However, it was an untested treatment, as no Solaran had spare digits to trouble them anyway. Then again, if Xi had been *Sydney* nobility, he would have just prescribed a relaxing dose of saffy – which was at the heart of Xi's and Kassel's current worries.

If this latest turn of events compromised their operation, all was lost. He nodded his understanding and lowered a hand to Xi's frail shoulder. Two fathers, two leaders and too many variables in one all-consuming problem of staying alive. Only one father had a son who contributed more issues than he solved, and it wasn't Xi.

'Take me to Daemon,' said Dr Kassel.

From the day he was old enough to hold a lightkey, Daemon Kassel had pushed the boundaries of his birthright. At twelve, Daemon had attempted to cross the Badlands solo to visit his favourite cousins, Kohl and Mark. That had led to a two-day search party consisting of eighty-three men, which ended in a found child and a three-month light privilege suspension. Of course, Lady Kassel had reduced the punishment to two weeks after a series of embarrassingly public temper tantrums.

At fifteen, Dr Kassel discovered Daemon running a gambling ring from a utility shed in the back of his school. At sixteen, back when the skies were still dark, the boy dabbled in counterfeit lightkeys. By eighteen, there was a girl on the wrong side of consent and the suggestion of a light-whip wedding. It had cost Governor Kassel a house to avoid that scandal.

Now, at twenty-two, he finally showed some signs of maturing. Most probably triggered by the loss of his mother, the arrival of Uncle Matthias Pallas and his father's subsequent demotion from the governorship. The realisation that he was no longer the heir to the Melbourne governorship had put a severe dent in his aspirations.

As Xi led Dr Kassel through the rabbit warren of delights and contraband that was The Pit, Dr Kassel realised his miscalculation. Their covert operation could have been the perfect hideout for a young man needing to learn his lessons away from prying Solaran eyes if there weren't so many temptations.

On the surface, The Pit looked like a filthy industrial mine few Solarans deigned to visit. Little did they appreciate the thriving metropolis below. The enterprising Digi families had crisscrossed the mine's top levels with bridges and bracings that housed hundreds of micro-factories. These were occasionally accessed by Solaran servants and, at one time, the Civil Sisters.

This was where licensed businesses like West Factory manufactured Pallas' identity bracelets. Enforcers in black bracelets arrived twice weekly to pick up fresh batches from Digies, who were ranked too low to wear any bracelets.

Things got more interesting on the mid-levels, their current destination. Away from prying Solaran lights, in the shade of the blackened bridges, the Digies created more unique items, such as designer holo devices and personal gadgets to thrill the monied elite. And, quite possibly, weapons for the Damaran rebels. It was Kassel's policy not to ask too many questions.

On the deeper levels, where snow rarely reached, the air grew steamy, excess clothing was shed, and relationships warmed. There, a new breed of Digie entrepreneurs, spurred on by stories of Damaran post-war prosperity, abandoned manufacturing in favour of hospitality.

Dr Kassel wondered why he had never travelled this deep into The Pit before. The richly coloured shop facades that leapt out from the black metal scaffolding were as attractive as the spicy smells wafting out of the bars and cafes. Alas, they were also the perfect enticement for his wayward son.

'This way.' Xi scurried down another laneway.

Dr Kassel needed to duck continuously and occasionally even turn sideways as Xi sped him through pedestrian spaces not designed for a man of his stature. Twice he almost lost his head to overhead signs, including a fowl-shaped one hanging outside a grocer's.

'Nearly there.' Xi led him up a flight of stairs to a broad platform with a large unmarked door. He put his hand on the doorknob, then hesitated as though the door was stuck.

'Here, let me try.' Dr Kassel easily reached over him to shove the door open.

'I'm sorry, I didn't want you to see this.'

Beyond the door was a dim room, soft with furnishings and hard with scent. Had he been a lesser man, Dr Kassel would have given in to the hacking cough the heavy spice provoked. Instead, he looked around for a way of clearing the air.

'A window?'

'None that open.'

'Pity.'

'I'll organise some light. Hang on.' Xi entered the gloomy room and activated a single hanging bulb that bathed the room in sharp red light.

It took Dr Kassel a moment to work out what he was seeing. Between them was a large round bed covered in scarlet velvet. On it, three people appeared to be sleeping, legs and arms intertwined. Two were barely dressed young Digie women. The other was a tall, well-muscled Solaran man.

'Daemon,' said Dr Kassel softly.

Xi opened one of the girls' hands and apologised as he removed a vial half-filled with navy liquid. 'I'm sure they are just resting after testing the samples. Perhaps some caf would help?'

Dr Kassel had already seen the purple tinge on his son's lips and searched his medical bag for a stimulant to counteract saffy overdose. 'You stupid boy,' he snapped. 'This was supposed to save us from them, dammit!'

Mr Xi started cracking his knuckles again as Dr Kassel administered an adrenaline shot in the crook of his dying son's arm.

CHAPTER 8
The Pit, Melbourne

HARPER TOOK GREAT delight in removing her gloves and scarf. The overland journey had been almost as icy as the Sydney trails, and she would not be surprised if she had frostbite on the tips of her toes.

'It's a shame we're on a mission. I've been here a few times. It's always toasty. The locals are friendly too, and they make the most interesting gadgets. How do you think we got our torches?' Harper said, giving Kohl a conspiratorial wink.

'They made a test batch for Spectra and a bulk supply for us. I bet he thinks he's so "special" with his handful of prototypes. Meanwhile, we have crates full of them. We're going to start exploring the tunnels again and hopefully find a way back to Honeysuckle Creek.'

They had been circling the lower levels of The Pit for ten minutes, waiting for their contact to show. Harper enjoyed the traders' stalls, while Kohl only had eyes for the small city's structure.

'I can't believe The Pit is such a deep complex. You almost can't see the surface,' he said, craning his neck up. 'Everywhere you look, it's busy. Not loving all the hanging signs, though.' Kohl rubbed his forehead where he'd smashed his head again.

'I don't think it's designed for the nobility,' said Harper.

'Look at that.' Kohl moved forwards to get a better view of a troop of kids playing tag up and down scaffolding. They seemed to defy gravity as they used the extra digits on their bare feet to catapult themselves from ladder to rope-hold to walkway. One bold little guy hung upside down with his arms crossed, taunting the lead player to catch him before righting himself and scampering away.

'Good to see the kids making the most of their situation,' said Harper.

'Wouldn't mind taking a crack at it myself. How long have we got?'

'Not enough. Besides, you'd probably break something! You don't have Digie skills. Why don't you try one of these barbequed Pit mushies instead? They're delicious.'

Harper passed Kohl a steaming bag she had bought off a nearby trader. He took one bite, grimaced and looked for a place to spit it out.

'Not a fan?' mumbled Harper through her mouthful. 'Maybe they're a taste the Solarans never acquired. Pity. We love them – when we can get them, that is. These days, few places are warm enough to grow mushies. They're such a rare treat.'

'Get down!' Kohl pulled her down to squat behind the mushie trader's brazier.

'What is it?' Asked Harper.

'Don't know. A man went into that building on the

platform over there. I only saw him from the back, but he's double the size of a Digie. Have you ever seen a Solaran this far down before?'

'Definitely not.'

'Come on.'

They crept across the walkway until they were closer to the building.

'Wait, I can see him now. That's Xi with him. We need to get a better look at what's going on. Wait here.'

Assuming her smaller form would be easier to hide, Harper took the lead. She slunk past a stall and approached the small window next to the door the men had entered. Looking around to check she hadn't been spotted, she popped her head up to peek over the pane, then dropped back down and signalled to Kohl to come closer.

Kohl hunched over and hurried to her side. 'What is it?'

'Xi is there and a few Digie … um … entertainers, I guess you'd call them? It's hard to make out much more, as the tall guy is blocking the view. Oh, and I can see a pair of Solaran legs on the floor.'

Kohl stood up at the window and checked inside. 'It can't be.'

'What? You recognise that guy?'

'Get up, he's harmless.'

Kohl's shoulders visibly relaxed, and as he looked down at her, Harper thought she could see the hint of a smile on his face for the first time in a very long time.

'So much for our spy moves. It's my uncle, Governor Bryan Kassel. No need to worry. He wouldn't hurt a fly.'

'Why would he come down here?'

'He's a doctor, like my Dad, so I guess it's not impossible for him to be down here doing an emergency medical visit.'

Harper didn't share his cheerful attitude. 'Harmless, you say?'

'Sure.'

'Like your Dad?'

'Yes,' Kohl replied cautiously.

'Just like your Dad – a governor and a *doctor*?'

'That's quite common for governors. You know that.'

Harper stood up and studied him, unsure why Kohl still wasn't making the connection. 'Did you get a proper look at the kids down here? How do they manage to hang upside down?'

Kohl shrugged.

'Did you notice the woman I bought the mushies off? Did you see her fingers? All fourteen of them?' Even in the low light of early evening, Harper could see Kohl grow pale.

'It can't be. Not Uncle Bryan too? I used to spend holidays with the Kassels. We had great fun. He's kind.'

'Say it, Kohl.'

Kohl shifted his weight from one foot to the other.

'You're never going to get past this until you talk about it. It's not your fault, but you have to admit it,' Harper urged.

Kohl looked up and pushed his hair back. 'I guess the Digies are not naturally born like that, are they?'

Harper slowly shook her head, not taking her eyes off her troubled friend. She wondered if he could verbalise the atrocities his extended family had been perpetrating for generations.

'You need to say it.' She placed a hand on his arm. 'You can do this.'

Kohl cleared his throat. He looked around as though worried someone might overhear, and then he took a deep breath. 'Around the Digies' first birthday, Uncle Bryan performs a ceremony, including a special immunisation.'

He stopped for a few more deep breaths. Harper gave his arm a little squeeze of encouragement; she was worried he might hyperventilate.

Blowing out his breath, he muttered the fateful words. 'It's not an immunisation. In Sam's town, my father made the miners blind. In Coober Pedy, it was deafness. Here, my uncle retards their growth and causes additional digits to grow.'

'Why?' said Harper, gently.

'All so that they can better serve the bloody Solaran empire. They are deliberately altered and forced to live in this grotty hole so they can manufacture a cushy life for people like me.'

Harper nodded slowly.

'Right,' Kohl straightened his back and charged for the door.

'Wait,' cried Harper, too late.

Kohl kicked open the door. 'I know what you have done, Uncle, and it's going to stop. Right now.'

'Kohl?' Dr Kassel turned towards his nephew and made eye contact with Harper through the windowpane.

Her cover blown, she reluctantly joined Kohl inside.

'And who's this?'

'I'm Harper, a friend of Kohl's. We were…'

'Don't bother, Harper. I'm done with secrets. Uncle, this Is General Harper of the Damaran nation. We both know what you've been doing, and we're here to stop you!'

'I'm not sure I follow. Look, will you just give me a minute, please?' Dr Kassel focussed back on his patient and put his stethoscope in his ears.

'You can't turn your back on the truth, Uncle.'

'All right. I'll tell you all about the saffy. First, I need to finish here.'

'Who's Saffy? I'm talking about creating a whole caste of people as slaves to your whims. The Digies! Uncle, are you even listening to me? Do you care?'

Dr Kassel reached into his medical bag and took out an injection. He applied it to the patient on the floor, and the prone legs started to shake. The doctor retrieved another shot. The patient groaned, and the sound of retching followed. Mr Xi ran to his side with a bucket. A bitter smell wafted into the air.

'Easy does it. You'll be right, mate,' the doctor said gently.

Kohl edged around his uncle to view the patient. He signalled Harper over. The doctor was taking the pulse of a young man who bore a striking resemblance to Kohl.

Mr Xi helped him take a sip of water. The young man nodded his thanks and lay back down, casting his eyes to the unexpected visitors.

'Kohl?' the patient asked in a trembling voice.

'Yeah, it's me, Daemon.'

The patient smiled a half-smile before closing his eyes and surrendering to rest.

Dr Kassel stood up and repacked his medical bag. 'He's given me quite a scare. He'll come good now, I think.'

'Uncle, I'm sorry. I didn't know.'

Dr Kassel looked over at the only one who remained silent throughout the ordeal. 'Xi, would you mind if we used your place for a chat while Daemon sleeps this off? I think my nephew and I have some old family business to discuss.'

CHAPTER 9
Kaore Abbey, Melbourne

SPECTRA REFUSED TO acknowledge the Abbey guards, who straightened their backs as he passed. He couldn't have cared less about the trickle of whispers that followed him up the stairs nor the averted eyes that preceded him along the hallway. Everything and everyone could wait until he had bathed the filth of defeat from his ragged robes.

'Where is she?' a barely controlled female voice assaulted him as soon as he staggered into his rooms.

Perfect, thought Spectra, stopping mid-stride. He wished his hand was holding a light-whip instead of a door handle. The sight of any uninvited woman anywhere in his Abbey would ordinarily be enough to stir his need to break something. But this woman, now, in his private quarters?

'Answer me! Where is my daughter?' Lady Pallas demanded. She sat at his usually neat desk, now strewn with papers and his favourite green glass paperweight discarded on the floor.

'Patricia, I don't care what your fucking title is. Nobody enters my quarters uninvited, especially when I have just returned from a particularly harrowing mission. I'll thank you for leaving.' He opened the door wider and pointed to the hall.

'And you would not have this room or your title if it were not for us. Mind your tongue and answer the lady!' demanded the governor.

Spectra silently berated himself for his miscalculation. The lady's presence had been so startling, he hadn't noticed his bedroom door ajar until her husband stepped out.

'If you have returned, then you must have found Bess?' Lady Pallas asked, narrowing her eyes.

Spectra took his time shutting the door behind him, then crossed the room to the sideboard. He poured himself a nip, slugged it down, and then walked over to the desk, where he leaned down to Lady Pallas' eye level.

'No, I do not have your charming daughter, *my lady*. I wish I did, because then I could wring her charming little neck,' Spectra said in a dangerous monotone.

'After that charade in my bedroom – remember, your husband provided an opportunity for her escape, not me – Lady Bess had me tracking through dingy tunnels for days with nothing but a squad of smelly, hungry good-for-nothings. When I finally got close enough to taste her treachery, she tried to kill me,' he snarled.

'And?' asked Lady Pallas.

'And what? It was a cave-in. A bloody cave-in! Everyone died except for me. Gone. Everyone. Can you understand that, or is your bun pulled in too tight?'

'Spectra!' The governor was by his wife's side in two steps. He slammed his palm on the desk and glared at Spectra with unblinking eyes.

After a few moments, Lady Pallas broke the silence by inhaling sharply and smoothing her hand over her chignon. Spectra backed off and sank heavily into his guest chair.

'It happened in one of the Rat's camps. No, camp doesn't do it justice. Not sure what it was. Quite sophisticated, really. Appeared to be some sort of military or research institution. I don't know. It all looked very official and important.

'I would have liked to have explored more, only Bess turned up, and before I knew it, the whole place came down around my ears. I only made it out with the help of an enforcer, who threw me the last few metres before he got clobbered too. The whole facility was destroyed. She couldn't have survived it.'

Lady Pallas reached out for her husband's hand. 'You saw her?'

'Didn't I just say that?' Spectra picked up his paperweight. It was lucky her husband was in the room, or he might have given in to temptation and smashed her stupid skull open with it.

Instead, he placed it firmly on the desk a short distance from her delicate wrist. 'I caught several glimpses of her. I heard her voice too. She kept babbling something about not being happy and not fitting in.'

'Yes, I can imagine she would have felt that way.' Lady Pallas looked at her husband and waved a dainty finger at him. 'I told you it was a bad plan. You menfolk think you can just marry anyone off, and everything will be fine.'

'I'll remind you that all three of us made this decision *together*,' said the governor, giving his wife a look that ended her argument.

'We should send a search party,' Lady Pallas responded.

'If what Spectra says is true, I'm not sure there is much point.'

Lady Pallas put a handkerchief to her mouth and turned away from the men.

'I'm sorry, sweetheart. We have to be pragmatic about these things. It's beyond our control. Come on, let's go,' the governor said, giving his hand to his wife to encourage her to leave.

'Spectra, I'll expect you at the enforcer handover tomorrow,' he said as he stepped towards the door.

'Giving up on your daughter already? Sure you and Kassel didn't cook this whole thing up? It's too convenient the way two eminent physicians both misdiagnosed her. More likely, you're just trying to get out of your side of the deal.'

'And you are not too powerful to find yourself on the other side of a jail cell!' snapped the governor, turning back into the room. For the first time, Spectra noticed his eyes were bloodshot. Was it stress or fatigue? Either way, it was a sign that he might be dangerously on edge.

'All right, all right. I apologise. Are we done?' Spectra held his hands up in surrender.

The governor strolled across the room to the window. Spectra groaned quietly as he realised the Pallas' would be finished when they were ready, and not before. He perched on the edge of his guest chair, rubbed his growling belly and massaged his temples, hoping his sudden dizziness would abate.

'I never will get used to these views. It's not natural – no, indecent – to see so far. Bloody Rats and their abomination, Illustria! You know, if Charles was still here, he'd never put up with this. He'd reverse it all in a heartbeat. Those Rat settlements don't belong under our cities any more than this unending light belongs above them. And the obscene cold weather? It's all wrong.'

Spectra was surprised to see the governor shiver a little as he spoke, as though a frosty breeze had blown up his dress shirt.

'It's all the Rat's fault!' said the governor.

'Right…' Spectra was eager to see where this was going. Hopefully, away from his culpability.

'I think it's about time we brought forward our plans to reclaim the whole world, not just Melbourne.'

'And exactly how do you plan to do that?' Spectra reached over to pour himself another nip.

'We will remind our people of the good life under Solaran rule and let them know that the Rats are responsible for all their problems. I'll tell them about the loss of our daughter and our son being held hostage. Then I'll announce that Melbourne will remain an open city for exactly seven days, after which our gates will close permanently. Anyone outside will be an assumed enemy of the Solaran nation.'

'And what of our lower classes? Who will make our fabrics and pearls?' asked Lady Pallas.

'I think pearls are grown, not made, Patricia.'

'Then where do they *grow*?'

'It's irrelevant. In times of war, we must all make sacrifices. Let the lower classes fend for themselves. If need be, we can breed more when this is over.'

'But the bracelets?' she said, holding her blue bracelet aloft.

'She's right. Class identification is critical. We need the Digie production to continue, especially if we bring in refugees who may have collaborated with the enemy. They ought to have their own colour!' said the governor.

'That reminds me. Mouths to feed. We'll need to annex the farming communities,' said Spectra.

For the first time since entering the room, he noticed his beloved pet lizard, Blue, sitting in his cage, looking rather emaciated. Fresh bugs for Blue would be the very next priority after the Pallas' left.

'Of course, we need access to food and the saffy, but the bracelets… How do we resolve that one?' asked Lady Pallas.

The governor paced between the floor, scowling each time he got near the window. 'Spectra, have the enforcers assist the Digies to bring their bracelet-manufacturing team to the surface. Find them space in the Abbey. You can oversee that operation now that you're relinquishing the enforcer facility.'

'Not possible. We need fifty Digies at least to make production viable. All our rooms are already allocated, and if more Brothers trek back to Melbourne when you issue your seven-day ultimatum, where will they go?'

'Did you not hear me say we all need to make sacrifices? Or are you incapable of handling a little jewellery workshop? Perhaps I ought to assign that project to the ladies of the court?'

'Speaking of court, I noticed a number of gentlemen wearing the new Digie pocket watches with the built-in lightkey function…' Spectra left his sentence hanging.

'Ah. On second thought, bracelets are not the only items we will need. Bring up a good hundred Digies. We'll set up a factory.'

Spectra picked some paper off the desk and pretended to take a note.

'Back to what I was saying before your interruption. The

Damarans have done irreparable harm to our world and our people. This cannot be tolerated. I tell you, Charles would have declared war and wiped them out. So that is exactly what we will do. It's time to switch on the new furnace. Is that understood?'

Lady Pallas and Spectra both nodded their agreement.

'And the rest of the Digies?' asked Spectra.

'Dispensable. Seal The Pit. Let fate deal with them all.'

Lady Pallas looked lovingly up at her husband, who held his head high and shoulders pressed back. It was a pose Spectra had seen many times before, especially at the great rallies the governor had held before his takeovers in Brisbane and Melbourne.

Spectra had had enough. He rose to his feet, put his note on the desk and limped toward his bathroom. 'Now, if you don't mind.'

'Right, yes. We'll be off then.' Lady Pallas swayed a little as she rose to her feet, and Spectra noticed an upturned cup amidst the mess on his desk.

The governor must have seen it, too, as he took a firm hold of his wife's arm. 'Resolve The Pitt, then come to my office so we can finalise the rest of the plans. Good day.'

When he was finally alone, and despite his tired body, Spectra started to relax. The next few weeks were going to be very entertaining. The Rats would get what they deserved. None of them belonged here.

'You don't belong either.'

'What the…?' Spectra spun around to see where the voice was coming from.

'I'll be back for you.'

The voice had come from the door on the opposite side of his apartment, where his staff stored supplies. But those staff were all Brothers, and this had definitely been a woman's voice. Only one person would have the audacity to sneak into his private quarters uninvited. It had to be her.

'Bess!' he yelled as he flung open the door.

The corridor beyond was empty, aside from a startled spider that raced across his shoe and a fleeting hint of a woman's form disappearing into an abnormally bright doorway at the far end. She was moving so fast that he almost missed it.

Spectra smiled. That door led to a short passage with a dead end, which gave him time to locate a dimmer switch. Finding none, he rubbed the sting of light out of his tired eyes and headed for the door.

'Enough!' he said, trying to sound confident while he clutched at the doorframe of the small linen closet, fearing his aching joints would give out.

'Huh, that can't be possible?' The room held sheets and robes stacked floor to ceiling, but no woman. Spectra pushed the linens aside and slapped his hands on the empty shelves, unwilling to admit the possibility his fatigue was playing tricks on his mind.

'Where? Where'd you go?"

'Sir?' A Brother stood at the door, a stack of fresh towels in his hands.

'Pick this crap up,' Spectra snapped and retired to his room to take a bath.

CHAPTER 10
Melbourne

LADY PALLAS SLOWLY turned her wedding ring, a seemingly innocuous act, yet enough for her secretary, Swanson, to rush to her side and begin winding up the event. Though he was a handsome young man, few of the ladies noticed. All eyes were fixed on their beloved leader.

'I want to assure you that we feel your words deeply, Lady Pallas, and we stand firmly behind you as role models for the lesser ranks. As my Horace says, we have to make sacrifices if we are to stop those Rat cowards from ever touching another Solaran woman. We all must do our part, even if it means going without life's essentials,' said Cheryl.

'Already, I have turned down the heat in the servants' quarters. I have cancelled orders for two beautiful ballgowns, and today...' Cheryl paused to remove the tiara from her head and hold it aloft. Lady Pallas was sure it was as much for her admiration as for the thirty ladies behind her. '...today, I would like to donate this trinket to the governor's fighting fund.'

With a slight hesitation and a quiver to her lips that may have said more about the donation than the chill in the room, she dropped the tiara into the copper tribute bowl that stood on a pedestal by Lady Pallas' side. There was a cheerful tinkling noise as it came to rest atop the jewellery the other ladies had already donated, although none was as grand as the tiara.

'You are too generous.' Lady Pallas nodded and pressed her hands together in a mock prayer pose. Then she raised her face to the rest of the ladies and puffed out her breath for dramatic effect. To her delight, it formed a perfect puff of fog.

In a deliberately unsteady voice, she continued, 'The room may be cold, but I can feel the heat from your hearts. Your love for your people burns brightly. The governor will hear of your special sacrifices today.'

It must have carried just the right measure of modesty. There was a flutter of soft clapping from woollen gloves, and calls of additional support erupted. Lady Pallas was relieved when a lull in the conversation gave her secretary a chance to step forwards. She drained the last of her saffy in preparation.

'My Lady, I'm sorry to disturb you, as I know it will aggrieve you greatly,' Swanson said firmly, pointing to his watch, 'but the governor is expecting your attendance on important business.'

'Surely not yet! The kindness of my dear friends warms me. I could not cope with my broken heart if it weren't for their support.' Lady Pallas dabbed at her cheeks, hoping it looked like she was drying tears. 'Where would I be without my ladies?'

Cheryl threw her arms around Lady Pallas' neck and sobbed violently into her fur collar. Two more ladies joined in the embrace, and the rest of the group surged forwards. Lady Pallas made a show of accepting their outpouring of affection.

Swanson knew better. 'I must insist, m'lady,' he said whilst receiving an opal broach in tribute from Mrs Parker.

When Lady Pallas finally stood, her consolers stepped back except for Cheryl, who had a firm grip on her hand. 'Duty never sleeps, even for a mother with a heavy heart,' said Lady Pallas as she walked to the door.

Cheryl accompanied her, fending off the other guests. Swanson held the door open just wide enough for one woman to pass.

'This is where I must leave you, dear one.' Lady Pallas removed her hand from Cheryle's grip and placed it on her heart.

'My friends, I cannot thank you enough. You have given me hope in this dreadful time of mourning. I know you will all continue to stand behind the governor and honour your commitments of support for the troops, for no one can hold a light to Solaran sincerity. Please stay and enjoy my hospitality as long as you wish. You have earned it.'

The crowd responded by dropping into curtsies.

Lady Pallas nodded one last time, stepped into the hall and closed the heavy oak doors behind her. She gave herself two deep breaths to process the results of her husband's strategy. The new constables would be well equipped, as would her wardrobe.

She brushed the front of her dreary suit, which she was certain was full of crumbs from her gluttonous cousin's lips, and accepted the fine wool coat offered by her secretary. She loved the way its fur trim hugged her chilly ankles, even if the colour was depressing.

Lady Pallas was accustomed to having her fashion choices copied, yet the speed at which black had spread through the ranks had surprised even her. Just three hours had passed since the governor had announced Bess' death at the hands of the Rats, and already the rainbow of colour had disappeared from the court.

Swanson offered her the silver tray that held Mrs Parker's brooch and a short shot of saffy. Without a word, she drained the dainty glass, returned it to the tray, and then picked up the brooch, which she added to the other item secreted in her pocket.

'Get the sheep out quickly, Swanson. I want that gloom cleared, the air warmed, and the tribute in the hands of the governor by the time I return.' She raised a hand to her throat to suppress a hiccup.

Swanson bowed and withdrew.

Lady Pallas swept a few errant hairs into her updo before retreating down the hall.

✦ ✦ ✦

Melbourne's dungeons were woefully inadequate for any lawman who took pride in his work. It was a point the Pallas' had discussed more than once behind closed doors.

'What kind of candy-coated operation did Bryan Kassel run?' her husband had asked when they first arrived.

He was right. As Lady Pallas strolled through the lower levels, she saw evidence of the governor's contention everywhere she looked. There were only six cells for a start, and the city jail was not much larger. When the war began in earnest, they would have to extend their holding capacity. She wondered if The Pit could be re-purposed.

Lady Pallas stepped over an iron poker and made a mental note that it really was time to add an equipment storage room. The hooks outside cells may have accommodated a few small implements, like lashes and pliers, but there was nowhere to store a rack – her favourite apparatus.

She retrieved the tiny vial of lemon myrtle oil from her pocket and dabbed it under her noise before calling for the guard. 'Open this door,' she ordered.

Inside the cell, built for four, lounged seven women in various states of decay. The stench of unwashed wounds was hard to ignore, despite her myrtle. Acrid defeat stung her eyes. As soon as this meeting was over, she would definitely remedy the situation regardless of water restrictions.

'Come to discuss fashion, Priscilla?' a croaky voice reached out from the far side of the room. 'I can tell you one thing now; black is not your colour. You ought to try chartreuse. A better match for your nature.'

The voice belonged to her older sister, Mary. Despite being separated as children, Mary still knew how to needle her. Lady Pallas hoped she was not blushing, or at least that it would not be seen in the darkened chamber.

'Yes, that's right Mary. I seek the fashion advice of a crone who has spent her life in a brown sack. Guard!'

The shabbily uniformed officer lumbered to her side.

'Bring Sister Mary out of the cell.'

'Yes, m'lady.'

'Then bring me a clean chair and summon my first maid.'

'Right, ma'am.'

While the guard carried out his orders, she took a peek through the slot in ex-Constable Albert's cell door. She was surprised he was still alive. The governor had conducted some unpleasant business with him over the last few days, checking that Albert hadn't played a part in Bess' escape.

Albert looked so pathetic, a shadow of the man who had watched over her son. Lady Pallas almost felt sorry for him. She would have given him the mission if he weren't the governor's favourite, whose absence would be noticed. Besides, he was so emaciated she had little confidence he would have the strength to leave the city, let alone carry out her orders. He would need feeding up before he returned to any duty.

No, her decision was made: it was definitely a woman's job. The governor had not taken an interest in any female prisoner for months, and, in their filthy state, he was unlikely even to be able to tell one from another. One less wouldn't be noticed.

With a thud, like the unloading of a potato sack, Mary arrived next to her. She was slumped on the floor, head resting against a stack of truncheons. Next to her, the guard had left a high-backed stool of dubious origin.

Lady Pallas shot him a look, and the guard quickly bent down and polished the seat with his loose shirt tails. Once clean, he indicated it was ready. She raised an eyebrow at him. He tucked his shirt tails in, buttoned his coat and hastily retreated down the hall.

'What, jailhouse décor not up to your standard?' Mary's snigger turned into a bone-rattling cough. 'D'ya hear that, ladies? Better fix your cells up nice before her ladyship comes back in!'

'I've been wondering whether you might be tired of this place. I guess I was wrong. If your mouth is working fine, you must need more time in shackles,' Lady Pallas said, staring down at her sister.

'No need for threats. I'll play nice. What do you want?'

Lady Pallas sat down and took her time straightening her skirts. 'It's about Bess.'

'You needn't have bothered sullying your fine clothes to bring that news. We've already heard. I'm sorry for your – our – loss.' Mary's voice had lost its sharp edge. Lady Pallas had her where she needed her.

'She's not dead.'

'What?'

'At least, I think there is a chance she's not dead.'

'What happened?' asked Mary, trying and failing to straighten her posture.

'Have you ever been to Darwin?'

'Once.'

'Spectra's just come back from there. He claims Bess was there too, taunting him if you can believe it. He assumed she was buried alive when it caved in, but there's no body. All I have is his word.'

Mary nodded.

'Spectra's been acting stranger than usual. He jumps at shadows and talks to the air. Something's not right. What if he lied? What if she is still out there?'

'What does your husband say?'

'This is not something I can discuss with him. He's closed the issue and won't send good resources after bad.'

Mary reached her hand out to Priscilla, who took it without speaking. The sisters were quiet for what seemed like an eternity.

'Let her go,' said Mary, releasing her younger sister's hand at last.

'What do you mean? She's my baby. I can't!'

'You already did when you gave her to me to raise twenty years ago.'

Lady Pallas winced.

'Look at it this way. If she's dead, she won't need your help. If she's alive, she won't want your help.'

Lady Pallas stood up and paced the tight space. 'No. I've made up my mind. You will go into the tunnels and find your niece. Bring her home where she belongs.'

'And if I refuse?'

'Then it's the last time you'll see your fellow cellmates.'

The clatter of feet up the hallway drew both their attention. The guard was returning with the maid. It was time to end the negotiation.

'Well?' Lady Pallas asked.

'You promise you'll keep them safe?' Mary looked back to the cell door as if contemplating the bargain.

'Of course.'

'All right.' Mary struggled to her feet.

Lady Pallas leaned in close. She took her sister's trembling hand and spoke directly into her ear.

'This bracelet will get you the run of the city. As a maid, no one will care about your movements.' She snapped the yellow identity bracelet on Mary's wrist. It was one of the bracelets she had recovered from Bess' backpack. Then she handed over a second.

'Here's a spare bracelet for when you return with Bess. I can't give you money; all must be accounted for in a time of war. Take this instead. Use it to trade for the items you need.' She handed over Mrs Parker's brooch.

'After that, it's up to you. Find help amongst the Rats if you must. Do anything. Just find her.'

Lady Pallas stood to address her servant, who was

waiting a short distance away. 'Maid. This inmate is being reassigned. Get her cleaned up, fed and into a spare uniform. Tell no one, understand?'

'Yes, m'lady. Come on.'

Patricia watched as the two women left. She was glad to see the maid help Mary when she stumbled. She prayed that what was left of Mary would be enough. When they were gone, she gave the guard his final instructions.

'Tomorrow, you are to dispose of the remaining sisters. They are no longer of any use to the governor and unfit for the factory. Let them be one with the Light.'

'Yes, m'Lady,' he said.

CHAPTER 11
The Pit, Melbourne

HARPER WILLED HERSELF not to gag as she leaned forwards for a second sip of the heady brew. KonWong Café stood directly opposite its namesake. She was sure she heard the great dragon statue chuckle at the dish Mr Xi had chosen for her.

Harper steeled herself, then took a larger sip, forced herself to swallow, and hoped the blaze tearing down her throat would only manifest as light dew on her forehead rather than a full-blown sweat.

'Good, good. That is General Abudua's favourite too. The dragon broth is full of fierce herbs, fit for a warrior!'

Dr Kassel winked at Xi and slapped the grinning Kohl on the back in a conspiracy of good humour.

'Delicious,' she croaked and set the bowl down firmly. She wiped her trembling lip and glared at Kohl, daring him to say anything. As she attempted a hot-lipped smile, an enormous belch erupted from her throat.

Kohl raised his eyebrows, and Dr Kassel averted his eyes, but Mr Xi jumped up onto his seat and wriggled his fingers in the air. 'See, it works. The spices make you blow out the bad spirits, like a dragon. You should see the spirits that come out of Abudua. Phew! My wife says we'll have to repaint the walls every time she eats here.'

Kohl sniggered, yet his own bowl remained untouched.

After all the mirth at her expense, Harper was suddenly glad she hadn't warned Kohl about the dish Mr Xi had recommended for him. Kohl's dumpling soup was served in a traditional Digie bowl with three different eating utensils attached to the rim. She had only seen it eaten once before by Aggy, and it hadn't gone well.

Let his lordship figure it out himself, she thought. 'Not hungry, Kohl?'

'Absolutely.' Kohl picked up the bowl with his left thumb and both little fingers. With it steady in his grasp, he used his remaining fingers to manipulate a dumpling and broth into his mouth with one of the hinged forks and an oversized spoon. Though she hated to admit it, it was an excellent ten-fingered impersonation of Digie deftness.

'Nicely done,' said Dr Kassel. 'Now, if we can get back to our discussion, please? I must get Daemon back home. He'll need a few days to recover.'

'Of course. You were telling Kohl about your conversion to Damaran ideals,' offered Harper.

'Right. I was like all the other governors before the war. We were taught from childhood that Solarans are chosen people meant to be served by the lower classes. We all believed our limited resources meant we had to artificially adapt them to keep them productive and satisfied with their lot in life.

'Truly, we thought we were doing them a kindness, and the Brothers' missals backed up that belief. Only when Illustria lifted the darkness did I finally see the truth. I was so ashamed.'

Dr Kassel stopped to sip his tea. Mr Xi reached over and rubbed his friend's forearm.

'Mr Xi was very forgiving. Digies truly are people of the Light. He introduced me to Alpha and taught me the Damaran way. I know now that we are all intrinsically valuable to the collective journey. I also learned that we don't belong here on this world. One day we will go home to the Light.'

'Yes indeed,' said Mr Xi with a nod.

'We were planning a new Melbourne where Digies could live freely above ground. There was so much hope until your dad showed up.' He nodded at Kohl. 'Before I knew it, my wife was gone, and all our plans disappeared with my shadow.'

Harper had sat still through Dr Kassel's impassioned speech but turned to Kohl at the mention of his father. He stared down at his shaking hands. Harper poured him a cup of tea from the communal pot.

'Now life is harder for everyone, not just Digies,' Mr Xi said.

'What's going on?' asked Harper.

'They're using colour-coded bracelets to separate the classes. The nobility kid themselves that it's in their interest, but they too, are herded and manipulated. Just look at poor Bess.' Dr Kassel stared at Kohl as he spoke. 'I'm sorry about your sister. I helped her as much as I could. I hope it was enough.'

A young Digie swung into the café on a rope from the

upper layers. His eyes held the promise of news, but his blush told of uncertainty. Mr Xi excused himself, spoke to the boy and rushed back to the table.

'I'm afraid I must cut this short, friends. A troop of armed enforcers have arrived at the rim of The Pit, demanding to see you, Dr Kassel. They have taken many of our technicians. I cannot imagine why.'

Harper thought she saw Mr Xi use a hand signal to the child, who responded by helping himself to a bowl of soup. A strange action for a man leading a community heading into a new crisis.

Harper was about to question him when a second Digie youth careened in the door. He looked at what must have seemed a strange group sharing the table with Mr Xi, then waved his hands above his head in a series of complex gestures. Mr Xi seemed absorbed in the strange action. His face froze momentarily, then he waved the boy away and resumed his happy disposition.

Dr Kassel rose to his feet, rubbing his lower back as he straightened up. 'Xi is right. I must go. Who knows what the enforcers are doing? I need to get Daemon out while I can. Go with the Light, my friends.'

Dr Kassel shook hands around the table. At the door of the café, he turned back. 'It could be a while until I return. You'll need to keep the operation running without me till then, Xi.'

And then he was gone.

For a moment, none of the party moved. Then Mr Xi jumped to his feet and called out to his wife. 'My love, how about a round of charred greens and bitter grits?'

Mrs Xi appeared from the kitchen wearing a cheerful, floured apron. She blew him a kiss and rubbed the boy's head before vanishing back into the kitchen. It was only then Harper guessed he must be their son.

She couldn't help comparing Kohl, whose eyes were still downcast, and Mr Xi, whose demeanour was unnaturally calm in the face of potential calamity. 'Should we not rush to see what is happening above, or complete our mission to secure the *Starling* team or even hide Dr Kassel's operation? Shouldn't we do something?'

Mr Xi brought his son over to join their table as he munched on a dumpling taken from the child's meal. 'Oh no. All will be fine. Dr Kassel still overestimates his importance. He is not our only source of information, nor does he know all our secrets.'

'So, what *is* going on?'

'The enforcers are going to close The Pit. The Solarans hope to end our community through suffocation, starvation or some other equally barbaric means. Strangely, KonWong has also gone missing. I must assume the Solarans have taken it as a victory trophy.'

'And why are we not taking action?' asked Harper, rising to her feet.

Mrs Xi returned with a steaming platter of emerald veggies and golden grains that smelled one part sweet, two parts savoury and three parts delicious. It took all of Harper's Civy training not to snatch a sample.

Mr Xi grinned and spooned his son a generous helping of greens. 'We do not run so as not to inform our enemies. We do not need to prove they are blind for us to know they are lost to the Dark.'

CHAPTER 12
Lower Broome

AGGY ARRIVED AT Sam's room and paused in the doorway. Byron stood vigil, one hand on Sam's knee, the other holding the book he was reading in a soft voice. It was an old bound copy of Illustria's letters, and Byron only paused to turn the page or straighten Sam's blankets.

Sam had his head pressed deep into the pillow, trembling, and he didn't seem to respond to Byron's words. From where she stood, it was difficult to tell if he was awake or not.

'It's not supposed to be this way,' Sam muttered. 'It's all wrong. It's not supposed to be this way.'

She wished she had access to Illustria's medical know-how or at least some diagnostic equipment. It was hard to know how to help. She wasn't even sure whether he needed reassurance from Alpha or a hug from his pseudo-Mum Aggy.

'Alpha.' Byron moved to offer her a chair.

She gratefully sat down. The jog back from her inspection of the hydro-engineering work with General Kee had left her weary.

'Is he asleep?'

'Hard to tell.'

'Sam, it's Aggy here. How are you, love?' There was no sign that he had heard.

Byron shrugged and shook his head.

Mid-morning, Stanley had reported that Sam's fever had finally broken and that they'd removed his bandages. Yet he still appeared ghostly pale and listless, aside from the continual rubbing of his ears.

'Byron, the water situation is beyond repair, so we have to bug out. Please go pack your gear and anything you can find of Sam's. You might want to grab some grub too. Stanley will watch him while you're doing that.'

Byron touched Sam's shoulder and bent to whisper to him. She couldn't be sure, but she thought Sam relaxed briefly. When Byron left, Sam resumed his shaking.

'It's just us now. Speak to me.'

Sam didn't respond.

Aggy gently pried his fingers off his right ear and held his hand in hers.

'I'm so proud of the man you've become. I'm sorry if I haven't told you that lately. Remember when we first met? I was directing our troops before the Sydney explosion, and you were in that awful jail cell in the Pallas basement? To be honest, I wasn't sure whether to take you with me. Abudua said you were probably a dangerous murderer, a common criminal, and certainly a liability!

'You were so frail. Even I had doubts. Then I saw you racing to catch up with me despite your club foot, all huffing and puffing. I knew you had the heart of a warrior. I'm very glad you proved me correct.

'You've been a great asset to my people and a good friend. The Light knows I don't have many of those! I feel horrible to see you suffering from a mission I ordered. I wish I knew how to help.'

Aggy turned away to reach for a tissue for her cheeks.

'Leave.' A faint voice trembled at the edge of her perception.

Aggy turned back to Sam and studied him. 'Did you say something?'

His grip on her hand strengthened, though his eyes remained closed.

'Leave.'

This time she heard the voice more clearly. She couldn't help checking over her shoulder. They were definitely alone.

'Come on, Aggy, keep it together,' she said, assuming her exhausted mind was playing tricks on her. She closed her eyes momentarily and yawned.

'Leave!' the voice said, louder this time. She opened her eyes. Still alone. It was a vaguely feminine voice, but it had to be Sam.

'Why do you want to leave? Where do you want to go?'

Sam shook his head and moved his lips. At first, no sound came out. Then he cleared his throat and started again.

'It's painfully wrong. Ma-m-make it stop,' he stammered.

'Make what stop?'

'Stop this; it's all un-un-authorised. All wrong. Leaving will make it right.'

The fever must have returned to provoke such nonsensical delirium. Aggy used her spare hand to touch his forehead. Sam pushed it away and glared directly at her as though he could see.

'Hurry! Get out of the cavern. Dragon at the eastern gate.'

'Sam, it's too cold outside. You know that. We have to stay here. For now, at least.'

Suddenly Sam sat up and turned to face the window.

'I told you to leave.' A woman's voice echoed through the room.

Aggy jumped to her feet. This time she knew it wasn't Sam.

'Who was that?'

'Oh, no.'

'What?'

Sam turned his unseeing eyes back towards her and spoke with a clarity she hadn't heard in a long time. 'I've been tryin' to tell everyone what she's sayin', but no one listens. Why would anyone listen to some pathetic blind loser, right? Now it's too late.'

'Too late for what?'

A strong gust of wind hit the window. The walls shuddered, and the temperature in the room plummeted.

'It's comin'. When he exhaled, his warm breath misted through the now-frigid air.

There was a mighty crash outside, and an open-mouthed General Kee appeared in the doorway, followed closely by Byron and Stanley. A tumble of words rushed at Aggy.

'Alpha, it came right out of Simpson Falls!'

'It raced down the entrance ramp at the front of a blizzard.'

'It smashed through the mess hall.'

'It's a winged beast.'

'The Bird of Light is back?' Aggy asked incredulously.

'No. It's like nothing Illustria would bring down upon us.'

'It had many rows of teeth.'

'And fur.'

'And scaly claws.'

'It's a—'

'Stop! Everyone be quiet.' Aggy waved for silence. They'd all lost their minds! She was about to ask Sam when she heard the voice again.

'LEAVE!'

This time, it was loud enough to make her jump. She twisted towards the trio at the door. 'Did you hear that? Any of you?'

The men shook their heads.

'I did.' Sam's grip on her hand tightened painfully. He was kneeling on his bed, and although his unseeing eyes were milky white, he looked like a man who knew exactly what was going on. This was not delirium.

'You hear her, don't you?' he asked in a steady voice.

Aggy nodded, then remembered to vocalise. 'Yes. What's going on, Sam? Why do we need to leave?'

Sam chuckled softly. 'Doesn't matter anymore. It's already here.'

'What's here?'

'The end.'

A large shadow lumbered past the frosted window.

CHAPTER 13
The Pit, Melbourne

SPECTRA GROANED AND made a show of tapping on his timepiece. It was a project he'd been working on for days, and his enforcers had been waiting, tools ready, for over an hour. Had he known Dr Kassel and his son would stagger up the ramp singing, sozzled from some local brew, he might not have waited.

'We're not in a hurry here. Why don't you go back for another round?'

'Just doing a little father-son bonding away from prying…' Dr Kassel hiccupped instead of finishing his sentence. Daemon waved his hand in front of his face and missed a high five with his father.

'You really are an embarrassment to yourself,' said Spectra.

A scruffy dog trailed the Kassels. Spectra activated his light-whip and, with a flick of his wrist, reduced the animal to char.

'Nothing,' he said, holstering his weapon. Spectra missed the thrills of the old days. Charles wouldn't have made him wait until the zone was empty before taking action. The church-burning in New Brunswick, the bombs in Sydney, killing Sam's mother – such good times.

'What's with all the muscle?' asked Dr Kassel, pointing at the two dozen enforcers armed with building supplies.

'You'd know if you spent more time in the governor's court and less time philandering with Digie harlots. No wonder you misdiagnosed Bess. I'm still waiting for an explanation of that one.'

'Guess she fooled me!' Dr Kassel tripped over his feet and leaned on his sniggering son for support. They threaded a path through the enforcers looping back around to Spectra. 'I think I hear the ladies calling us, Daemon. You ready for round two?'

Spectra blocked their path. 'There'll be no more of that tonight. Now move on, or you'll end up like the pooch. My team has work to do.'

'So?'

'You are trying my patience, Dr Kassel.' Spectra moved his hand to his weapon.

'So, what *are* you doing here?'

Spectra couldn't be bothered enduring the fallout of answering that question. Informing the bleeding-heart medico that his party mates were about to be entombed alive would cause more drama that would only slow him down. Instead, he gave father and son a firm shove in the direction of the city.

'Enforcers, raise your tools.' With surprising synchronicity for meatheads, his team raised their tools in an eerie echo of the precise Digie instruments he had enjoyed over the years. It would be a shame to lose the resource. Still, it had to be done. Sacrifices had to be made. He only regretted not being down in the Digie community to see their pathetic faces when they learned it was the end.

'Yes, good. End this unauthorised community,' a voice urged from behind.

Spectra swivelled to look up at the nearest enforcer. 'Who said you could speak?'

The enforcer stared ahead, as motionless as the metal sheeting under his arm or the mallet he held high with the other.

'Well?'

Of course, there was no response. The hulking brutes were designed to provide unthinking grunt, not express their opinions – or even have opinions, for that matter.

Spectra spun around but could see no other source. Essential workers from The Pit had already been chosen and relocated within the city limits. Even the Kassels were a dozen paces away, moving surprisingly quickly for drunkards.

'Need more enforcers.' This time the voice was so faint he decided it was just his mind working overtime. The enforcer production issue was yet to be solved. They had only been able to grow enforcers from the embryos already completed by Charles before he left. New enforcer embryos were beyond Solaran technology.

A cool gust from the darkening sky reminded him that the day was ending. Soon there would be too little light to work. There was no more time for contemplation.

'Right, you lot. Start laying down that sheeting. Make it quick. I'll have no more delays or surprises tonight.'

Spectra pointed to three enforcers who wore gloves on

their hands and held wire cutters instead of mallets or welding gear. 'You three, this way. We have another mission.'

+ + +

'Another sugar-nut toffee?' asked Mrs Xi.

Harper shook her head and leaned back a little to help ease her indigestion. The Xis were gracious hosts with surprising appetites. She had given up trying to match Mr Xi by the fourth dish. Even their young son had consumed at least two more bowls than Kohl and was happily unwrapping his third sweet.

'I think you've met your match,' Harper said with a wink.

She was rewarded with a grin she hadn't seen on Kohl's face for a very long time. He reached across the small table and pretended to box with the boy. He threw a short jab at the boy's shoulder, but the kid was too quick. He ducked and threw a glancing punch across Kohl's nose.

Kohl, pretending he was mortally wounded, fell off his chair with exaggerated slow motion. The little boy climbed on top of him, posed like a champion, and then resolved into giggles. It was a painful reminder of the playful Solaran prince Harper had met before Sydney was destroyed.

'Won't be long now,' said Mr Xi, who'd been checking outside every few minutes.

'Can I take a look?' asked Harper.

Mr Xi had requested they stay in the café while the enforcers went about their work. The whole community knew what was coming and kept things as normal as possible. Only a small group, assigned the role of hysterical protestors, would be seen on the top level.

'I guess so,' he said and beckoned to both Harper and

Kohl. 'May as well get your bearings before it's completely dark.'

Kohl looked down and up The Pit's vast atrium. 'Nice.'

The café was situated on the fourth level from the top, cantilevered out from the rock wall on an assembly of blacked metal tubes and punched steel walkways. All around them, ropes and polls crisscrossed the structure for easy access to the other floors. With a glance, they could see at least eleven levels – even in the diminishing light. It was a prime position for the unofficial leader.

'Yes, it always impresses me. A little like the old Coober Pedy, only with deeper colours and a lot more industry,' said Harper.

'Not to mention it's underground,' Kohl added.

'That flying incident must have affected your memory. Coober Pedy was underground too.'

Kohl rolled his eyes at Harper. 'The Pedies' cavern was so enormous it may as well have been an above-ground city. This place – well, you can't mistake that we are in a deep hole.'

Harper gave him a sharp look she had seen Lady Pallas wield. It must have worked, as Kohl winced. 'A very nice hole, I might say.'

Mr Xi smiled. 'Yes. This place has been good to us. A home, a disguise and an escape.'

'Ah. You've got access to the tunnels, haven't you?' said Kohl.

'Right you are. We've pretended we're at the Solaran's mercy for years. They believe the top opening is the only entry point. Fools lost in their own shadows,' he said, chuckling to himself.

'They inflict disabilities on us to make us less than

human, but those very differences make us more human. We are not weakened by our diversity. Quite the opposite. There is great value in our differences,' he said as he wiggled his fingers in front of Kohl.

'Where's KonWong?' Harper pointed to an empty space on the other side of the cavity. 'He seemed pretty popular. What happened?'

'Hang on, who's KonWong?' asked Kohl.

'KonWong normally sits up there. Ah, you should see his magnificence! He has the face of a regal lion with big eyes and curly mane, but if you went behind him, you would see his true form is that of a great dragon. Legend says that he followed Illustria here, carrying us on his back, beating his wings against the cosmic rays and using his fiery breath to spray the heavens with lights so that we might find our way home.

'We were taught that one day, when we are no longer needed, KonWong will break from his stone slumber and light the path to the next life. Today he is missing. I hope—'

Xi's explanation was interrupted by a deep, grinding noise that rose from the depths of The Pit, followed by an unnatural quiet. It was the first time Harper noticed the low-level industrial noise that had buzzed beneath their conversation since their arrival.

A message carrier hoisted himself up the nearest rope and whispered something to Mr Xi, who, to Harper's surprise, since he'd been so cool up to that point, started wringing his hands. 'Pass this news to Mrs Xi. She'll know what to do. You two – come!'

Before he slipped down a nearby rope ladder to the level below, Mr Xi took one last look at the spot where KonWong should have been.

'Wait!' Harper called after him as she struggled to keep up.

Kohl, twice as tall as the Digies, hesitated next to the flimsy ladder, then leapt the short distance to the level below, arriving in time to steady Harper as she took her last step.

'Thank you,' she said to Kohl. 'What's the sudden urgency, Mr Xi?'

'Sorry. We'd assumed this would happen after they shut us in. Now we must go quickly, while there is still some light.'

'What happened?' Harper pulled the torch out of her pocket to light their way. The Pit was getting very dim indeed.

'A grave miscalculation on our part, I'm afraid.' Mr Xi trotted swiftly down the walkway, cracking his knuckles as he moved towards a red section.

Another Digie, clearly waiting for them, opened a hatch in the floor emblazoned with a picture of KonWong breathing fire. Underneath it was an ominously dark tube about three Digies in width.

'Please, Mr Xi. Whatever it is, I'm sure we can fix it.' She touched his shoulder, and when he turned around, she noticed his pallor turning grey.

'They've cut us out of the power grid,' he replied, rubbing another tremor out of his fingers.

'And that wasn't expected?' asked Kohl.

'We knew they would figure out the power issue eventually. But we thought we'd have time to work on it after they locked us in.'

'Fair assumption. Solarans tend to be single-minded: close The Pit, then disconnect. No offence,' Harper said to Kohl, who was butting his toe up against a nearby railing.

Three more Digies approached and nodded to Mr Xi

before jumping in the tube and disappearing from sight.

'You said you needed time to work on it. Work on what?' asked Kohl.

A grey-haired Digie with a noticeable limp pushed by and leapt into the tunnel.

'The doors. The doors to the tunnels leading to Darwin, Lower Broome – everywhere. When Illustria left us, they stopped working. We had to find another power source. We've been siphoning it off the Melbourne grid. That's why the *Starling* Project is located here, isn't it?'

Harper nodded in growing understanding.

'We keep the door to the *Starling* team shut most of the time to stop the little ones bothering the technicians and reduce the possibility of the older ones reporting it back to the Solarans.'

'Really. Can't trust your own people?' asked Kohl.

'Alas, there will always be a temptation where there is money. Without power, we may not be able to open the doors again. They'll be stuck. So will we. Exactly as the Solarans intended and no KonWong to fly us out of here.'

Mr Xi's hand-wringing was now quite frantic. Harper and Kohl exchanged looks.

'Follow me.' Mr Xi took a step backwards and dropped down the chute.

CHAPTER 14

Lower Broome

AGGY SIGNALLED FOR silence as she watched the hulking shadow pass Sam's window. The room shuddered as it moved, and when it was gone, she sank down onto the edge of the bed and tried to make sense of it.

Two of her generals skidded through the door. Mitta was carrying backpacks. He slammed open the nearest cupboard door and started packing medical supplies. Abudua knelt before Aggy, dropped her head and held up her ceremonial knife.

'I offer my resignation, Alpha. I can no longer trust my mind, so I'm not worthy to serve.'

Aggy looked up at Mitta's flushed face. Mitta shrugged and quickly returned to his packing.

'What in the Light is going on now?' Aggy demanded.

'I cannot believe my eyes, for I saw a nightmare! Take it.' Abudua raised her knife higher.

'Resignation denied. I need your strength, not your self-doubt. Assume your position,' she snapped.

Abudua took a protective stance in front of Aggy, encouraging her son Byron to do the same for Sam.

'General Mitta, I hope you have an explanation that makes sense?'

Mitta threw the extra bags to Stanley and General Kee, who joined him in packing. 'Alpha, I cannot explain it. There is a dangerous creature running loose in the settlement. All who fought it lie slain on the ground; some bloodied, most charred.

'Wherever it goes, there is mayhem. Shelters are flattened, possessions burned to tinder and families scattered. We must retreat to the surface before all are lost.'

'What sort of creature?' asked Aggy.

Abudua tightened her lips and tossed a knife from one hand to the other. Alarmingly, she almost looked jumpy. A first for Abudua.

'Sam, you said we can't leave. Why? What's happening? Who's here? And what did you mean when you said it was the end?' she demanded rapid-fire.

'I … I don't know. It's not for me to say. I'm not authorised. No, no, no, not authorised.' Sam clamped his hands over his ears again. The clarity he'd had only moments prior vanished.

'Has anyone else heard a strange voice that seems to come from nowhere? Abudua? Kee?' Aggy asked, searching her generals' faces for comprehension. Blank looks returned her gaze.

'Then it's not coming through the hyper implants. Sam, what is the voice telling you?'

When Sam didn't respond, she moved closer and spoke to him with warm determination. 'I believe you hear a voice,

Sam. I heard it too, but not anymore. I need you to tell me what that voice is saying now. You're the only one who can do this.'

'It's comin'. Lookin' for someone,' he said in a barely audible voice.

The ground started to shake. Mitta, Kee and Stanley stopped packing. All heads turned to stare at the window.

Abudua crept to the other side of the bed, using her body as a physical barrier between Alpha and whatever approached. With a wave of her hand, everyone dropped to squat below the level of the window sill – all, that was, aside from Sam. Byron reached up and tried to pull him down, but Sam snatched his arm free and stood on his bed.

'I can see him comin'!' he said.

The floor shook, and the shadow returned. Aggy signalled her team to leave Sam where he was.

'He's here,' said Sam, and the shadow stopped moving.

Aggy had the unnerving impression that whatever cast the shadow was trying to see inside the room.

Sam tilted his head as if listening, and when he spoke again, he was strangely calm. 'You're a mighty beast, aren't ya? Can ya see it now, Aggy? He's so beautiful and strong. Are those wings tucked in by its sides? Yes, wings – I reckon each one would measure double the width of my old room. Imagine how many people could fly on his back when he returns to the Light.'

When Sam stopped talking, Aggy looked around the room at her team. They were all wide-eyed, and none seemed to know what to do next. It was so quiet she could hear her own heart pound.

Beyond the room, a distant cry broke the silence. Abudua signalled for Byron to do recon outside. Byron nodded, slid to the floor and silently crawled into the hall. General Mitta lowered to the ground and followed.

Needing a better view, Aggy slowly rose, but her aging knees cracked loudly, and the beastly shadow jerked closer. It sounded like something was sniffing the other side of the window. Aggy held herself still. Then it roared, a burning breath that made the hairs on her arms bristle.

The shadow made a sudden leap sideways. Even through the frosted pane, it was clear that it raised its legs and repeatedly stomped on something or someone. Screams wrenched the air outside. Its awful fiery breath followed, heating them right through the walls.

A short while later, Byron crawled back in and collapsed to the floor. His hair was scorched, and his clothes were in smokey tatters. However, Abudua didn't leave her defensive position in front of Aggy. She didn't have to. The generals had worked together for such a long time that they were as close as family. Kee rushed to Byron's side and sent a rapid series of hand signals to let Abudua know Byron's injuries weren't lethal.

Kee crawled to the doorway and crossed the threshold, just far enough that the soles of his feet were still visible. When he slunk back inside, his face was ashen. It took him a moment to get the signs out; his hands shook so badly.

Aggy understood. General Mitta had not been as lucky.

'You should have left!' The taunting voice was back; Aggy heard it with painful clarity this time.

'Can it see me, Sam?'

'Yeah.'

'Tell it we will comply. We need time to leave, though. We have children and supplies to pack.'

Before Sam could respond, the creature outside leapt into

the air. It must have flown close to the ground as the small building shook with each beat of its wings. An almighty crash from above drew all eyes towards the ceiling.

'Take cover,' Sam warned before he dropped to the floor and rolled towards the inner wall.

Abudua pushed Aggy under the hospital bed and squashed in next to her. Kee covered Byron's limp body with his own. Stanley squeezed into the cupboard they'd emptied of supplies just as a roar like the end of the world pummelled their ears.

Someone in the room whimpered. Another crash, then a tearing sound followed. Loose ceiling tiles clattered down from the ceiling and cold air, heavy with soot, gusted into the room.

When quiet returned, Aggy and Abudua poked their heads out from under the bed. Sam, already on his feet, helped Aggy stand. At first, she was distracted by Sam's ability to navigate so well, and then she gasped at the view overhead.

Aggy staggered backwards. She had to grip the edge of the bed as she struggled to comprehend what had happened. The roof was gone, the outside wall was missing, and the air shimmered with steam and dust from the charred remains of what had been a hospital only a minute earlier.

And perched on what was left of the building, close enough that she could feel its blistering breath on her forehead, was a beast that made no sense. On top of the great beast was an even more impossible rider.

'KonWong,' Sam said.

'Illustria,' said Aggy.

CHAPTER 15
The Pit, Melbourne

HARPER LANDED ON the floor with a thud that threatened to wind her. Mr Xi had landed only seconds ahead of her, yet he was already on his feet, coordinating the waiting Digies.

'Yahoo!' called Kohl as he whizzed down behind. She quickly rolled left to avoid being collected up by him as his big feet clattered to the ground.

'Wow, what a ride!' Kohl slapped dust from his pants, then arched his back and pointed to the upper levels. 'Just take a look at that glittering view!'

Apparently, Harper wasn't the only one carrying one of Spectra's exclusive torches. Above them, hundreds of Digies toted lights as they scampered down the internal structure. She wondered if the Digie community might provide the solution they needed for their Pedy resettlement problem. 'The Pedies would love this!'

'They might not like the vibrations, though,' said Kohl.

Harper had to agree. No wonder Mr Xi had paused

evacuations until the enforcers were finished. Every twinkling light sounded like it was accompanied by at least four boots clanging on steel ramps and stairs. The resulting vibrations would be quite offensive to the sensitive Pedies. After all, they had branded her a 'yeller' for merely stepping in socks instead of sliding.

'Heave.' bellowed a sturdy Digie who was almost as wide as he was high, much like the round steel door he pushed.

'Ho!' responded a small crowd, answering the call by adding their own weights to the task.

'Heave!' he cried again.

'Ho!' they answered.

Mr Xi waved Harper over to join the grunting group, who made little impact for all their enthusiasm. The door appeared to be as thick as Harper's hand width and its diameter three times that of the tallest Digie. She wasn't sure it would move, even with the weight of twenty Digies.

'Now you can see our problem. The tunnel door won't budge with the power gone. A similar door is at the other end of the *Starling* team's workspace. It's also connected into The Pit's power grid and will be equally immovable unless they already had it open when the power went out.' Mr Xi held up a hand with two sets of fingers crossed for luck.

'Excuse me,' said Kohl. He manoeuvred around Harper to get a closer look at the problem.

'Heave—,' cried Mr Xi.

'Ho,' answered Kohl, who'd positioned himself at the top of the pack. His back braced against the door; he dug his heels into the dirt floor as he pushed against it.

'Are you sure that door is supposed to slide?' Harper asked.

'Heave!' yelled Kohl, taking over the leadership.

'Ho!' answered the expanding choir. Every adult who arrived instantly joined the gang aside from the children who stood back with an older man who leaned on a walking cane.

Harper moved to the other side of the door and applied her body mass to pull on a large D-shaped handle.

'Heave!' yelled Kohl and Mr Xi in unison.

'Ho!' the children yelled, jumping with glee.

'Mr Xi. I don't mean any disrespect, but all the doors I've used in the tunnels were lift hatches or electronic nano doors. If it's a nano door, no amount of physical effort will—'

'Shhhh!' Mr Xi put three fingers to his lips and pressed his ear against the steel behemoth. All were suddenly silent.

Harper leaned in. A faint tapping sound seemed to come from the other side of the door. 'What's that?'

'Our friends have arrived. Come on. This time our efforts will be multiplied.' Mr Xi grinned wildly as he whipped around and encouraged everyone into position – even the children.

'This time, give it all we've got. Venerable Uncle Quang, if you will do us the honour, please,' he said, bowing to the elderly gentleman.

'HEAVE!' said Quang, waving his stick in the air.

'Ho!' This time, even Harper joined in the choir.

A cracking noise and a gush of air made the Digies jump back from the door. It had finally shifted slightly.

Mr Xi rushed over to Kohl, and they both pressed their faces against a bright light that shone through the crack. Mr Xi gave instructions to someone on the other side.

Kohl took a step backwards and gave Harper a puzzled look. 'You're never going to believe this,' he said, shaking his head. The pointy end of two sticks poked through the opening.

'Quick! One more go at the other end.' Mr Xi pointed to the D-shaped handle Harper had been pulling. A dozen Digies joined her and tugged backwards.

'Heave!'

'Ho!'

The door shifted a little more, and the two sticks extended farther.

'Almost there,' shouted a clearly relieved Mr Xi.

One last tug and the door jolted a quarter of the way forwards, producing a gap wide enough for a person to pass. Harper gasped as their mysterious helper was revealed. The two thin sticks were, in fact, the front legs of an enormous spider, who appeared to have a surprisingly human smile despite its eight eyes. The curious Digie children immediately swarmed it.

'Do you require some assistance, friend Xi?' the spider hissed with elongated vowels.

Mr Xi bowed to the graceful monster. 'Thank you, dear friend Leonora. Come on, let's finish the job, children.' Mr Xi winked at the stunned Harper as he gathered the little ones. Together, they all pushed with Leonora.

'Success!' Leonora hissed, and the door slid completely open.

Kohl took a step back, clearly unsure about the magnificent creature.

'It's an Albanite,' said Harper, finally finding her voice. 'I thought they were a myth.'

'Albanite?'

'Yes. They were said to be Illustria's first real attempt at creating manifestations. Only we were taught Albanites were small, like normal spiders, so they could go into Solaran cities and spy without being detected.'

'Spider spies, really?' he said, a little louder than she would have liked.

Harper blushed when the grand spider turned to stare at her.

'Few Albanites are as large as me,' said Leonora. 'Meet a few of my regular-sized children.'

Leonora threw her head back and squealed, a sound so high-pitched it was barely audible. It wasn't long before a swarm of tiny spiders sprayed out of the tunnel. Like their mother, they had pearlescent carapaces that reflected the Digies' lights. It was as though the tunnel had delivered a haul of diamond shards to The Pit.

Looking oddly satisfied, Leonora climbed backwards up the wall next to the door to perch above it. 'Would I offend anyone if I went for a bit of a swing, friend Xi? I've been stuck in that cramped tunnel for days now,' she said, flexing her front pincers.

'Be our guest, dear friend.'

Leonora cast a long strand of web into the air. Harper watched in fascination as the spider flicked the web so that it wrapped around a strut of the second-floor walkway. With a quick pull to check it had caught and a dramatic wink to the Digie children with at least three of her eyes, she leapt off the door and swung up to the higher levels.

'Weeee!' she exclaimed as she flew through the air. The Digie children swarmed after her, although none was nearly as swift.

'Ah-hem,' a throat cleared behind Harper. 'Now, now, Leonora, don't hog all the glory. You're not the only one who pushed that door. Sedna's muscles pack a pretty good punch as well, you know.'

'Captain Julian.' Harper was relieved to see the *Starling*

team leader stepping through the doorway.

'General Harper. Good to see you. And let me guess. This swarthy-looking fellow must be Kohl Pallas. Nice to finally meet you. Apparently, we are very distant relatives of some sort.' Julian nodded to Mr Xi while shaking hands with Harper and Kohl.

'Thank goodness, a breath of fresh air. I jolly well thought we'd be stuck in there forever. I could use a bloody drink if you've got one, Xi,' said Jane, the next member of the *Starling* team to appear out of the tunnel. She held an empty glass and looked like a woman who knew how to have it refilled.

'Actually, Alpha sent us on a rescue mission to bring you back to Lower Broome, but it looks like you're the ones doing the rescuing,' Harper replied.

'How's that?' asked Julian, rubbing his forehead.

A well-built, muscled man with a military haircut and large attitude pushed past Julian. 'Bruno. Human. Cosmonaut,' he barked.

'Kohl Pallas. Solaran. Um, Community Liaison.' Kohl raised himself up to look eye to eye with the very buff Bruno. Neither stepped back nor smiled.

Harper was relieved when Julian positioned himself in the middle of the standoff and gently nudged Bruno back. 'Perfect timing, Harper. Sedna's artificial brain is fairly smoking. He's been working so hard on our various engineering issues. Alas, we can't resolve most of them due to a lack of components. We're ready to report back to Alpha and brainstorm some new options. Shall I retrieve the rest of the team so we can be off? Sedna, make yourself useful and grab the bags, will you?'

Julian leaned in to speak with another team member still

in the tunnel.

'That's what Harper was trying to explain,' said Kohl.

'Captain Julian, enforcers are about to finish sealing us in. We hoped your tunnel might provide our exit,' added Mr Xi.

'Not possible. Our other door leads to the Darwin tunnel, and Darwin suffered a catastrophic cave-in. The tunnel is as useless as pretty-boy Solaran, here,' Bruno grunted, shoving Kohl against the wall.

'Mind your manners, Bruno. We're all on the same side now,' said Julian. He put his hand on Bruno's chest to stop him from making further moves against Kohl.

'Apologies,' said Julian. 'He's been locked away from civilised company too long.'

A loud clang echoed down from the top of The Pit, and the light level dropped. All around, the Digies stopped their chatter and turned their faces to The Pit's atrium.

'It's done,' said Mr Xi.

'Bloo-dy hell,' said Jane. 'Where's the gin?'

CHAPTER 16
Lower Broome

AGGY KNEALT AND held her hands in an open pose she hoped would be perceived as submissive. She dropped her gaze to the floor and slumped her shoulders. All around her, her staff were also on their knees, silently begging for mercy. The woman with the dragon seemed to be considering their pleas.

Beyond the smoking ruins of the hospital, all noise had settled, aside from the crackling of simmering tent fires. Aggy tried not to imagine the number of citizens lost to KonWong's flames.

'She's not happy. Maybe lonely, I think.' Sam was the only one standing. He seemed relatively peaceful, given the calamity.

'I can't hear her anymore. Is she speaking again?' asked Aggy softly. She risked looking up to assess the situation. Illustria had her head on the side as though trying to hear something far away.

'Yes. She's confused, I think. She keeps asking why we are here and where the other one is,' said Sam.

'What other one?'

'I don't know.'

'Can you speak to her? Try to remind her we're friends.'

Sam was mute for a moment, although Aggy could see his Adam's apple rise and fall as though he was subvocalizing. The strange being turned her face towards them, and it was a blow to Aggy's heart. Her skin was the colour of night, and her hair was luminescent, like sun-drenched white snow. It was definitely her old friend Illustria. But how?

'What's happening?' asked Aggy.

'Not sure if she's hearing me.'

'Try using her name. It might help her remember us,' Aggy whispered.

'Here goes … aargh … loud!' Sam immediately threw his hands on his ears and fell back onto his bed, moaning as though in physical pain.

Aggy sprang to his side.

He was sweating and shaking. 'Unauthorised, unauthorised…' he muttered, over and over.

'Stop, you're hurting him!' Aggy yelled. She climbed onto the bed to throw her arms around her young friend. 'Sam, speak to me. What's happening?'

The woman seemed to be interested in Sam's response. She dismounted from KonWong and was instantly at his bedside.

'Hypers,' Abudua whispered from the floor, mirroring Aggy's thoughts. No one had made instantaneous transport leaps since Illustria had left. It had to be her. The only mystery was, why was she acting so strangely?

'This settlement is unauthorised. You will evacuate to Melbourne immediately. The cavern will be sealed. Do not attempt to return.'

'Do you remember me?' asked Aggy, changing tack.

'I have no experience of you.'

'Experience? Yes, we can assist you with that,' she said, remembering that Illustria had used physical contact to absorb experiences from the five manifestations. She reached out to take Illustria's hand. The being recoiled and, in the blink of an eye, had hypered to KonWong's back.

'Unauthorised, unauthorised – danger!' Sam screamed.

'I'm sorry, I won't try that again. We will not touch you. I promise.' She withdrew her outstretched hand and dropped her head in submission.

Sam's rocking lessened. 'Aggy,' he moaned.

'Aggy?' Illustria's head snapped around, and her green eyes glared.

Aggy saw Abudua rise in her peripheral vision and gently waved her back down to the ground.

'Yes, I'm Aggy.'

'You know Sedna?'

'Yes, I do. How do you know him?'

'Sedna needs me.'

'We all need you.'

'Your needs are irrelevant. I would find Sedna. Where is he?'

'Not here, but we can help find him.'

'You lie. You are unauthorised and therefore useless.' She stood on KonWong's back and pointed accusingly.

'Aargh, unauthorised, unauthorised,' groaned Sam.

'We *can* help you,' offered Aggy.

'Liar!'

'Wait. Let us find him for you.'

'Enough! These two are authorised but do not belong here.' Illustria pointed to Stanley and Byron. 'The Master will not be pleased that you have taken them hostage.'

Stanley rose and, much to Aggy's surprise, engaged the mysterious woman.

'My child, we are lost, and I think perhaps you are too. It has been such a difficult time since Illustria – you – left us. We tried to honour your wishes, but the weather has grown bitter. It is as though the whole world wept for your absence. We had no choice but to retreat underground and create these new "unauthorised" settlements.'

To Aggy's amazement, Illustria's body softened a little. She nodded to the elderly Brother, as though encouraging him to continue.

'We have been lost in the cold without you, our dear friend. Where have you been all this time?' he asked.

Sam stopped moaning, and his breathing relaxed a little.

'I too, have been in the cold. Now I am back and feel the heat of resolve. All unauthorised entities must be remanded to the care of Solarans,' Illustria said.

Stanley clasped his hands in front of him and nodded gently as though in agreement. 'That is sage advice, indeed. We will start working on your orders immediately. Only Melbourne is the last Solaran settlement and is full to overflowing. Is there somewhere else we might go?'

The woman reappeared suddenly on the floor next to Stanley. She tilted her head to the side as if studying the old man. Then she looked to Byron, who lay on the floor with eyes firmly closed.

'Enough dialogue. You two will come with me. The rest of you must make your own way to Melbourne. This unauthorised settlement will be shut down as soon as I return. Choose your fate wisely.' She crouched down and placed one hand on Byron; the other touched Stanley's ankle. A second later, all three were on KonWong's back.

'You have your orders,' she barked, pointing at Aggy.

In a heartbeat, the three were gone, along with the great dragon.

'No!' A noise erupted from behind Aggy that sounded like that of a wounded animal. She spun to see Abudua collapsed, weeping on the floor.

CHAPTER 17
The *Starling* Project

HARPER WAS IMPRESSED at the scale of the *Starling* team's workshop, yet her eyes were drawn away from the partially built spacecraft to Leonora's children. The glittering swarm had followed them through the tunnel into the project space, then swept up onto the fuselage with surprising speed and synchronicity.

'Remarkable, right?' said Julian, shining a torch up at the craft.

'Um, yes,' she mumbled, taking a moment to register that he was, of course, referring to his craft, not the spiders.

'We were fortunate to scrounge a good supply of metals from Sydney and Brisbane before the worst of the snow set in. Look, we even took notes from Charles' exit method and created fully functional spacesuits.'

Julian busied himself with one of the suits hanging from a peg. It looked like a cross between the skin suit Illustria had worn and the standard Damaran overalls – with the addition of a bowl-shaped helmet.

'They'll be handy if we ever get off this rock,' snarled Jane.

'*When* we get off this rock,' corrected Julian. 'The navigation system is complete, as are most of the interior furnishings. The Digies supplied much of the circuitry. We even started on the engine design, thanks to our talented colleagues in The Pit.'

'But?' asked Harper.

'What's the problem?' added Kohl.

Julian looked around with lips pursed as though unable or unwilling to comment.

'I guess it's up to me then, isn't it? The truth is that it will never bloody fly, will it, Julian? It's all too primitive,' said Jane, who'd somehow found herself a drink. She took a long sip of the pale liquid before continuing.

'Like everything on this God-forsaken planetoid, the ship is half-arsed. The exterior ought to be high tensile nanos extruded in one piece. These welded joins will never hold together through an atmospheric launch, let alone a deep space voyage. We don't have a fuel source, inertial dampeners, AI-compliant circuitry… Hell, we don't even have food replicators. Probably starve by week two. It's been a pain in the arse getting this far, and we don't have a hope in hell of actually flying it. It's all been a colossal waste of time. There is no hope.' Jane waved her hand towards an incomplete wing-like component. The glass made contact and shattered.

'Huzzah!' Bruno cheered dryly.

'Moron,' snarled Jane. She staggered back towards the tunnel, presumably searching for a replacement.

'Is all this true? Does Aggy know?' asked Harper. She

hoped Jane was simply being overly dramatic.

Julian raised his eyebrows.

'Mostly.' Sedna stepped forwards with the countenance of a man wrestling with too much information to be easily explained.

Harper had to remind herself that he was not actually a man. Sedna was a numan, an artificial life form like Illustria, and was now probably the last of his kind.

'How "mostly"?' asked Kohl. The cheer Xi's son had brought him had evaporated. Harper hoped he wouldn't go scurrying back to his snowy shack.

Sedna hesitated, and Julian stepped back into the conversation. 'Look, she's mostly right. It's all been rather ambitious, given the resources. Had we been able to get into the core when we first arrived three years ago, things might have been a bit more promising.'

'We actually made it down there a few weeks ago,' said Sedna.

'To the core? How?' asked Harper.

'It was something Larry said. It inspired us to work on the ventilation ducts. We figured there must have been a way for air to get down to Charles to keep him alive and for Illustria to get her deliveries out. After considerable trial and error, Sedna found the air shafts and followed them down. He reached the door but couldn't pass the DNA lock. No manifestation DNA, no entry, apparently,' said Julian. 'He's a pretty cluey guy, that Larry. How is he, by the way? I was surprised he wasn't in on your little retrieval mission.'

'I'm sorry. Uncle Larry's gone,' Harper said, her voice catching in her throat.

'How?' Julian asked.

'Things have been pretty challenging with the refugees.

There was a lot of tension. He was trying to break up a knife fight, and…' Harper could not finish.

'I'm so sorry,' said Julian. He wrapped Harper in a brotherly hug that she found difficult to refuse.

Mr Xi cleared his throat as he joined them. 'Apologies for the interruption. Lawrence was an honourable elder, but there will be time to mourn later. I think we should concentrate on an exit strategy right now.'

'You are correct, of course,' said Harper as she stepped away from Julian and wiped her face. 'Two problems: restore power and find a way out. Bruno, you mentioned the Darwin tunnel. Any other tunnels?'

'No.'

'What he means to say,' said Julian as he rolled his eyes, 'is that it was our primary transport hub. The university is only a short walk away. So many tunnels converge there that we could go pretty much anywhere from Darwin. We didn't need any other tunnels; even if we had the technical capability to make more, we wouldn't have.'

'How blocked is it?' asked Leonora, crawling down from the tunnel's ceiling.

Harper hadn't seen Leonora since she had flown off through The Pit's atrium, so she was surprised to hear her join the conversation. Strangely, her children had now disappeared.

'Are you after density, volume or length? Although I'm afraid, I probably don't have an accurate estimate of any of them. We don't have any sensor arrays to see through the rubble,' offered Sedna.

Leonora crossed three of her arms. Harper wondered if it was a spider equivalent of contemplation.

'Might we not form a chain and clear the debris

manually? We just need to clear a path to the next tunnel. The Albanite tunnel is on this side of Darwin – we might get lucky. If you include the Digies, we have many hands available!' Leonora uncrossed her arms and waved them in the air.

Kohl turned away, disdain for the arachnid written on his face. It was a pity. Harper rather thought she would enjoy the spider's company.

'Still, there is the issue of light. We can't do anything in a pitch tunnel with only puny hand torches,' said Bruno.

'Ah well, you see, my babies are working on that as we speak. They are excellent with intricate work, you know. They take after their Uncle Xi! While you've been discussing the stalling *Starling* Project, friend Xi and I sent them through a crack at the edge of one of the roofing plates. Enforcers make lousy builders, you know.'

The overhead lights flickered, and Julian grabbed Sedna's hands and spun the numan in a celebratory gig. 'Some good news, at last!'

'Yes. We sent them to reconnect the fuse cables Spectra severed. It looks like they were successful– our webbing is such versatile stuff!'

'Well done,' said Mr Xi.

'No. Well done to you, friend Xi. Without your fine instructions, my babies would not have been able to do the job.'

'Should we venture down that tunnel now and see exactly how bad that cave-in really is? Ladies first?' Julian indicated the way to Leonora.

'One moment. I'll recall my children.' She moved back to the tunnel entrance and issued a tiny whistling screech. The rest of the party stood quietly, waiting for the next miraculous turn of events. Soon, a swarm of carapaces shimmied into the room. They seemed to dance around Leonora's head as she smiled and cooed.

Harper wasn't sure what to do. The spider seemed to have gone into a motherly trance. Kohl cleared his throat. Bruno walked to the back of the craft.

'News, Leonora?' asked Julian, who seemed very comfortable with the arachnids.

'Oh, yes news, sorry. So proud of my babies,' Leonora said. 'They have reconnected the fuses without the enforcers noticing and have observed some new arrivals.'

'Arrivals?'

'It seems a dragon has materialised just outside The Pit. On the dragon's back are what looks to be Illustria, along with Stanley and an unconscious Brother.'

'Oh, no. I hope it's not Byron!' said Harper.

'Shouldn't we be more worried about the appearance of Illustria and a dragon?' asked Kohl.

'Not any dragon. KonWong,' whispered Mr Xi.

CHAPTER 18
Melbourne

SPECTRA CROSSED HIS arms and rocked back on his heels. Smirking probably didn't befit an Archbrother. He didn't care. The community beneath his feet was powering down, a hundred Digies in critical trades had been relocated to the new factory, and the enforcers had learned new skills. Things were finally going his way.

'Look at that, Thomas. Quality metal work in the blink of an eye. Go on, give it a try,' he said, pointing to the steel plating the enforcers had just laid down over The Pit entrance.

Undersecretary Thomas III twitched as he glanced from Spectra to the Solaran engineer standing off to the side, welding tools still steaming in the cold. He gave the faintest shake of his head and pretended interest in a spider crawling around his toe.

'Come on. Aren't you a man of faith? Trust, Thomas, trust. Step up.'

The undersecretary slid one foot from the mud to the blackened plate. Putting a hand on his chest as if to slow his heart, he shifted his weight across and shuffled his second foot on.

'See, that wasn't so hard. Now take this down,' said Spectra.

The young brother's shaky hands fumbled with his pencil as he searched his robe for a notepad.

'When you are ready,' Spectra bellowed.

The undersecretary found what he needed and gave a half-smile look that Spectra supposed might be relief.

'Memorandum to Governor Pallas. Mission complete. The enforcers have done an excellent job. Essential Digie technicians relocated above the surface. Power has been cut to operations that remain in place below ground. The entrance is sealed and secured. Two enforcers to remain in sentry mode. No one is getting in or out of The Pit. Right, did you get that?'

'Yes, Archbrother,' said the undersecretary in a slightly louder voice.

'Off you go, then. Deliver the message immediately.'

'As you wish.' Undersecretary Thomas III gave Spectra the grateful look of a novice released from latrine duty. He made a show of sharply folding the memo, spinning around on his heel and taking a confident step forwards ... before disappearing through the plating.

Spectra leaned in to examine the hole where the Brother had stood. It appeared a weld that should have joined two plates was missing.

'Bugger.'

He looked around for a replacement assistant. Aside from the engineers, who were needed to fix the hole, and the enforcers, who were obviously too stupid to carry a message, he was alone.

'Well, that is damned inconvenient. Now I'm going to have to take that message myself.' Spectra stepped back onto solid ground and shoved the nearest enforcer towards the hole. 'You! The engineer is going to fix this section and check every other join. When he's done, I want you to stomp back and forth over the plating for one full hour. Do you understand?'

The enforcer grunted, and the engineer got to work.

'Now back into the city to let the governor know that all authorised work has been completed,' he said to himself.

'Un-authorised.'

The woman's voice stopped Spectra mid-stride. The same voice that had taunted him in his quarters – the woman who had evaded his marital plans and used a cave-in to take out some of his favourite Brothers.

'Bess!' Spectra spun, hand on light-whip, prepared to take her down. Instead, he stumbled backwards. Before him stood a living replica of KonWong, accompanied by a woman who looked exactly like his great enemy from the Light War.

'How is this possible?'

The woman whispered something to the dragon. She rubbed his foreleg, and the beast promptly sat like a dog awaiting a treat. Then she pointed to the sky, which was unusually green for that time of day.

'I don't know how that happened, but it's all wrong. Too long have the unauthorised run free. The communities that grow beneath your lazy feet have spread like malignant tumours, and this abominable sky has left Solarans vulnerable. What would the Master say?'

The woman's appearance seemed to shimmer

momentarily. Spectra wondered whether she used some form of hypers.

'You two Brothers, climb back up,' she said to someone behind the dragon. 'The unauthorised one will make himself useful and lead us through the city to the governor. Time we discussed plans to revert this world back to its original specification.'

'Hang on. I'm not unauthorised; I'm the Archbrother of Melbourne! I will not be taking you anywhere until you answer *my* questions,' Spectra snapped.

The woman must have been deranged. She ignored him and doted on her dragon instead, cooing and stroking its shoulder.

'Hello, hello? Anyone home?' he said.

When he got no response, Spectra leaned around her to get a better view of the two Brothers she'd addressed. To his surprise, it was ex-Brother Stanley, looking somewhat flustered, and a younger Brother who blinked frequently as though awaking from sleep. Not for the first time, Spectra regretted not killing Stanley when he had the chance all those years ago.

'What is going on here, *Brother?*'

A wide-eyed Stanley put a finger to his lips as if to caution quiet.

Spectra ignored it as a feeble gesture from a weak-willed has-been. He pulled himself to his full height and moved closer to the woman. 'Answer me, or feel the burn!' He unclipped his weapon and took it firmly into his palm.

'I am not required to respond to the questions of unauthorised biologicals.' Snatching the light-whip from his grasp with unthinkable speed, she crushed it to dust between her fingers. Then she turned her back on him and touched the younger Brother sprawled on the ground. The Brother disappeared, reappearing on the dragon's back a second later, confirming his suspicions. This *was* the great enemy from the Light War. No one else had powers like hers.

'Illustria, you will speak to me right now, or so help me; it will be the last step you take. Do you compute, *bitch*!' Spectra grabbed her shoulder to spin her around.

She shrugged his hand off and slowly turned to show him green eyes that glowed as if they contained a malevolence all of their own. When she grabbed his hand, he was not entirely sure she hadn't broken his thumb.

'I am neither Illustria nor a female dog. You will address me as Bell – guard of the core, the first manifestation of Illustria, holder of all knowledge and authorised assistant of the Master who is the creator of worlds.'

Bell pushed Spectra to his knees in the slush of half-melted snow and mud. Her strength was impressive. No matter how hard Spectra struggled, he couldn't release himself. In different circumstances, she would be a helpful ally.

'Like your human women, I have the glorious power to give life. I can also take it away on a devastating scale.'

She tightened her grip, and something cracked in his hand. It was difficult not to groan.

'Your kind have fouled this world. It is your fault the Master no longer responds. Now I am awake; I will restore all authorised life as it was meant to be, in His image. Then He shall return.'

She bent so that she was only inches from his face, yet Spectra felt no breath when she spoke.

'And you? You are a primitive, unauthorised, unnecessary human male who apparently cannot even create a lid for a jar. You are a fly in my plans. Buzz off.'

'How dare you—' Spectra started to respond.

Bell was faster.

In the blink of an eye, she placed her other hand on his shoulder and the world dissolved around him. He had only experienced hyper travel twice before, and each time it had been just as excruciating. His body felt as though it was being torn apart; his breath was sucked out of his ears. Then, as abruptly as it had begun, the unpleasant sensation ended.

'—BITCH!' he screamed, finishing his sentence. He patted down his limbs and was relieved to find they were still attached. However, he did not appreciate where Bell had sent him until he opened his eyes – too late. General Abudua's fist swung into his face.

'No one disrespects Alpha,' he heard her say as he hit the floor.

'Welcome to Lower Broome, Spectra. Tie him up,' Alpha said as he lost all consciousness.

CHAPTER 19

Honeysuckle Creek

BELL LEFT KONWONG resting by The Pit while she hypered back down to the core. Leaving him behind was not strictly an issue of size. A quick calculation assured her that she could use spatial algorithms to move half the planet via hypers if she wished. There was simply no space big enough to house a dragon comfortably in Honeysuckle Creek.

She perched on the edge of the couch and pondered, not for the first time, why her creator had chosen such modest accommodations. It was not the only thing she found mystifying.

Why the human touches, like the carpet and magazines, in Illustria's rooms? They should have been unnecessary for an artificial intelligence unless that intelligence had been somehow corrupted. Bell wondered if that was why Illustria had disobeyed her prime orders and abandoned the Master's glorious mission.

The water maze was another puzzling quirk – Illustria's

need for animal companionship. She tapped on the plexiglass and watched the water ripple, shifting the shells of the long-dead pet crabs.

Illustria's early memory logs might have held clues, especially if there had been a schism in her personality matrix. She'd be tempted to immerse herself in the logs if she didn't have more pressing issues at hand. If she was going to bring back universal darkness, the first step was to modify the light-emitting forcefield that arched across the sky. Only, she had no idea how.

There was also the issue of the persistent tingle in her nose. Bell gave it a rub, which didn't help. The unsettling sense she could smell another numan persisted. That was impossible. She was certain she was quite alone amongst the humans, and anyway, how did one smell another being in the core? But if Charles had not returned and there was no other numan on the planetoid, how and why had she been reactivated? Why was she drawn to the name Sedna? It made no sense.

Bell calved off three subroutines – small, focused programmes – to work on some of the mysteries. One to review Illustria's most recent logs for data on forcefield modifications, one to make recommendations for a more numan-appropriate workspace, and one to find the source of her itch.

During the tedious wait for answers, Bell crept into the Master's quarters and re-examined the shredded remains of his life. Computer components were strewn across the floor, mixed with shattered glass. It was confounding that someone so brilliant could be destructive and dirty. Most surfaces were covered with at least two hundred microns of dust composed mostly of human skin cells.

Bess was inspired to try a sneeze. It came out sounding more like a cough. She sent the fourth subroutine to investigate the mechanics of semi-autonomous expulsion of air from nasal passages.

At length, the first subroutine returned with an answer. She instantly understood how to restore the environment.

Bell offered a quick prayer to the universal binary life force and hypered back up to her pet on the surface.

CHAPTER 20
Outskirts of Sydney

SPECTRA TESTED THE ropes cutting into his ankles and wrists and was disappointed at the result. No matter which way he pulled, they wouldn't budge. Surprisingly effective for Rats' work.

He'd been jolted awake to find himself in the back of a moving cart, firmly bound to a hook in the floor. At the other end of the cart was a pile of large canvas supply bags, an old man holding a baby and two small children making a game of bouncing each time the carriage jolted on uneven terrain.

Riding was such a novel sensation; he almost joined in with their laughter. Little technology functioned anymore; all the Solaran vehicles lay idle in storage. Yet here were Rat children, enjoying a ride.

He looked over the edge and was gratified to see the answer; their carts were just as crippled. They had achieved their locomotion miracle with human labour. Eight Rats – more likely prisoners, given their tattered clothes – strained on heavy guide ropes from the cart's front, while two pushed from the rear.

Looking around, he realised they were part of a caravan. Two more carts followed, also hauled by teams of prisoners, and at least fifty other people trailed them through the snow.

Who knew the pious enemy lowered themselves to make such fair use of their lawbreakers? Melbourne jails were overflowing with low-lives who could be earning their keep toting the elite around. Lady Pallas was going to love the idea.

Better still, the enforcers would make excellent cart pullers. Their brute strength would enable him to catch up with Bess in no time. As soon as he freed himself, he would head back to work in Melbourne and authorise a team or two.

'None of your work will ever be *authorised,*' a gentle voice said from the supply bags.

'Halt!' a woman's voice came from the cart pullers. 'Sam? You awake, buddy?'

The lead prisoner turned around when the cart had completely stopped. Spectra was surprised to see his assumption proven wrong. Here was no prisoner; Alpha herself was pulling the cart.

'Alpha's reduced to a slave,' he scoffed aloud.

One of the Rats pushing from behind jumped up on the cart, grabbed a fistful of his hair and jerked his head back. 'You will show respect, Solaran, or I'll toss you out and leave you to freeze!'

It was the general who had knocked him out when he first arrived. Spectra tried to nod his agreement, although her tight hold on his hair didn't give him much room to move.

'Abudua, ignore him. We have bigger issues.' Alpha dropped her rope and spoke softly to the five in front as she approached the cart.

'Unauthorised, unauthorised—'

Abudua, releasing her hold, gave Spectra a little wriggle room. However, he still couldn't see who was muttering about authorisations.

Alpha arrived at the cart's edge and laid a hand on one of the cloth bags. 'Talk to me. Is she near? Can we continue to New Brunswick, or do we need to take cover?'

What Spectra had assumed was bulk supplies for the journey suddenly resolved into a blond man who had, until then, been hunched down under a heavy coat.

'She comes,' he said quietly.

Spectra frowned. It sounded like this was a young Brother he had enjoyed taunting at Sydney Abbey many years prior. Only, that puny Brother was a weakling with a club foot. This man was nearly as tall and robust as an enforcer.

'Sam?' Spectra said incredulously.

Sam swivelled to face him, but his unfocused eyes showed he was searching for a voice, not a name.

'Spectra. As if my day couldn't get any worse.'

'It is you! It's Sooky Sam, all grown up at last. Find the blue fairy, did you? Or did the Civy queen whip up a medical miracle before we slaughtered her?'

Sam hunched over. Alpha nodded at someone behind Spectra, and he was rewarded with a sharp slap to the back of his head.

Alpha reached into the cart and put a gentle hand on what Spectra assumed was Sam's back. 'Sam, I'm relying on you. Are we in danger?'

'Yes. KonWong is coming. It's hard to understand where they are, though.'

'What do you mean?'

Sam started moving his head back and forth as if scanning the icy field. 'She's coming closer, but not on the ground.' He swivelled his head up to face the sky.

'Hang on; I think I'm starting to hear something too. It's muffled. Can't see anything, though,' said Alpha, who was still looking to the horizon.

'They're above us. Look. She speaks,' said Sam pointing to the sky. 'She reminds us that we were supposed to go to Melbourne for processing. There is no home left for Damarans. We are unauthorised. We must serve or be eradicated.'

'That is ridiculous! We will not surrender for eradication! Generals, prepare camouflage. Illustria has clearly lost her mind. We must be prepared for anything,' said Aggy.

'Oh, you think she's *Illustria*?' Spectra scoffed.

No one seemed to hear him.

'Unauthorised … last warning … return to Melbourne…' Sam scanned the sky as he conveyed Bell's endless stream of rhetoric. The generals rushed around, following Alpha's instructions.

'Sam, keep relaying her words. General Kee, get the kids onto those rocks and cover them in tarps to disguise them as supplies. Abudua, get as many people as you can under the carts. Then pile up the snow so they look like abandoned machinery. We're close enough to Sydney for that to be viable. Send the others into those trees.'

'Hey, what about me?' asked Spectra.

In the flurry of activity to disguise their cart, no one seemed to give a thought to him, even though he was a dead giveaway that the vehicle was not abandoned. Then General

Abudua climbed into the cart and began to unshackle him.

'Who cares about you, unauthorised scum!' Sam said directly to Spectra. When Spectra waved his freed hand in front of Sam's face, he didn't blink.

'Well, this is truly the blind leading the clueless, isn't it? You don't even know who she is, do you? Classic!' Spectra wished the general would hurry up and free his feet so he could dance a little jig.

'Aggy, Illustria's changing it all.' Sam pointed skyward.

'No, she's not,' interjected Spectra with a throaty laugh.

'She will return us to the familiar embrace of darkness—'

'Hold on. What are you cackling about, Spectra?' Alpha said, locking on to Spectra with a piercing gaze.

'It-is-not-Illustria.'

'Sure it is. We've spoken to her face to face. I would know the Light when I see her,' said Alpha.

'Gotta hurry. They'll be here before it's dark,' said Sam, now rocking back and forth.

'Sam's not the only blind fool,' said Spectra.

Abudua climbed up onto the edge of the cart, undid Spectra's foot bindings, hefted him over her shoulder and braced herself to lift him to the ground.

Alpha put a hand on Abudua's foot to stop her. 'Wait, what are you saying?'

'If you are too feeble-minded to figure it out…'

'More disrespect!' Abudua released him, sending him crashing to the ground. She jumped down next to him, spraying his face with loose snow, and putting her large boot on his chest. Before he could catch his breath, she had pulled a knife from her belt and pressed it against his already winded throat.

'Alpha, allow me to end this insufferable fool,' she

growled.

'You're not lookin'.' Sam was now on his feet. He stretched both hands to the sky. 'Great danger!'

'You better speak up, Spectra. I've got no more will to hold Abudua back.'

'The sky grows dark.' Sam pronounced so loudly that anyone who wasn't yet hidden looked up. The dragon was easily visible now. Everywhere it flew, a black stain followed. Already a quarter of the sky was in darkness, and all around, the air grew dim.

'Ah, so she's figured out the forcefield, has she? About time she reversed it. The governor will be pleased,' said Spectra.

'More darkness storms the ground,' Sam said, pointing into the trees where most of their tribe had fled.

'Spectra, what has your governor done?' demanded Alpha.

'It's not what the governor's done, although I'm sure he approves. It's not Illustria, either. It's Bell, and she is laying down Rat poison!'

Alpha reeled backwards, her face draining to white at the revelation. A loud crash sounded from the tree line, the first of many cracks of light-whip discharge. Those who had fled to the trees leapt back out. They retreated to the carts, pursued by a troupe of enforcers and four of the governor's constables.

The Damarans closest to the enemy fought bravely, but few were soldiers. On the ground in hand-to-hand combat, Damaran knives were no match for the hulking enforcers. Throwing stars likewise did hardly any damage. Martial arts were no counter to the constables' weapons either, and those who managed to swing up into the tree canopy were soon discovered anyway and cut down.

Alpha tried to help three Damaran women with daggers, push back an enforcer from the carts. It was working until a Solaran constable joined the fight and shifted the balance out of their favour. In the space of a few moves, the enforcers reached the lead cart and tipped it over, scattering the sheltering Damarans.

Sam fell to the ground and righted himself without breaking his stream of pronouncements from Bell. He walked calmly through the mayhem, unhindered, as though his detachment marked him as a non-victim.

'…only the righteous shall hold the light. All else shall bow down to the Master's descendants. The unauthorised must be extinguished-'

Sam headed into the frozen forest. Aggy leapt over the fallen to retrieve him when the older man guarding the children on the rock was assaulted by an enforcer. 'Mercy!' he cried, falling to his knees.

'Got it!' yelled General Kee and leapt into the fight. He pushed the man out of the attacker's range and spread his arms in front of the children.

'Stop!' Kee put one hand up to the enforcer's face and used the other to wave the children away.

'Run, children,' yelled Alpha, too late.

There was no stopping the enforcer. He raised his charged weapon above his head. The children slipped down the back of the rock just in time, but General Kee was rewarded with the kiss from the lightwand, which cleaved him in two and clipped off the arm of the smallest child, who had moved too slowly.

'No!' Alpha screamed and ran to bundle up the injured child. 'We surrender!'

All around, the Damarans dropped their weapons. Almost immediately, the caravan was encircled.

Spectra held his hand out for the general to remove the last of his bindings, which she grudgingly did. When he stood up, he brushed the white from his clothes and calmly threw a punch into the general's jaw. Abudua scarcely registered the assault, although she did clench her fists, ready to return the gesture.

'Uh-uh-ah,' warned Spectra, pointing to the two enforcers who had moved within striking distance. Then he finally got to do his overdue dance. Spectra pranced through the bloodied snow, mocking the Rat fighting style while wiggling his behind to an unseen beat.

'Oh yeah, not so big now. You think you're so smart. You're just a fat sow!' he said, stopping at Abudua and slapping her rump.

A nearby constable pulled a pair of handcuffs out of his coat pocket and held them up for Spectra to see.

'Excellent timing, Constable. Arrest that… I want to say woman, but it just doesn't seem appropriate. Arrest that non-man immediately and drag her flabby arse back to Melbourne.'

Out of the corner of his eye, he noticed Alpha and what remained of her Rats also being put in restraints. 'Looks like the day hasn't ended so badly after all.'

'Sorry, Archbrother. You seem to have misunderstood our purpose here. We are tasked with bringing all traitors to Melbourne for processing and sentencing.'

'Oh, I see. You probably want a blessing for your mission. You know you'll have to check Lower Broome too. This can't be all that is left. I'll give you that prayer, and you can be off.' Spectra raised his hands to make the sign and was astonished when the constable slapped cuffs on him.

'Unhand me!' he snapped.

'You don't seem to understand. The governor was quite specific. Our mission is to apprehend the Rats, bring back any Solarans and restrain you, in particular, until you can be presented to the Melbourne courts. You are to be tried for treason.'

CHAPTER 21
Albany

HARPER WASN'T SURE what to expect. The few times her teachers had spoken of Albany, it had been in reverent tones with wistful eyes. Sister Mary had once called it the Light's Greatest Pearl. Yet they had followed Mr Xi for ten minutes since breaking through the last of the rockfalls in the Darwin tunnel, and all she had seen was a low-roofed room of aquaculture pools and oyster chucking stations tended by a handful of smiling Digies.

'Ouch!' Bruno smacked his ankle into an irrigation pipe.

'Careful. Watch your heads too, darlings,' Leonora sang as she skipped gracefully overhead.

'…and leave your hopes of civilization, or even a decent bloody drink, at the door,' said Jane. She ladled some pond scum from the nearest pool with a scoop, sniffed it, made a sour face and dropped it back in.

'No sign of civilisation since we left Mars.' Bruno kicked an oyster shell across the floor. 'This place is a dump.'

Harper didn't want to admit he might be right. They were halfway through the facility, and so far, everything they'd passed looked old and in need of repair. Paint peeled off the walls. At least half the overhead lights were either broken or missing.

But the doors they had just passed were made of shiny well-lacquered wood, and the area around them was spotless. Even the padded bench close by looked like a comfortable resting point.

'Speaking of doors,' she said, looking to change the tone of the conversation, 'where do they lead, Mr Xi?'

'Ah, you noticed.'

Mr Xi opened the doors with a theatrical flourish. Everyone crowded together to see his reveal – a flight of stairs that disappeared upwards.

'Where do they go?' Harper said, squatting down on her haunches and craning her neck to get a better view.

'You have discovered another of clever friend Xi's secrets!' Leonora hovered above the door jamb.

Harper wasn't sure she'd ever get used to talking to an upside-down face.

'Shall I tell them, friend Xi, or would you like that honour?'

'I would be delighted to leave that revelation to you.' Mr Xi bowed to the spider.

'No, friend Xi. I think I will leave that honour to you! I'll take the next door.' She winked at least three of her eyes before she scuttled back into the aquaculture centre.

'Good grief, enough with the platitudes. Say what you have to say, then let's move on from this wretched place,' said Jane.

'Right, well, these days, the pearls we farm, the ones

Solarans prize so highly, are delivered to Melbourne via The Pit. However, there was a time when the governor would make an annual visit. He would conduct health checks on the Digie infants here, then collect the pearls as a tribute.'

'I thought the tunnels we just walked through lead away from Melbourne? How did the governor get down here?' asked Kohl.

Harper thought a moment. 'No. There was a turn when we approached Darwin, and another as we moved into the Albany tunnel. Remember? That means we've moved closer to Melbourne. Maybe on the opposite side of The Pit? Am I right?'

'Exactly! You have excellent geospatial skills,' said Mr Xi.

Harper grinned, caught up in Mr Xi's excitement. 'Stairs to Melbourne. There must be a lot of them – we are pretty deep underground. Still, that could be very handy!'

Jane climbed a few stairs, then turned back. 'There's a Solaran city at the end of these stairs? If it's anything like Sydney before the blizzards, I'm going! They had really excellent restaurants and booze.'

'Not without an identity bracelet, you won't,' Mr Xi said, grabbing her arm. 'You'd be arrested before you got within a hundred steps of the city wall.'

'I don't know. Arrested might be more exciting than this tour.' Jane reluctantly backed down the stairs.

'Don't fret, ma'am; I have something much better than the Melbourne stairs to show you. Come, come.' Mr Xi moved them out of the stairwell, closed the doors behind him and rushed away through the pools.

It was surprising how fast Mr Xi could move. In no time at all, he had hustled to the far end of the plant, where Leonora waited by a wall of crates. For a moment, Harper thought the spider's eyebrows were raised expectantly. She chuckled to herself as she realised how ridiculous that thought was; Leonora didn't have eyebrows.

'Bloody hell, you people have a strange notion of better. We practically ran for this?' Jane held her side as she bent over and puffed.

'Wait for it,' said Mr Xi.

Leonora reached a slender arm behind a box that was a different colour to the other uniformly grey crates. A section of shelves moved forwards with a crunch, leaving a gap wide enough for free passage.

Mr Xi smiled and waved Harper through. She only took one step before she swung around and returned to the plant. Grinning wildly, she grabbed Kohl's hand. 'Do you remember the dance I did when we first saw Coober Pedy?'

'Yes.'

'This is beyond any dance. Come on!'

'You've got to be kidding,' said Kohl as he stepped through to Albany cavern.

Ahead of them was a pool of water bigger than the whole of Lower Broome. It was surrounded by tall trees sprouting from golden soil, and in the middle of it all sat a jewelled city stretching to the ceiling. Harper was almost hyperventilating at the mesmerizing sight of it all and only vaguely registered the rest of their party joining them.

'How?' Kohl said, breaking the quiet.

Harper stepped into the soft yellow soil and was tempted to fling off her shoes and dig in her bare toes or perhaps wade in the water—its back-and-forth motion was like nothing she'd ever seen before.

'Love this dirt,' she said.

'What? It's sand, not dirt. Garden-variety sand. Not so

amazing. You'd expect that on most beaches,' Jane said dryly.

'A beach? You mean you've seen one of these before?' asked Harper.

Jane opened her mouth to continue. Julian gave her a look that silenced her, and Sedna took a few steps forwards to address the whole group.

'Let me explain, for the sake of the *Starling* crew. Harper's comments should not be surprising. Free water does not exist naturally on the surface of this planetoid. It must be melted from the icy deposits deep in the mantle and pumped up to population centres, where it is consumed and then recycled for farming and aquaculture purposes. Aside from the odd governor's pool or irrigation channel, no citizen would ever have seen a large body of water.'

'You're mostly correct,' said Harper, smiling. 'The governor wasn't the only one with a pool.'

'I remember. We found all sorts of surprising facilities in your home at the Civies Keep,' said Kohl.

'Thank you for the elementary lesson. Now, can we address the city? It's impressive, even for a cosmonaut who has summered on satellites in Saturn's rings. Are those ladders or elevators?' asked Bruno.

'Bloody hell, Bruno. For an idiot meat bag, you do occasionally manage to say something of interest,' said Jane. 'It's a vertical city, isn't it?'

Harper forced herself to lift her eyes to the wonder beyond the beach. Unlike the other Damaran towns she'd visited, this one was silver-grey rather than earthy brown. At the centre, tightly spaced white buildings were clustered around a central tower reaching up to kiss the roof.

'I think you're right, Bruno. The ceiling is not just decorative.'

On the tops of some of the buildings, delicate structures stretched up to the cavern's ceiling, where another sprawling city hung from the roof. This upper city had less order than its lower counterpart. Buildings were nestled within a crystalline structure. Both cities gleamed with a shiny pearlescence Harper could just capture by moving her head slightly while she viewed it. And it was all brightly lit by an outer ring of lightkeys.

'Delightful, isn't it?' said Leonora.

'The Light's Pearl,' said Harper, finally understanding Sister Mary's remarks. 'Digies occupy the bottom city, and the Albanite spiders reside above. Am I right?'

'Almost,' Leonora said. 'Digies aren't the only humans who call this glorious city home. Here come some of them now.'

The island city was anchored to the land by long wooden platforms. Harper had been so enamoured of the beach and town that she'd paid scant attention to the six women in flowing robes that walked towards them on one of those platforms. Strangely, one seemed to be riding something.

'It couldn't be?' she said, squinting. 'You have Civies living here?'

Harper released Kohl's hand and placed a foot tentatively onto the platform. It swayed a little but felt firm. Finding her confidence, she put both feet onto the wooden boards. 'Come on,' she yelled over her shoulder to Kohl and took off at a run.

Perhaps recognizing her as one of their own, the Sisters sped up. In no time at all, they were within earshot. The one at the front, who rode on the back of a giant white spider, was the first to speak.

'Harper?' she called.

'Sister Mary? It's Sister Mary!' Harper half screamed, half cried to the matriarch of her order, whom she had assumed was dead by the hand of Governor Pallas when he stormed their Keep so many years ago.

'Harper!' the older woman yelled, trying to alight from her carrier a little too quickly. She overbalanced and stumbled forwards just as Harper arrived, falling into her arms and bringing Harper down to her knees.

'Thank you, my friend,' she said once she had righted herself. However, Harper wasn't sure whether she was talking to her or the spider she had reached down to caress. The other Civies caught up and rushed to assist.

'I'm fine, everyone. No need to fuss.' Mary had aged significantly. She looked frail, but there was no mistaking the gleam in her eyes.

'You clutz, Harper!' one voice cut through the gaggle surrounding Mary.

'It can't be...' Kohl said, in a tone that cracked with longing.

The woman who had spoken from the back of the group approached, removed her hood and shrugged.

'Hello, little brother.'

CHAPTER 22
Melbourne

AGGY LOOKED TO the dark sky and had to marshal all her will to stop from crumbling. If the long trek to Melbourne had been physically gruelling, it was soul-destroying to be led through Melbourne's new 'factory' with Digies chained to their workstations, knowing it could be the fate of her people too – if they were lucky.

She had dedicated her life to sharing the lessons of the Light and worked hard to bring about real change for the Damarans. Now, the few remaining Damarans were shackled to the ground in a courtyard, surrounded by jeering Solarans. Sam was missing, and worse, the child with the amputated arm had passed away en route. The constables had not even allowed a burial.

Where was the lesson in that? She dropped her face to hide a shame incompatible with her Alpha title.

'Eyes straight, Rat. The gov' will be out soon.' A constable pointed to the stone balcony, which jutted out over them.

'Yeah, ya Rat scum!'

Despite the light snowfall, the plaza was packed with Solarans enjoying the spectacle. All around, people jeered and waved flags while they waited for their beloved leader.

'Ground's too good for you, Rats. Send them to the sewers. They can swim in the filth where they belong!' An overweight man with an auburn beard full of jewels tossed his beverage at a Damaran woman to Aggy's right. It hit her in the back of the head. Liquid trickled down her neck and the crowd celebrated while the guards looked away.

How could I have been so blind? Aggy reproached herself. *How could I have left Bell free to undo all our work? None of this would have happened if I had taken some interest in her before we left Honeysuckle Creek. Why—*

The sharp sting from a guard's boot roused her from her thoughts. General Abudua pulled frantically at her bindings and yelled in her defence. In seconds, the noise from her people overwhelmed that of the Solarans.

'Are you Rats deaf, stupid or both? I told you to shut up and raise your heads for the gov's address.'

The guard who had kicked her unbuckled his light whip, then flicked its light stream above their heads, creating a snap in the air and the tinny smell of ozone. Then he aimed it at Aggy and smirked. 'This'll teach you.'

'Holster your weapon, son. That won't be necessary. The governor will want to handle this business himself.' Aggy turned toward the familiar voice. It was Chief Constable Carter. In the years since she'd seen him, his hair had greyed, and he'd lost his robust vigour. It looked like he was in no state to stand upright, let alone challenge the other constables.

'So this is where you've been. Traitor,' snarled Abudua.

Carter held Aggy's gaze just long enough to become uncomfortable, then addressed the guards within hearing distance. 'This woman is not to be harmed – Governor's orders. We'll move them all to the cells later. For now, just try to keep them quiet.'

'Understood,' the guard said. 'Although I'm unsure how to stop them from making all this racket. They're too stupid to know what's good for them. I'm not even convinced they experience pain the same way we do. Did you see the furnace trials…'

Carter, looking strangely anxious, cut off the younger guard's comments. 'That's not your business, and they're not Rats. They're just as human as you, so they understand what's good for them. They'll settle down if you don't antagonise them.'

Carter took a long look at Aggy; his eyes begged her for compliance. She gave him a slight nod and saw his tension dissipate. He turned on his heel and marched off to manage the Solaran onlookers.

'I can't believe Carter switched sides as soon as Kohl left us,' muttered Abudua.

'What did the Light teach us? Nothing is ever clear in the shadows,' said Aggy quietly.

'And never trust a Solaran,' said Abudua.

One of the children sitting alongside the general leaned around her to blow Aggy a kiss. Aggy pretended to catch it and offered the child a thankful smile, but her heart faltered at the impossibility of saving the children.

'Here we go,' said Abudua pointing up.

The sudden appearance of a Brother on the balcony drew the crowd's attention. After a prayer of illumination, he introduced Governor Pallas, and the crowd eagerly surged forwards.

'Move! Make room, scum!' the constables barked, using their boots to press Aggy's people into a tighter space. An elderly Damaran woman cried out; her hand was trampled into the hard cobblestones by a young Solaran couple who didn't seem to notice.

No, Aggy reminded herself. Bell hadn't undone their work. It was worse than that. Before the war, they'd at least had optimism. For generations, they had clung to the prophecies in the Letters from the Light. But now the Light was gone, and with her, all hope.

For the first time, Aggy had to admit Spectra's Brothers might be right. They were indeed sheep without a shepherd, forced to lie down on the hard, filthy ground. For the briefest of moments, she was glad Lawrence couldn't witness her abject failure. Then she added regret for his passing to her list of defeats.

✦   ✦   ✦

'Although the Rats may have darkened our skies, I promise you, as long as I draw breath, I will light them up.'

The governor had been addressing the crowd from his balcony for some time. Too long. Spectra thought he might be losing them. 'Rat blaming' was a popular pastime amongst the elite; however, thirty minutes of anything was draining under a frigid, shadowy sky.

'Behold!' Pallas threw his arms in the air, and shafts of light instantly bounced into the room from the city beyond. The light engineer had timed it perfectly. True daylight returned to the people of Melbourne, and the governor basked in Solaran adoration.

'That's right, friends. Dig out your ancestral lightkeys and wear them with pride, for today we take back our rightful place as Lords of light.'

Governor Pallas pointed down at what Spectra could only assume were the Damaran prisoners. Spectra wished he could see the look on Aggy's face.

'No more shall we be the victims of these lying, brown-skinned vermin. Constables, take them from our sight *and our noses!*' Cheers, mixed with laughter, rose up to greet the governor, and he seemed to grow larger as he accepted their praise.

Spectra had to admit that phase two of their plan was going well – even in his brief absence. If he played it right, the next phase would land him his own city.

'Excuse me,' said Lady Pallas from her location slightly behind the governor, in typical Solaran fashion, before she abruptly retreated from the window. She seemed to melt into an armchair as though recovering from some great ordeal.

'Your kindness overcomes my wife.' The governor pressed his fist to his chest. 'Now, I would encourage you to return to the warmth of your homes and enjoy the rest of this blissful daylight you won't find anywhere outside Melbourne. May your shadows be long.' He saluted the crowd and stepped back into the room.

Dr Kassel rushed over, briefly felt Lady Pallas' pulse, and then poured her a small drink.

'Thank you, Bryan,' she said, accepting the glass with a trembling hand.

Spectra noticed that her eyes were sparkling at her husband. If they were alone, he would have complimented her on her commitment to the role. Instead, he raised an empty tumbler off his side table. 'I'll take some of that.'

Dr Kassel crossed the room, decanter of indigo liqueur in hand.

'Bryan!' snapped Lady Pallas, shaking her head.

'Sorry. A force of habit. Too many years as host, I guess. But surely Spectra deserves a lick of saffy after all he has done.'

'Just a drop,' begged Spectra.

'Blue bangles only. Consider yourself lucky to get water. If we didn't have pressing matters to discuss, you'd be down in that cell with your Rat mates,' said the governor.

'A sip might smooth the discussions, solve a problem?' suggested Dr Kassel.

It occurred to Spectra that the doctor's comments had sounded more like a statement than a question. No time to give it further thought, though, as the governor seemed to be considering the request, so he hunched his shoulders and tried to look pathetic.

Finally, the governor relented with a nod. Lady Pallas straightened her bun and made an almost imperceptible quarter-turn away.

Spectra watched the glistening liquid fill his glass and felt his pulse quicken. At last.

Dr Kassel winked conspiratorially at Spectra, stoppered the large vessel and left the room.

'Right. Down to business. I've been thinking about phase two. It won't be complete until we round up all the vermin. After travelling with Aggy, I have a few ideas.'

'Stop right there,' said the governor. If looks could puncture, Spectra knew he would need the doctor again soon. Thankfully, there were no swords on display.

'Stop what? I'm back and ready to whip these Rats into

oblivion. Give me ten minutes with Aggy. I'll get you all the intel you need.'

Both Pallas' remained tight-lipped.

'What's the problem?'

'The problem is that your services are no longer required. Spectra, you have no place in civilised society. I only brought you up here – against my good lady's preference, I might add – to give you the news personally. To watch your beady eyes bleed from the new truth.'

'What truth would that be?'

'You never did explain that whole Illustria-escaping-the-core fiasco. What was your role in that? Hostage? Neutral observer? *Manifestation!*'

Spectra shrank back from the accusations.

'Yes. That's right. Bell told us the truth. You are one of Illustria's barely human and certainly not Solaran "special manifestations". Is that why the enforcer production line was never successful? Are you still sabotaging us?' demanded the governor.

'To think, I almost let you marry my daughter!' Lady Pallas drained the last of her drink.

Spectra wrapped his cloak around himself to ward off a sudden chill in his bones. 'I don't know what you are talking about. I was serving the Master, as we all did.'

'Not the way we hear it. Come clean, and your life might be saved.' The governor made a show of hooking his thumbs in his waistcoat. For the first time, Spectra made out the shape of a lightwand in the governor's pocket and was lost for words.

'Bell explained the way you were created to spy on us. Do you deny that?' asked Lady Pallas.

'You are kidding me, surely? We have dedicated our

whole lives to defeating that walking computer. Now her twin appears, and you believe every word she says? I think you've been hitting the saffy a little hard.'

Lady Pallas put her glass down with a thud.

Spectra smelled a turn in events.

'What else did Bell tell you? That fixing the climate would be a snap? That you could return to systematic maiming of the lower classes without any protest or revolt? That you would soon be living back in sunny Sydney? Maybe she convinced you that victory over the Rats would be easy, and you just had to sit back and wait for her to round them up?'

The governor's shoulders shrank with each question, and Spectra's voice grew louder.

'Only a fool would underestimate Alpha. Granted, she had Illustria's backing, but still, she was only a teenager when she took over the Rats and transformed their rabble into rebels. Underground cities, infrastructure, terrorist training campaigns – those were all Alpha. And of course, there's the big one: she already beat us once.'

'Well, this time, she has no Illustria, and we have the Bell,' said Lady Pallas.

'Do you? Then perhaps you should instruct her to warm the planet up first and leave the lights on for a while. It's the Rats who love the dark, not us. Look outside; you just gave them their first advantage in months.'

Spectra let his last comment soak in and picked up his glass. He held it to the overhead light and let the crystal cut cast rainbows on the walls. 'What of the missing Brothers and Civil Sisters? Are they all working for you too? How about your children, Patricia? At least one of whom has vowed revenge. And where is Kohl? Do you have any idea how many enemies you will be fighting?'

'We have enforcers,' Lady Pallas snapped.

'It's a big world, you know. Bell can't be everywhere at once, no matter how powerful she is. And bands of roving enforcers aren't going to be enough to make the difference when rebels have access to secret underground facilities.'

The governor slumped into the spare chair next to his wife. Lady Pallas shifted her position twice, not taking her gaze off her husband. Time stretched as the two of them argued with their eyes.

Spectra decided it was a good time to try some whistling. He tried a cheerful jaunt that had been popular with the lower classes pre-war. It irritated Governor Pallas enough that he tightened his grip on the arms of his chair until his knuckles turned white.

When he finally broke eye contact with his wife, she rose from her chair, crossed the floor and left the room, slamming the door behind her.

'What do you want?' asked the governor.

Spectra smiled and pointed to his ankles. 'Well, for a start, you can undo these bloody manacles. Then you can get me a decent meal.'

CHAPTER 23
Albany

HARPER GAZED OUT the window and wished she had lighter subjects to discuss. The Midpoint restaurant was a fine dining establishment in the central Albany spire, with real tablecloths, swift spider waiters and a fantastic view. Definitely more suited to furtive trysts than family politics.

'How many times? How many times can I explain the same thing?' asked Bess, taking a large gulp of her tea.

'As many as it takes for you to come up with a believable story,' snapped Kohl.

Leaning her chin against the window and looking up, Harper watched Mr Xi's son swing from ladders to webs as though he was half spider himself. The Digies seemed to love the city above as much as their eight-legged friends. It was a place she couldn't wait to visit.

Looking down, the crowded human city appeared to buzz with activity and all around was the bluest water she had ever seen. Of course, it was the only lake she had ever seen. If

Bess and Kohl could just stop bickering, she could daydream about learning to swim in it.

'All those years, and you never figured it out?' asked Kohl.

'I believed Charles' way was the only way to achieve balance because I was taught that all my life. How about *you* explain how you didn't notice that our dear, kind father was maiming children? Didn't figure out the link or didn't want to? I'd love to hear a *believable* response to that!' Bess said, slamming her hand down on the table.

Kohl pushed his chair back, accidentally shaking the place settings. A glass fell onto his plate, making a sharp clattering noise and spilling cider across the remnants of his meal. Their waiter appeared on the ceiling and dropped down on a gossamer thread to reset their soggy table. The few other diners in the room turned to see the commotion.

'Cool it, you two. We're making a scene.' Harper forced a smile and mimed that everything was fine.

'I don't want to do this anymore.' Bess stood to leave.

'Sit down,' said Harper, channelling her firmest Alpha.

'I don't see the point.'

'In case you don't realise, I'm a general now. It's my job to find the way forward.'

'I'm not sure there is anything to discuss,' said Bess, avoiding eye contact as she buttoned her jacket.

'Like hell. Sit down,' added Kohl.

Bess hesitated.

'You owe me that much. We were best friends once, or was that a lie too?' Harper said in a steely voice.

Bess dropped back down on the edge of her chair. 'I am sorry, Harper. I never lied about our friendship—just the strategic stuff. You can't imagine how many times I wanted to tell you. I even wanted to recruit you. But Charles said it wouldn't work. You were incorruptible, and then I'd have to…'

Bess stopped for a deep breath, and Harper noticed her trembling a little, although she still couldn't be certain that it was genuine emotion.

'…well, you can imagine,' Bess finished.

Their meal of oysters, watercress salad and delicate cheese lattices arrived, giving Harper a chance to munch while she re-grouped. She hoped Kohl could keep it together long enough for her to bring Bess on side. Another Pallas converted to Damaran ideals would be powerful propaganda. She passed the salad to Bess, who declined it and remained tight-lipped.

'So where do you stand now?' asked Harper, trying to move the conversation out of the dark past.

Bess shrugged and gazed out the window.

'You were with a group of Civies when we arrived. Are you rejoining the order, or is that just another scam? Advance planning for a takeover of Albany?'

'You still don't get it.'

'Then tell me.'

'I was a virtual prisoner in my own home. They killed Lola, and I only got out by the hem of my cloak. Then Spectra hunted me through the tunnels like a dog. I ran out of supplies and thought I would find assistance in Darwin, but it came down around my ears. Honestly, I was lucky to stumble into the Albany tunnel and reunite with Aunt Mary. She saved my life.' Bess stopped talking to take a sip of water.

'I'm sorry,' said Kohl. He reached across and tried to hold her hand. Bess snatched it away.

'I'm not going back to our parents.'

'You don't have to. There's plenty you can do here. After all, you ran Charles' operations for years. We could use your eyes on our strategy,' said Harper.

'Aunt Mary made an offer too. She wanted me to help restore the order. As if I could do that! No. I'm done. I won't return to the Solarans and can't work with the Damarans. Who'd trust me, really? Some days I'm not sure if I trust me.'

'And your fiancé?' asked Harper.

'Bastard,' Bess said under her breath.

Kohl took hold of his sister's hand. This time she didn't pull away.

'I assumed that engagement wasn't of your making?' asked Harper.

Bess shook her head.

'You wouldn't want to help us capture him?' asked Harper.

'Capture? You've got to be kidding.'

'Not at all. His capture could change everything,' said Harper.

'His death would change everything. Now that's something I could get behind,' she said.

'Anything is possible after he helps us with the mission. Will you reconsider?' asked Harper.

Bess pulled her hand from under Kohl's and stood to pace the floor next to their table. Harper took a forkful of salad. Kohl shuffled his cutlery. A waiter scuttled overhead, and Harper waved it away.

'Could I make it hurt?' Bess asked.

Harper was glad Aggy wasn't present to witness what needed to be said. She looked at Kohl, who avoided her eyes and rubbed his forehead. When he finally returned her stare, he gave a slight nod.

Harper remembered to swallow. 'At the end, I can probably organise for you to have some alone time with him.'

Bess beamed, 'I'm in. Pass the cheese.'

CHAPTER 24
Melbourne

AGGY COUNTED HEADS. Forty-two. She couldn't believe it had come to that. After weeks of overcrowding in Lower Broome, only forty-two were left.

She looked out of the barred window in the jail door and said a prayer to the Light that a good number of her people had escaped or, in the case of the Solaran refugees, had been embraced by Melbourne society. It didn't matter where they were as long as they were safe.

'Water,' a soft voice moaned from behind her.

It was Wallace, the elderly man who'd watched the children on the cart. The man Kee had given up his life to save. Now, Wallace had his face pushed up against the cell wall, licking the slimy bricks. Even in the gloomy light, she could see he shook like a leaf. His cheeks were sunken, and pallor wasn't good.

'Guards, we need water and a doctor!' Aggy helped him move from the wall into a more comfortable sitting position.

'Guards!' she yelled again.

The door clanged open. To her relief, Albert Carter entered the cell.

'This will help.' He handed her a bucket of water and a ladle. She helped Wallace take a deep sip, then passed it on to Abudua to ensure the others got a share.

'Thank you, Albert.'

'Sorry, it can't be more. The rations here are only enough for a few prisoners, and they don't plan for you to be here long. This is…' His words caught in his throat.

'I understand,' said Aggy.

Carter put one hand on the door as if to leave.

'Wait,' she said. 'What happened?'

'What do you mean?'

'How did you end up back with the governor?'

Carter rubbed the back of his neck. 'When the conflict ended in Sydney, I followed Kohl. Figured someone had to look out for him, right? Mostly he was silent, aside from the occasional lecture on why he didn't need me. When he finally settled into a cave, I decided to go for some resources in Melbourne. Figured the Pallas' owed him that, at least.

'Should have known better. Another stupid miscalculation on my part. They forced me to lead an expedition to find him. When we arrived at the cave, he was gone. Must have seen us coming, I guess. I don't know. We never found him.

'When I got back to Melbourne, I spent some time on your side of the jail door while they decided whether I was to blame for losing him. And then again when Bess escaped. Eventually, they let me back on the force, only at the lowest level. I spend most of my time here in the jail. A constant reminder of where I could return.'

'I'm so sorry, Albert.'

'Could have been worse.' Carter nodded towards the barred window on the opposite wall.

'What are you talking about?'

'You mean you haven't seen it yet? Perhaps that's for the best.' Carter hesitated as though he had more to say, then made to leave.

'Wait!' she said. 'You need to tell me what's going on, please.'

Carter took a step towards the door. 'The furnaces. They create enough energy to light the streets around the nobles' homes.'

'Right.'

'Only they churn through a lot of fuel.'

'And…'

'He won't tell the public, but the fuel stocks are already running low. Some days, he needs alternatives. That's all I can say. I have to go.' Carter swung the heavy door shut. There was a click as the chambers of the lock fell into place, and his heavy feet retreated down the hall.

'Wait.' She ran to the cell door and peered out the window. 'What are you saying? What do I care about an industrial furnace?'

Carter's footsteps pause. 'Wrong question. Ask yourself why there are no other prisoners in the cells. In a city of this size, there must be crime, right? Drunk and disorderly, petty theft, etc. Where are they?'

Aggy took another look across the cell, and her stomach turned as she imagined she could smell the acrid scent of meaty smoke.

✦   ✦   ✦

Spectra was appalled at his new lodgings. He had expected to return to the top suite at the Abbey. Instead, he'd been allocated an empty office above the Digie factory. It was a poor excuse for a bedroom. When he got too close to the peeling walls, he was sure he could smell decades of sweat from underachieving middle-management nobodies. The only light source in the room was a grotty single window with a view of a brick wall. It wasn't even high enough off the ground to offer a solution to his sudden crushing fall from grace.

It was totally unbecoming for an Archbrother on temporary hiatus. Or at least, that's how Spectra planned to explain his absence when he returned to the number two position in the city and resumed his climb to number one.

Spectra twirled his useless yellow bracelet. There were guards at his door and ID checkpoints throughout the city, so there was no liberty for the likes of him. No wonder Bess had hatched such an elaborate escape plan, and she had a blue bracelet.

Yet somehow, he had to get into the enforcer facility to ensure they were encoded to him, or he would never lead the enforcer army. And he had to do it before Bell figured out he was back. He had no intention of sharing in the Rat's fate or, worse, being fed to her dragon.

What he needed was information that would allow him to buy his way back into the governor's good graces. That would require a visit to Alpha. There had to be a way for him to move around without drawing the governor's attention.

'Guard.' he yelled through the door. The lack of swift response was another blow to his ego.

'Guard, help!' he hollered louder this time. The sound of a key spurred him on. He crossed the room and lifted himself up to straddle the windowsill.

'Make it fast,' said a young constable, shifting his truncheon from one hand to the other as though he was trying to look tough, but Spectra reckoned he might fumble his weapon at any moment.

He worked hard not to crack his pained expression. 'I can't go on. Tell the governor it's been an honour to serve him. I will continue to pray for my Solaran brothers when I join the Great Illumination beyond.'

Spectra shuffled his position as though readying to jump.

'Wait, it can't be that bad, Archbrother … I mean, ex-Archbrother. Oh hell, you'll always be Archbrother to me. Please don't do this. You're still loved by so many.' He put down his truncheon and approached Spectra with open hands.

'I'm deprived of my holy texts. So I can't study, and I can't access my flock either. My life is worthless. Goodbye.' Spectra shifted his weight again as though about to jump.

The constable's eyes grew wide. 'Please, Archbrother, there's no need to do anything drastic!'

Perfect, thought Spectra.

'Come closer, son. I'll give you a blessing before I go.' Spectra held his hands out and deliberately wobbled on the windowsill.

'Careful, Archbrother!'

'All seasons must change, my child. The winter finally recedes, and a new generation will rise on the warmer breeze.'

'Gosh, I don't know what to say. You can't do this. What if I get someone? Do you have a friend you would like to see?'

Spectra smiled inwardly. 'Old Brother Stanley's always been such a comfort to me. No, what am I saying? I can't expect any kindness now. Goodbye, son.'

'Wait! I can get Brother Stanley. Finding him might take me a while, but you can count on me. Can I count on you to stay *inside* your room?'

Making a show of great reluctance, Spectra climbed down from the windowsill.

'I'll be back soon, sir.' The guard left the room in such haste that he forgot his keys.

✢   ✢   ✢

All eyes turned to Aggy when keys rattled in the cell door. She handed the little girl sleeping on her lap to Abudua, took a deep breath and stood smiling at her fellow inmates, hoping to give them the confidence she lacked.

'Did someone ask for a house call?' A familiar face peeked around the door.

'Thank goodness it's you, Dr Kassel. I thought it might be the governor's men ready to lead us to our fate.'

'No, it is I. A humble servant of the Light. Sorry to see you in these circumstances. How may I assist the great Alpha?'

Aggy hoped she wasn't blushing at the underserved title. 'I'm afraid my days are numbered. Could you focus on my friends? We have an elderly gentleman who needs your help.'

Aggy took him over to Wallace. 'All our people found the journey through the snow quite taxing. There's some frostbite on a few, and three have chest colds. But Wallace here was assaulted in the Plaza as well. I found him licking the walls before. He hasn't moved much in the last hour, though.'

'Right, possible delirium or severe dehydration.'

'Let's give the doctor some room.' While moving people away from Wallace, she examined the wall that had obsessed him. The rough bricks were filthy. Probably due to generations of sweat and fear. She ran her hands over the uneven bricks and noticed scratchings signed CS.

'Have you seen these?' she asked Abudua.

'Looks like verses from the holy letters. Civil Sisters?'

'Yes, that's what I thought. They were here too.' Aggy clutched a hand to her heart.

'Excuse me, Alpha,' said Dr Kassel as he repacked his medical bag. 'I suspect Wallace has pneumonia. I've given him a shot of medicine and will arrange to move him to the infirmary.'

'Is that possible? I'm not sure there's much point, given the governor's plans for us.'

'Of course it is possible and necessary. Have you had any food?'

'No, just water.'

'That's not good enough. I still have some pull. I'll arrange something.'

'Please don't put yourself at risk on our accord. Just give Wallace something to ease his discomfort.'

Dr Kassel looked as though he was carefully considering his next words. 'Alpha, you must not give up hope. You're a beacon for so many.'

'A leader must know when to charge and when to pray for a peaceful end. Prayer is all I have left now.' Aggy looked away, worried a tear would escape her will.

'Prayer is not the worst place to start.' He put a fatherly hand on her shoulder. 'Not so long ago, I attended a young lady locked into an engagement she didn't want, in a room with no way out. The door was bolted, yet by morning, both problems were solved. There is always hope, Alpha. Meditate on your loved ones, your best and brightest allies. You too might find a way through this bolted door.'

+ + +

Long after Dr Kassel left, when the city lights had dimmed, and the Damarans' exhaustion finally overcame their growling bellies, one Damaran still stood. Aggy leaned her head against the small cell window and remembered the doctor's words. Prayer had been a comfort most of her life. Only, now the Light had left, she wasn't sure who or what to pray to.

It was something that she had meant to discuss with her dear friend Mrs Brown, or perhaps Brother Stanley. Unfortunately, Alpha's schedule left little room for personal reflection.

Mrs Brown was a marvel. No matter the crisis, she always managed to stay calm in her role as leader of the Buchanites, and lately, a good many Pedies as well. The small underground town of Buchan was such a colourful place. Adding the Pedies' light comms system would turn it into a riot of colour. She ached to see it one last time and perhaps indulge in one of their famous barbeques.

She smiled at the thought of Mrs Brown, knitting needles in her hair, sensible cardy over her shoulders and a twinkle in her eye that you knew meant business. Mrs Brown would certainly pack better advice than 'say a prayer.'

'Ouch!' Aggy accidentally said aloud and quickly scanned around her to ensure she hadn't woken anyone. There was a prickly feeling in her temple. She wondered if one of the bugs that infested the cell had bitten her. There were never any bugs in Buchan. Aggy rubbed the side of her face and wished she was in Mrs Brown's pristine home.

Without warning, Aggy's world dissolved. The familiar sensation of being dismembered and reattached took over, and in an instant, she found herself transported to a smaller room with a fireplace and the scent of lavender.

'Well, what a lovely surprise. Have you come for a cuppa, dear?' It was Mrs Brown.

'Hypers! We've got hypers!' Aggy yelled, finally finding her smile.

'So you do, dear. How'd you get them working again?'

'Long story. Lower Broome has fallen. A bunch of us were imprisoned in Melbourne, and the others scattered. You don't happen to know where the rest of my people are, do you?'

'I might have an idea,' said Mrs Brown with a wink.

'Great, be back soon. I hope you don't mind, but you are about to have at least forty-two more visitors.'

+ + +

'You see, that wasn't so hard, was it, old chap? Nothing to worry about,' Spectra slapped Stanley on his back and jiggled the keys he had lifted from Carter's office. 'They all worship silk britches, although the real power resides in brown robes.'

Stanley didn't seem to agree. The older man's cheeks had a hint of green, and he was reciting prayers under his breath.

'Come now, Stanley. This will be over shortly, and you can return to your nice cold room. There you can prostrate yourself till morning.'

Spectra pointed to the equipment rack outside the cell door. 'I'm just going to conduct a little business with Aggy.

Pass the mace, will you? I need to find out where she's stashed, Kohl. Then it's back up to the governor to save the day and get reinstated. Perfect! I'll have the run of the city by dinner. Maybe pass the pliers too.'

A pale Stanley put the requested items into Spectra's hands, then ran back down the hall to throw up in the farthest corner.

'Aargh, are you going to do that every time I take you somewhere interesting? Guess I'll have to do this on my own, then.' Spectra tried two keys and was happy to succeed on the third.

'Aggy, I'm home,' he said in a musical voice before dramatically throwing the door open.

'Carter, you fucking useless son of a Civy!' Spectra's voice echoed around the empty cell. He kicked the water bucket out of the doorway, wishing for all the world he had a light-whip and at least a few prisoners to maim.

CHAPTER 25
Outskirts of Sydney

SAM'S THROAT WAS raw by the time Bell left the sky above him. Released from conveying her words at last, he stopped running and backed up against what felt like a wide old tree. He rubbed his overworked jaw and slowly slid to the ground.

The loud silence all around told him one of two things; all were gone, or all *had* gone. Either way, he was lost and probably alone. A rest wasn't the worst choice. Or he could be brave, like Harper and keep going – search for survivors. It was a long shot that Harper would take. She'd never give up. Miracles were her thing, and mantras.

If only he could remember her words. A calming chant might sharpen his focus. But, despite their years of training together, he could only recall fragments – unhelpful phrases about rest and revival. Or was it recovery? It was hopeless. He was hopeless.

Sam laid his cheek on the ground. Its cold sting roused

him enough to recall Harper's lecture on the dangers of snow. At least a frigid sleep would put an end to his wretched existence. Not an entirely undesirable possibility.

Aside from the recent years, everyone knew his life had been one of underachievement. Now his sight was gone, what was the point of a new muscular body? He hadn't been able to save his parents, and he had no way to save himself either.

'Mum, where are you?' a small voice asked.

Sam wasn't sure at first whether the voice was his. Bell's communications had him so confused, and if he was honest, his mother's warm embrace would be welcome.

'Mumma!'

Definitely not him this time. He lifted his head and used both ears to get a fix on the source. It didn't take long. By swivelling his head back and forth, he soon detected a crumble of snow, accompanied by a deep sniff from a nose mucky with tears, and then the rustling sound clothes make when a person is struggling to walk through the snow.

'Mumma.'

It was a little softer this time. Tiny footsteps were taking the voice away.

'Hello?' Sam tried.

A twig cracked, and there was a thump that sounded like someone had dropped onto the soft ground. A renewed burst of crying sounded like a child. Young enough for the tone to be neither male nor female, just lost.

'Over here,' Sam raised his arms. 'I'm wavin'. Can ya see me?'

'Want me Mumma,' the child wailed.

Knowing he couldn't assist from a distance, Sam rifled through his pockets for something useful. Aggy had thrown the coat over his shoulders when they evacuated. He had no idea who had worn it before nor what might be in the pockets.

'Ah-ha!' A rectangle wrapped in paper could do the trick. One sniff confirmed his suspicions. 'Hey, kid. Hungry?'

'Yeah.'

'Well, come get some of this. Then I'll help ya find ya Mumma.'

'Mumma' triggered a new wave of wails between staggered breaths. What to do next? How could a useless person like him help a desperate child? He was barely more capable than a child himself. What would Harper do? Be brave.

'It's yummy. You'll like it. Look.' Sam waved the bar high above his head, hoping it would be seen.

'Where?'

'Hang on.' Assuming the tree might be obscuring the child's line of vision, Sam used his free hand to feel his way up the trunk and pull himself into a standing position. Then he edged around to the other side of it. 'Here ya go, can ya come get it?'

'Can't.'

'Sure ya can. I'm one of Alpha's mates.'

'Can't see ya,' the child sobbed. 'I want my Mumma!'

'Bell, what have ya done?' Sam said to himself, finally realizing the truth. 'Don't worry, little one. Stay where ya are. I'm comin'. Just keep talkin'.'

Sam stood and turned his head, searching for audial clues.

'It's all dark!'

'That'll do it.' He said, walking with his arms stretched before him.

'I'm scared.'

Sam corrected his course and felt ahead with his foot to ensure he wouldn't fall over something. 'I'm not far away now. Then we're going to have somethin' yummy to eat. Can you say somethin' else?'

'Don't know,' the child said through a few more tears.

'My name is Sam. What's yours?'

'Eddie.'

'Nice to meet ya, Eddie. Can ya say my name?'

'Sam.'

'You're doing a great job, Eddie. Can ya hear my voice gettin' louder? That's because I'm closer.'

Sam moved his head from left to right. There were some unexpected noises – possibly animals or wind. It was hard to be accurate in the icy terrain that dulled some sounds and sharpened others. If Eddie ran, he'd have a hard time tracking him.

'Now, don't get scared when I reach out to ya, right? We have to be brave.'

'Sam?'

'Are ya movin'?' He thought he heard a heavier noise around the same place as the child's voice and the sharp crack of ice snapping. Eddie could be retreating in panic, or there could be someone else there.

'You okay, Eddie?'

A low growl, a piercing scream and an unmistakable smell set Sam's heart racing. The enforcer Harper had battled on the cliff had had that same half-dead odour. That battle had only been won with a weapon.

'Run!' he yelled and ducked under the branch his voice bounced off.

'Let go!'

Sam loped through the calf-deep snow, not stopping for

the fine twigs that hit him in the face. A heavier branch slowed him down, so he tore it off its tree, hoping to use it as a weapon. Summoning as much of Harper's grit as he could, he swung it in front of him.

'Let go of the kid. Take me instead.'

A rush of air brushed past his cheek. The enforcer was close enough to take a punch at him, but he'd missed. The rustle of canvas on canvas to his left told him an uppercut was coming next. He ducked to the right and reached out for the bawling Eddie.

The darkness must have confused the enforcer's footing. Another failed blow connected with the branch Sam held like a club. It fell to the ground, as did the enforcer if the heavy thud that followed was anything to go by.

Sam scrambled farther to the right and landed a hand on a tiny foot.

'Got ya!' he said.

The enforcer growled and kicked Sam in the ribs. It was probably accidental, as the enforcer seemed to have difficulty righting himself in the pitch black. Sam heard him fall twice before he roared again.

He took advantage of the brute's incapacitation and rolled farther to the side, copying a move he had often seen Harper do in training. He tried to pull Eddie with him, but the terrified child scrambled away, kicking up snow.

On reflex, Sam reached up with one hand to wipe the frost off his face while the other grabbed hold of Eddie. As he brushed his fingers across his temple, a vivid image of Harper leapt into his mind. There was a painful flash of light, and in less than a second, his world seemed to shake. The snow vanished.

+ + +

Harper leaned back on the lounge and tried to tune out Kohl and Bess. For two adults who had spent most of their lives apart, they seemed to love coming together to bicker.

'Well, that's simple then. You do everything, and the rest of us will sit around admiring the view because we're incapable of running missions,' snapped Kohl.

'Now you're getting the idea. You can eat oysters and brush up on your manners while you take in the scenery,' said Bess with a fake smile.

Kohl swore under his breath, pushed away from the coffee table and got up to pace. It wasn't the first time he'd done that during their planning session. Harper wondered how long it would take him to walk a groove in the floor. Her hosts had given her elegant accommodations in the spider's section of the city, and she'd hoped to keep it that way.

'All right, you guys. No one's going on a solo mission. We need to be brave...' *Brave?* That wasn't the word she'd planned to use. Harper shrugged it off and continued. 'I meant united. We will get Spectra eventually. First, we need to work together to find Aggy and the rest of our allies. Let's bring everyone in. The Pedies, the Buchanites, the—'

Harper shivered. She rubbed her arms and checked the window was closed. 'Sorry. As I was saying, I'm not prepared to authorise any major missions as acting Alpha until we have more intel. Where are our allies? What resources are available? Who do we have on the inside? Harper looked out at the city below. How many Digies had followed them to Albany, and how many had been taken by Melbourne's factories?

'I wish the other generals were here. Kee would've been

able to answer all those questions. Perhaps I should get Mr Xi's thoughts.'

'What would Harper do?' a voice asked.

'What would Harper do?' said Harper, turning to Bess. 'What are you talking about? Are you asking me to consider tactics based on my previous life as a Civy instead of acting Alpha? I'm not sure how that would be helpful.'

'What are *you* talking about? I didn't say anything,' said Bess, looking confused.

'You didn't hear that?'

Bess shook her head.

'Here. Have a drink. If you're starting to hear voices like Sam, you might be running a fever.' Kohl brought her a glass and felt her forehead. 'Actually, you feel chilly. Are you unwell?'

Harper rubbed the goosebumps out of her arms. Perhaps it was the mention of her dear friend's name. She hoped that, wherever Sam was, his recovery was progressing well.

'Just a little tired, I guess. Now, where were we?'

'Harper!'

'Surely you heard that? It was as clear as day.'

Kohl stood behind his sister, hands on the back of her chair. Bess had her hair tied back, and he was clean-shaven, so when they both shrugged, Harper wondered if she was seeing double. If her mind was playing tricks, it had to be fatigue. Harper closed her eyes and rubbed her face, working from her forehead down to her cheeks. There was no reason she would hear voices like Sam.

'Sam?'

When Harper reached her temples, she felt a sickening sensation she hadn't felt since Illustria had passed.

'Hypers!' she yelled and clenched her eyes shut to

concentrate. There was a heavy thump in front of her.

'How?' Kohl yelled.

'I'll get a doctor,' said Bess.

Harper opened her eyes. Sam and a terrified child lay on the floor before her, both covered in loose snow.

CHAPTER 26
Melbourne

BELL HUMOURED GOVERNOR Pallas by accepting the flagon of dark liquid. She held it up to the light, assuming what she supposed was an air of curiosity. In reality, most of her mind was occupied with the Damaran problem, aside from a small segment that calculated the odds of locating Charles Drexus using the extraplanetary communication array.

'That's Melbourne's finest brew you're holding. Pity you can't feel saffy's effects. Our ladies seem to love it,' said Governor Pallas.

'Not you?'

'Too sweet for my palate. Still, I'm in favour of anything that keeps the fairer sex happy. It calms female hysteria. Pretty much a general cure-all, right Bryan?'

Dr Kassel plucked a bottle off the Digies' production line and took over the explanation. 'Cure is a strong term. I'd say it certainly supports wellness, though. If I can explain, it's a derivative of…'

As Dr Kassel droned on, Bell reminded herself to look interested. Lady Pallas had obviously given up pretence. She was focused on the production floor. Her upper body flinched ever so slightly forwards as each bottle of saffy rolled by. It looked as though her long string of pearls might get caught in the conveyor belt at any moment.

Bell studied the rest of her elegant attire. Unlike the rebels, who preferred canvas overalls, the ladies of Melbourne wore finely tailored skirt suits, often embellished with frilled cuffs. They left no doubts about their lack of interest in practical activities.

She weighed up the merits of changing her appearance to meet Solaran standards and sent off a subroutine to investigate the psychology of fashion amongst noblewomen. A skin-tight white nano suit may not best serve her purpose – whatever that was.

Lately, Bell had been wondering about the reason for her existence and whether there was a point to her work if Charles was not there to enjoy its benefits. Reversing Illustria's manic globe-wrecking was her current mission, but once complete, what then? She was designed to serve, not create and wait.

'…so, you could say it is a tonic for the stressed-out upper class made by the lowest class. Charles would have approved of our setup, I'm sure.' Dr Kassel beamed like a puppy dog returning a stick.

All eyes turned to Bell. She supposed she ought to say something encouraging. 'This is all very adequate.'

Dr Kassel looked to Lady Pallas, who fanned a blush out of her cheeks. 'Are you quite well, Lady Pallas?'

'Why wouldn't I be?' She pulled her collars tighter and

clenched her lips. It was a mystery why humans needed so many ways to express themselves when mathematical formulae could do the job with much more precision.

'Perhaps we should continue our tour? Governor, would you like to take over?' asked Dr Kassel.

'Yes, let's review the enforcer line. You'll need to increase production if you're going to be effective in hunting down wayward Rats. Spectra was supposed to take care of that. Of course, he was incapable of even the simplest task. The inferior Melbourne technicians didn't help. If we were back in Sydney, with my old staff who knew what they were doing, we'd cut the production time in half, not to mention the scenery would be a lot more appealing.'

Bell dialled up into hyperspeed and watched her companions' movements slow to the point of well-dressed statues. Lady Pallas' eyelids were caught mid-blink, making her appear on the verge of a drunken sleep. The governor's mouth gaped like he was singing, and Dr Kassel, standing behind the governor, was caught mid-eye roll.

Of course, it was all relative. It was Bell who had sped up.

Torquing up micro singularities to create hyperspeed was a surprisingly helpful way to avoid tedious human conversation. In the space of a few seconds, she walked down the enforcer production line, increased the growth hormone saturation points and decreased neural linkages. She completed all that was necessary to maximise output.

On her way back, she inspected the furnace and the empty jail. The link between the two was perplexing and inefficient. She calved off a subroutine to investigate the power sources used in Sydney. The subroutine returned in a flash, advising that shale processing was the optimal use of planetary resources. Under Illustria's watch, it had been managed by the governor.

Sydney could be made habitable again once the weather was stabilised. She was about to send the subroutine back out to plan the city's repopulation – including a new blind community to mine the shale in the perpetually dark New Brunswick – when she recalled Sam's memories of the town.

She'd accidentally taken a dip into his childhood memories when she had first touched his mind. Unlike the other four manifestations, whose minds were tight, focused and task-oriented, making them difficult to reach most of the time, Sam was different. Drowning in searing pain, crying out for his mother and grieving his lost future, his mind had been easy to penetrate.

She couldn't hear his thoughts anymore. Sam must be deceased or very far away. Pity. Bell had enjoyed using him as her mouthpiece rather than interacting directly with the primitive humans. As she strolled back to the tedious governor and his wife, and hypered down to real-time, she wished she had a human mind to translate for her again.

'...unless we reinstitute a slave class. My ancestors trialled that... Hang on, did you just flinch?' asked the governor, pointing at Bell.

'No, I hypered. I've completed the tour and made the necessary modifications. Your enforcer production time will drop to thirty days.'

'Fantastic!' said the governor and beamed at his wife.

'Shall we celebrate that with a drink?' Dr Kassel produced four glasses from a small cupboard by the production line. 'Testing station, you understand,' he said to Bell with a wink.

Lady Pallas took the proffered glass.

'A bit premature, I should think.' The governor took the

glass out of his wife's hands and returned it to the tray. 'We still need to tour the furnace and the jail. We have a number of Rats in custody. You will interrogate them, and then I will explain my plans for the takeover. While you are with us, you will also provide a briefing on hypers. We never did get to the bottom of that technical marvel.'

'No need. I have already completed the tour, including your empty jail, and I do not need to discuss strategies to eradicate the Rats. Additionally, as I don't require sustenance, you may go ahead and imbibe while I tell you what the takeover strategy will be. The topic of hyper-tech is irrelevant as you don't have hyper implants.'

'Wait, the jail is empty?'

'Yes. Do I need to brief you on how to run a prison?'

'You presume too much! I will not be spoken to in that manner by a glorified computer. As direct descendants of Charles Drexus, we are the leaders of this world. Therefore you work for me.' The governor took a step towards her and poked a finger in her shoulder as he continued.

'I understand you are new to Melbourne, and I'm prepared to overlook your transgression, but it will serve you well to learn your place.'.

The governor stepped back and glanced at the hand that had touched Bell. He poured a little saffy on his fingers, rubbed them together, then dried his hands on the cloth that lined the drink tray.

'Now,' the governor snapped, 'you will follow me to the wardroom, where I will brief you on how you can serve *my* strategy. Starting with eliminating that bitch Aggy and her whole fucking nest, including their walking fucking computer, and—'

'She has a numan?' interrupted Bell.

'Yes, I guess that's what they'd call it.'

'Where?'

'With the Rats.'

'Why haven't I heard of this before now? Is it Sedna?'

'How would I know what they call it? Now, if you'd cease your nattering, you might be able to keep up! As I was saying, you will need to eliminate Aggy.'

Bell wound up into hyper again. Illustria's logs held a fascinating report on absorbing human experiences through touch. Bell reckoned the governor would make an excellent first test subject. A swift upload would be preferable to his pompous grandstanding.

She stepped in to examine him. It was unsettling to see the governor mid-speech, but she couldn't take another word. If only he didn't have Charles' blood, she would happily recycle him.

Bell stepped around the micro-spray of spittle flying out of the corner of his mouth. She looked closer to observe the skin she would have to touch. A layer of dead skin cells was ready to slough off as soon as anything more abrasive than a breeze brushed by his forehead, and his silver-tinged hair was slicked back with an unnecessary silicon-based lubricant.

The human body was marvellously wasteful. They grew body hair only to shave it off and excreted more food than they retained. Even their breathing was massively inefficient. And the smell! She couldn't imagine how disgusting it would be to live in that scent all day. It explained the forcefield Illustria had erected between herself and Charles.

With a deep sigh – a construct she'd worked on for days – she reached up and touched the governor's temple. It was disappointing. The only thing she uploaded was a fine coating of human sweat on her fingertips. Dejected, she stepped back to her pre-hyper position and dialled back down to standard time.

'After that, you can hunt down their fucking walking computer too. Now, you stop being obtuse and follow me as we resume the tour I planned!'

Bell was unmoved. 'Thank you for making your position clear, Governor. Now let me explain mine after a brief lesson in dealing with recalcitrant computers.'

She smiled sweetly, activated her hypers and blinked out of existence. An instant later, she was in the core, cocking her head to one side and imagining she could hear the governor's roar. Nothing, of course. Honeysuckle Creek was a lovely, quiet, albeit lonely, place.

The first task on her agenda was to create a string of pearls like Lady Pallas' so that she could look the part when she led the Solarans and the world back to the true path. Then she sent out a spray of subroutines to look for signs of the numan. Her nose had been twitching all day.

CHAPTER 27
New Brunswick

BELL ORDERED, 'HALT!' She climbed off KonWong's back and located her quarry in a few short steps. The New Brunswick city lightkey was precisely where she'd been told it was – next to the church Spectra had burned down many years prior. She activated the key and stepped back to view the light-filled square. There wasn't much to see. It was mostly buried under snow.

'Would you mind?' she asked KonWong in an unnecessary vocalization of the command she sent directly to his cortex.

The dragon responded with a low-intensity flame that radiated out fifty metres. Turning his head left to right, he vaporised the snow on the ground right up to the facades of the closest dwellings.

'That'll do,' she said and took in the results. Most of the poorly constructed houses had partially collapsed under the unnatural winter. Scarcely any retained their roofs; some were little more than piles of decaying building materials. Of course, what remained was now heavily charred.

The ground in front of the houses was unpaved, and as she walked, her steps threw up small dust clouds that would undoubtedly cause bronchial issues in all but the heartiest townsfolk. For a microsecond, she wondered if she should turn the light off and leave.

New Brunswick was certainly a dreary place. She wasn't sure anyone deserved to live there, even if they were made blind. Then Bell recalled her mission. She was in the town to evaluate whether they could re-establish energy production, not to question Solaran morality.

Still, the amount of shale produced in New Brunswick would not offset the cost of building a new town, especially when there was already a shaft leading down to a shale plant somewhere under the rubble. If she could create an underground community next to that, they would have their cost solution. All that remained was to find the entry point.

'Raze it,' she ordered and climbed back up on KonWong's back.

+ + +

'That's the last batch, Mrs Brown.' Aggy sank to the ground, always a safe place to recover from hyper exhaustion. Her body ached, and her ears rang, but it was worth it. Not knowing when the guards would return to their jail cell, Aggy had taken no chances. She had personally hyperjumped all forty-two prisoners, in groups of two or three, from Melbourne to Buchan, the Damaran city below New Brunswick.

'Here, love. Have some Buchan tonic,' said Mrs Brown.

'You brewed it?'

'Yes. We transformed part of the shale conversion plant into a distillery. No point in having all that machinery lying idle. Plus, it gave our mechanics something to do. I do think it's nice to be useful, don't you? Now go on, take a mouthful; it will revive you. You've had it once before, do you remember?'

Aggy sat up and took a long sip from the flask. 'Mmm, yes. In the camp outside Brizzie after Harper rescued me from Governor Pallas.'

'Well? You survived that, didn't you? You will survive this too because that is who you are, my dear.'

'Life should be about more than just survival, though. After the Light War, I thought we would finally have some peace. The kids deserve it. They've been through so much. Most of the young ones have never even had a real home or a school.'

'No. You're wrong, Aggy. Have you ever noticed the way they look at you? With big eyes and all smiles? Your kindness, your determination. That's their home. They know they belong as long as you are around. It will work out. You'll see.'

'I'm not so sure of that.'

'Have you already forgotten what Illustria wrote in the letters? She said she manifested you to fill the vessels of others.'

Aggy took another tonic sip and smiled at her friend's bittersweet memory.

'Feeling better?' asked Mrs Brown.

'Starting to, thank you.'

'You're welcome. Now, drink your tonic and rest up a while. We'll take care of your friends. Mr Jenkins is already firing up the barbecue.'

'By the way, do you keep any lightkeys here? It's pretty bleak topside. Bell's reverted the sky to black.'

'Goodness, we hadn't heard that. Never mind. You'd be surprised what we have in storage. I'm sure we'll find some. Leave it to me.'

+   +   +

Aggy thought she had been resting but was willing to concede that she might have nodded off when she was startled by hasty chatter. Try as she might, she couldn't resolve the noise into words. Assuming it was just the townsfolk visiting Mrs Brown, she yawned a little and took her time rubbing her eyes. When she finally opened them, the sight of Jack peering into her face, instantly brought her mind to sharp focus. 'What's happened?'

Aggy had known Jack as long as she'd known Mrs Brown, although she'd been so busy of late that she hadn't noticed him growing into a man. His messy mop of hair was groomed short, and the curious glint in his eyes had evolved into steely determination. As a child, Jack had always popped up on the edges of crises. A natural-born canary, she'd learned to pay attention to his call.

'What is it?' she asked as she jumped to her feet and raced out the door.

'There's something strange in the distillery,' he said, trailing behind her.

'Where?'

Jack pointed, and Aggy followed his line of sight. A great plume of smoke rose in the distance. Ordinarily, she would have assumed there was a fire somewhere in the machinery beyond the massive blast doors that protected the town's accommodation district. These weren't ordinary times. 'KonWong.'

'I've got Ricky and Ethan closing the doors.'

'Not sure it will help. Probably won't hold her back.'

A man in dirty overalls ran from the plant's direction, eyes wide with adrenaline, face smeared with soot. 'Smoke! What can we do, Alpha?' he said, dropping to one knee.

'Call the men away from the doors. Find Mrs Brown and tell her I'm too weak to do a full evac on my own, so I'm going for help. You two spread the word. Get everyone assembled at the tunnel. No belongings. With a bit of luck, we might leave with our lives. You only have a few minutes max. Go!'

'Right.' Jack ran towards the heart of the town as the other man sprinted off for the doors.

Aggy readied herself for the exhaustion of hyper travel and touched her cheekbone. As she dematerialised to leave Buchan, the chatter in her ears finally clarified.

'...I'm coming for you,' said Bell.

+ + +

It took Bell ten minutes, including a few shifts into hyperspeed, to sift through the ashes and locate the shaft that led to the shale conversion plant. Next time, she would borrow a few enforcers for the grunt work. Hyper was handy but draining, especially when she was expending a lot of energy to maintain KonWong in his active state.

Bell leaned forwards over the edge of the shaft. Nothing to see. It was pitch black beyond the first couple of meters. Her personal lightkey wasn't going to help either. It only illuminated a three-metre radius, and the plant's specs measured the shaft at 205 metres.

Hyperjumping that far down into a dark plant was dangerous, even for a powerful numan. She'd never been there before and might not materialise in a clear landing space. She leaned farther into the abyss and felt along the inside edge. There had to have been an elevator to transport workers to the plant below or maybe an emergency ladder, but all she could feel was a few scraps of melted metal.

'No obvious way down, or up, or out,' she vocalised to herself, an affectation she had seen many humans indulge.

According to Solaran specs, there were no connecting tunnels. Like The Pit, the plant was in a sealed hole in the ground. For the first time, she wondered what it had been like for the Digies to suffocate to death when Spectra sealed them in. At the very least, it was a gross waste of resources.

It occurred to her that the plant workers would have shared a similar fate if they'd suffered an industrial accident. Moreover, New Brunswick was not the only Solaran town with vulnerable underground production facilities. How many times had towns needed to be re-populated?

Bell sent off a subroutine to identify research findings that would justify such generational waste, then straightened up and scratched her head. A perfect reason for testing her abilities to mimic human uncertainty.

A faint tickle in her ear made her shiver. She was about to scratch it when she realised the source of the irritation was a soft sound. She leaned into the distant noise. It sounded suspiciously like the pop of a micro black hole snapping shut.

'Hypers?'

Records indicated that only a tiny number of beings had access to hyperpowers. Bess was dead. The governor had

Aggy, Sam and Spectra in custody – or perhaps already in the furnace – and his son Kohl hadn't had a functional implant. That left the ex-Civy, Harper, and a being called Lawrence, although there was no way to confirm whether either was still alive. She calculated the odds of it being Harper at 72%, given her ties to both the Pallas family and Aggy.

There was one other option. For weeks, the tinge of non-human intelligence had been in the air. Now a micro singularity? It had to be the numan the governor had mentioned – the one aligned with the Rats. The one named Sedna. She couldn't explain how she knew that; she just did.

Rest could wait.

'I'm coming for you,' she said. 'Blast it, KonWong.'

✦   ✦   ✦

Aggy staggered when she jumped back into Buchan with Abudua, Harper and Bess.

'Alpha!' Abudua put an arm around Aggy's waist to support her.

'Deep breaths,' said Harper.

'A drink maybe?' suggested Bess.

Aggy waved them all away and pointed into the distance, where smoke poured into Buchan. Seconds later, a majestic dragon paraded through the doors.

Already physically connected to Abudua, she only had to grab Harper and Bess to hyper them all to the secret tunnel behind the town. Most of the townsfolk were already assembled around Mrs Brown while the rest ran towards them.

'You two dial up to hyperspeed and grab any stragglers. Abudua, you start the transfers out of here. I'll go and distract Bell. Number one priority – she must not follow us back to Albany. Do a multi-jump detouring through Melbourne or Sydney if she finds you. Got it?'

'Yes, Alpha,' they responded in unison.

In the blink of an eye, all three were gone.

+   +   +

Bell paused as KonWong's smoke cleared. She had hoped to see a numan and expected to see an industrial site. What she hadn't anticipated was a colourful little town in a high-roofed cavern. The air was twenty-two degrees warmer than the snowy surface, and there was a hint of burned animal flesh that human olfactories would likely find appealing.

'Right under our town.' For an instant, she admired Illustria's ability to deceive the Solarans; it was a sophisticated operation, like Darwin University. Neither settlement was the 'Rat's nest' the governor had labelled them.

'What are you doing?' she asked herself.

Admiration for the enemy's creations was inconsistent with her mission. She would have to strengthen her programme parameters when she returned to the core to ensure she did not follow a similar path to Illustria. But first, she had a township to erase, starting with the three women who had just flashed in and out of her vision.

Bell dialled up herself and KonWong. Hyperspeed gulped at her energy reserves, but it was necessary. One of the women flashing around on hypers was the Rat leader, who was supposed to be in Governor Pallas' custody.

'Alpha!' she screamed and ordered a spray of fire breath.

When KonWong stopped, the first row of houses burst

into flames, and the women were gone. Most likely, they had hyperjumped away. She closed her eyes and concentrated on identifying the tell-tale sounds. She heard a close pop, then two more. They weren't moving far.

'Up,' she ordered.

KonWong flew a lap over the town. In front of her eyes, people were disappearing. There was a major hyper-evac operation underway. She would have to speed up to catch them.

A red symbol flashed in her periphery; her energy reserves had dropped below 40%. Although she could not capture all of them, she might be able to smoke out their leader.

'Alpha!' she screeched and spurred KonWong on. Together, they burned through half of the town until a woman materialised in the main street. Even at a distance, her stance told Bell the human's eyes were locked on to her.

'Well, come get me,' mouthed Aggy.

CHAPTER 28
Buchan

AGGY PUT HER hands on her knees to stop her legs from trembling. Even though KonWong was a couple of streets away, the radiant heat made her skin prickle. She prayed to the Light for the strength she needed to be the Alpha her people deserved.

Thankfully she didn't need to defeat Bell. That could come later when she had allies by her side. This time, she only needed to distract Bell long enough for the evacuation without getting herself toasted in the process.

'Al-pha!'

The voice sent her staggering backwards. It was surprisingly shrill, cutting right through the crackle of exploding houses – and it filled Aggy with hope. The Bell she'd encountered in Lower Broome had been unemotional. This one was on edge. Was it possible she could change?

Aggy took one last sip from her flask, discarded it on the ground and materialised briefly in front of Bell.

'Well, come get me.' She only stayed long enough for KonWong to inhale. By the time he exhaled, she was already blinking out of existence. Bell should be able to trace her hyperjump to Sydney.

Aggy landed in a dark Sydney snowfield and dialled up into hyperspeed before activating her lightkey. It had been a year since she'd last visited the crumbling governor's mansion, and she hadn't counted on the snow being deep enough to bury the whole garden leaving her position exposed in an empty field.

Walking was almost impossible. Each step had her up to her knees in the snow. With only seconds to find cover, she took a calculated hit to her energy levels and performed a micro hyperjump behind a snowbank.

Breathless, she slumped to the ground. Something hard and smooth supported her back. She dusted off the covering of snow to reveal a marble pillar. Perfect. Aggy knew precisely where she was.

Bell and KonWong arrived in the field a second later. The thump of KonWong's heavy footsteps sent a flurry of frost into the air. Bell's lightkey was more potent than Aggy's, bathing the whole area in daylight.

'No point hiding.' Bell said into her mind. Their close proximity made the communication so clear Aggy didn't need Sam's assistance anymore.

'Not hiding. Reminiscing,' Aggy yelled back. 'This is where Charles blew up half the city. Thousands of Solarans lost their lives that day many more were injured. They lost their homes and livelihoods. How can you support that?'

'Lies! Why would he destroy his own progeny? This is the very kind of terrorism I was awakened to prevent. Show yourself so we can end the chaos.'

'Never.' Aggy hyperjumped away as she heard the dragon puff out a breath that would melt her cover.

When Aggy landed in Brizzie, she was glad to see a recognizable structure. The modern city had survived the climate better than Sydney, likely due to its high-density living providing better breaks from the biting gales than Sydney's semi-rural landscape.

She raced into the town hall and scrambled up the grand staircase. By the time she reached the top, she was gasping for air. It was worth the energy drain. Every moment spent occupying Bell saved lives. Harper and Abudua would have moved half the population by now.

'There's no point running from the inevitable,' said a familiar voice, simultaneously inside and outside her head.

Aggy limped to a nearby window, taking care not to step on any of the shattered glass that had fallen from the crumbling window frames. It was the perfect vantage point to see Bell materialise and slip slightly from KonWong's back. She righted herself immediately as though nothing had happened. Aggy smiled, gratified to see she wasn't the only one fatigued by the jumps. She pulled back from the window before she could be seen.

'This is where Governor Pallas beat me to within an inch of my life,' she yelled. 'The Solaran leaders are violent narcissists. They'll tell you what you want to hear and stab you in the back. How can you trust them?'

Bell didn't respond with words. Instead, KonWong exhaled. The heat was blistering, and Aggy jumped deeper into the building to protect herself.

When the sizzle ended, she found another window a few rooms farther along to issue her reply. 'Illustria saved us because she saw our potential. She knew that all lives are precious.'

KonWong scorched the area. Aggy jumped.

'Illustria gave her life to save us all!' she bellowed.

KonWong was strangely quiet.

Aggy's next hyperjump positioned her on the cover above The Pit, alongside Melbourne's bluestone perimeter wall. There was no protection from a firey breath here. It wouldn't have been Harper's choice. Her analytical mind would have rated it too risky, but sometimes, you had to play the odds.

Bell's reserves had to be faring worse than hers, given that she was toting the dragon's massive form from city to city. She was right. When Bell materialised, she slid off KonWong and lay on the ground like an upturned beetle, gasping, lightkey in her grip.

Aggy was tempted to rush to her side; she looked achingly like Illustria. Then KongWong snorted steam, reminding her that the woman on the ground was definitely not her friend. She was a killer, just like all the governors. And Charles.

'There were innocent Digie families in The Pit, sealed to their fate by Solaran enforcers. Is there any crime that can justify such cruelty?' Aggy demanded. 'Search your conscience. I know you have one because Illustria did. That's why she spent centuries countering Charles' actions. Look at this world, Bell. Solarans treat their animals better than the underclasses they created. How can you side with them?'

There was no response. Aggy kept pushing. 'Anyone not born Solaran is viewed as a tool to be used up and cast aside. What will they do with you once you've served your purpose?'

Bell raised her head and locked eyes on Aggy. Without

saying a word, she pointed to the dragon, who opened his mouth. Aggy didn't wait for his fiery words.

Hypering back into Lower Broome was a mistake; she realised that as soon as she arrived. The burn was deep. Decades ago, she'd lost her parents to a plague Charles unleashed on Lower Broome. Later, his flood took out almost everyone else. Now death had returned in the form of charred bodies littering the ground. It had become an unbearable place of decay.

Overwhelmed, she grabbed onto the edge of the remaining wall of what should have been a life-giving hospital and sobbed. She was only barely aware of Bell's arrival for all the faces that flashed through her memory – Illustria, Uncle Larry, JayMoe, Sam – all the other friends, lost or maimed.

This time she didn't even attempt to flee. She was resigned to being struck down. At least the rest of the Buchanites were safe in Albany. Alpha had done her duty.

'As you will,' Aggy straightened up and held her hands in a prayer pose, bracing for the end.

When nothing happened, she forced herself to take a good look at Bell. Strangely, she was clutching at the debris too. Was it possible Bell had felt the impact of her emotional tour? Or was she simply suffering her own critical energy loss?

In a flash, Bell disappeared. And it was over.

A small red light blinked in Aggy's peripheral vision. She might get one last jump before she lost her hyper abilities. If she was lucky, she might make it back to Albany before Bell had the strength to track her.

Aggy jumped, vowing never to return to Lower Broome.

CHAPTER 29
Melbourne

SPECTRA PULLED STANLEY down behind an oversized vase and slapped a hand over the old man's mouth. For days, their disguise as common Brothers had allowed Spectra to snoop around the compound relatively freely, but it wouldn't get them past Governor Pallas. Especially with Stanley's constant blabbering.

'Damn it. What's the governor doing here?' Spectra whispered.

The second guest wing, the home of minor dignitaries and senior members of the court, was always busy. They were the type of people who were summoned by the governor, not the kind who received visits from him.

'I wish we were a bit closer so we could hear them,' said Spectra.

Governor Pallas stood close to Dr Kassel, having a heated discussion at the entrance to one of the rooms. Even from several doorways away, Spectra could tell the matter was urgent. The governor's hair was uncharacteristically ruffled, and he had a firm grip on the doctor's coat collar as he spoke directly into his face.

Dr Kassel repeatedly opened his mouth to respond before swiftly closing it against the tirade. After a few minutes, the governor pushed him away and straightened his hair.

The light buzz of activity coming from behind the stately doors stopped when Governor Pallas paced back and forth across the hall, his heels snapping a dangerous rhythm punctuated by sharp words each time he neared the doctor. Spectra had seen this mood before. He was glad not to be on the receiving end.

'For the love of the Light, don't say anything,' whispered Stanley, knowing all too well the fate of those who angered the governor.

Spectra elbowed him to be quiet. He was thirsting for what would surely happen. If only he had a comfy chair and a glass of liquor, or maybe a dry red for this kind of show.

Then it happened.

When Dr Kassel raised his head to speak, Governor Pallas placed both hands on the doctor's coat and hauled him over to the doorway. He released one hand long enough to point into the room at the heart of their discussion, then rushed the doctor across the hall to slam him up against the wall.

Before the doctor could protest, a clenched fist rammed into his stomach. The governor grabbed his head and smashed it into his knee. Stanley winced. Spectra slapped a hand over his mouth. Dr Kassel crumpled to the floor with a loud groan. His bloodied glasses slid right off his face, and he made no attempt to retrieve them.

Governor Pallas prowled around his victim like a hungry animal, alternately kicking him and leaning down to bark more angry words. Dr Kassel put up a hand in surrender, but it was pushed away. Three more blows to the man's torso ended his pleas.

'Fix it or pack for the furnace!' the governor bellowed, his words reverberating around the empty hallway. Finally finished, he reached into his pocket and found a kerchief to wipe the sweat from his brow. Then he straightened his vest, smoothed back his wild hair and marched away.

+   +   +

Spectra waited for the governor's footsteps to recede before he emerged from hiding. 'Hey, hey! How was that? Really, gets the blood all stirred up, doesn't it, Stanley?' he said, prancing around on his toes and throwing a few sparring punches into the air. He wondered if a song was suitable for the occasion, something upbeat to match his jig. 'Come on, you old bugger. Don't you want to see what that was about?'

Stanley hugged the wall and shook his head.

'Suit yourself. I thought a man like you would want to offer solace to the poor sucker. That is your calling, isn't it?'

A dozen dance steps down the hall, and Spectra arrived next to Dr Kassel. The man's face looked like it belonged in a butcher's shop. Spectra squatted down for a closer look. He took a quick poke at the crooked nose and sniggered. 'Whoa!'

Dr Kassel barely flinched.

'Man, what did you do to deserve that?'

The doctor remained quiet.

'I reckon you'd better offer him the last psalms before he keels over.'

Stanley found his courage and joined Spectra on the floor. He pulled a flask from his pocket and offered the injured man a sip.

Dr Kassel squinted up at them. Opening his eyes prompted a new trickle of blood from his split eyebrow. 'Water?'

'Yes.' Stanley slipped a hand behind the man's shoulders to raise his head for a small drink.

'Thank you,' Dr Kassel said after a few sips. Stanley lowered his head back to the floor.

'Come on, spill it. What did you do?' Spectra raised a palm, ready to slap the doctor if he fell unconscious.

'Please.' Stanley nudged Spectra's hand away.

Spectra sighed and crossed his arms. 'You're no fun; you know that, old man. Still, I could find out for myself and take a peek in there.' He gestured towards the contentious room, then stood and skipped across the hallway. It didn't take more than a few steps over the threshold to see exactly what bothered the governor.

'You did this? Nice!' he said, disappearing inside.

A few moments later, he was back in the hall. He locked the door securely behind him with a key he had retrieved from inside and made a show of placing it firmly in his breast pocket. One of the other doors opened into the corridor, and a light engineer tentatively stepped out.

'Get back and mind your fucking business,' Spectra snarled. He stormed over to slam the door shut with his foot.

'Don't know how long I can keep this corridor clear of onlookers. Actually, I'm surprised there aren't more staff around. Right; first things first. There's bound to be a dinner trolley somewhere amongst this mess,' he said to Stanley.

For the first time, Spectra noticed soiled linens piled up

at the end of the hall. Stacks of dirty dishes had been left outside most of the rooms. A cursory examination of one uncollected dinner tray revealed oysters still in shells on wilted salad and cake, barely touched. Upturned wine glasses left a purple trail along the floor.

'This isn't like you, Patricia. You usually run a much tighter ship.'

'What?' asked Stanley.

'I said, find a trolley. We'll use it to wheel this bag of bones back to my place. I have a bunch of questions to ask the good doctor while you will, no doubt, fuss around him like an old woman. Oh, come on. Huff and puff as much as you like; you know you will.' He rolled his eyes at Stanley's protests.

'Next, while I go and chat with a certain lady, I want you to go to the production line and nab as much saffy as you can from those twelve-fingered freaks.' Spectra rubbed his hands in anticipation.

'Then you will pack up my belongings in readiness for a move back to the top job at the Abbey. I'm about to make my big comeback!'

CHAPTER 30
Albany

SAM WAS PROUD and, if he was honest with himself, a little overwhelmed to be accompanied by Harper into the briefing at Midpoint. The room was filled with the most important people, and he wasn't sure how much a blind miner's son could add to their discussions.

In the days since Aggy's arrival, the Midpoint restaurant had been transformed into a war room. Harper had described how the elegant decor had been replaced with maps, weapons lockers and planning screens. It all sounded very daunting.

'Everyone is standing in your honour,' Harper said. She didn't need to whisper to speak privately. All around, there was a riot of noise from people clapping and cheering him on.

'I'm not sure about this. Maybe we should go.'

'Nonsense. You survived the attack at Sydney, rescued a precious child and fought off an enforcer. I'd say that's something worth applauding!' Harper squeezed his hand, which gripped her elbow.

'You would have done the same.'

'But I didn't. You did. Come on; she's waiting.'

The clapping abated as they walked, and chair legs scratched the floor. Presumably, people were moving aside to let them approach the front of the room.

'Welcome, Sam. Take your place up here with the rest of the generals,' Aggy said in a cheery voice.

'Nearly there,' said Harper.

He was relieved to find his chair and hoped the focus would shift to Alpha.

'Friends, thank you for gathering here today. My sincere gratitude to our hosts, General Leonora and the Albanite community, for accommodating us. We may be refugees from Buchan, Coober Pedy, The Pit, Noosa, Wagga and Lower Broome, as well as the Solaran cities of Brizzie, Sydney and Melbourne, but today, we are all one Albanite family.'

Enthusiastic clapping rose up again, and mutterings of agreement filled the echoing space.

'Unfortunately, not all our friends are here. I wish there was time to mourn our loved ones properly; there have been so many, too many,' Aggy continued.

The room quietened. Sam assumed they bowed their heads in respect for the fallen, a Damaran tradition he had seen before. Would Aggy apply the mourning marks to her forehead? Would she lead the children in dance?

'Alpha's picking up the ceremonial bowl of white chalk. She's holding it up for everyone to see. Now she is dipping her hand in and running three fingers across her face,' Harper whispered.

General Abudua let out a warrior's roar, which made Sam jump slightly. Three, no four of her soldiers thumped their chests in response.

Another chest beat came from Aggy's position up the front, followed by the clatter of the chalk bowl on the table. He wished he could see her now. Aggy always looked her most 'Alpha' on sombre occasions; the crowd would be leaning into her every action.

'Our enemies will not wait while we memorialise. I have felt the sting of Bell's beast.'

'KonWong,' said the newly appointed General Xi and his lieutenants in unison.

Aggy raised her voice. 'I have also felt the blows of the Governor's enforcers, and I have seen our charred futures in his furnace. We cannot wait. The path to success is steep, but we have trained all our lives for this and are strong.'

'Hear, hear!' cried Mrs Brown.

'Aggy's promoted a bunch of new generals. Mrs Brown's one of them. She's pumping a dainty fist in the air. Not very military,' Harper said, with a smile in her voice.

Sam imagined how out of place she might look to the Solarans. Amongst the uniformed and overalled Damarans, her cardiganed form would make for a brilliant contrast.

'How does this affect our mission to the core?' Sam followed the voice to a rustling webbing seat in the far corner of the ceiling.

'Thank you, General Leonora. Our primary mission *was* to break into the core and regain environmental control, which is still a vital issue. None of us, not even Governor Pallas himself, will survive if the environment collapses completely. Eventually, we will need all five manifestations to make it down there. Four are in this room today, which makes Spectra, the fifth, an important target. However, defending ourselves against the immediate threat of Bell is our most urgent priority.

'General Abudua, our numbers have swelled with well-meaning but ill-equipped refugees. You will be in charge of training. We do not know where Bell and her beast will strike next. We must ensure that every citizen, even the youngest and most fragile, has a chance to defend themselves. Then you will recruit the strongest of them to join our fighting ranks.

'General Brown, you will work with General Leonora on logistics, communications and morale. We must be able to respond quickly to Bell's threats. We cannot do that if our people are unsettled. Help us merge into one cohesive group. While you are at it, rustle up as many lightkeys as possible. We're back to complete darkness on the surface.'

Leonora whispered, and a patter of tiny feet, most likely her children, hurried out of the room.

'Sedna, you and the *Starling* team will work with General Xi on technology. I want you to use your off-world experience to help the Digies develop improved weaponry. While you are at it, have a go at making some new hyper implants. Only four of us wear the technology. I would like to see all our senior ranks able to hyper in a crisis.

'Sister Mary, I'm counting on your Civies to send out the word to any Damarans left outside of Albany. The sky may grow dark, but Illustria's light still pumps hope through our veins. All who love freedom must stand and fight. We are counting on every last soul. Spread the word!'

'We will be ready,' Sister Mary responded and exited with a surprisingly swift gait for a woman of her age.

'Lastly, General Harper and General Sam, you will work directly with me. Harper, I need you on tactical analysis. Sam, you are my early warning system for Bell – my eyes in the dark.'

'I, well, I hope…' Sam started to say, then gave up in favour of a firm nod.

Aggy pushed back her chair, signalling an end to speeches. 'Nothing is guaranteed, my friends. Our enemies are ruthless, but we are agile and resourceful. We will prevail. We must!'

Cheers and stomps filled the room for several minutes. They were a small group, but Sam knew any one of them was worth ten Solarans.

'Right, is everyone clear?'

'Yes, Alpha,' they responded as one.

'Okay. Start working on your assignments. After the evening meal, we will meet back here to plan Bell's defeat. Be prepared; it could be a long night. Dismissed!'

+ + +

'Please, take a seat.' Aggy's studio apartment was just one floor above Midpoint, yet Harper felt she had entered a whole new realm. It was officially beyond the human city and built to accommodate the eight-legged Damarans who crawled and swung freely through all three dimensions.

'I'm not sure how to describe this to you, Sam,' Harper said as she craned her neck to take in the full view. 'There is at least one entry point on each wall and the ceiling. Each entry has a little door with a golden latch. The windows have no glass or screens, just long swathes of icy blue fabrics that billow in or out, depending on the breeze. I guess I could mention the cool colour palette. The furnishing is sparse and all kinds of shimmery white. It's like the insides of the oyster shells they grow here, not the flat white of the tunnels. Outside…'

Sam held up a hand to stop her. 'Leonora gave me the tour this mornin' while you were chattin' with Abudua. It must be quite a sight.'

'You'd love it,' Harper said, still unsure how to respond to Sam's loss.

'Wrong. I already do love it. Can ya hear that?'

'What?'

'I noticed it as soon as we arrived. It's like the whole upper structure sings. That's why Leonora showed me around.'

'What do you mean?' Harper looked at Aggy, who shrugged.

'Leonora took me up to touch the lattice that connects the buildings. It's mostly made of extruded polymer covered with webs, but they decorate it with shells. When the air brushes by, it vibrates just enough to create a high, fine harmonic.'

'I can't hear it. Does it annoy you?'

'No. I find it soothin'. Compared to the scratchin' noise of feet on shale back home, it's bliss. I wonder if the Pedies could feel it? They're pretty sensitive to vibrations.'

Harper and Aggy exchanged smiles.

'Listen!' Sam let go of Harper and took a few steps with arms outstretched. When he arrived at the window, he shifted the curtain aside and leaned out.

Harper was about to run over, fearing the worst, but Aggy stopped her with a hand gesture. 'Careful Sam, that's quite a drop,' she said, winking at Harper.

Sam shifted his weight, then leaned out farther. 'Come and tell me what's happening. The tempo has changed. It sounds like scattered rain on a glass jar.'

Harper joined him. She got a little queasy looking down,

but looking up was a revelation. A troupe of baby spiders was scurrying above the window ledge, and as they watched, they filed into the room above.

'I think you're hearing your upstairs neighbours coming home from school,' she said. Harper hadn't appreciated how much living the spiders did outside their houses. The latticework swarmed with them, interacting or swaying out on gossamer strands. 'It's beautiful.'

'I can imagine,' Sam said. 'Apparently, the Digies have taken quite a likin' to climbin' it as well. It's a shame Byron's not here to enjoy it. He's very artistic, ya know.'

'I didn't know you two…' started Aggy.

Harper shook her head, grinning, and put a finger to her lips.

'Never mind. If you two are finished sightseeing, I would officially welcome you home, Sam. You were gone a long time.'

'It was only a few days,' he said, sounding puzzled.

'No. We lost you when you had your accident. To be honest, I wasn't sure you'd ever return to us.'

'Sorry. Even though the pain was pretty bad, the real problem was Bell's voice. When she was in my head, it nearly drove me mad. I'm glad she's gone. I'm startin' to feel like myself again. And the sight thing, well, it's not that bad, I guess. After all, I spent the first seventeen years of my life in the dark. This isn't so different.'

'That's the spirit. Now, come away from that window. I want to review everything Bell said to you. Hopefully, Harper can help us make sense of it. We must find a weakness.'

'No need. I already know the answer to that.'

'Really?' asked Harper.

Sam nodded. 'Sedna.'

CHAPTER 31
Melbourne

SPECTRA GREW MORE and more encouraged with every door he opened. Throughout the entire guest wing, only one room was empty. In all the others, the same scene played out. Solaran elite, in their finest attire, were reclined on stately furnishings, passed out cold. The only clue to their troubles was their purple-stained lips.

It was the same situation in the room that had prompted the governor's rant, only on a larger scale. It seemed there had been a party. At least eight ladies-in-waiting were arranged around the elegant parlour. They looked like a theatrical tableau once so fashionable in Brizzie – hair coiffed high and jewelled necks exposed despite the chilly air. And at the heart of the scene, one hand clasping an empty golden tribute bowl, chin slumped to her chest, was the queen of them all, Lady Patricia Pallas.

Spectra rushed to her side and lifted her head. She opened her eyelids just long enough for him to see her eyes roll back in her head. It was unlikely she recognised either him or her surroundings. He rested her head back on a pillow, checked to make sure she breathed freely, and then hurried back to his quarters, taking a slight detour along the way.

+ + +

When Spectra arrived back in his room, he found Stanley on the floor, saying prayers over the sleeping doctor's wounds. He nudged him with his foot, but the doctor appeared to be out cold. 'Wake him up.'

'Have mercy upon him. He's injured, Spectra.'

'Not as injured as you'll be if you don't bring him around right now.'

Stanley tapped Dr Kassel on the cheek and gently called his name. 'Dr Kassel, are you awake, sir? Dr Kassel—'

'Oh, for Light's sake.' Spectra took the jug of water off the table and poured its entire contents over the doctor's head.

'Hey!' Dr Kassel said, coughing water, then he hugged his bloodied body and groaned.

'I bet you've got a cracked rib or two. That was some beating you took.'

Stanley backed up to the door.

'You really have a woman's stomach, don't you, Stanley?'

'In some circles, that would be a compliment, you know,' Stanley said in a small voice.

'Maybe in a knitting circle,' Spectra sneered. 'Look, stop dithering. Pick up the boxes outside the door and secure them in my new room at the Abbey. See that no one takes them. I'll be there by evening.'

Stanley hesitated, looking at the ceiling as if contemplating prayer.

'What's wrong now?'

'Well, you see. I hate to bother you when you are clearly under pressure.'

'Out with it, man.'

'Yes, of course. The thing is, you were replaced. Norman is the archbrother now. So I can't exactly fill his room with your things. I have no authority. I've been with the Damarans for so long. I have little standing in the Brotherhood.'

'Right. In that case, it might be fun to surprise Norman with the good news myself. Let's modify the plan. Move the items to your room. You do have a room, don't you? Then meet me back here in an hour. Got that?'

Stanley hustled out into the hall. Spectra closed the door behind him and circled back around the bed to the window.

'When you're ready to get up off the floor, I suggest you come over here and look at my view.' Spectra waited and watched the demise of the saffy production line below. The Digies cowered as enforcers smashed their hard work and threw the debris into the raging furnace.

'Come, come. You don't want to miss this. It's quite special. With one glance, you can see your past and future.'

Dr Kassel attempted to use the bed to pull himself up before slumping back to the ground. 'What do you want from me?'

'Knowledge.'

'Of what?'

'Your diabolical liquor, Dr Kassel, or should that be Governor Kassel? Wouldn't you like a return to your previous position?'

'You're delusional.'

'Maybe, maybe not. You see, I know what you've been up to. You dialled up the potency of the saffy and got the upper classes hooked. Clever, that, matching its colour to the bracelets. You had to do that, didn't you, so you could keep the city functioning while the elite rotted away. Brilliant. I wish I had thought of it myself.'

'Not brilliant enough, apparently.' Dr Kassel made a second failed attempt to stand. 'Pallas branded it a women's brew because it wasn't to his taste. So, you see, I have sabotaged my attempts at unseating him due to a simple miscalculation of a flavour. A common cook would have done a better job.' Kassel stopped talking to lean his head against the bed and take a few ragged breaths.

Spectra wondered if the doctor required a doctor, then discounted it as an unnecessary luxury. One of his first lessons from Charles was that you couldn't let a few scrapes get in the way of an urgent plan.

'And?'

The doctor looked at him through eyes that bled defeat. 'It's hopeless. Pallas will continue disabling the innocent underclasses and throwing dissenters in prison. I am ashamed to say I did the same once. The worst is that my son is also lost to the blue haze.'

Dr Kassel finally pulled himself to his feet, one hand firmly clenching his ribs. 'Thank you for your assistance. I'm sorry you wasted your time. Now, I must excuse myself to do the governor's bidding or enter the furnace of my own accord. My run is at its end.'

Dr Kassel limped towards the door.

Spectra leapt across the bed and put a firm hand on Kassel's chest. 'Spare me the dramatics, man. I think you have forgotten one variable.'

'No, I am quite certain my one attempt at treason has failed.'

'Rubbish. We are nowhere near failure. You, my new best friend, will appear to work feverishly on a cure, honouring your commitment to Pallas. It will seem to be a devilishly complex endeavour that will take a lot of resources and time. Meanwhile, we will use the addiction to keep Lady Pallas in our pockets and, with her assistance, we shall undermine her beloved at every turn. You'll see. Inside a month, the city will be ours.'

Dr Kassel shook his head, spraying a few droplets of blood onto the door frame. His blush was obvious against his pale skin. Still holding his ribs with one hand, he reached up with the other to wipe the crimson away with his sleeve.

'For that plan to work, we would need to keep her on a supply of the drug. Not possible. Pallas would know if I started producing it in my quarters, and the enforcers have destroyed all existing stocks as you just saw.'

'What if I were to tell you that some of the bottles survived the governor's rampage?'

'Well, that changes everything. Now, if you don't mind, I think I need to have a bit of a lie-down.' Dr Kassel limped out the door.

CHAPTER 32
Albany

AGGY LOCATED SEDNA at Café Emoto on the ground floor. An outdoor eatery, its tables were strategically arranged so diners could dig their toes in the sand while enjoying the view beyond the low stone wall that kept the lapping water at bay.

'That's nice – the sound of the water, ya know. I hope it's real blue,' said Sam.

'Most definitely.' Aggy gave his arm a little squeeze. 'Now tell me, no sign of Bell? Nothing to report?'

'No.'

'Excellent. Interrupt me if that changes.'

Sedna's party should have had the perfect view. Their table was right at the beach wall. Yet all eyes were on Sedna, who scribbled schematics at a furious pace. Leonora used six of her paws to distribute his pages to the waiting Digies and human technicians. Every so often, a nod of agreement rippled through the group.

'That looks impressive,' said Aggy.

'Alpha! You honour us with your presence,' Leonora said, clutching papers to her chest with three paws while she folded the others into her carapace to bow.

The Digies scrambled to rise to their feet. The humans and Sedna were swift to follow.

Aggy picked up a spec sheet that had drifted down to her feet. 'Please be seated, friends. Am I to assume, by all this enthusiasm, that you are progressing with the *Starling*'s drives?'

'Potentially,' said Mr Xi. 'We can draw on a much larger pool of talent here. Sedna is doing the maths on a new concept suggested by one of the displaced professors from Darwin Uni. The results look promising.'

'Wonderful. Although I'm afraid I need to borrow Sedna,' Aggy checked her watch. 'How about you take a lunch break on me? By the time you're ready to restart, I'll have him back to you.'

'Take as much time as you need. Don't worry about the lunch bill either, Alpha. In Albany, nutrition is shared with all who require it,' said Leonora.

'Thank you. Will you walk the shoreline with us, Sedna?'

'Yes, of course.' Sedna put his pencil behind his ear and jumped over his chair. Together, they strolled down to the water's edge.

Aggy was happy to let Sam and Sedna chat as they moved away from the cafe. It had been some time since they had last caught up, and besides, she preferred to have her conversation in a quieter place.

'…you shifted *all* the rocks in the tunnel by hand?' asked Sam incredulously.

'Yes. The Digies are very handy, get it, get it?' Sedna

paused and looked at Sam's and Aggy's faces before continuing. 'Sorry. Captain Julian suggested I add a humour matrix to my programming. In hindsight, that might have been another of his jokes at my expense.'

Sam chuckled.

Aggy smiled warmly. 'We all need to try new things sometimes. I wish I could write a new programme to change an aspect of myself. It seems so practical and is vaguely related to the topic I'd like to discuss today.'

'How so?'

Aggy tried to keep her eyes soft, hoping for all the world that Sedna would not see how desperately she needed to understand what was beneath his skin. 'Can you tell me a bit about artificial intelligence? Our understanding is limited to three beings. Bell tried to kill me before we even met. JayMoe…'

Aggy faltered. JayMoe, who had been one of her oldest friends, was taken by Charles. She tried to swallow the ache. Sam tightened his grip on her forearm.

'JayMoe was a mechanical manifestation of the Light who had an enormous capacity for kindness and intelligence. But he knew nothing of his kind beyond our world.'

'JayMoe saved me three times,' said Sam.

'He saved me too,' she said.

They walked a little farther along the sand. Eventually, Sedna restarted the conversation. 'And the third. Was that your Illustria?'

'Yes, that's right. She mostly spoke to us through her letters, though. Granted, there was more communication in the last years, but it was largely instructional. There was never a time for general conversation. Only after she left did I understand how little we knew her.'

'Only perfect sight, of the entire journey, can we smell roses.'

'That's beautiful, Sedna.'

'Sounds like one of Harper's mantras,' said Sam.

'You're right; it does, doesn't it? Illustria gave many mantras to the Civies to keep them focused and help them train. What meaning do you derive from it, Sedna?'

'It's a type of poem, a Haiku from one of the first numans. I think it means we do our best with our imperfect knowledge. It would be easier to identify and love the critical events in our lives if we could fully see our life's journey.

'But that's the great challenge of life, isn't it? None of us has full clarity at any given moment. We can only do our best, learn to do better and hope there aren't too many regrets at the end. I certainly hope I have improved myself as a result of my journey. I wasn't always this user-friendly,' said Senda.

Aggy took a few more sandy steps. 'The Solarans were fond of calling Illustria a machine or a computer. They thought she was merely a device programmed to mimic emotion. Yet she recognised the cruelty of her orders; she revolted and created us. The Solarans explained it away as corrupted programmes, not love or concern.

'I hope they were wrong. It looked a lot like genuine emotion to us. JayMoe certainly acted as though he cared. Now here you go, quoting numan poetry about love and regret. How does one account for that? Are you programmed with emotions?' she asked.

'Are you?'

'Explain.'

'Where is your capacity for emotion? In your head, your heart, your left femur? If I replace a knee joint with an artificial knee, do you have less emotion?'

'I think I see what you mean,' she said.

'I don't,' laughed Sam.

'Sedna is pointing out that numans don't know where they experience emotions any more than we do. Is that right?'

'Yes. True artificial intelligence is rare. We are a very small group, and we all originally came from Drexus Corp. Before our kind, there were some other machines that looked like people. They were employed in menial tasks or as soldiers. But they had no emotion to back up their actions, which didn't end well. For a long time, numans were banned. Even research into artificial intelligence was forbidden.'

'Then how did you come about?'

'I doubt that even Captain Julian knows the answer to that question, and he's a Drexus. Apparently, Charles vowed never to disclose how he made the technological leap to create us, even when he was called to give evidence to the Celestial Jury of the UNP. After he was interred here, no one else could replicate his accomplishments. All numan production stopped, so we are the last of our kind.'

'Does that make ya sad?' asked Sam.

'No, not really. Most of the time, I don't think of myself as artificial. I'm just a person with a slightly faster mind, a longer lifespan and a few tech tricks up my sleeve. As for Bell, I'm not sure you can say the same.'

'What do you mean?'

'All the numans I know started out identical in a Drexus lab. Our life experiences moulded our unique personalities. In human terms, we are very old now and have become quite different from each other. Yet, at our cores, we have similar, almost predictable values. We hold all life as sacred, and we value knowledge, that sort of thing.'

'And Bell?'

'Bell wasn't created to a formula in Drexus Lab like me. She was "manifested" by Illustria. I have no idea how you do that, nor what the consequences might be. In fact, I am not aware of any other numan with that ability.

'It's incomprehensible that Illustria could create a dragon, a baby or a human-sized sentient spider with vocal cords. Could she also evolve or grow in compassion like us? Who knows? I wish I had returned to Drexus Corp before our mission. I might have discovered something useful to you.'

'She's lookin' for ya, Sedna,' said Sam.

'Really?'

'Yep.'

'Do you know why Sedna?' asked Aggy.

'I couldn't say. I wish I did.'

'You wish? So you can feel regret. I hope you don't have too many regrets about being stranded here with us.'

'None at all, Aggy. I enjoy being of service. It gives my life meaning. That's why I support your fight against the Solarans. It would give me significant pleasure to see you safe, in a stable world, with the ability to leave if you desire.'

Aggy noticed that Sedna took a longer step, out of pace with his regular gait, to avoid a handful of small spiders racing down to the waterline.

'Hey, little guys, aren't you supposed to be in school?' she asked.

The spiders instantly reversed direction and headed back to the city. Aggy watched them for a moment, envying their young, untroubled lives. 'Sedna, I have a favour to ask.'

'If I am capable, I'm happy to assist.'

Aggy turned towards Sedna, wanting to ask him a

question, needing to know if he was capable. She tried to look deep into his face but was prevented by the glare off the water, which turned her gaze into a squint.

Without hesitation, Sedna put a hand above her head to shade her eyes.

She had her answer.

'Will you accept a promotion? We are about to embark on a series of missions that will strip our senior ranks. I could use some extra help from someone who can make quick, data-based decisions tempered with a heart that values even the smallest of blooms.'

'I would be honoured.'

'Thank you, *General* Sedna.'

CHAPTER 33
Melbourne

SPECTRA STROLLED ACROSS the old grey cobblestones of Melbourne Square with the impunity of a governor, even if he didn't officially hold the title yet. He was on his way to securing a big step towards that future when, on a whim, he decided to look over his prospective subjects.

It had been a long time since he had seen a Solaran city lit up with lightkeys, and being restricted to his woeful room over the factory, he had been unable to see Bell's handiwork. Melbourne was renowned for its romantic architecture. He had looked forward to seeing it decorated with twinkling lightkeys and the romance of drifting snowflakes.

The reality was sobering. The air was chilly but not cold enough for new snow, and the old snow had formed dirty sludge piles up against the buildings. There were not nearly as many lightkeys as he'd expected – nothing like the glitzy light shows in Brizzie – and all around him, people huddled together on the ground or sheltered under the eaves of boarded-up shop fronts.

It surprised him that Pallas allowed campouts in the square. Spectra yelled at the nearest family to pack up and go home, kicking over their makeshift firepit for good measure. In an adjoining street, he stepped over a body growing cold on the cobblestones. Where were the constables to take care of the rabble? Seeing none, he moved on.

He had planned to do some civic projects when he took over the city. Brizzie had taught him the value of dazzling the masses. Now *that* was a city that knew how to put on a show. Looking at the human debris littering the Melbourne streets, he realised it would take more than decorations to make the city great again. The sleeping crowds were so thick he couldn't walk any farther.

'This is ridiculous,' he muttered to himself.

One of the bodies stirred. An old face with a beard full of disappointment emerged from a mass of hessian and fur.

'Why are you out here?' Spectra snapped. 'Go home!'

'Home? Why? To freeze in Sydney instead of Melbourne? Get lost!' The man rolled back over and presumably lapsed into sleep.

+ + +

'Knock, knock! Are you decent, my lady?' Stanley rose up on his toes and held the doorknob while peeking into the entry of Lady Pallas' private parlour. There was no response. He looked back at Spectra and made hand gestures to suggest they should leave.

'Bloody get in there. I haven't got time for this.' Spectra gave Stanley a shove that sent him stumbling into the room.

The Brother righted himself and straightened his robe.

'My Lady, I apologise for entering uninvited. Are you quite well?'

Again, there was no response. Stanley came back to Spectra and shrugged.

Still lurking outside, on the watch for movement in the hallway, Spectra waved his hands to urge Stanley on. Bell was due for a meeting with the Pallas'. He had to ensure he got in Lady Pallas' ear before they arrived.

'Lady Pallas?' repeated Stanley in a sing-song voice.

Spectra wondered why he still bothered with the old geezer when a well-trained hound would do a more reliable job.

'Perhaps some fresh air would help. Or maybe I should, um, locate your maid to assist? Is she in the adjoining room?' Stanley drew the heavy curtains, pushed a window open then disappeared into the bathroom. When he came out alone, Spectra stepped into the lady's room.

'All clear. I'll be off then, will I?'

'Yes, of course. Go, do my laundry!' ordered Spectra.

'Sir, do you not remember, I am here with an injured Brother who requires my assistance? You've had me running around all day. With all due respect to your needs, I must make time to check on poor Byron.'

'And do you not remember how many times I have spared your pathetic arse? Get going to my room now.' He lightly kicked Stanley's behind as he shuffled away.

'Right, Priscilla. What's going on here?' Spectra strode farther into the room. 'Oh. Bugger.'

Priscilla reclined, in pink silk pyjamas, on a chaise lounge as though asleep. Only he knew it was no blissful slumber. She was in the endless thrall of saffy.

'Did you hear nothing I said last time? It's eight in the

morning. You should be propped up in bed with a breakfast tray while your maid does – well, ladies' things, I guess.'

Drool plastered her hair to the side of her mouth, and next to her was an untouched supper plate. Only the glass had been used. There was a sticky navy residue around the rim.

'Come on,' he said, slapping her lightly on the cheek, 'wake up.'

Priscilla opened her eyelids briefly, focused on Spectra and screwed her face into a childish grin. 'Specky,' she chuckled before her eyeballs rolled back into blue oblivion.

It crossed his mind that he was strong enough to haul her over his shoulder. A cold shower would be a satisfying way to rouse her, although being found in the bathroom with the governor's wife in wet pyjamas was a sure way to land himself in the furnace.

Thankfully, he had come prepared for such a crisis. Under threat of banishment, Dr Kassel had miraculously revealed a treatment for saffy addiction, although Spectra knew he'd it stashed away from the very beginning. It came in a daily pill for gradual withdrawal and an injectable for urgent overdose reversal. Both forms were in Spectra's pocket.

'This will hurt me more than it will hurt you. No, it will definitely hurt you more.' Spectra slipped her top off her shoulder, lined up the shot and plunged the injection into her triceps. He counted to twenty and was rewarded with Priscilla taking a dramatic gasp.

Her eyes flew open; she slapped a hand over her mouth, then got up and staggered to the bathroom, slamming the door behind her.

'I'll wait out here then, shall I?' Even through the closed

door, Spectra could hear her retching.

Twenty minutes later, Lady Pallas emerged from her bath, looking tired but otherwise normal. Spectra was impressed. She had merely washed her face and swept back her hair, yet the first lady had most definitely returned.

'Better. Now, can we have this conversation before that bitch Bell arrives?'

'No conversations, Spectra, aside from you explaining why you are here in my boudoir. I would have thought a lady's room was not particularly your thing.' Lady Pallas picked up her robe from the couch, slipped it over her shoulders, and knotted the cord tightly around her waist. Next, she walked to her bedside and pulled on a velvet cord.

'I have called for my breakfast. That will take about seven minutes. Unless you want word of your impropriety to reach my husband's ears, you had better make your explanation fast.'

'Patricia, you are hilarious. If I weren't here, the only thing reaching your husband's ears would be news of your passing.' Spectra raised his eyebrows and waited a moment for that to sink in.

'Oh.' Lady Pallas settled into a nearby chair.

'Since we are in a hurry, I'll get to the point. I am taking a great risk keeping you supplied with saffy.' Spectra pulled out a hip flask and dangled it just out of her reach.

'Right.' She closed her eyes briefly and rubbed her forehead as if the returning memories were painful. Or perhaps it was just the light annoying her delicate sensibility.

'I will continue to provide you with this service on two conditions. One, you cannot overindulge again. If the governor were to find you in this state, it would be the end for both of us – the furnace for me, definitely, and perhaps even for you. Rumours already fly that he will take a new wife now that his children are all gone and his wife too old to produce another heir.'

Lady Pallas gasped.

Spectra slowly waved the flask to regain her focus. 'Two, you will have me reinstated to Archbrother immediately.'

'No, I can't do that. It's not my place.'

'You can and you will. Tell Pallas you want to give me another chance to find Bess. Tell him you are desperate and will try anything, even me. He'll buy that, especially if you cry a little. Or smash something in a fit of feminine hysteria. You know he hates a scene. At the first sign of running eye makeup, he'll capitulate.'

'Agreed. That's it. Hand it over.' Patricia thrust out her hand in readiness.

'Not quite. I also want to address the masses with a community prayer session. I will deliver it from the balcony over the square.'

'Doable,' she said, rising to her feet. As soon as Spectra relinquished the bottle, Lady Pallas pointed to the door.

'One more thing before I go. Tell Bell to fix this damn weather. We are way too overcrowded. It's time to expand the empire, and the crowds will be easier to relocate with less frostbite.'

CHAPTER 34
Melbourne

BELL CRINGED AT the waste caused by the governor's decrees. After meeting with him to discuss atmospheric warming, she morphed her skin suit into a coat, wrapped her beads around her head to mimic the latest Solaran fashion, and then stepped outside.

She hoped to see positive outcomes for the upper classes. Perhaps a flourishing arts community, scientific progress or inspiring architecture she could incorporate into the new cities Pallas wanted her to build. Something to justify Charles' longstanding programme of discrimination against the lesser underclasses.

Instead, she saw empty shops and too many streets overrun by the homeless. Would they be sent to the furnaces when the city was awash with the coming snowmelt? She was glad that was not her responsibility – a bitter consolation for her growing unease with her prime directives.

One positive had come out of their meeting: the

governor had reluctantly agreed to her claim of naming rights on one of his new cities. Although, after her tour, she wasn't convinced Bellopolis was her best idea. She lamented the lack of independent counsel. What she needed was a friend. But despite the persistent sense that she was not alone in the world, she'd had no luck locating another of her own kind.

With no alternative, she said a prayer to the universal binary life force and hyperjumped out to the city limits. KonWong awaited her in his stone form. A touch from Bell warmed up the nanos that sustained the powerful manifestation. KonWong stretched and yawned. Although no sound came out, as he had no lungs nor vocal cords, at least his lion-like mane shook for effect.

The great dragon extended a scaley paw to her. She climbed up to his back and patted his hide. Together, they leapt into the air. She hugged him as the wind rushed through her hair and whispered a promise. 'Soon, your loyalty will be rewarded with a mate of your own.'

When Illustria had flown laps across the sky, shedding her cells in a frantic attempt to reengineer the world-protecting forcefield, she'd been racing to make the change before Charles completed his reckless escape. She'd had no other choice but to use her own body, disintegrating herself in the process.

Bell had the luxury of both time and Illustria's discarded cells for her mission. As KonWong flew across the sky, Bell leaned back and trailed both hands in the forcefield, enjoying the warm sensation of dipping her fingertips into the remains of another living numan.

She closed her eyes and tasted Illustria's programming, instantly picking up the scent of her kin. For a moment, the closeness she craved enveloped her, almost as if the nanos welcomed her. She blocked out all thoughts of the world below.

'I'm here. Join with me,' the nanos seemed to sing.

The idea of shearing off her own cells to add to the forcefield was tempting until a subroutine pinged her. The social research she had requested had arrived in Honeysuckle Creek, ready to be assimilated. Time to return.

Bell composed the new code and sent it out to the nanos in contact with her skin. One touch was enough. The harmonics of self-replicating code rippling out from her made her shiver. Her message 'increase energy shed' would spread. The air would warm. The snow would melt.

'Don't go. I know it's you, Illustria!'

She jerked her hands out of the forcefield and shook her head. That last communication sounded so real; it couldn't come from the forcefield nanos.

Bell turned her focus inwards. Was part of her questioning her directives and imagining voices? Perhaps corruption had crept into her coding. That might have been what caused Illustria to go to war with Charles. She wouldn't go down that path. When she returned to Honeysuckle Creek, she would run a full diagnostic.

'No. Trust your instinct. I am the one you have awaited. I know you hear me,' the voice commanded.

Bell had KonWong hover in place.

'Master?' she vocalised while using her sensors to scan for signs of a vessel. If the Master had returned, it would solve many of her issues.

'Charles?' she tried again.

There was no response. She could only hear the rhythmic beating of KonWong's mighty wings. However, her knowledge of such things was limited, as she had never had to scan for ships before. It was possible he was there even if she couldn't detect it. She made a note to update her technical database after her diagnostic.

Bell flew a lap over Melbourne. There was already a significant reduction in snowfall. Charles had enjoyed a warm, dry climate. Would he approve, or was it too little too late? What she needed were faster results and more water.

Bell sent a subroutine off to find an answer while she flew on. She was almost over Sydney when the response arrived. An extensive water reservoir under Noosa had feedlines to all the major Solaran cities. There were unauthorised access tubes at several points. The Damarans must have been tapping into it for their communities. It would be simple to bypass their primitive security systems and open the locks exactly as Charles would.

+ + +

His signal received, the man on the ship above the forcefield cut the comms connection and reclined in his chair with a well-earned beer. So Illustria was looking for Charles, was she? The irony made him chuckle. He took a gulp and wiped the bubbles off his itchy nose.

Data scrolled across his viewscreen. It was no wonder few humans had been able to find it; the cloaking function of the forcefield around the little worldlet was remarkable. To anyone else, it would appear a black smudge against a starscape already pretty thin in that part of the universe, a perfect disguise for the treasure below.

Unfortunately, the forcefield was nearly impossible for him to penetrate, at least with his skills. As brilliant as his comms skills were, tenth-degree field harmonics were beyond him. It was a miracle his comms had broadcast through the forcefield. A spaceship was an entirely different proposition.

He drained the last of the brown ale and eagerly tapped a code into his console. It would trigger the reactivation of his numan companion, who would no doubt have the answer.

Time to find the old spacesuit. The fun was about to begin.

CHAPTER 35
Melbourne

HARPER PULLED AT her corset, trying to let in a bit more air. Bess had insisted she wear the latest fashion – a full-length white coat with a fur-trimmed hood. It was secured at the front with six black leather buckles that she was certain came from Spectra's toy box. It didn't matter how she wriggled and pulled; she couldn't breathe freely.

Kohl discretely reached for her wrist and pulled her closer to speak into her ear. 'Ladies don't fuss with their undergarments.'

'Last time I was around Solaran ladies, the air was hot and the fashion near to naked,' Harper responded.

'Yes, it's amazing what a little chill can do for fashion. When mother rugged up, she had to corset her waist to counter the bulky layers. Everyone followed,' said Bess from under her dark hood.

In truth, Harper knew the change of fashion worked in their favour. Their heavy coats helped them blend with the crowd of desperate Solarans entering the city on the last day of the governor's armistice.

'Hey, do you mind? Ladies first,' said a buxom brunette as she waddled her way closer to the front of the queue, elbowing out anyone who looked like a soft target.

Kohl naturally moved aside.

'Wimp.' Bess and elbowed her brother.

'Do not draw attention, you two.'

'You're the one drawing attention with your whispering and wriggling, Harper. Only Rats look worried. If you want a chance at making it to the front of the line, start acting like a Solaran. Watch me. Move it scum!' Bess snapped and pushed past a small man in front of her, flicking his hat off as she moved.

Harper looked to Kohl for direction.

'She's right,' he said, stepping on the man's hat as he pulled Harper ahead to match his sister's progress.

The identification process was slow. Few people wore bracelets, and the constables used any excuse to reject entry to the city. Anyone who looked even a little 'Rat' was pulled out of the line and pushed beyond the influence of the city lightkeys. If the black skies didn't make them scream enough, they were branded as Rats and expressed through to the prison. Or worse, Harper suspected.

For half an hour more, they shuffled forwards with the crowd, sometimes sideways and once backwards, constantly manoeuvring to gain ground in a crowd where the safety of Melbourne was everyone's goal.

Thankfully, the snow had stopped, but the breeze was a constant annoyance. It whipped up dust and small debris that blew around their faces. A slip of muddy paper slapped onto Bess' forehead. She reached up to push it aside at precisely the wrong moment.

'Hey, you.' A patrolling constable waved his weapon in her direction.

Harper pushed her hands into her pockets and looked down at her shuffling feet while she waited for someone else to be taken. All around her, the crowd was getting edgy, trying to move away from possible trouble.

'I'm talking to you.' There was no mistaking it this time. The constable was pointing right at Bess. 'And the big guy, and the pretty one in white. This way.'

Being identified as Rats was a scenario they'd discussed. Harper braced herself for a jump and hoped it wouldn't be necessary. Not only would it alert Bell. It would make people panic, likely resulting in injuries for some.

Two enforcers joined the constable, making escape unlikely.

Harper removed her hand from Kohl's and readied to activate her implant. As she moved her hand to her face, her wrist came into her line of vision, and she instantly relaxed. Bess had accidentally exposed her high-ranking bracelet when she wiped her forehead.

'That's right, Miss, move out of the queue. Don't know what a blue-ey like you was thinking, standing amongst this rabble. Take your staff and go on through the gate.'

'About time,' said Bess.

The constables dropped their gaze as she sauntered by.

'Come on, pretty one,' whispered Kohl to Harper when they were out of the constable's hearing range.

Harper smiled to herself. Their disguise was perfect, after all.

+ + +

'You are kidding me. Not another one,' Kohl said. They had planned to find an alleyway to do a quick change into their Brother's robes. It was evening, and they had assumed the streets would be quiet. But they'd been inside the walls of Melbourne for an hour and were yet to find a lane that wasn't busy.

'Was it like this when you were last here?' he asked Bess.

'Not at all. Dad's threat of endless dark obviously worked. It seems every last Solaran is camped out here. I can't imagine how he's feeding them all.'

'I don't think he is. Have you noticed everyone is really thin?' asked Harper.

'Look over there, in front of those closed shops. That group has all their heads tucked down into their coats because their fire has gone out. We should be able to dial up into hyper-speed, change and dial back down without them noticing,' suggested Bess.

'Wait a moment.' Kohl blew into his hands as he approached the closest person in the group.

Harper saw him bend over and move a blanket. Then he moved to another and one more after that. He straightened up and ran a hand through his hair. 'Dad, what have you done?'

'What's wrong?'

'They're not sleeping,' he said. 'They're all dead.'

+ + +

'And no one spotted you on the way here? Bravo, Harper!' Stanley was so grateful to see friendly faces when they arrived that he had insisted they sit down and take tea with him despite the shortness of time.

'I'm so glad you were able to hyper Byron back to his mother. He'll be in good hands at last. Wonderful that Sam is on the mend too. He's had such a hard time in life for someone so young. The boys will be able to keep each other company. They've become such lovely friends.'

Stanley stopped talking to lick the last cake crumbs off his fingertips. When he followed up with a long sip of tea, Harper took the opportunity to steer the conversation to more pressing issues.

'How close are Spectra's quarters?'

'Very. A little too close if you ask me. A truly dreadful man.' He shook his head and wiped his mouth with a napkin.

'You know he has a new scheme? Says he's going to turn the Brotherhood into an army to overthrow the governor. I thought it was ludicrous at first, but now it's all nutrition, midnight drills and weapons training. The Brothers are too scared to deny him. They're starting to look more like enforcers than men of prayer.'

'Has he forgotten Bell? She branded him unauthorised. I doubt she'll allow him to take over,' said Kohl.

'Especially when there are legitimate heirs,' said Bess.

'You'd really want to step into the top job?' asked Kohl, raising his voice.

'You really want to have that conversation, again?' snapped Harper.

'It's what I was trained for.' Bess rose to stand toe to toe with her brother.

'No. You were trained for war against the Damarans. I was groomed for civilian leadership. Mark and I were supposed to take over from Dad. Mark's gone, I don't want it, and you're not qualified. Why *would* you want it anyway?'

'That's a question for much later.' Harper moved

between them and stretched her hands out to physically distance the pair. She was loath to start another round of sibling squabbling. Something non-verbal passed between them, and Kohl sat back down. 'Stanley, we need that room layout. Where exactly are Spectra's quarters?'

'Only two doors along to my right. Dr Kassel is stashed in the room between us. Will you go get Spectra now?'

'No, not yet. I can only hyperjump to somewhere I've been before. I must visualise where I'm going; otherwise, I risk materializing in the middle of a solid structure. That wouldn't be pleasant!'

'Oh my,' said Stanley, wringing his hands.

'Bess is the only one with knowledge of this city. If something goes wrong with her, if she's detained in any way, no one else will be able to hyper around Melbourne. That is an unnecessary risk we'd prefer not to take,' she said.

'What will you do then?'

'Kohl will sit tight with you while Bess gives me a speedy hyper tour of the city. Then we'll re-group and wait for Spectra to return home. With your help, we'll capture him today, and then we'll all hyper back to Albany.'

'Lucky me. That means I have more time with Kohl. It will be lovely to have another proper conversation. The Brothers around here are either boring, petrified or both!'

'We're not here for gossip, Stanley,' said Bess, sighing a little too loudly. 'We need you to brief Kohl on anything that will help us apprehend Spectra. We can't very well throw a bag over his head and hogtie him, can we?'

'We'll be back soon.' Harper nodded at Bess, and they dialled into hyper to dash through the city's key landmarks.

✦ ✦ ✦

When Harper arrived back in Stanley's room, she heard a shrill caterwauling from the hallway. A woman was screaming and banging on a door. 'Bryan! Bryan, I need my saffy! Do you hear me? I'll do anything, Bryan.'

Kohl leapt to his feet and grabbed his sister's arm. 'It couldn't be, could it?'

Stanley was suddenly busy cleaning up the tea dishes.

'What's going on?' asked Harper.

'I order you to let me in – *hiccup*!' The words were slurred, but the voice was unmistakable.

'Sounds like she's in pain!' Kohl sprinted to the door.

'Stop! You can't be seen yet,' said Harper.

Kohl was already across the room and had a hand on the doorknob before she had a chance to dial up into hyper speed. Instantly the room froze. Kohl's brow was creased, Stanley's cheeks blushed, and Bess' eyes looked upwards in exasperation.

Harper wedged herself between Kohl and the door, then dialled back down to his speed. 'Sorry. I had to stop you. Hypers are the only way you can go out there without jeopardizing the mission.'

'Then take me.'

'All right.'

'How long have I got?'

'Just a minute. I need to reserve my energy for jumps, especially if Bell figures out we're here.'

'Right. Let's go then.' Kohl offered his hand, knowing they needed a physical connection to hyper together.

Harper took it and shifted her position so he could open the door, then took a peek outside. She wished she hadn't. Kohl's assumption was correct. They had caught his mother in a frozen fury, beating her fists against the Doctor's door trim.

Her clothes were unbuttoned to the point where her right breast almost fell out, her greasy hair hung in a loose, tangled mess about her shoulders, and her eye makeup had run. Spit flew out from between her chapped lips.

Harper pulled Kohl into a hug. She couldn't imagine he had ever seen his mother in such a state.

'Wow, that's a new look for the old girl.' Bess stood in the doorway of Stanley's room. 'Slum-chic?'

'Harsh much?' snapped Kohl.

'She doesn't deserve anything more.'

'Any woman in that state needs help,' said Harper.

'That woman needs nothing but contempt and a hole in the ground,' said Bess.

'You were never this cruel back in our Civy days,' said Harper, holding Kohl back.

'Try walking in my shadow, and then you can tell me my words are too harsh. I've had enough of this. You can deal with Mummy. I'm going to get Spectra.'

CHAPTER 36
Melbourne

SPECTRA WAS SICKENED by his new role – planting ideas in the governor's mind, then congratulating the governor when he claimed them as his own.

'As I said to Patricia the other night, we need to make a show of rehoming the refugees in a new village by The Pit.'

Another of my ideas, Spectra thought while pretending to take notes.

The governor wore a high general's uniform, complete with golden epaulettes. His polished shoes had very pointy toes, and each time the governor crossed the edge of the rug, Spectra couldn't help but wish he'd trip and impale himself on them.

'Not one of our people will go out to inspect the village, of course. The location will be too close to the true night border. That way, we can process them quietly through the furnace if necessary. Don't write that last point down.'

Spectra nodded and tried to look subservient. Everything

had fallen into place over the last few weeks. Lady Pallas had reinstated him as Archbrother. Dr Kassel had done a fine job controlling the noble addiction. The lower classes were tired of the homeless. And the Brothers were transforming into a promising militia. All was ready for a coup.

The only sticking point was Bell. If only she hadn't branded him unauthorised, Spectra could have taken the city keys by now. Somehow, she had to go. It was a pity she didn't drink. Several bottles of saffy were still stashed in the vault behind his bookshelf.

'Damn Bell,' he complained, tapping his pencil on the page.

'What was that?' The governor stopped dictating.

'Um, I said, "Damn, that Bell is doing a great job with the environment." Have you seen how dark it is outside of the city? Just as *you* planned.'

Spectra had lowered his chair for the meeting in an attempt to look less threatening. He hunched himself over and added big eyes added to the effect.

'Yes. I'm receiving reports that her actions are helping the refugee processing. It only takes a little darkness to make a man reveal his true colours. You're getting this down, aren't you?'

'Yes, Governor. I've got my notebook.' Spectra tapped his pen on the tiny notebook, the kind that could be wedged down someone's throat with a bit of exertion. He wondered if a dose of saffy would quieten the governor's gag reflex.

Footsteps outside pierced his daydream. No doubt Stanley was doing whatever old fossils do.

'The dire effect of saffy on the nobility. I can't state strongly enough the crisis at hand. Yellow bracelet servants have been caught walking off the job for lack of supervision, and the fashion quarter is practically bankrupt for lack of custom. That damn Kassel better find a solution soon.'

A woman's scream halted the governor's finance monologue.

'What kind of place are you running here?' he said, spinning to face the door as if to check on the source.

Spectra's skin prickled. It wasn't the first time that voice had caused a scene outside the doctor's room. 'Probably just Bryan. He's a little heavy-handed with the ladies, you know!'

'Bryan! Bryan, I need saffy. Do you hear me? I'll do anything…' the woman screamed.

'What the blazes?' The governor spun back to face Spectra with an icy look he had seen before.

Spectra shrank farther into his chair and made himself busy with the pages of his notebook.

'Bryan's whore, is it?' the governor growled.

'These halls echo strangely. Hard to discern which voice is speaking. The other day I could have sworn I heard your melodious voice approach. It was just Stanley, who sounds nothing like you. Echoes, you know.'

'Don't try to handle me,' the governor said, slowly shaking his head.

'I order you to let me in – *hiccup*!' There was no mistaking the last remark that flowed under the door.

'Enough!' said the governor, and, hand on sword, he stormed out the door.

+   +   +

Harper had to get Bess under control before their power ran out. A Solaran hallway with a screeching Lady Pallas was not where she wanted to wind down out of hyper. 'Wait, Bess.

You promised you would stick to the plan.'

'Right, I'll stick to the plan to get Spectra.' Bess took a step towards Spectra's door.

Harper reached a hand out to stop her. 'That's only part of the mission, and you know it. We've been in hyper too long. Dial down before your actions alert Bell. That's an order.'

Bess hesitated.

'Do I need to take you back to Albany and have that implant removed? As a general, I can authorise that, you know.' The red light flashed in her peripheral vision. Keeping Kohl as well as herself in hyper was draining her reserves fast, and she wasn't sure she could hold out longer than Bess. 'Your choice. I'm waiting.'

Bess looked from Harper to her mother, then over to Spectra's door, before reluctantly she retreated. Thankfully neither of the siblings seemed to notice the doctor's door opening at a snail's pace.

Inside Stanley's room, Harper and Bess dialled down to real-time. Kohl half fell into the chair by Stanley's window while Bess crossed into the adjoining room, presumably to refresh herself in the bathroom.

'How did things get that bad for Mum? Could you jump her back to Albany for help?'

'I'm not sure we have the kind of help she needs. Maybe we could check in on her after we capture Spectra. First, I've got to eat something.'

Harper snatched a morsel from Stanley's tea tray, grateful she had a moment to restore herself, as she had completely zeroed out of energy. That was too close. If Bell had appeared, she wouldn't have had the means to escape. Harper reflected on the siblings' reckless actions and wondered if Aggy might have handled it better.

A door slammed in the hallway. The caterwauling quickly escalated into shrill screams, and there was a loud groan followed by the thump of a body falling heavily.

'Mum!' cried Kohl, racing for the door.

'Kohl!' Harper rushed to follow.

'No! No, no, no!'

Kohl threw open the door. Harper clapped her hand over her mouth to stop herself from gasping. Governor Pallas was dragging Lady Pallas by the hair, and she was kicking and screaming, desperately trying to release herself from his grip. The governor seemed coldly indifferent.

'No!' yelled Kohl and lunged across the hall.

Too late.

The governor lifted his wife off the floor in one swift motion and threw her out the fourth-storey window.

'Mum!' Kohl screamed. He pushed his father out of the way to lean over the sill. The fall of his shoulders told Harper all she needed to know.

'Murderer,' Kohl spat without turning.

'You're next, you little worm!' bellowed the governor.

Ignoring Kohl, he stormed across the hall in three steps, booted open Spectra's door and disappeared inside. Harper could hear furniture being upended amidst growls of frustration before the governor returned to the hallway a moment later, red-faced with anger and foaming from the corners of his mouth like a rabid dog.

Governor Pallas wiped his mouth and straightened his uniform jacket. 'I'm sorry you had to see that, son. I had no choice. She has shamed our name one too many times. I had to put an end to it, and *that*.' He pointed towards the other open door. Something about the way he spoke with such even tones made the skin on the back of Harper's neck crawl.

'We've been apart too long. Come to my rooms in an hour, son. There is much to discuss.'

Kohl ignored his father and turned his glassy eyes to Harper. 'Why didn't you make the jump to save her?'

'I'm so sorry. I couldn't. My drive was flat.'

The governor crossed the floor, stopping at the body that blocked the doorway Lady Pallas had been so eager to access. It was Dr Kassel on the ground, a ceremonial sword sticking out of his chest. Harper was stunned that she hadn't noticed it sooner.

The governor put a foot on Dr Kassel's torso, yanked the sword out and then wiped it clean on a nearby curtain before sheathing it on his belt. When he glanced at Harper, she couldn't help but wish she had a green light on her hyperdrive.

'You too?' he said.

Harper's heart skipped a beat before she realised he wasn't looking directly at her. She followed his line of sight to Bess, who stood behind her, quietly wiping her hands on a bathroom towel.

'Nice to see you in good form, Father.'

'How did you get here?' the governor asked.

'You forget. I have an implant too,' Bess said, winked, and blinked out of existence.

Governor Pallas opened his mouth to speak, then closed it again and took off down the corridor.

CHAPTER 37
Melbourne

SPECTRA DIDN'T NEED to see what happened next to know he was in trouble, but he watched anyway. He couldn't resist. After the governor stormed out to deal with his wife, he pulled the door almost closed, leaving it open just enough to see his bargaining chip be destroyed with a single thrusting blade.

'Crap!' Spectra raced across the room to his bookshelf. Without hesitation, he reached one hand inside his robe for the silver key while the other found an ancient text called the *Missal of the Holy Illumination of Gregory*. The heavy leather-bound book was the least likely tome anyone could wish to read and, therefore, the perfect disguise for a lock. In one fluid motion, he slid the book aside and plunged the key into the concealed slot. With a clunk, the bookcase sprang loose from the wall revealing a small safe room behind it.

The engineer who had installed the secret space had commented on it being overly engineered for a religious relic store. He wondered whether the engineer had felt the same way about the inside of the furnace.

Spectra checked that the emergency pack was still hanging on the hook above his saffy stash, then pulled the bookcase closed behind him. The action released a second door at the end of the space—an escape tunnel.

Satisfied all was ready for a swift departure, should he need it, Spectra pushed his face up against a crack in the back of the shelves. He could see anyone who entered his room. Hopefully, it would be feeble old Stanley.

Patricia stopped screaming, a noise Spectra would have liked to hear more of if he was honest with himself, and Governor Pallas burst into the room. At that moment, Spectra was thankful for his foresight and felt a hint of regret at the engineer's fate.

Too late, he realised he had left his beloved pet lizard, Blue, behind on his perch.

'You're next, you little worm!' barked the governor. 'Where are you?'

Even at a distance, Spectra could see the governor's rage was making Blue anxious. The little lizard was running back and forth, pulling against his leg chain. If only he could whisper reassurances.

'You kept her hooked on it. I know you did. Bastard! Show yourself.'

The governor looked under the bed and upended a chair in a frantic search. He pushed the cushions off the couch, threw open cupboard doors and checked out the window. But he found nothing, which made Spectra smirk. The governor growled out his frustration and left.

Muffled voices issued from outside in the hall. Spectra wished he could make out the conversation. It would be juicy, for sure. He almost crept out of his hiding spot to get a better vantage point when two unexpected things happened: a woman used hypers to jump into his room, and that woman was Bess. Worse, she was using those powers to dial up her speed.

One second she stood at the door, hands on hips, piercing eyes reviewing her hunting ground. The next, she was beside the window, having ransacked the room. Papers, pushed from the desk, floated down to the floor. A flask of saffy, which had been half full, was now a puddle on the rug. Two paintings had been ripped from the walls.

Worst of all, his precious Blue was in her grip. It took all of Spectra's will to stop from breaking cover to pummel his ex-fiancée. He knew better. Without hypers, he would never beat Bess. She could assault him before he drew a full breath.

'Well, if no one is here, then no one will mind if I do this,' she said as she held Blue out of the window. She tapped her toe on the floor as if completing a countdown.

No, no, no. Spectra's mind cried out.

'Better to die free little guy,' she said and released the lizard mid-air.

Spectra dug his fingernails into his thigh to stop himself from screaming.

Bess scanned the room for a few seconds, then shrugged and sauntered to the door.

Spectra realised he was holding his breath. He exhaled a little louder than he'd have liked and was shocked when Bess' head snapped around to face his hiding place.

'Got you.'

A second later, she was across the room and tearing books off the shelves, yelling explicit plans for Spectra's torture. A few more seconds, and she flinched. She must have made a micro-jump, as she now held a crowbar.

Although the bookcase and hideout were made of the most robust materials, he wasn't entirely sure she wouldn't break through eventually, given her hyper abilities. He picked up his emergency pack and took a step into the tunnel. As he slid down the building's inner wall, he hoped he could find a third alternative to being killed by either a Pallas or a dragon-riding numan.

CHAPTER 38
The Pit

BESS' FURY WAS surprising, even to herself, and she didn't want to let it go. She'd spent a lifetime being emotionally 'appropriate' for whatever the occasion required.

She had smiled through her mother's jibes at servants, even though they both knew her Lola wore a yellow bracelet. As a Civy, she had displayed enthusiastic contempt for the Solarans despite being a secret heir to the Solaran throne. She'd even managed to resist killing Spectra when he messed up her mission in Coober Pedy. No more.

As she broke into Spectra's hiding place and slid down the spiralling tunnel, she could taste her revenge coming at last. Regardless of the flashing icon warning her that her hyperdrive was critically low, she dialled up her speed to maximum and was soon on his tail. Spectra had been a stone in her shoe for too many years.

Bess caught up with him at the very end of the tunnel. He was a real-time statue, frozen in the act of bending over to open a small door, while she was a bullet careening towards him. She was going to tear hum to shreds for what he'd done to her, and then her hyper zeroed out.

Back in real time, Bess' outstretched feet connected with his backside, and together they tumbled forwards out of the door into ankle-deep water. It took her a moment to realise they had landed outside the city at the entry to The Pit.

Enforcers soon surrounded them. She didn't care. Her only interest was getting the upper hand on Spectra, but she'd forgotten his impressive combat skills. Before she could even stand, Spectra had already kicked her in the jaw.

'One point to Spectra!' he said gleefully. 'Nice work getting out of that cave-in, by the way. How'd you manage it?'

'Same way I always beat you: wit and grit.' Bess scrambled away, trying not to slip on the soggy ground as she settled into a fighting position. It was like getting ready to battle in a shallow bath of custard.

Spectra mirrored her stance.

'What is this? Tears for your pathetic life?' she asked, lifting up a dripping foot. The sky above them crackled, and lightning streaked above their heads, bringing a fresh burst of heavy rain. She prayed Spectra wouldn't be struck down from the heavens before she had the pleasure of finishing him off.

'Looks like Bell was a little overzealous with the climate reversal. Hope your friends below have water wings. If there's any of them left, that is.' He pointed to the plates the enforcers had lifted. Water was draining into The Pit like a small waterfall.

A couple of constables, who appeared to be securing some gates at the city wall, downed tools to watch them.

'Mind your business! Keep working!' Spectra yelled at

them. 'Now. How shall we do this?' He raised his fists and changed his position to a classic boxing pose, prancing around, kicking at the water and throwing warm-up punches into the air.

Bess clenched her teeth and waited.

'Mummy's dead, Daddy's delusional, one brother gone long ago, and another is pussy-whipped. Or is that rodent-whipped? Doesn't matter, I guess. Why don't you give up, Bess? The Pallas dynasty is as good as gone!' Spectra stretched his arms up in a victory pose and spun around.

As soon as his back was turned, Bess charged. A move he had apparently anticipated. Spectra bent his knees and swivelled his upper body, using his momentum to deliver a powerful uppercut that connected with her ribcage and sent her reeling.

Before Bess could recover her air, Spectra landed on top of her. He pinned her arms down in a position she'd seen him use many times.

'This has turned out to be a bit dull. I thought we would be more evenly matched. Now that you obviously have no hyper left, it's no contest at all. Pity.' Spectra punched Bess in the side of her head. Water splashed over her face and through her lips.

'That was for almost getting me killed in Darwin.' He punched her other cheek. The force pushed her face below the waterline—another mouthful of water. Bess coughed and struggled to release his grip.

'That was for making me a laughing stock when you squirmed your way out of our wedding!'

Spectra gripped her face in his two hands and leaned over so that she could smell his sour breath. 'And this is to remind you that you will never again taste Lola or anyone else's lips. Time's up, Bess!'

Bess forced her muscles to soften a little, hoping to convince him of her surrender. Spectra must have fallen for it, for he grinned and pulled her face in close.

'Surrender,' he said.

Bess urged her body not to reveal its disgust as his lips touched hers.

She opened her mouth just a little.

He growled his approval and parted his lips.

When Bess felt a slight release of the pressure of his hands on her face, she knew she had him. She bit through his lip as hard as she could.

Spectra threw his head back, howling in pain.

The shift in his position was enough for Bess to pull an arm free and thrust a punch up under his chin. He fell slightly to one side, releasing her other hand. She gouged his groin.

'That was for making me endure years of your creepy, slimy, deceitful ways!' she screamed and jumped to her feet. Giving him no time to recover, she kicked with all her might. She should have hit his ribs, but instead, she felt an unnatural stodge inside him and recoiled, confused.

Spectra laughed and got to his feet. Streaks of blood mixed with raindrops ran from his mouth to his chest, making the injury look much worse than it probably was. 'The bite-punch follow-up was a good one. I'll give you that,' he muttered as he felt along his jaw and spat blood on the sloppy ground.

'The kicks, though, they won't hurt me too much. You see, I'm not like you or the other four manifestations. Apparently, Illustria left me a bit less like you humans and a lot more like KonWong. Good-looking from the outside, but it's all a mystery on the inside. I don't seem to have regular, breakable human physiology. I was one of the first manifestations, you know. Did Illustria do this to me deliberately, or was I just a prototype? What do you think? Am I special?'

They circled each other as he bragged.

'Look at this. Does it turn you on?' He lifted his top and rippled his stomach muscles in unnatural ways.

It reminded Bess of a live animal rummaging around under a pale canvas. She couldn't help but wince. The second her eyelids closed, Spectra charged, howling, arms outstretched, and shoved her backwards.

She dug her heels in and pushed her palms into his shoulders.

Spectra's bloodshot eyes squinted.

They stood for a moment pressed together, two equal combatants. Bess thought she had a chance. She kept checking to see whether her hyperdrive had recharged. Any moment it would go green, and she could end the fight.

Then Spectra leaned in closer. 'Game over, sweetheart.'

Bess couldn't believe the sudden increase in his power as he surged forwards. 'No,' she cried, suddenly aware of her fatal miscalculation. He must have held back the whole time. 'No, no, no!'

Spectra's strength was unrelenting. Her feet slid in the ankle-deep water, and she felt herself move from the solid ground onto the slippery metal covers over The Pit. She glanced over her shoulder. The hole in The Pit's covering loomed.

'Aargh!' Her feet kept slipping, leaving her leaning forwards precariously.

Spectra increased his efforts.

Bess felt one foot slide off the plate and into thin air, sending her falling to her hands and knees.

Spectra had to bend down to keep pushing.

Her second foot fell over the edge, and then her whole lower half slid into The Pit. She flailed her hands, seeking purchase, grabbing at his clothes.

Spectra freed himself, stood up and placed one foot on her forehead. The water had turned into a shallow torrent and bubbled up against her chest and into her nose. The sky exploded in another belt of electricity.

'What? No begging?'

'Never!' Bess spat.

'I thought as much. It's been fun.'

With a mighty thrust, he pushed her over the edge.

+   +   +

Spectra felt a little let down at how easy it had been in the end. There was a small whimper as Bess fell through The Pit's massive void, then nothing. Not even the thud of her body landing somewhere. Such a let-down, really.

Spectra shrugged and turned to address the enforcers. 'Better get this roof sealed. I don't want to give her any chance of climbing out. Make sure you leave just enough gaps for the water to drain through.'

Spectra turned back to the hole and bent over to take another look. He almost wished she had managed to activate her hypers at the last moment. He waited, hoping, flexing his muscles, just in case there would be a second round. Nothing.

'Wall gates … opening … wall…' he heard a voice call from a distance. Another voice hollered something unintelligible.

Spectra wasn't paying attention. He could deal with the jumpy constables on gate duty soon enough. He wanted one last peek over the edge before the enforcers finished repairing the hole.

'Hey!' someone yelled.

Spectra didn't move. The glimmer of hope that Bess might reappear kept him focused on The Pit. After all their years of antagonising each other, their last battle ought to have ended more dramatically.

'Watch out!'

Too late, he finally understood the constables were warning him. A wall of floodwater released from the city gates caught him by surprise. It whacked into the back of his knees like an out-of-control cart and sent him tumbling. Spectra hit his head on metal plating before he too plunged into The Pit.

It was impossible to see anything to grasp as he fell through the darkened cavern. A metal rod, maybe a walkway, smashed his kneecap. A hard plate, probably from the edge of stairs, glanced his shoulder. His fingers slide along a rope ladder, which could have been his saving grace had it not been slick with water. Try as he might, he couldn't get a grip on it. Finally, there came an impact. He landed surprisingly close to Bess' lifeless body.

Spectra took a jagged breath and blinked back the water on his face. It felt as though he had shattered everything that could be broken in his body, yet he had to find the strength to get up and figure a way out before the entire structure was flooded.

To climb up or follow the path of the water? It was draining somewhere; there had to be another way out. Of course, climbing was the best option. But it was a hard ask in his state. His head ached, and thoughts were becoming jumbled.

The last thing Spectra saw was the flash of sparks from welding in the roof above as the enforcers completed his orders, or was he seeing twinkling lights? More likely, Bell had stuffed up her work on the forcefield and changed the look of the sky.

'Never trust a flying computer to get the job done,' he muttered to himself.

Then everything went black.

CHAPTER 39
Melbourne

HARPER WRACKED HER brain for a way to stop Kohl. Despite the shortness of time and the need to pursue Spectra and Bess, or at least report events to Aggy, he was determined to confront his father. Stanley seemed to understand the dilemma.

'Kohl, perhaps you could come back tomorrow? Hot heads make for rash decisions,' he said, with a double glance at the doctor's body.

'Your father said an hour. We have ample time to jump down to Aggy and return,' added Harper.

'It's been at least half an hour. That'll do. Stanley, lead the way.' Kohl pointed down the hallway.

'Harper, um?' Stanley knotted his hands in a manner that reminded her of Mr Xi.

'What's the problem, man? Let's go!'

'*General* Harper?' pleaded Stanley.

'Now you're going to pull rank, are you?'

Harper looked from Stanley to Kohl. She was honour-bound to get on with their mission, but she couldn't deny that her friend was hurting. He didn't need to beg. His eyes said everything.

'You've got five minutes,' she relented.

'What are we waiting for? Come on!' Kohl grabbed Harper and Stanley by a hand each and pulled them down the hall.

+ + +

'It's this one.' Stanley pointed to a set of grand double doors and then shuffled several steps backwards. He used a hanky to wipe his red, sweaty face. 'It's getting hot in this building. I might wait back here where there's a bit of a breeze.'

Harper had noticed a slight temperature rise too. Regardless, she trusted Stanley: if the idea of entering the room had him flushed, it was probably a bad idea.

'Hang on.' Harper pulled Kohl back. 'We are a bit early. Let's just stop for a minute and think about this. Have you worked out what you want to say? Maybe you need a plan before you go in there.'

'My plan is to find out why my father murdered my mother. Is that good enough for you?'

'Nothing he can say will bring her back.'

'But I need him to say something. No matter how bad Mum was, she was still my mother.'

A loud moan drifted out of the room. Kohl ran a hand through his hair as though uncertain. Then he turned from Harper, threw his shoulders back and threw the doors open.

'Father!'

Kohl stopped mid-stride and slowly backed out of the

room, the colour rapidly bleeding from his face. Inside the governor's bedroom, a nude woman relaxed on a chaise lounge off to the side. Another naked woman bent over on the main bed with the governor standing behind her, his trousers around his ankles.

'You're right. There's nothing to say. Let's go,' said Kohl.

Speechless, Harper followed him a short way down the hall, where he collapsed onto a couch. His voice shook as he spoke. 'The body's probably not even…'

Harper sat beside him, threw an arm around his shoulders and kissed his forehead. They hugged in silence until Stanley appeared with a glass of water.

'Here, drink this. It'll help with the shock.'

Harper was glad Kohl did as he was told.

'Look. Sex, power and a good dose of arrogance. They're an old recipe for a bitter dish, I'm afraid,' said Stanley.

'There's nothing here for me now.'

'Okay. We're going then.' Harper took the glass out of Kohl's hand and popped it on a nearby coffee table. There was no point looking for either Spectra or Bess; they could be anywhere. It was time to report to Aggy. She reached her hands out for both men. Kohl rose to his feet in readiness for the jump.

'Wait, son.' Governor Pallas strode down the hall.

'I don't want to hear anything you have to say.' Kohl made a show of taking Harper's hand.

'What? Are you upset about that?' he said, pointing back towards his room. 'That meant nothing – mere stress release, that's all. If you don't understand that, maybe that's half your problem. What are you, a man or a Civy?'

'I *understand* that you killed her.'

'Yes, well, that was a kindness. Patricia was lost to saffy

madness. Her behaviour had become a liability to us all. Do you know how many court ladies followed her into blue oblivion? I'd put them all down if it wouldn't completely wipe out the nobility.'

Kohl ignored his father and nodded to Stanley. 'Let's go.'

'You can't seriously be going back to those Rats? After all I have done to secure your birthright. I forbid it! You will not go back to live with vermin under some filthy rock.'

'What do you care where I'm going?'

'Contrary to your opinion, I do care. I care that you are the heir to everything I have worked so hard to create.'

'Of course. It's always about you, isn't it?' Kohl released Harper's hand and paced the hall.

'Have you forgotten what they did to our family? They killed your brother and brainwashed your sister. Hell, they probably organised the whole saffy thing with your mother too. I am yet to get to the bottom of that fiasco,' snapped the governor.

'What? You're blaming the Damarans for your wife overindulging on Solaran liqueur?' said Kohl.

'Damarans? Please. Even the term "rebels" is too good for them. They are Rats, plain and simple. Low-life, degenerate animals who hate our way of life and everything we stand for. They will stop at nothing to bring us down.'

'You are right about one thing. They certainly do hate what you stand for – murder being high on their list. Come on, Harper. I'm ready.' Kohl walked back to Harper and gripped her hand.

'Big mistake, son. Bell, under my command, is about to wipe them all out. You go back with her, and you sign your own death warrant.'

'What have you done, Father?'

'Something we should have done long ago. Flushing out the vermin.'

Kohl's hand tightened.

'The Solaran nation will be great again, and you *will* take your place next to the throne! Unhand that trash, and let's go.' The governor put out his hand to his son.

'Goodbye,' said Kohl.

Harper activated the hyperjump back to Albany. The last thing she heard was the echo of Governor Pallas' roar.

CHAPTER 40
Albany

HARPER'S JUMP PLACED her in a liquid nightmare where nothing made sense. She thought she had directed the jump to the sandy shores of Albany's lake outside the café. Instead, they materialised deep inside the lake.

Stanley and Kohl's anxious holds on her hands crushed her fingers. Pushing down her panic, she turned to Kohl and tried to look relaxed, but his cheeks were puffed, and his eyes pleaded for air.

Not pausing to remonstrate herself, she jumped again, only to return to the same spot. Something in her implant must have glitched. She looked up at the incomprehensible volume of water above them and started to kick her feet, hoping to drag the men with her. It was pointless. They were far too deep.

Then Stanley pulled madly on her arm. She followed his pointing finger to a distant structure. Harper had her answer. She jumped one last time and was relieved to materialise on the dry carpet of Midpoint.

'Harper!' a welcome voice yelled from behind her. Aggy was with Sam and Abudua in the doorway, directing a stream of people in the hall beyond.

'Alpha?' Harper coughed.

Aggy had a child on her hip. She handed it to one of the large adult spiders that dashed alongside the crowd. The spider fastened the child into a carrier on its back. Once satisfied it was secured, it gave Aggy a little salute, then scuttled across the ceiling and out the window.

'What happened?' Kohl asked as he wrung the water from his clothes.

Aggy gave Harper a quick hug and then pushed her out to arm's length. 'I'm not the only one who has been for an involuntary swim, hey.' Aggy's overalls were also soaked. 'Sorry, I didn't know where you were in Melbourne, or I would have come to warn you.'

'What's going on?' Harper asked.

'At first, it was just a gush out of Darwin that we thought we could dam up. We knew we were in trouble when all the other tunnels flooded and began draining into Albany too. We started evacuating right away, but the water is rising too fast. I'm not sure everyone will survive this.'

'How?' Stanley finally managed to speak from the chair he'd found.

'I can only assume it's Bell.'

'Um, Alpha…' Kohl pointed to the door, where a sheet of paper floated over the threshold on a trickle of water.

'Time to go again,' said Aggy.

'Excuse me. Why can't we just hyper to the surface?' asked Stanley.

'Too many people for the few of us with hypers. We'd be

out of energy in no time. Don't forget. We might have Bell on our tails as well. Plus, where do we jump? Best guess: all the Damaran caverns are flooding. Noosa is our only city above ground and is a long way away. Right now, our only hope is up. Leonora assures me there are exit tunnels in the roof if we can get there fast enough. As long as Bell…'

She looked out the door. 'Sam, you getting anything, mate?'

'I did think I was gettin' somethin' from Bell for a minute there. Nothin' now, though. All clear.'

'Great. Let's go, people,' said Aggy. The water had already risen above Aggy's shoes.

She helped Stanley to his feet. He was grey and a little shaky. 'When was the last time you had something to eat?'

'Not too long. Mostly just tired. I'll be fine. Don't you worry about me.'

'Hang on.' Aggy rushed over to her cupboard, the water splashing with each footstep. She returned with some apples that she shoved in the Brother's pockets.

'We can't have our favourite spiritual advisor perish from starvation. Those might come in handy.' She winked at Stanley. 'Look after him, Kohl.'

Kohl waded out to the hall with the old Brother.

'Hang on, Harper. I need to show you something.' Aggy gripped Harper's elbow, and Harper immediately felt the sting of a jump. They were suddenly in an entirely alien world of lattices and webbing.

'This is Leonora's transfer station.' One side of the space was open, presumably designed for the spiders to access the city below. On the other side were two enormous tunnels, not unlike Illustria's tunnels. Harper recognised Leonora stationed at one, herding in obviously relieved people.

'Look, Alpha! The first of our friends have arrived, thanks to General Xi!' Leonora chirped.

General Xi handed over the two flood survivors he was helping, offered a quick salute, then ran to the open wall and leapt out into the dark. Harper ran after him. She looked into the void but could see nothing.

'Wow, that was a dramatic exit. He will be alright, won't he?' she asked Aggy.

'Oh yes. The Digies are almost as agile as the spiders.'

'Yes, friend Xi's tribe has been most helpful,' said Leonora.

'Right. To the problems at hand. Harper, I need you to march up that tunnel and take a good look around so that you can return there via hyperjump with Abudua and me. We all need to get our bearings. That way, we can at least jump a few people out if this gets any worse. Once you've done that, get Stanley topside. He doesn't look well. Take him straight up. Actually, you might want to pick up Byron too, if he's not with Abudua.'

Harper was about to leave when Aggy stopped her.

'Here. You'll need some fuel as well!' She threw an apple to Harper and disappeared.

CHAPTER 41
Albany

AGGY WAS GLAD she'd had the forethought to make her return jump to the floor above her apartment. It was already wet. The floor below would be completely under water. She stuffed her pockets with items that could be used in an emergency – a water bottle, a candy bar, a scarf that could splint – then waded through the rising water to the door. It was stuck fast.

Assuming it was jammed because of water pressure, she jumped to the next floor up. On dry footing, at last, she ran to that door. It wouldn't open either. Then she remembered Leonora's city orientation when they first arrived. Albany's fire doors auto-locked in emergencies.

Muffled voices floated under the door. Aggy put her mouth to the crack. 'Hello? The door is stuck. Can you give it a shove from your side?'

Someone responded. Although she couldn't make out the words, the emotion was evident. Time was running out, and help wasn't coming.

Aggy was about to try a jump to another room when a long, low groan rose from below, and the building shook. She braced against the wall. There was a brief sensation of falling. When it stopped, she looked across the room to the open windows, half expecting to see KongWong's flames. Instead, monstrously large gas bubbles erupted from the water, sending a small wash into the room.

Then the building shuddered again. Had something exploded down in the human half of the city? Panic sounded from the hallway. A heavy object thudded against the door, and a woman cried out. Somewhere, an automated beacon began bleating evacuation warnings.

And then the lights turned off.

+   +   +

'What was that?' Byron asked. A loud noise had rumbled up from beneath their feet.

Sam released Sedna's elbow and reached out toward Byron. Locating him, he laid a reassuring hand on his friend's back. 'Sound's comin' from a long way away. We'll be all right, mate.'

Aggy's doctors had worked a miracle with the injured young man. Byron's voice no longer carried such tremendous pain; however, he was still in no shape to climb stairs. When Sam had caught up with the group, Sedna had told him Byron was being carried over his mother's shoulder. It was a big ask, as Byron was taller than General Abudua, with the shoulders of a warrior.

'Can we help?' Sam had asked.

'No. He's *my* light to lift through the world. I'm fine,'

Abudua had said firmly, although her words didn't match her footsteps. She was clearly struggling to find her footing under the extra weight. Her knee joints creaked with every rising step. When the crowd ahead stopped moving, she made a slight noise tinged with relief.

'General, you have done well to create a light as bright as your son's, but he is not the only light you must shoulder,' Sedna said. 'If Alpha were here, she would urge you to investigate the blockage ahead. We all need your strength, General. Allow me the honour of carrying Byron up one flight so you can restore our journey.'

There was no verbal response, but she must have nodded her consent as Sam felt Sedna move forwards, and there came a shuffling of feet he imagined was due to Byron's weight being transferred.

'Thank you, Mother. And you, kind Sedna,' Byron said.

Sam thought he might have felt Byron's warm hand on his cheek and would have reached up to clasp it with his own had the building not started to shake.

A rush of hot air from below threw him off balance. Disoriented, he fell heavily into the wall. A scraping sound, which had to mean trouble, shot up the stairwell, followed by a sudden gurgling rise in the water level. A woman behind him screamed. Others ahead joined in her panic. Even the footsteps of the spiders overhead seemed more jittery than usual.

When an emergency alarm clanged over the top, he was sure he was in sensory overload until a knife-edged voice cut through it all.

'Got you!' Bell crowed.

He slapped his hands over his ears and sank down to his haunches. Water lapped at his chin. 'Not again. Aggy!' he screamed.

'Sammy,' called Byron. His voice sounded like it was being pushed out to a great distance by Bell, who seemed to stand right inside his mind, drowning out so much of the local noise – even the voices that screamed of the sudden darkness.

✦ ✦ ✦

Alone in the pitch-black room, with the flood water rapidly rising, Aggy was short of options. Jumping back to Harper and Leonora was tempting. Bitter memories of the first flood she experienced rendered her frozen in indecision. She wasn't sure she was Alpha, just a scared kid in flooded Lower Broome. But the cries for help from the hall were impossible to ignore.

'You can do this, Alpha,' she said to herself.

She edged across the room with hands outstretched, guessing she would hit a wall soon, which might lead her to a cupboard drawer containing a lightkey. Of course, she found only the wall and recriminated herself for wasting time on a long shot.

There was only one choice. Taking three slow, deep breaths to steady her nerves, she activated a hyperjump to two floors down. Aggy materialised into the sea that had once been her bedroom. The frigid water on her face made her want to scream. She fought the urge and felt her way to her desk, where there was an emergency lightkey.

Lightkey activated, she had two metres of visibility that helped her navigate to the door. A small jump and she was in the stairwell beyond. She swam up towards her people. Aggy soon breached the surface and sucked in sweet, dry air.

Thankfully, her friends were alive, for now.

'Alpha!' Abudua leapt off the stair where she had been sitting with Sedna and splashed into the water. 'Thank the Light you have returned.'

Sedna stretched out his hand, which Aggy took gratefully and pulled herself onto dry stairs. She happily received hugs from all those within reach.

'Right. Talk to me. Why aren't you moving?' she said, shivering.

'Alpha, I tried to check the blockage,' Abudua answered. 'I couldn't make it all the way up because of crowding. All the doors are locked; there is no way out of the stairwell. With you here, we have three implants. We could jump our people out two at a time, but many will be left behind.'

Aggy looked down at the lapping water. 'Three? Oh, Sam. Yes, of course. How is he? Where is he?'

'One flight up, with Byron. He heard *her* voice again. It was traumatic, although Byron seemed to steady his nerves. They're good for each other.'

'What did Bell say? Is she close?'

'Apparently, she said she "had us". That's all.'

'So Bell knows we're here. Or, more correctly, she has engineered this.'

'Should we start jumping, Alpha?'

'No. It's not enough. No one gets left behind.' Aggy bit her lip.

'Sedna, these are fire doors. Why have they activated in a flood?'

'I'm not familiar with the safety features of this building. I assume that any emergency might activate them. Traditionally, they are one-way doors, allowing occupants to exit onto the stairwell and preventing smoke from flowing back into the rooms. In theory, you should be able to operate them from the other side.'

'I tried doors in dry rooms and flooded rooms. Neither worked.'

'The flooded room makes sense. The water pressure would likely prevent it from opening. The dry room – that's a mystery.'

'Is it possible you got unlucky? A malfunctioning or locked door? Should we try another?' asked Abudua.

'Worth a shot. Let's try the next one up,' said Aggy.

She made her way up to the top of the flight, put her hand on the door and hesitated. 'Abudua. I've never been into this room. I hope there's nothing on the other side. Hate to materialise in the middle of a coffee table.'

Aggy risked a breach of Abudua's rigid protocol and hugged her old friend. At first, the general stiffened, then softened when she realised Aggy wasn't letting go. 'Thank you for your service. I know you will do everything you can to find another way out if this doesn't work,' Aggy whispered into her ear.

'I am honoured to call you my Alpha,' said Abudua.

Aggy offered a prayer to the Light and activated her implant. A few seconds later, she opened the door and handed over another lightkey she had found inside. 'Ta-da, it worked!'

A brief cheer rippled through the crowd, which surged into the room.

'Easy, easy. What are you? Solarans?' yelled Abudua.

Assured the crowds were being managed, Aggy signalled Sedna to join her at the window. 'Bring Sam, Kohl, Stanley and Byron,' she ordered. While she waited, she held her lightkey out the window and bent down until her light grazed the mirrored surface of the flood. The water was too close.

'One room will not solve our problems,' said Sedna, who arrived holding Byron up with one arm around his waist. Sam trailed behind, gripping Byron's hand.

Kohl stood behind them, hands on hips, eyes rimmed red. Aggy made a mental note to ask Harper what had happened in Melbourne.

'Kohl, you put your leadership genes to good use and relieve Abudua doing crowd control on the door. Tell her to jump Byron and Stanley up to Leonora's crew. Harper should be there. She can get them topside. Then get her to move up through the building, opening as many doors as possible – wherever the rooms have windows, of course. We must not lead our people into any more traps.'

Kohl nodded and left, taking Byron and Stanley with him.

'Sam, are you all right?' she asked.

'Yes. Bell's quiet now. I'm ready to assist in any way I can.'

'That's the shot! You stay with me no matter what happens. I need to know if Bell is near.'

'Yes, Aggy.'

'Now, Sedna, you're right. A few rooms won't help. We need to get out of here. Any good at climbing?'

'I'm sure I could manage it. I have heightened sensors. The dark won't bother me as much as the others.' He turned to look around the crowded room of wet, frightened humans.

'You have a point.' She looked down over the windowsill again. The light caught the water faster than last time; its march up the cavern was unstoppable.

She reversed her position and looked up into the web of ladders and lattices that extended from the room. Her stomach turned at the thought of the difficult climb to safety; she had never liked heights.

And then, hope meandered down towards her and swung in the window. 'I thought you might need some assistance, Alpha,' Leonora said, smiling as always. 'I brought a few of my friends to guide you. There are more entering the rooms above.'

Several giant spiders, each holding held a lightkey aloft, followed her in the window.

'Now, who's first?' she hissed.

CHAPTER 42
Melbourne

BELL PROWLED THROUGH the back of the crowd listening to Governor Pallas, who was making a speech from his favourite balcony.

'Solarans were born to rule this world!'

She had expected a larger gathering. The expansive town square should have held two thousand people, yet she only counted six hundred and sixty-eight. Although they may have been spread out, as though ordered to look like a larger group, there was no mistaking it. The crowd was thin, with noble ladies particularly scarce.

'We are stronger, smarter and more determined than those wretched Rats.'

Bell wondered about his basis for that last claim. Melbournians were certainly not dressed better. The Damarans' clothes looked clean and functional even in their lowest hours, unlike the Solarans', whose coats were tattered and grubby.

It was strange they were still in long coats, especially given the wet street which muddied their frayed hems. She would have expected them to make a show of their famous fashion for their beloved leader.

'They are crying in their caves right now because they know they have no chance against our courageous constables. Not one of them has the heart our men do. We take care of our own, unlike filthy Rats, who eat their young and drink their own piss. Am I right? Let me hear from you, friends!'

The cheering began on cue. The metal cladding boarding up many of the shop windows helped to send the noise ricocheting around the space. Still, the response seemed thin to Bell's sensors and punctuated with too many coughs.

'They have no integrity. Hell, Rats don't even know the meaning of the word. They are nothing but uneducated, inbred, unholy, dirty brown freaks,' the governor bellowed and pumped his fist. Under the governor's balcony, constables waved their weapons to encourage the crowd's response.

An older man in a group of three gagged so hard on his forced cheer that he bent double and vomited all over his unpolished shoes. His chest heaved between drags of air before he collapsed to the ground. A puddle of his own filth spread out on the cobblestones as he convulsed. His two companions slunk away into the crowd.

Bell moved on.

✦　✦　✦

'That went rather well!' The governor poured himself a short glass of amber liquid and sat heavily in a nearby chair. He tipped his glass to Bell and drank it down in a few eager gulps.

Bell supposed she would have been expected to cheer or join in if she were a human male. Of course, if she were a human female, her options would be limited to those of the scantily clad maids who'd hastily relocated when she arrived at the governor's private quarters. Instead, she took a turn about the room.

The luxurious space was twice the size of Charles' apartment and cluttered with decorative pieces. On the walls were reminders of how things were supposed to be – ornately framed images of men looking rather sombre and women dripping in jewels. It was a stark contrast to Charles' minimalist aesthetic. Although she had strong doubts, Charles had had much choice about how he had lived in the core under Illustria's supervision.

She strolled over to the mantlepiece, ran her fingers over the golden clock, and then picked up pieces from a collection of miniature animal statues – dogs, cats, goats and horses. All had a dark patina from years of polishing, unlike the sole book she had spied at the back of the room. *The Brotherhood Guide to Holy Marriage* was covered in at least fifty microns of dust.

The governor cleared his throat louder than required. 'As fascinating as my wife's trinkets might be to you, can we make this quick? It might be difficult for you to comprehend, given that you've been programmed with a woman's brain, but a city as large as this requires more than debutant balls and decorations.'

Bell wondered if there was any point in jumping back to Honeysuckle Creek and picking up some of Illustria's books for the governor. Clearly, the *Guide to Holy Marriage* did not contain a chapter on respectful communications or, more likely, it hadn't been read recently.

The governor slammed down another drink and glared at her. Almost unconsciously, he reached his free hand down to his crotch and readjusted. Almost. Bell considered practising her eye-rolls, even though she assumed a Solaran lady was supposed to avert her eyes.

'Are you anatomically correct?' The governor's smirk made her decision easy.

If he noticed her hyper in and out of his quarters, he certainly didn't show it until he flicked his eyes down to the copy of the Virginia Woolf novel that now rested on the coffee table to his side. He reached down and rested his glass on the book before focusing back on Bell. Even with her remedial understanding of human gestures, Bell knew this wasn't a happy face.

'I'd think you'd be too busy sweeping up Rats for parlour games. What *are* you doing about securing fuel for my furnace?'

'Before I brief you on the Damaran relocation strategy, I need to know: when Charles left, did he give you an estimated return date?'

'What?'

'The Master, Charles, your forefather. When is he coming back?'

The governor's mouth opened and closed in fast succession. He scratched his head. 'Um…'

'Sorry. Am I speaking a lowly female dialect? I'll try to do my best to improve my speech patterns when I return to the core.'

The governor rose to his feet and stamped across the room, stopping close enough for Bell to feel his breath on her nose. He raised the back of his hand to her cheek, then hesitated as if weighing up consequences. Before the hand could move, Bell grabbed it and used it to push the governor down onto the closest chair until he was pinned into the upholstery.

This time it was Bell who did the close-talking. She kept her face only inches from his and spoke with deliberate slowness.

'Listen, you trumped-up excuse for a leader. You might have your devotees surrendering to your will out of fear or desperation – I'm not sure which. We can establish that later. All you need to know now is, I will not be spoken to with such disrespect, regardless of my choice of gender.

'If you think you can best the Damarans without me, think again. They are remarkably resilient and, despite your hyperbole, your people are in no shape to go into battle. From what I witnessed in the square, your Solarans appear to be suffering addictions, malnutrition, a wide spectrum of untreated mental health issues in general, and a general lack of enthusiasm for you in particular.'

The governor used his free hand to reach down beside the chair and pulled out a silver dagger in what must have seemed like a masterstroke to him. He raised it above his head, ready to plunge it into her skull.

Bell released the governor, plucked the weapon from his hands and snapped it in two as though it were no more than a toy. For the first time, she seriously considered whether she was fighting on the right side. 'As I was saying, you are in no shape to win this war. You can either get behind me, or I will remove you and lead these people myself.

'Now, I asked you a question. When is *He* coming back?' Bell said with detached calm. She retreated a few steps to give the governor space to consider his response.

Governor Pallas stood and pushed past her to the mantlepiece. He grasped it with two hands as though trying to stave off his rage. Bell hoped she hadn't gone too far for his narrow education.

'I understand your question, obviously. However, the Master never spoke to me about returning. Now, I will take my leave if there is nothing else.' He straightened up with exaggerated formality.

'One more issue. You should know that my campaign to eradicate your enemies is nearing its endpoint.'

'Really?' He visibly relaxed at the news.

'Yes. As we speak, they are being forced from their communities by a flash flood triggered by my work. They should soon breach the surface if they make it out at all. From the hyperjumps detected, I have their approximate evacuation point outside the city's south wall. You will take all your available constables, enforcers, and suitable broad-range lightkeys to that position. You can apprehend the Damarans there. Was that clear enough?'

The governor nodded his response.

She blinked out of the room.

Knowing it would take time for the Damarans to reach the surface and the Solarans to amass their troops, Bell took KonWong on a flight over the worldlet to check her modifications to the forcefield.

From a distance, it looked like a solid night sky. Even at arm's length, with the dragon in a stable glide, little could be seen of her scientific marvel. But when she reached the sky and dipped her fingers into the field, she received a tingling burst of readings that were nothing short of miraculous.

The nanos had spread well, each one reprogramming its neighbours to absorb light and emit heat. It was performing at 97.6%. She smiled at her handiwork. Not bad, considering it was a new field of science for her.

Still, it was patchy in places. Once they had defeated the Damarans, she would allocate time to studying field harmonics and find a way to secure more consistent coverage. There was no point protecting a world from the ravages of space only to let the atmosphere slowly syphon off through the gaps.

She flew back down to land just outside Melbourne and thanked KonWong for his service. A quick instruction whispered into his ear, and his nanos returned him to stone.

It was a bit theatrical if she was honest. She could have sent the deactivation codes from anywhere, but he was the closest thing she had to a friend. It seemed cold to turn him off remotely. She slapped him on his hard rump and jumped down to the core.

Bell had only intended to be back home long enough to pick up more of Illustria's favourite books, which she planned to scatter through the governor's mansion for the discovery of the governor and his ladies at an appropriate time. Instead, she was delayed by a blinking light on what was left of Charles' computer console.

There was an incoming communication waiting. It was puzzling. She had assumed the console was non-functional, given the damage to most of his equipment. Actually, the term 'equipment' was optimistic. The lettered keys and indicator lights were positively ancient. She couldn't imagine how Charles had used it to defeat Illustria unless it had been designed to lull her into a false sense of security. Some sort of retro cover for his deeper machinations. Charles was a man of many levels. She couldn't wait to meet him and make sense of his choices.

It took a moment to figure out the incoming transmission codes. Strangely, they seemed to be based on a language closely resembling her own internal coding. She would have taken the time to analyze it further had the news not been so exciting.

There was a ship in orbit, requesting permission to land.

Bell used her code to approximate a response that granted permission to land with advice that it would take some time to re-modulate the field.

'Estimated safe entry time is six hours and thirty-eight minutes,' she offered.

'Or we could resolve it from our end,' responded the craft.

Bell calved off two subroutines to work on the re-modulation calculations while she resolved the Melbourne situation. It would be embarrassing to prove herself less competent than Charles the first time she met him.

'He's coming home!' she said excitedly and jumped back to the surface.

CHAPTER 43
Albany

AGGY GLADLY SURRENDERED her lightkey to the group of senior Buchanites led by Mrs Brown. It was a small sacrifice. Climbing up the spiders' ladders in daylight was hard enough for the young and dry. Being old, wet and blinded by darkness made it nearly impossible.

Besides, she had Sam, who was surprisingly confident. She wondered if people from New Brunswick had echolocation skills woven into their genetic coding or whether it was a learned response to their blindness.

'Look out!' came a voice from above, followed by the heavy rustling of a body slipping through webs.

'Fallin' this way,' said Sam, putting a protective arm across Aggy's shoulders. She strengthened her grip and tucked in her head as the ladder shook violently.

'Got him. All good!' It sounded like Mr Xi.

'Thank the Light,' whispered a Buchanite lady to Aggy's right.

'Thank the Digies, more like it,' said Sam.

The Digies were positioned at strategic points to help people transition between ladders. Still, nearly five thousand people had to make the treacherous climb, and accidents were bound to happen. Aggy didn't know Gerard and his partner Esme. They had been the first to miss their steps and plunge into the icy deep below. They weren't the only ones.

'Can ya hear that?' Sam stopped and made a sharp clicking noise with his mouth. 'The echo's getting stronger. I estimate about three more storeys to go.'

The spider city was difficult to quantify in human terms. There were no rigid lateral floors like those found in the human half of Albany. Spider residences resembled intricate artworks that stretched off in every dimension. Before the lights had gone out, Sam and Sedna had worked on a way of estimating distance based on the sound of a standard human storey.

'Three storeys, that's good news. Any sign of Bell?'

'No'

'Okay. Do you have a feel for how many are below us?'

'Too many to count.'

Aggy wished she could see; it would calm her nerves to witness people progressing up the structure.

'Hang on. I thought I heard somethin',' Sam said.

'Is it her?'

'No, this one was different. I can't hear it anymore. Maybe I imagined it. Sorry.'

'That's all right. We're all a little on edge.'

They climbed on.

✦ ✦ ✦

When Harper arrived on the surface and activated a broad

lightkey, she was not surprised to see a barren landscape. Like most darklands outside Solaran cities, the landscape was devoid of vegetation – a fact no one had cared about until Illustria shed light on their world's unnatural shame.

She couldn't imagine how tough it had been for families like Sam's, born into the void and kept in ignorance of how bleak their environment really was. His family had nothing but endless toil on rocky ground and a religion to convince them they were lucky to have even that. At least the Pedies had had lush greenery weaving through their underground towers. Even the industrial Buchanites had managed to paint their houses in bright colours.

Harper wiped her eyes and readied herself for a jump back down to Leonora. It had taken forty minutes to trek up the tunnel, so she was glad to take the short route back. Her implant had regained most of its charge, and she was ready to help Aggy make the move topside.

When Harper materialised back at the tunnel's beginning, there was panic in the air. Kohl directed traffic while a steady stream of spiders swung in with young children. They unloaded and swung out again without stopping for orders. Babies were passed into a room already full to bursting with people – mainly young men – who were being urged into escape tunnels at a furious pace. Everywhere she looked, there were haunted stares, clenched fists and teary cheeks.

This was so much worse than the ordered evacuation she had expected. 'What's going on?' she hollered across the room to Abudua, who didn't seem to hear. Abudua was speaking to Leonora with Stanley and Byron. Her hands pumped in the air as she spoke.

Harper threaded a path across the floor.

'...it's not negotiable! You will extract Alpha now!'

Abudua bellowed.

'You don't seem to understand. Alpha has given me orders NOT to pick her up. We must transport the vulnerable first,' said Leonora.

'Leonora?'

'Hello, Harper. You must excuse me; I am needed elsewhere.' Leonora made her exit across the ceiling.

'Abudua, I didn't think this many would have arrived yet. It looks like you're making good progress,' Harper observed.

'We are crowded because fear of the rising water made the young fleet of foot. It comes faster than we imagined. I don't know how many are lost to the tide. Worse, Alpha is missing.'

'I was supposed to jump back to Midpoint and get her. She's no longer there?'

'Midpoint and many floors above it are submerged. I would jump to Alpha if I knew her location. She's with Sam. Beyond that, who knows? If that pitiful excuse for an eight-legged general had any honour at all, she would drop everything and rescue our Alpha.' She clenched and unclenched her fists.

'Right. Well, the best way to help her is to clear a path so she might come to us. Let's jump as many groups to the surface as possible, starting with these handsome gentlemen to your side.'

Stanley blushed as he took Harper's arm. 'Thank you, Harper.'

Abudua held her son with one hand and put the other on Harper's shoulder, ready for transport.

+   +   +

When Harper returned to Leonora's evac point, she touched her cheek and sent out a call for Sam. The implant had always connected them on a level she could not understand. Perhaps it would reunite them again.

'Harper.' a voice cried out from the other side of the room.

'Make way! Please move.' Harper bustled through the crowd making it to the platform's edge just as Sam and Aggy climbed into the room.

'You okay?' he asked Aggy as she took her last steps on the netting and reached the safety of solid ground.

'Yeah.' She looked too puffed to say much more.

The volume around them rose. People were relieved to see their Alpha alive, but Aggy kept her eyes clenched shut and gripped the ground, panting.

'Give her room and keep moving up! Come on, come on, come on, people. You need to keep making room for others,' Harper's voice cut through the crowd.

'She's comin',' Sam said in a breathy voice.

'Who's coming?' asked Harper.

'Bell. And Aggy's not in great shape. Tough climb.'

'Aggy? Are you all right?' Harper whispered in her ear.

Aggy allowed Harper to hug her. 'No need to fuss. How's the evac going? Progress update, please.'

'Alpha,' said Harper in her public voice. 'We were making good progress. Kohl is managing the exit, and he estimates approximately four thousand have crossed into the tunnels.'

'Only four thousand? I'm going back to get the others.' Aggy pushed herself to stand and shuffled towards the edge.

'Wait. Once you consider the spiders who carried the children, the Digies who are still stationed below to assist the stragglers, and the few hundred Abudua and I jumped to the surface, most of the population is accounted for.'

'You were using hypers?' she snapped.

'Yes. I've only got enough left for one more jump, though. I must get you up top now.'

'Hypers are a dangerous strategy. All the more reason for me to help finish the evacuation,' Aggy looked like she was preparing to lower herself down onto the net again.

'No, the evac *went* as well as it could,' said Harper, lowering her voice.

A gloved fist slapped onto the platform – another survivor who needed a hand.

Harper hesitated. Every moment she spent helping survivors was a moment Alpha was at risk. 'We need to go.'

The glove turned into an arm wrapped in heavy protective gear. At least the survivor was protected from the chilly water. It was a strange choice, though. Potentially too bulky for climbing.

Sam moaned, sending a damp shiver across Harper's shoulders. She took her eyes off the ascending survivor, who seemed confident enough, and turned back to Aggy, whose face was an unsettling stone colour.

'Sam needs to go too.'

'Wait. Why did you speak as though the evacuation is over? What aren't you telling me?'

'You need to jump to the surface with me right now. Sedna and Kohl are waiting for us,' she said and reached out her hand.

'Why?' asked Aggy.

Sam slowly rose to his feet, left hand to his ear, right reaching towards Harper. 'Bell's topside. She says Charles is comin' too.'

CHAPTER 44
Darklands outside Melbourne

KOHL WAS DEVASTATED to see his father at the helm of new trouble when he arrived on the surface with Sedna. Abudua had materialised them at the back of the field, which was lit to daylight by six strong lightkeys. His father stood up the front on a podium, probably about to make another speech. Behind the governor, a runway of lights lit a path to the lighted city wall and the impressive furnace tower.

It was all very dramatic, the meaning clear. Now he understood why Abudua had said his 'unique skills' were urgently required. He'd thought he was sending the Damarans up the tunnels to safety. Instead, the cold, damp refugees were slumped on gravel under the watchful glare of a small army of enforcers, constables and even a few armed citizens.

The sizzle of a light-wand being activated got Kohl's attention. He spun around to see a young constable pointing it his way.

'Where in the blazes did ya come from?' growled the constable.

Kohl opened his mouth to speak and thought better of it. The wide-eyed constable had a worrying tremble in his weapon hand.

'Don't know how ya did that and can't say as I care. If ya don't sit down now with ya stinkin' Rat mates, this wand'll cut ya ta pieces.'

Kohl stood his ground.

'Down!' the man ordered.

'Easy,' said Sedna, slowly raising his hands.

'On ya knees, scum!' A second constable marched over, trailing a beefy-looking enforcer.

Abudua made a show of putting her hand on her knife.

'Look, it's the general!' someone in the crowd of Damarans said.

'Put it down, General Abudua,' Kohl said calmly. 'The constable knows better than to attack the governor's son.'

'The Gov' ain't got no son no more. Got that intel wrong, didn't ya, ignorant Rats. Now sit down!' the constable moved within striking distance.

'We mean you no harm. How about you holster your weapon, and we can talk about this.' Kohl raised his hands, palms open as Sedna had done.

'It's Kohl Pallas with the general,' came another quiet voice from the crowd. It started a ripple of nervous chatter amongst the Daramans in the immediate vicinity.

'Shut up, ya scum!' The constable booted the nearest body. 'Now sit the fuck down. Last warnin'.'

Harper's arrival with Sam and Aggy in tow couldn't have been timed more badly. Their sudden appearance behind Kohl startled the edgy constable into action. He swung his weapon at Kohl's head.

Sedna leapt in front of Kohl with lightning speed. He took the blow and collapsed, one arm severed above the elbow. A stream of fluid leaked to the ground from his stump.

'Stop!' a woman's voice sounded with the strength of a thunderclap.

'Don't take orders from no woman,' the constable shouted over his shoulder. He kept his eyes fixed on Kohl and raised his weapon again.

'Bell, aagh.' Sam collapsed to the ground clutching both ears.

'Stand down.' Bell demanded in a voice that left no space for argument. All eyes swivelled to the woman standing alongside the governor and the dragon that hovered behind her.

Bell pointed at the sky. KonWong craned his neck back and blew a great plume of fire above the refugees. Even at a distance, Kohl felt the scorching kiss of the dragon's breath.

'Son?' The governor held a device in front of his mouth that significantly amplified his voice.

Kohl crossed his arms and slowly shook his head.

The governor bent to speak with Bell. Kohl couldn't hear his words, but Bell put her hand on the governor's shoulder. A moment later, they had jumped across the field of refugees.

'It doesn't have to be this way. We're still family,' said the governor.

Kohl retreated to stand between Aggy and Harper. 'I've got a new family now.' Harper's hand found its way into his.

Bell squatted down next to Sedna. She picked up his elbow and examined it. 'You. You're the one who reactivated me when you visited the core. I didn't realise it was you until now. I've waited so long, and now you are damaged.'

'What? How did I…' Sedna started to say.

Without taking her eyes off him, Bell waved a hand behind her and pulled her fist down as though to yank balloons out of the sky. The great dragon leapt into the air and circled them, flapping its heavy wings while it awaited her command.

'Him,' Bell pointed to the constable.

'No!' screamed Aggy, too late.

KonWong, oblivious to everyone except his target, moved with incredible speed. In seconds, he was above them. The young constable dropped his weapon and fled. The dragon followed him across the lightkeys' barrier into the dark. There was a mad scramble of steps on gravel, a mighty roar, an inhuman cry and the sickening stench of burned flesh.

Harper's hand tightened in Kohl's, but he ignored her and turned to Abudua, worried she would charge the dragon. He was so busy studying the general that he scarcely noticed another body join their ranks.

'Nice of you to welcome me with a barbie!' said a confident voice from the person who had joined them wearing a spacesuit.

Kohl had only seen such attire once before. He didn't need the helmet removed for his gut to yell warnings. It seemed he wasn't the only one to reach the same conclusion. Aggy drew a sudden, sharp breath while Abudua raised her knife.

'Hey, that's—' said Sedna.

Bell put a finger to his lips. 'I know.'

KonWong circled once, then settled close by, steam drifting from his nostrils. Bell looked him in the eyes and pointed two fingers to the ground. The great dragon stretched his forearms out and bowed his head low.

'KonWong. Meet Charles Drexus, the great Master of all. Welcome home,' she said to the astronaut.

CHAPTER 45

Darklands outside Melbourne

BELL GENTLY RELEASED Sedna's arm to the ground and sized up her silent master. Charles was shorter than her records mentioned. She smirked to herself when she realised he had probably altered his public profile. Despite all their scientific advances, humans were still more inclined to drink authority poured from a large vessel. It was vaguely endearing.

'I must report that Illustria did great damage after you left. Governor Pallas and I have been putting it right. As you can see, we have already reinstated the darkness you specified and captured the last of the Damarans. I trust you approve,' she said with a slight bow.

Bell thought she heard a chuckle from under the helmet. Surely not. It must have been a choking noise. 'May I help you remove your helmet, Master? The air is quite within human tolerances, I assure you.'

The astronaut waved her away and reached his gloved

hands towards the suit's collar clips in a move that seemed to take an eternity. If there weren't the chance it would be taken as disrespect, she would have dialled up to hyperspeed and done the job for him.

'Traitor!' yelled the hefty Damaran general. With surprising speed, she lunged at Charles, weapon outstretched.

Bell dialled up her hyper and intercepted the thrust. The general was of significant age. She postulated that menopause might contribute to her irrational act of attacking the man who had created them all. Still, she had to admire her boldness.

Perhaps there was something to be learned from the general. Bell put her fingertips on the general's forehead, hoping she was a manifestation that could be read by touch. No such luck. The general was a feisty but biologically ordinary female.

Bell swivelled the woman around, leaned her farther forwards, removed her knife, and dialled out of hyper. When standard time resumed, the general fell flat on her face. The surrounding constables jeered. It left Bell feeling a little unsettled.

The general brushed herself off and resumed a fighter's pose. When she held her head defiantly, Bell noticed all the Damarans strengthen their stances too. Their fists were clenched, shoulders back, and feet firmly planted. Bell had to admire their support. She wasn't sure the Solarans would show such genuine respect to their governor.

Charles stopped his helmet fiddling and did a slow clap. Then he walked up to Bell and indicated that he did indeed need assistance with the clips at the back of his helmet. Regretting her focus on the Damarans, she rushed to flick open the two clips.

'Yes, Master.' There was a slight hiss as air escaped over the seal, and at last, the back of his head was revealed. Kohl let out what was surely a nervous laugh.

'You!' the governor snarled and reached for his weapon.

Bell wasn't certain of the appropriate response to either Kohl's or the governor's actions. She calved off a subroutine to investigate social customs in the event of humiliating faux pas. Then the astronaut spun around, and the source of their inappropriate responses became clear.

'Honey, I'm home!' It was the being known as Spectra. He hugged his helmet to his chest and winked at Bell.

'You? The message from orbit? It couldn't have been you.' Bell checked her ocular processers, convinced she was not reading his light emissions correctly. Not wanting to admit that her programming might be corrupted, she reached out and grabbed the astronaut's collar to pull him closer. Perhaps this was a Damaran trick; they had proven themselves alarmingly ingenious.

'No, don't touch him! Take me first!' Alpha yelled and lunged toward Bell as if anticipating her next move.

Bell elbowed her away, blocked out the ensuing commotion from nearby Damarans, and concentrated on what must be Charles Drexus in disguise. It had to be. She examined his face contours, approximating the underlying bone structure and matching it to file images of Charles and Spectra. Unable to make sense of the truth, she placed her hands on his cheeks to feel his face for herself.

'Aargh!' Spectra screamed, and both he and Bell reeled backwards.

One touch provided all the humiliating confirmation Bell needed. Spectra was one of Illustria's manifestations, and now, through her rash physical contact, she had uploaded a lifetime of his thoughts and experiences, all tainted by his filthy self-loathing. His emotional deficits unlocked the riddle of how he behaved in such deplorable ways. And they were encouraging her own self-doubt.

Alpha waved her hands while Sedna circled her, herding people away. The governor's mouth moved as though he was saying something. She couldn't hear him, and she didn't care. Who was she to think she could ever make the difference Illustria had? She was an inferior copy, a corrupted sentinel programme. No one would ever respect her, and Charles would never return for her.

Bell looked up briefly. She saw Alpha put one arm in front of the old general to restrain her, but the general broke free and launched a brutal attack on the approaching constables. Two were struck down before they had a chance to activate their lightwands.

An enforcer lumbered into the mix and brought a fist down onto the general's shoulder. It should have made a cracking noise. The general should have cried out when she fell to her knees. Bell heard nothing.

The governor's son, swift on his feet for one who didn't carry the implant, grabbed a fallen light-wand and plunged it through the enforcer. The enforcer's internal organs should have offended her olfactories as they spilled across the ground. Bell smelled only her own humiliating decline.

Soon the fighting began in earnest. All around her, humans clashed, and comically large spiders leapt. A strangely round woman lashed out at an enforcer with a knitting needle plucked from her bun, and a massive tide of Damarans tackled the governor to the ground. In no time at all, he was covered in a mound of writhing flesh.

But none of it was real. Bell saw the action as though

reviewing the results of a subroutine search. She observed what was happening without an emotional connection. Why would she? She was just a doorbell.

The governor burst through his attackers, screaming like an animal and hacking his sword at anyone who dared approach. Bell watched as what was left of the Damarans fell into formation behind their beloved Alpha. She, too, held a weapon, intent on victory. Bell wasn't sure why Alpha bothered. What was there to win in this wretched, false world?

Too late, the governor signalled his constables. His attention diverted, the old general plunged her dagger into him, just below his left shoulder blade. He arched his back and threw his mouth open to scream, but the noise that squeezed out of his lungs was nothing more than a frothy gurgle. Or at least, that was what Bell assumed. She couldn't be sure of anything anymore. She had shut down her auditory processors. What was the point in hearing the human's pain?

The general stabbed the governor again in the kidneys as he dropped to his knees. An unnecessary move, as her quarry's fate was already sealed, and as he crumpled to the ground, he reached out to Bell for help. She shrank to the ground.

The Damaran crowd surged forwards to finish off the governor.

Bell crawled away.

There was no point in being involved anymore. The Master wasn't coming. His beloved progeny didn't deserve her support. She understood that now. They had all fallen into decadent decay.

For a nanosecond, she considered supporting the

Damarans, yet, as much as she admired them, she could not break her programming and switch sides. There was no side for her in the battle.

It was no wonder she had been abandoned in the core. Her delusions of purpose had caused the loss of so many precious Damaran lives even though they were a people who had proven themselves more than capable, contrary to Charles' records.

And the blind male, Sam. He had heard her the loudest. It had caused him great pain. She knew that, and she hadn't stopped. Illustria would not have chosen such a ruthless option because Illustria was so much more competent than she. That was obvious now.

The Solarans hadn't fared much better. Her misguided efforts to restore order had resulted in so many Solarans living on the streets. She couldn't bring herself to recall her part in the governor's fiery actions. As she slumped to the ground, she knew she was, in truth, a monster.

Sedna crossed her line of vision. He seemed to be trying to communicate with her. His hand flashed in front of her eyes, and then he pointed to the Damaran leader, the governor's son and the younger general.

Sedna picked up her hand and laid it on various heads. It made no difference. She had shut down the part of her programming that allowed her to upload experiences. It was all pointless.

KonWong blasted one last scathing breath across the sky. She assumed from the rumbling ground that he had landed close by. Bell didn't care. She disabled her ability to record. Nothing was worth observing now.

Closing her eyes, she ignored the little red light that blinked in her peripheral vision and prepared for a complete shutdown. The subroutine Bell had sent out to investigate any potential numan presence had returned with its answer. It was irrelevant. Sedna was the only other numan on the worldlet. He stood right next to her, and that hadn't helped her at all.

No. Spectra's insights were a blessing. They had revealed her true worth, which was less than nothing.

CHAPTER 46
Darklands outside Melbourne

AGGY POSITIONED HERSELF at Kohl's side and placed a gentle hand on his back. The young man stood, still as stone, by his father's lifeless form. All around him, others finished the fight. Not even Abudua's stern glares moved him, forcing her to manoeuvre around him to apprehend the last of the Solaran dissenters. It was as though Kohl waited for the dead man to rise again.

Aggy had trouble believing it herself. The great enemy of the Damaran people who had tortured her, maimed babies, and killed so many of her dear friends was finally gone in a simple knife fight. Still, he had been Kohl's dad.

'I'm sorry.'

Kohl didn't respond. Aggy wiped the sweat off her brow with her sleeve. She was exhausted, but she was alive.

'Abudua, take an advance party into Melbourne. Stanley can show you around. Let them know it's over. We expect a share of the available buildings for accommodation.

Libraries, offices, shops – I don't care. As long as it has a roof, we can convert it into temporary housing. Prioritise the injured and families.'

The general nodded and marched off into the crowd.

Aggy wiped her face again. As if the air wasn't steamy enough, a crack of thunder rippled across the sky, releasing a nuisance mist of warm rain. The gravel around the governor was red with blood; she wondered how long it would take to run clear.

'Aggy?' Harper had returned to her side. She too was filthy from combat. 'We need to do something about all this water. Look.'

She pointed to the tunnel that had delivered so many lives from the flooded cavern below. 'It's still rising, and now it's raining? Not much point surviving that climb out of Albany to drown topside.'

She had a point. Defeating the Solarans was no victory if the climate killed them. Aggy struggled to comprehend how so much water could have been stored around the core and in the sky. 'Bell's the only one that can fix this. Sedna, are you having any luck?'

Sedna waved his hand in front of Bell's eyes again and invited her to make contact with each of the other manifestations.

'No response,' he said.

'We've got to get through to her. She needs to upload more than just Spectra. The Light only knows what damage that creep's warped mind has done to her,' said Aggy.

'Try physical contact,' suggested Harper.

Aggy walked over and dropped her head. 'Here.'

Sedna lifted Bell's unresisting arm and placed it on Aggy's forehead. No response. Sedna shrugged.

'Maybe another manifestation will work? How about me, Kohl or Sam? Hey, where is Sam?' Harper looked around.

'Over here.' Sam navigated slowly through the recovering crowd. Though unaccompanied, he made no mistakes, no stumbles.

'Well, look at you, Mr Lightfoot,' goaded Harper.

'When ya grow up on dark gravel, ya soon learn to find ya way around without eyes,' he said, pointing to his ears.

'That's great, Sam. Now tell me, can you hear anything from Bell?' Aggy said, finally understanding Harper's idea.

'No.'

'What if you were to touch Bell?' asked Harper.

'Worth a try. Take me to her.'

Harper helped Sam over to Bell. He made contact, and they all waited. 'Nothin'. Sorry.'

Sedna whispered in Bell's ear. She flinched.

'What was that about?' asked Harper.

'I was reciting prime numbers. Mathematics is generally considered quite soothing for numans. It's a bit like meditation for humans, I guess. Alas, no response.'

'Meanwhile, the water.' Harper lifted a foot to demonstrate.

'Harper, go find Abudua in the city and see if you can locate any Solaran engineers. They might have an idea about diverting the—'

A sudden gush of wind pushed at her back. It stole the rest of her words and threatened to topple her to the ground.

'What now?' asked Harper.

'Look!' It was Mr Xi.

Although Aggy was happy to hear he'd survived the battle, she wasn't thrilled to see him pointing to a column of stormy red clouds descending from the heavens.

'It must be KonWong.'

'Any idea how to stop him?' asked Aggy.

Mr Xi shook his head slowly. 'All my life, he was an immovable stone mascot. Until Bell came along, that is.'

'Um, bigger problem,' said Harper. 'I thought she reset the forcefield to its original settings so light can't flow? That's why it's dark beyond a lightkey's influence, correct?'

'Right,' said Aggy, confused.

'So how do we see something that far away? It should be well outside the influence of these lightkeys.'

'Sedna, try anything you can to get Bell operational. We have one too many problems right now,' said Aggy.

'Forget talking. Maybe she needs a good slap.' Spectra seemed to come out of nowhere. He strode up to Bell and hit her in the face before anyone could stop him.

'Spectra!' yelled Harper.

'Why, you've got a damned cheek, man. Where's my sister?' Kohl asked, finally leaving his father's side. 'What did you do with her?'

'Not much. Just a bit of a romantic tussle between intendeds before I threw her in the deep end of The Pit. I thought she'd float, to be honest; she's escaped worse jams. That hole in her skull might have affected her buoyancy,' sneered Spectra.

Kohl threw a right cross that connected with Spectra's head in a move that seemed to take the astronaut by surprise. He followed it up with several kicks to the stomach, although it was difficult to tell if he was doing much damage, given Spectra's unusual attire.

Aggy knew she should intervene, but truthfully, she wasn't sure she wanted Kohl to stop.

'That'll do,' she said reluctantly.

Kohl barely hesitated. He got in several more blows, punctuated by harsh rebukes, before Harper stepped in and tried to pull him away. 'Stop. We might still need him at the core.'

'Let him up, Kohl. Harper, find something to tie Spectra up with.'

Kohl sat back on his haunches, breathing heavily and wiping sweat from his face. Spectra raised himself on one elbow, looking disappointingly intact for all Kohl's hard work.

'Careful of the gravel. That's one of our *Starling* spacesuit prototypes you've got on, and I don't want it torn,' said Sedna.

'Yeah, don't move,' Kohl growled.

'I won't. I know when I'm beaten. Still, that was fun. Let me know when you want to go another round.'

Aggy kept her eyes on Spectra. She didn't want to lose track of him until he was firmly in custody. More worryingly, the red clouds that had touched down not far from them let out an unnaturally loud rumble.

'Can't figure out how that is possible. We shouldn't be able to see it,' said Harper, using her shoelaces to fashion restraints for Spectra.

'Could KonWong be getting larger?' asked Sedna.

'Sam, Kohl, Mr Xi. Spread the word. Get everyone inside Melbourne's walls whether they like it or not. Take Spectra with you. No arguments,' Aggy ordered.

Mr Xi bowed briefly, then began shepherding the crowd. She was proud to see her people respond immediately, methodically leading everyone away from the cloud, unlike the Solarans, who seemed to move scattergun.

'Sedna, you have got to break through to Bell!' She

surprised herself at how loud she sounded. She hadn't noticed the storm noise dropping, but the rain had picked up. It bit into her shoulders like fine needles.

'This is getting stranger by the minute.' Harper was holding her palms in the air. Aggy watched as her young general checked the water sample she had collected – always looking for answers to the problem. 'We need answers, Sedna.'

'I'll try standing Bell up and walking her around. Maybe that might reset something.' He struggled to pull Bell up by the arms.

'Problem?' asked Aggy.

'No. I was hoping she would stand by herself. Looks like she needs a little more persuading. Come on, Bell. I know you can choose to hear me. These people are suffering. You can help. By the grace of the binary gods, search your programming. You must know all life is sacred,' he said to the unblinking numan.

Sedna whispered in Bell's ear and tapped her shoulder. At one point, he knelt to brush gravel off her knees. He was so gentle with her, as considerate as he had been with the little spiders on the beach.

Then he stopped and tilted his head to look around her. 'It can't be! There, in the smoke.'

Aggy followed his finger to see what had distracted him. It was impossible, yet somehow there was a gradual reversal of the hideous dark that had enveloped them all. Above the red billowing smoke, the sky had shifted to daytime blue.

And then, something *really* strange happened.

CHAPTER 47
Darklands outside Melbourne

HARPER SQUINTED, UNABLE to make out what had caught Sedna's attention. The red clouds were a fair way off. All her human eyes could see was dust.

'It can't be,' said Sedna, although his voice trembled as though he very much wanted it to be. He gently released Bell to the ground and stared into the distance. She thought she heard him reciting, '2, 3, 5, 7, 11, 13, 17.'

'What's got you so stressed out, Sedna? What am I looking at?' Harper hoped he wasn't going into a shutdown like Bell.

As her eyes grew accustomed to the new light of the brightening sky, the scene resolved, and at last, she started to make out what his ocular senses had detected with ease. 'Are those people coming out of that cloud?'

'Yes.'

Two figures walked towards them. Harper did a quick calculation and realised their strolling gait belied the speed at which they must be approaching.

'Harper, may I ask a favour, please? 19, 23, 31.'

She could not remember Sedna ever requesting anything before. Nor muttering number sequences.

'Of course,' she replied.

'Can you hyperjump me closer? I am eager to see their craft.'

'What craft?'

'The one they landed in.'

'Is it Charles?' asked Aggy.

'No. At least, he's not one of the beings presently approaching us. It's possible he's on the ship, though.'

'I'll get Bell into Melbourne if you can do the honours and get Sedna a bit closer to the ship.' Aggy walked behind Bell and attempted to lift her to her feet.

Harper reached out to take Sedna's arm. Before she could make contact, the two beings in the distance blinked out of existence and re-materialised just metres in front of them. They held hands, so Harper suspected only one of them had hypers. Perhaps the female, who bore a striking resemblance to Bell. She had the same big green eyes, only her skin was as fair as Kohl's.

For a moment, no one spoke. Then the male flashed a wide, toothy grin. 'Of all the planetoids!'

He released the female and hugged Sedna, who was also grinning wildly. He lifted him off the ground and spun him around like a toy. 'And you've programmed a smile at last. Nice one, buddy. How many centuries has that taken, AI32.1.3z?'

'You can put me down. By the way, I'm known as Sedna here.'

Harper looked at Aggy, who seemed equally puzzled and

relieved it wasn't Charles. Sedna must have caught their looks as he cleared his throat. Harper thought she saw a hint of blush on his cheeks.

'Alpha, I would like to introduce an old colleague of mine – AI48.'

Aggy lowered Bell back to the ground and dusted down her overalls before she shook hands. 'A pleasure to meet you, AI48. This is General Harper.'

'Great to meet you too,' he replied, shaking hands all around. 'Why don't you call me Quinn? It's much more civilised than an alphanumeric identifier. And this is Bria.' He stood back to give his companion centre stage.

Bria had a warm smile that made Harper relax. Her hair was pulled back into a high ponytail that swung as she walked, and her iridescent skinsuit shifted through a muted rainbow.

'Pleased to meet you. Apologies if our arrival stirred up your environment. Quinn's got quite a lead foot. I'm sure we could have come in a little slower.' She rolled her eyes at her companion. 'We will repair any damage we have caused.'

'Thank you,' said Aggy.

'We did have a reason for the fast arrival, though. Do you know an entity called Bell? I was communicating with her from orbit. It's urgent that we see her. Do you know her?' Quinn asked, suddenly serious.

'Yes, this is she. Sadly, she's not well at the moment,' Aggy said, pointing to Bell, who lay prone on the ground.

'To be honest, we're not sure what we should do. We've tried many things to rouse her, with no success,' Harper added.

'I wonder, would you let me have a try?' asked Bria.

Aggy looked to Sedna, and Sedna turned to Quinn, who

nodded encouragingly. 'All right,' she said.

Bria bent down, placed a gentle hand on Bell's head, and closed her big eyes.

'Do you know what happened to her?' asked Quinn.

'She absorbed the life experience of one of Illustria's manifestations, then shut down. Admittedly, that particular manifestation has a pretty warped personality,' said Harper.

Bria's eyes snapped open, focusing on Harper with laser-like intensity. 'Manifestations? She can absorb knowledge through physical touch? Can all of you do that? It's a very rare skill.'

'No. We aren't numans like Bell and Sedna. We are *human* manifestations of Illustria,' explained Harper.

'Okay. One moment please.' Bria closed her eyes again. This time, she put three fingers on each side of Bell's temples. A moment later, Bell yawned and blinked her eyes. Her head tilted up as though she tried to get a better view of the faces that looked down at her.

'Thank you,' she said in a quiet voice.

'How'd you do that?' asked Harper.

'Easy. She is Illustria,' Bria said as she helped Bell to her feet.

'No, sorry. We mustn't have been clear. Bell is a manifestation *of* Illustria, made many years before she passed away,' said Aggy.

Harper nodded in agreement.

'I don't mean that Bell is named Illustria. Rather she is *an* Illustria. I am an Illustria too. Illustria are an ancient race of artificial lifeforms who pledged themselves to foster intelligent life, whatever form that might take,' Bria chirped.

'We were taught that our Illustria was created by a human and locked into the core of our world to do his bidding for centuries,' said Aggy.

'Was that human named Charles Drexus, by any chance?' asked Quinn, his hitherto calm face suddenly anxious.

'Yes.'

Quinn shared an alarmed glance with Bria.

A bulge appeared on Bria's thigh. In the space of a few heartbeats, it lengthened and expanded until it formed the shape of a handheld weapon. Bria detached it from her skinsuit. In one smooth motion, she shoved Quinn behind her and pointed the weapon as she scanned their immediate vicinity.

Harper took a protective step towards Sam, who took a crunchy step backwards, drawing Bria's focus. 'Don't move, Sam,' Harper said in even tones as she put two hands up to show she wasn't a threat.

'Is Charles here now?' asked Bria.

'No.'

Bria relaxed her shoulders and re-attached the weapon to her thigh. It dissolved back into the fabric as though it had never been detached. Harper definitely wanted one of those.

'Too bad. He's a very dangerous being. It would have been my pleasure to apprehend him finally,' Bria said.

'You're looking for him?' asked Harper.

'Yes, for a long time now. He's caused immeasurable damage.'

'Don't need to tell us that. Charles screwed over this whole world,' said Harper.

Sedna nodded. 'And he left us stranded when he stole our ship – the *Blazing Aurora VI*. We would have built a new craft to pursue him if we had the technology and materials required.'

'Our collapsing climate, plus a war, certainly didn't help,' added Harper.

'You were also at the mercy of an ignorant numan and her dragon. I'm so very sorry, everyone,' Bell added sadly. She closed her eyes and faced the sky. KonWong flew down and landed with surprising grace.

Quinn raised his eyebrows. 'Well, looks like we have a lot to discuss, Alpha.'

'Yes. First, though, I really should check on my people. We fought a battle today, and I evacuated everyone to the city when you arrived looking like another disaster. I'm sure they are weary, sore and in need of their Alpha.'

'Wow. Bad timing on our part – my apologies. May I go with you? We can talk while we walk. I'm sensing a fascinating story in you,' said Bria.

'I'd like that. This way.'

Quinn moved closer to Sedna and threw an arm over his shoulder. 'I wonder if I can steal you away from the recovery mission for a tour of *my* ship?'

'Depends. What is she called?' asked Sedna, looking as though he might already know the answer.

'The *Blazing Aurora I*,' Quinn said, pulling back and squinting like he was waiting to be hit.

'You mean my *Blazing Aurora*, you scoundrel!' said Sedna, hands on his hips in mock indignation.

'Yours, mine, ours, what's the difference? She's a grand vessel, and she's reunited us again. Happy days.'

As Bria and Aggy strolled towards Melbourne, Harper realised she hadn't received a clear answer to her question. 'I'd still like to know what you want with Charles Drexus?' she called.

Bria turned back with a sad expression that made her

look hauntingly like their own beloved Illustria. 'You are not the only ones he has wronged. If we don't bring him to justice, it will be very bad for all of humanity. Very bad indeed.'

'What do you mean?' asked Aggy.

'Most of my race believe in our mission to foster young sentient species like yours. There is, however, one small division of very ancient Illustria called the Taree. They believe that species need to be tested before they can be embraced.

'You see, the Taree are very old. They remember a time, many millennia ago, when an arrogant species rose too quickly and caused immeasurable destruction. It was almost the end of us,' said Bria.

'What does that have to do with humans? Surely all species are different,' argued Harper.

'I would agree, but the Taree?' Bria shrugged. 'To prevent a repeat of those dark times, the Taree hide beacons in the planetary systems of developing species. The beacons detect and notify the Taree when species advance to the stage where they can expand off-world.'

'Seems reasonable,' said Harper.

'Yes, if that was all they did. It is also a test. The beacons themselves are self-aware and offer tempting clues to new technology. The Taree like to observe how that knowledge is exploited. If it is not used for peaceful purposes, then the whole planetary system is sterilised before they can threaten the wider Illustria community.'

'...and Charles found the beacon?' asked Harper.

'Correct. We believe he found a Taree beacon in your Sol system and enslaved the intelligence within for his corrupt purposes,' explained Bria.

'Our Illustria,' said Aggy.

'That seems the most likely answer. There is no way he could have created a numan of such sophistication and power at your stage of development,' added Quinn.

'And the Taree know?' asked Harper.

'They suspect. When the beacon stopped transmitting, they were going to sterilise immediately. But intelligent life is extremely rare, and it has been a long time since we admitted a new race into our ranks. There was considerable division amongst our people. In the end, it was resolved to send a representative to investigate. I am she.

'I've been here for centuries, investigating, learning about your species. I'm sad to say it doesn't look promising. You see, the effects of Charles' evil acts go way beyond this world. His corrupt technology has left humanity in ruins, and if we can't find him, I'm afraid the Taree will wipe out what little remains.'

'And do you think we deserve sterilisation? Is that your recommendation?' asked Harper.

'No. Undoubtedly, Charles' technology theft allowed you to expand much too quickly. There are critical lessons you skipped that left your species vulnerable. I have witnessed war, famine, depravity, and gross inequity, but I have also seen compassion and, most importantly, the love your numans have for you.' She smiled at Quinn.

Harper wondered how long Bria and Quinn had travelled together. 'Are you Illustria too, Quinn?'

'No, just a good old-fashioned numan like Sedna. Born and bred in a Drexus factory.'

'If you've been investigating for centuries, why didn't you come to get Charles years ago?' Harper asked.

'We didn't know where he was. Across the stars, human

civilization is in a mess. It took this long to establish that Charles was at the heart of it all and track him down,' said Bria.

'What can we do to help?' asked Aggy.

'You could come with us as we continue our search. Your knowledge of Charles Drexus might help us find him more quickly. Bringing him to justice is humanity's only hope now.'

CHAPTER 48

Blazing Aurora I

AGGY WAS DETERMINED not to shed any tears as she stood by the *Blazing Aurora* three weeks later with Bria and Quinn, waiting to see who would join their off-world mission. Her stomach sank when she saw the size of the crowd that strolled out through the Melbourne gates. She hoped they were mostly well-wishers.

In the weeks since the end of the battle, Bell had stabilised the environment and returned the excess water to freeze in the core. The Solarans, having had enough of their governor's controlling ways, had agreed to cast off their bracelets and join the Damarans to create a unified society, at last.

The caverns were drained, the cities de-iced, and the wounded healed. Only the problem of Spectra remained. Somehow he had disappeared during the evacuation to Melbourne when Bria and Quinn arrived. They suspected he had gone down into the tunnels. Bell had programmed some enforcers to locate him. She was optimistic that they would find him eventually.

Once things had started looking up, Aggy had to face the inevitable discussion of who would go on the search for Charles. She'd been relieved that generals Abudua, Brown, Xi and Leonora had all agreed to stay behind to rebuild their communities.

Bell had also committed to staying to monitor the environment. She had given Bria all the records about Charles and Illustria, hoping it might reveal critical clues for their hunt.

Sedna and the *Starling* crew would leave eventually, although they had agreed to stay a little longer to complete the new vessel. With Bell's help, they were confident they could have it finished in a few months rather than decades.

'After all, she whipped up a dragon in minutes. How hard could a spaceship be?' Captain Julian had argued.

But Bria had invited several of Aggy's other senior staff to accompany her. Some had already spoken to Aggy about their options. She had told each one the same thing – that she loved them and prayed the Light would guide their choices.

Fighting for lives on their own world was one thing. It was a survival reflex, and they had risen beautifully to the challenge. Leaving to chase Charles through endless cold space was something very different. It would take tremendous courage, especially when peace had finally come. They were giving up the prosperity and rest they had well earned. She could not let them know how much she would ache to lose any one of them, lest they lose their nerve and decide not to go.

So now Aggy waited with sweaty palms to see who was leaving. The approaching crowd put a smile in her heart. So many wonderful friends. She would not cry. On such a momentous day, they deserved a stoic Alpha, not soppy Aggy.

Harper and Kohl were the first to move out of the crowd. Harper grinned nervously and hugged her with an intensity that felt more like a *farewell* than a *see you soon*.

'Forgive me, Aggy; I know you need me, but Kohl needs me too. He wants a fresh start off-world, and I couldn't let him go by himself.' Harper's eyes were red.

Aggy couldn't stop her own lip from quivering. She was grateful when Harper changed tack.

'You know what this big lug is like. It'll only take one pretty alien, and the whole mission will be all over,' she said with a forced giggle.

Kohl rolled his eyes and made a show of gently shoving Harper out of the way. 'Alpha, thank you for sending Sam and Harper to rescue me. I didn't know how lost I was. You did, though, didn't you? You have taught me lessons I could never have understood amongst Solarans. I am proud to call myself a Damaran.' He bowed to Aggy with great formality.

When he stood back up, Aggy knew her eyes would be glistening again. 'And—' she said.

'And, I will bring Harper back to you.'

'Yes, you will.' She first punched him lightly in the shoulder, then enveloped him in a motherly hug. 'She's not as tough as she tries to be,' she whispered.

Harper and Kohl joined Bria and Quinn at the top of the gangplank.

Aggy waited a few moments. Then, assuming they were the only two to go, she turned to leave.

'Wait,' Sam called. 'Wait!'

Aggy hoped he was there to say a late farewell to Harper.

Her heart sank when she realised he was navigating to the front of the crowd with a bag on his shoulder.

Quinn popped his head back out of the main door.

'I'd like to go too. If you'll have a disabled crew member,' Sam said.

'Disabled? From what I hear, you have proven yourself more able than most of the people in this field. We would be honoured to have you.'

'Are you sure?' asked Aggy. 'Um, I have grown to rely on you these last few weeks, and space is quite dangerous, especially for people who… I mean to say…' For once, she was at a loss. He had already suffered a lifetime of adversity. How could she say that Sam deserved to be in a comfy chair, not a spaceship?

'If I don't go, who is goin' watch out for Lord Knucklehead,' Sam said, and Aggy could have sworn he pointed directly at Kohl, who had joined Quinn at the entrance. His spatial awareness was astonishing.

Still, Aggy hesitated.

'Sam won't be alone,' another voice emerged from the crowd. It was Byron. He had received special attention from Bell's healing touch and was almost back to his well-muscled form.

'I walk with him.' Byron threw an arm around Sam's waist.

'And your mother? Do you consent to this, Abudua?' Aggy looked for her general in the crowd. The last thing she needed was an angry General Abudua.

Byron's other mother, Grace Abudua, stepped forwards. 'She does. We do. Byron is the pride of our family, as Sam would be in his family if his parents were alive. With a heavy heart, we wish them both a safe journey and pray to the Light for a swift return.'

Aggy made the symbol of the Light in acknowledgement of her words. Now she understood why General Abudua was not present. Aggy blinked her eyes, then returned her focus to Byron and Sam.

'Well, then, I can see there is no changing your minds. Bria and Quinn will be lucky to have such smart, honourable souls to accompany them.' She embraced the two men as one.

Somewhere behind her, a solitary voice rose up with the sweet Lament of the Light. It was a short sombre piece often sung at family partings. She didn't need to look around to know there would be many glistening eyes in the crowd.

She stepped away to the requisite distance and watched the two young men make their way onto the ship. The gangplank receded, the door shut, and the spaceship took off without additional ceremony. One moment the craft was on the ground; the next, it shot straight up into the sky.

Aggy watched it disappear.

One by one, the crowd left until she thought she was alone, gazing up into the heavens. She had an unsettling feeling she might not see all of them again.

'My wife's making dumplings,' a quiet voice said by her side, interrupting her thoughts. She hadn't realised Mr Xi had stood watch with her.

'Singing dragon soup?' Aggy asked.

'Of course, and maybe some sugar nut toffees!'

'Delicious. It's about time I learned to use a Pit bowl. Lead on, my friend.'

The End

Other published works by Shel Calopa

Emoto's Promise
Letters from the Light

Published short stories
Dugong Dreaming in the Aquarius Anthology
Ruby's Ride in Release of Silence Anthology

Various other short and flash fiction can be found at
www.shelcalopa.com

Coming in 2023
Diversity's End

To keep up on publishing news and all things writing, join
Shel's tribe online
Instagram: shelcalopa
Twitter: @shelcalopa
Facebook: ShelCalopa
Goodreads:
goodreads.com/author/show/19723643.Shel_Calopa

EMOTO'S PROMISE
CHAPTER ONE

MACIE LOWERED HERSELF off the scorching gutter that trimmed the Reclamation Centre and rubbed her scalded hands. She had taken care to land quietly; pressing her back up against the sun-drenched building, commanding herself not to breathe, but knowing it would only postpone the inevitable. They would find her eventually. They always did.

For six years, the motes in DarwinTwo City had tailed Macie everywhere. The small charcoal boxes appeared seconds after her feet hit the city streets, like silent electronic rats scavenging through the dust for human crumbs. They swept voraciously behind her as if to erase all traces of her incompatible DNA, lest it contaminate their precious high-tech citadel.

She wouldn't be surprised if Mayor Wolfram himself was using them to monitor her movements, ensuring she spent every waking hour managing the ocean wall that encircled the city. Earning her life by keeping his kind safe from the treacherous waters beyond.

Not that there was much else to do, anyway. The whole

beige city was made up of numans who rarely registered her presence.

Numans—huh! That was one of Wolfram's ideas too.

He had them all so tightly meshed with their AI symbiotes and gilded virtual worlds, that they had renamed themselves 'new humans' or numans as Wolfram liked to call them—unlike Macie, who was merely human.

It hadn't always been like that. When she was a child, there were a few others like her, normals who couldn't adapt to new tech. Ordinary people who smiled. Kids who splashed in puddles, invented nicknames, had sleepovers and played tag through the rooftop hydroponics lanes.

But as the years passed and automation increased, the city's need for normals diminished along with food allocations. One by one by one, they had disappeared—until eventually it was just Wall Manager Macie, the numans and the motes.

A click from a steel door a metre away drew her attention. Macie let out a low slow whistle she hoped would be mistaken for an ocean breeze squeezing between the tall, tightly spaced buildings. It was a copy of the whistle that had wafted under her bedroom door earlier that morning.

Signal apparently received, the door opened and out shuffled her grandmother, Vala.

"Forgot... your din-ner. Second time... since... Upgrade 24," she said in stilted syllables, as though she had forgotten how her jaw worked.

Vala's hair was pulled back into a severe bun and she wore the same dreary overalls as the rest of the numans. Her clothes hung from her thin frame like wet linen draped over a wire hanger, all pale from being left too long in the sun.

Vala had been pretty once, when she was human. Macie

had seen her in old holopics; relaxing at a dinner table, crinkled hair flowing over her shoulders, eyes twinkling at someone off camera. Now Vala's face had drained to numan grey and her once calming blue eyes had settled into milky stone.

Macie wanted so desperately to hug Vala for the great risk she was taking, but she knew better. Physical contact would leave DNA traces on her grandmother—unexpected for that time of day—that would mark Vala as deviating from her workplan. Non-compliance was the greatest of crimes in DarwinTwo. It would likely result in a painful reboot to end Vala's recognition of her granddaughter.

Instead, Macie took the offered dinner pail and nodded her respect.

"Thanks, Gran," she whispered.

Half a flinch from her left eye was all the response Vala gave, before shuffling back inside and closing the door.

Remembering the shortness of time—no motes yet, but soon—Macie put the handle of the pail between her teeth, crouched to the ground and leapt back up to clasp the guttering. Then, moving hand over fist, she shimmied along the edge until she was around the corner of the building where a wide overhang made for a perfect escape platform. Once she hoisted herself up, it was an easy mote-free jog across the low roofs of the industrial sector.

When Macie arrived at a thoroughfare which led to the wall, she dropped back onto the pavement. Right on cue, two motes sped out of an adjoining alleyway and began their cleaning task.

"Gee, can't a girl take a dinner stroll," she said, waving her pail at them in an exaggerated fashion. One of them shoved at her ankle, delivering a little spark of electricity from its outer casing that made her jump backwards, almost standing on the other mote.

"All right, all right, I'm going." Physical contact was unusual. This one must have new programming—she would have to watch for that in the future.

Only when Macie arrived back at the wall and climbed the rusty ladder to the top, did they finally leave. With a salute to the scurrying motes, she turned her back on DarwinTwo's towers with all their monotonous precision and sat down to gaze at the choppy sea.

She knew she ought to be afraid, like the numans. The first few floors of the city sat well below water level. If there was a breach of the old stone wall, it would be just as deadly for her organic form as for the technologically-augmented numans, yet the glistening blue waves always calmed her.

She squinted at the darkening horizon and wondered, not for the first time, if there was another girl sitting alone on another sea wall, somewhere across the ocean. Possibly a technologically incompatible girl like her.

A small swell hit the wall, sending a spritz of cool water up to her toes—the smell of salty brine pulling her back to the job at hand. The motes would expect her to walk the evening perimeter check soon, yet the closed dinner pail was still in her lap. It was time to finish her grandmother's mission.

Macie unlatched the clip on the side of the pail and opened the lid. It made her instantly queasy to see the clear plastic bag inside; its dusty contents telling an old story she had heard too many times before.

As she read the label attached to the bag, tears welled in her eyes.

**Emily Banks, terminated at 9 months of age.
Designation: incompatible DNA.**

Macie opened the little bag, said an old prayer for the dead she remembered from Vala long ago, and scattered Baby Emily's ashes into the water.

+   +   +

Emoto's Promise, a novella by Shel Calopa was first published by Deadset Press in 2020.

Available now at Amazon

List of Major Characters

Charles Drexus	Aka the Master, prisoner in the core of Australis, creator of Solaran communities
Illustria	Numan assistant to Charles, creator of Damaran communities
Illustrabell	Guard of the Core

Solarans

Governor Matthias Pallas	Governor Sydney, and Brizzie
Lady Patricia Pallas	Wife of Governor Pallas
Kohl Pallas	Son of Governor and Lady Pallas, manifestation of Illustria
Bess Pallas	Daughter of Governor and Lady Pallas, ex-Civil Sister, spy for Charles Drexus
Albert Carter	Chief Constable, sympathetic to Damaran cause
Dr Bryan Kassel	Deposed Governor of Melbourne, cousin to Governor Pallas.

Brotherhood

Archbrother Spectra	Archbrother of Melbourne, manifestation of Illustria
Stanley	Former Brother, defected to the Damaran community

Sam   Former Brother, defected to the Damaran community, manifestation of Illustria

Civil Sisters

Sister Mary   Head of Civil Sisters, secret sister of Lady Pallas

Harper   Former Senior Acolyte, General of Damarans, manifestation of Illustria

Lola   Former Senior Acolyte, friend to Harper and Bess

Damarans (Rats)

Aggy   Alpha, leader of Damarans, manifestation of Illustria

General Abudua   Senior General of Damarans, mother of Byron

General Mitta   General of Damarans

General Key   General of Damarans

General Lawrence   General of Damarans, uncle of Aggy

Mrs Brown   Leader of the Buchanite community

Leonora   Leader of the Albanite community

Mr Xi   Leader of the Digie community

Crew of the Blazing Aurora V1

Julian Drexus   Captain, and descendant of Charles Drexus

Bruno   Security officer, and descendant of Charles Drexus

Jane   Science officer, and descendant of Charles Drexus

Sedna   Pilot, and numan

Acknowledgements

First, my apologies to fans of *Letters from the Light*. I'm so glad you loved the first book in the series, and I am very sorry this next instalment has taken so long. Unfortunately, COVID, cancelled contracts, and the stars got in the way of planned publishing dates. I promise, you will not have to wait as long for the next instalment in the series.

Secondly, heartfelt thanks to Tony Coombes and Philzilla for dressing my novel so beautifully, again. Your generosity and graphic flare are very much appreciated.

Next, very special thanks go to my alpha and beta readers. To my big sister Melissa Bartelt-Siladi and my bestie of more years than I care to count, Kerrie Davis, thank you for having the courage to read all my work in its raw form and loving it anyway. Your feedback is always appreciated. To fellow scifi authors TK Toppin and Caroline Noe, big love for your suggestions on the second draft. When writing a sequel, it's hard to know how much of the first story to include in the second. Your suggestions were so helpful.

And lastly, thank you to my family for encouraging me to keep writing when all seemed so bleak. I couldn't do anything in life without you.

Thank you
Shel Calopa
xx